WESTMINSTER BLUES

Paul Gubbins

 New Generation Publishing

La Vivo ŝajnas monstra maro;
sur ĝi la Homo – ludoŝip' ...

Life is, it seems, a monstrous sea;
upon it Man – a child's toy boat ...

Julio Baghy: *Sonĝe sub pomarbo* (*Dreaming under an Apple Tree*)

London. October 2014.

It was as if his knee would no longer take his weight. It wasn't a question of pain: of that there was none. Or very little. Pain, he reminded himself, grabbing at the banister to support himself, pain, like any tormentor, requires a victim, something on which to work its malice. But here there was nothing. A void, an emptiness, where his knee should be. Or so it seemed.

He was sweating. Rivulets rolling down his back, his front, leaking into his crisp, white shirt, rendering it clinging, clammy, uncomfortable. Not that this was entirely unexpected. The knee had felt distant, in a world of its own, ever since he got up. It wasn't the first time. There were good days, bad days, though these seemed to be increasing, but for weeks on end it gave no trouble. But this was different. It had never given up like this, never scared him into believing he would fall, keel over, forcing him to grab for support.

What was especially alarming this time was that he was on stairs. Had there been no handrail, he might have tumbled a whole half-flight to a certain bruising, perhaps broken bones. Or cracked his head wide open on the floor below. And all this on the way to a meeting with the PM.

He removed his hand from the banister to consult his watch. The polished wood where he had seized it was stained with sweat. Already it seemed to be soaking in. You should always leave your mark on any government office in which it is your good fortune to serve, the old hands in the bars and dining rooms at the Palace of Westminster had told him. Not in this way, of course. And the cleaners would be angry. The Poles and Lithuanians who frequented the Foreign and Commonwealth Office after hours took great pride in burnishing the vestiges of empire.

His watch read 10.59. Already he was late. Some sort of feeling, however, was returning to his knee. Gingerly, and supporting himself once more on the banister, he placed a cautious foot on the step below.

"You okay up there, Mr Ryder?" One of the security staff startled him. "Anything I can do?"

"No. Fine, thank you. Just ... just a touch of pins and needles."

"You want me to take your case for you?" the man asked.

"No. It's fine. But thank you."

The security man, looking faintly disappointed, nodded, and resumed his boredom by the exit.

The knee was returning. It would just about take his weight if he leaned on the banister. Once on the level there would be less risk of falling and, while the afflicted joint was rediscovering itself, he could shuffle, if necessary dragging his leg, across Downing Street to number 10.

He almost wished he had handed his case to the security man. That way he wouldn't feel quite so lopsided, unbalanced. But he had to manage this himself, whatever it was. He couldn't give in to it.

All the same, when he next had the opportunity, he'd go and see Ellie. Not the fancy London consultant with whom he was registered and whose name he couldn't recall. Ellie. She'd sort him out. She always did. The thought of Ellie made him feel better. He could already feel strength returning to his knee.

***

Leaving the Downing Street entrance to the FCO he cast a quick glance towards the security gates ... the plebgates, as they were now known ... bordering Whitehall. It was probably too early for the long-lens snappers but you could never be sure. He hoped his walking appeared normal: any deficiency, any deviance, any supposed weakness would be pounced on and plastered over the pages of the following day's tabloids. A stumble, a slight fall: "Another Downing Street Trip-Up" ... the headline writers would have their sport. Fortunately he was a nonentity, hardly a household name. Hardly a government name, come to that. Parliamentary under-secretaries of state barely figured on the roadmap of power: he was a minor, unclassified by-way along which might shamble the occasional political horse and cart. It was his job to follow the horse. Clear up the mess. So what did the PM want with a shit-shoveller like him?

As if by magic the door to number 10 swung open as he approached. Clearly, they'd been expecting him. No wonder, because he was late. "The prime minister's waiting for you. In the study," a voice said. And another: "If you'd come this way ... please, follow me."

Portraits, former residents ... inmates, he thought unkindly ... of number 10, great and good, hated and loathed, forgotten and half-forgotten; a faint gnawing in the knee; then the study, with Adam Pemberton, prime minister, first lord of the treasury and minister for the civil service, in an armchair in the corner next to the fireplace. A table lamp, behind him, seemed to grow from his head, while the glow from the lamp lent him a ghostly halo, making it difficult to distinguish his features.

"Sit down," Pemberton said, motioning to another armchair, on the opposite side of the fireplace, and so placed that the table lamp appeared now in its rightful spot, by the wall, its light no longer beatifying the person sitting before it.

"I've no doubt, Tom ..." the prime minister began.

"With respect, sir ... it's Tim."

"What?" Pemberton shot a quizzical look across the fireplace, as if to check that the person opposite could truly be trusted to know his own name. "Tim ... of course. I'm sorry," he said, looking down at the paper in his hand. "It's been a difficult week."

"It most certainly has, prime minister. Very difficult."

"As it happens, that's what I want to talk to you about. This week."

Pemberton looked at him, as if expecting him to say something, but his under-secretary of state remained silent.

"This referendum ... this result ... as you'll be well aware ... is a disaster. Not what we were expecting ... hoping. And after the Euro elections ... UKIP ... to say nothing of the riots ... it's a mess. A complete and utter mess. Independence for Scotland means I shall go down in history as the man who took the united out of the United Kingdom."

"Oh ... I hardly think so, prime minister. No-one can attach any blame ..."

"Of course they can. And will. Mind you ... it's not all bad. At least the election after next will be fought without the Scots ... none of those ranting Scottish socialists to bolster the opposition. It's the end of the Labour Party ... unless they're stupid enough to go into coalition with what's left of the Lib Dems, and they're welcome to that, but either way the Labour Party'll be condemned for eternity to a handful of seats in a dozen or so godforsaken places in the north of England. Nothing against the north, of course," the PM added quickly. "I mean ... I know you represent somewhere up there ..."

"It's not all doom and gloom. In my constituency ..."

"Yes, yes, quite. Save it for prime minister's questions. Back to the matter in hand. This Scottish business ... it needs to be watched. And that's where you come in."

"I do ...?"

"If we're to manage this exit from the union ... salvage at least something from the wreckage ... I ... that is, we ... need to know what's going on. Need to be able to anticipate ... take action accordingly. I mean ... god knows there's so much to sort out."

Pemberton sank back in his chair. He was looking older, wearier. Threadbare. The press made fun of the PM's bald patch which, they noted with glee, seemed to be spreading. From where he was sitting Ryder couldn't see the top of the prime minister's head but, facing him, in close up, it struck him the man was exhausted. He rarely saw the prime minister at close quarters: in fact, he realised with a faint thrill, he had never been this close to him. Seeing him in the house, at a party conference, once at an FCO reception for some African leader or other, wasn't the same thing. At moments like that he was performing, on public view: here he was on home ground, more relaxed, more unguarded. Ryder wasn't sure which he preferred: the actor without his makeup or the figure striding the public stage.

As if reading these thoughts, the prime minister gathered himself and leaned forward, urgency in his voice. "What I want is intelligence. I want to know where they're going ... what they're doing. And with whom. This currency union with the pound, for example ... how serious are they? Or now they've got what they want in their referendum are they going to plump for the euro? Same with the monarchy. Are they going to stick with it ... or cave in to the republican wing? There's no knowing what they'll get up to. Besides, I need to know how this'll play out in the rest of the union. Northern Ireland, for instance. I mean ... there are more Catholic kids in schools over there than

Protestant ..."

He's rambling, Ryder thought. Lost the plot.

"In years to come they'll be looking to Scotland ... see how the Scots did it ... broke away ... then throw in their lot with Dublin. So I want to know what the buggers are thinking. Find out, perhaps, even now, even after the vote, but before the legislation's done and dusted, if there's any way to bring them back to the union."

Ryder gasped. The PM couldn't be serious. The referendum was a done deal. The Scots had spoken ... a strong turnout, a clear enough mandate for independence. They were set to reverse the 1707 Act of Union, end over 300 years of common history. Surely there was no turning back.

The prime minister was talking again. "This is where you come in. You've contacts north of the border. A Scottish wife ..."

"Margo's American."

"What's that?" For the second time that morning Pemberton was wrong-footed. He glared at the paper he was holding. The cretin that compiled those notes would be for the chop; no question of a safe seat, whatever the public school and the Oxbridge credentials.

"American. But third-generation Scots. With much of the family ..."

"Just so. Still in Edinburgh. And not without influence. All those relatives ... an MSP, a judge, I believe. The corridors of power. That's what I want you to tap into."

"But surely ... the Scotland office ..."

"History. It's all very well having a Scotland office when Scotland's part of the UK. But if Scotland's in effect a foreign country ... and it will be, unless we can do something ... then it makes sense to bring it under the FCO. Besides, in the referendum, the Scottish office played the government card. And, as we know, backed the losers. So the Scots are hardly going to trust it. Not any more."

"I'm still not entirely sure ..."

"I'm giving you responsibility for Scotland. A watching brief. Eyes, ears ... that sort of thing. Get up there, get talking to people ... and report back."

There was a tap at the door, which slid gently open.

"Sorry to disturb you, prime minister, but five minutes ..."

"I know. Thank you."

Pemberton lumbered to his feet. "So ... all clear?"

Ryder stood up. The knee gave a twinge: barely noticeable, the pain was passing. "I've got my hands full with our position paper for the global warming summit in ..."

"A parliamentary under-secretary never has his hands full. All frills, no thrills. You know that as well as I do. And stuff global warming. It can wait. Give it some eager Lib Dem ... not that there are many of them around these days ... so when it goes pear-shaped you're not around. From now on your priority is Scotland. And you report directly to me."

"Might I ask ... is this official? I mean ... is there to be an announcement? If so, I'd like to let my wife ... Margo ... know before she reads about it in ..."

"Semi-official. We'll keep it under wraps for the moment. See what happens. There'll be official contact, of course, via the Scotland office, before it gets wound up ... but let's just say ... you remain below the radar. And now, if you'll excuse me ... it's scouts and guides, or whatever they call themselves these days. Awards and presentations. A most worthy cause," Pemberton boomed, assuming his public persona, and striding towards the door.

There he paused, turning to look back into the study. "You ever a boy scout, Tom? You never know ... some of those skills might come in useful north of the border."

With that, Pemberton was gone.

***

Tim Ryder MP sank back in his first class seat on the Pendolino that would whisk him homewards. At least, he hoped it would whisk him. Railway privatisation, he knew, had not brought all the benefits his party had promised in the dying days of the Major government. Trains were still delayed, and nowhere was it written that privatised lateness was in any way superior to the old state-run British Rail kind. Late was late in anyone's book ... and, while train managers would walk through first class distributing claim forms, constituents wrote to tell him this was not always the case in standard and wanted to know what he would do about it. The answer, of course, was to write back politely and say he would approach the train company in question. Which, in turn, would reply that at the time of the complaint it was experiencing staffing difficulties, now resolved, and nothing similar would occur again. Staffing difficulties, indeed. Privatisation wasn't meant to be like that.

Ryder peered furtively through the window at the people, bowed and bent, scuttling along the platform, squinting at their tickets to find their carriage and their seat. He wished the train would start. At moments like this he was a goldfish, in a tank, on display, visible to any passing constituent who might recognise him and resent his taxes being squandered on first class travel for already overpaid MPs. He wondered how many votes, even marginal constituencies, had been lost because of a glimpse of an MP in a first class seat at a table laid for complimentary refreshments. With a general election next year it didn't bear thinking about.

In the first six months after his arrival in Westminster he had made a point of travelling standard. It was impossible to work, though. He found himself at least in partial agreement with the party grandee who had enraged the press by saying that in standard you found the wrong sort of person. There was an element of truth in this: stag parties, hen parties, particularly in the run-up to the weekend, charging up and down the gangways, shouting, singing, brandishing bottles, throwing up and monopolising the toilets, all determined to have a good time at the expense of everyone else. To say nothing of football supporters. The quiet zone was worse: the haunt of service engineers chuntering into phones about wiring diagrams or replacement parts for defective photocopiers. Not that these days first class was much better. Recession or no recession, it was generally packed, as it was this evening, with expense-account suits ... of which, Ryder reminded himself, he was one ... and post-war baby boomers, radiant with retirement, relishing their senior citizen railcards. Take the quartet opposite: the miniatures of gin already open, the tonic doing the rounds. The golden generation, Ryder thought, not without resentment, with its cradle-to-grave health service, university grants and jobs ... pensions ... never in doubt. Where had it gone wrong?

An announcement that the train was ready for departure, and the doors about to close, allowed him to relax. Ryder enjoyed train travel: despite mobile phones, despite internet access, there was still a sense of isolation, of being cocooned. Perhaps it was to do with the womb, being carried everywhere for nine months, warm and safe: a perfect prelude to train travel.

The mother as engine driver: discuss. That would make a good question on an undergraduate philosophy paper. If anyone still studied philosophy. The sixth-formers in the schools he visited in his constituency all seemed to be doing media studies, film studies. Or politics, god help them. But perhaps he was being invited to the wrong schools.

The teacup in front of him began to rattle and Ryder realised the train was moving. One of the baby boomers turned and glared at him, annoyance etched on her face, and, lifting the cup, he slid a doily onto the saucer beneath it. A retired teacher, Ryder decided. A glance spoke louder than words.

He looked out of the window. Already the lights of the station were disappearing as the Pendolino engaged with the gloom of a damp October evening. This was the London he liked best: not the sights, the sounds; the museums, the galleries, the theatres; none of its blue-plaqued history; not even the majesty or romance of the Palace of Westminster; no, none of these; but a train, accelerating up Camden Bank, putting the metropolis behind him, telling him that in just over two hours he would be back home ... if not precisely, then almost, at any rate in the part of the world he called home. Thank you, train, he would say to himself, as, having gathered speed, it raced past a lineside pub named, strangely, the Windermere. Tonight it would be too dark to make out the Windermere, but he knew it was there. It was a signpost, a signpost in an anonymous sprawling north London suburb that told him he was heading in the right direction. He sometimes thought he should visit the Windermere, see what it was like, see what relationship it bore to the lake after which it was named. But he knew he never would. Why spend any more time in the capital, let alone its faded, jaded suburbs, than absolutely necessary?

"I take it it'll be your usual, Mr Ryder?" a female voice broke in on his thoughts. He looked up to find Eileen, one of the regular attendants, looming over him. How she had learned his name was a mystery. Perhaps it went with the job. Or else she worked for MI5 reporting on who went where. Since 9/11 and the twin towers, all those years ago, you could trust no one.

"It'll be tea, milk, no sugar ... and we've a nice choice of either prawn or chicken sandwiches. I'd go for the prawn. Very tasty, the prawn."

Ryder would have preferred the chicken but, not wanting to appear churlish, let alone get on the wrong side of MI5, decided on the prawn. Anyway, it wouldn't do to offend Eileen: he was one of her favourites for, even with a full complement of customers, she had come down the carriage to serve him first. He rather imagined Eileen fancied him, despite being a matronly ten years or so older, since she was especially attentive, plying him throughout any journey with unwanted water, nibbles and nuts, crisps and biscuits. She looked lonely, Ryder thought: probably divorced, living in a bedsit, kids moved away. He felt sorry for her: probably she depended on the contact with people her job brought. She was the sort of person he ought to talk to, find out at first-hand if the government was doing enough to help low-paid people like her. But why? He already knew the answer.

"Thank you," he said, flashing his politician's smile, but at the same time trying not to give too much encouragement. "That'll be excellent. And the prawn sounds delicious."

"Right you are, Mr Ryder, sir," Eileen said, adding her usual quip. "Don't go away."

Ryder caught another critical look from the ex-teacher across the aisle. Why has this fellow been served before us? Why haven't we got our sandwiches, our complimentary tea and coffee? Serves you right, Ryder thought. You lot ... you baby boomers ... you've had your own way all your lives. It won't do you any harm to wait.

The tea, and the sandwich, plus a pack of custard creams and a pair of boiled sweets, came almost by return. It struck Ryder that Eileen had them ready even before she checked what he wanted. He nodded his appreciation, tipped a measure of milk into the tea and drank it at once. He was thirsty: the meeting on overseas aid he had left to catch his train had been as stuffy as the room in which it was held. He turned to the prawn sandwich but, even before he had wrestled it from its cardboard, Eileen had swept past and replenished his tea.

"Say if you want any more," she announced. "Plenty more where that came from."

"Why haven't we ...?" the ex-teacher began, leaning from her seat.

"Only got one pair of hands. Busy this evening ... what will it be? Tea, coffee?" Was that a wink, a hint of complicity, she cast at Ryder?

The sandwich was disappointing. The prawns, over-refrigerated, were rubbery, devoid of taste. He was grateful for the second cup of tea with which to wash them down. Settling back into his seat, and wondering if he should start on the custard creams, he looked out into the fleeting night but, apart from a few distant lights, could distinguish nothing. Perhaps they were already north of Watford.

He wondered if there were scout groups in Watford or, indeed, any of the communities through which they were passing. He assumed there were. The PM had seemed particularly exercised by the scout movement, but what had tying knots, erecting tents, collecting badges, to do with anything? Let alone help him in his new role? And what exactly was that role? But wait. Scouting ... that was it. Pemberton wanted him for a scout, sourcing information, gathering intelligence. Behind enemy lines. Like Churchill, in the Boer War ... hadn't he been on some sort of scouting mission when he was captured? Not a good omen. But scouts, Scots ... Scots, scouts ... it was starting to make sense. He hoped he wouldn't have to wear shorts or one of those ridiculous necktie things. And a toggle, or woggle, whatever it was. Or cook beans over a campfire ... all that smoke ...

A mobile was ringing. Somewhere far away. But getting closer, louder. His mobile ... a strident, insistent, old-fashioned telephone ring. He stirred, opened his eyes ... a half-empty cup of tea, unopened biscuits ... and squirmed, reaching deep into his trouser pocket, twisting in his seat, and meeting the disapproving gaze of the woman opposite.

"Sorry," he mouthed, extracting the mobile from the folds of his tailor-made suit, where it blared in momentary triumph before he hit the reply button.

"Hello ...?" he said, having failed to register who was calling.

It was Margo, irritated he had not answered at once, to tell him she had the car in the usual spot round the side of Lime Street station.

"Whatsatime?" he slurred, still half-asleep. "I mean ... not already."

Margo told him the train was due in ten minutes and wanted to know if he had been drinking.

"Certainly not," he muttered into the phone, shielding it with his hand. "You know I don't. I mean ... not in front of people. Just had a bit of a doze, that's all."

Margo said she thought to be on the safe side she'd do the driving.

"Fine," Ryder yawned. "See you in couple of minutes. Love you, hun."

No sooner had he ended the call when Eileen bore down on him, removing the tea and sandwich wrappings and depositing a bottle of water on his table.

'You have that," she said. "Goodness, what a night. Up and down the whole time. You were well off out of it. Wish I could have joined you."

Ryder felt himself blushing. As Eileen moved away down the aisle he caught a smirk on the face of the ex-teacher. A man, very likely her husband, though cast in a coarser mould, leaned across to him. "You're on there, mate. Go for it," he said, guffawing.

Blushing again, Ryder turned to look out of the window. He could see lines of carriages under the lights of the Edge Hill sidings, as his own train coiled round the curve leading to the sandstone cutting which, were Lime Street station a stately home, would constitute an avenue paving a path to its Victorian grandeur. It was here, Ryder reflected, that the modern railway was born ... and where William Huskisson MP, president of the board of trade, had become apparently the first person to be knocked down by a train. Perhaps that was why Mrs Thatcher had been so wary of railways.

"Goodnight, Mr Ryder," Eileen said as, a few minutes later, he stepped onto the Lime Street platform. The air, even under the station canopy, was chill, damp, with a tang of the Mersey and the Irish Sea beyond, and Ryder felt his senses sharpen.

"Thank you," he said and, without thinking, "See you again."

"I expect so, Mr Ryder. Enjoy your weekend."

Ryder nodded and set off down the platform. At the end he turned left, took the side exit, and soon found Margo with the Range Rover. He climbed gratefully into the passenger side.

"Home, hun. Home," he instructed. "It's been one hell of a crazy week."

So saying, and guiltily inhaling the aroma of expensive leather, he shut his eyes to resume his interrupted slumber.

Northaven. October 2014.

It wasn't until Saturday evening that Tim Ryder could unwind and he and Margo relax over a bottle of wine. Californian ... it had to be, at Margo's insistence. It reminded her, she said, of the sunshine and the vast, cloudless skies she left behind when she moved to the dark and cluttered island she now called home. It was a way of keeping in touch, of not forgetting. It worried Ryder sometimes that perhaps, even after all this time, Margo had never quite settled in Britain. In the years following their marriage, and when Alastair was little, she spent most of July and August with their son at her parents' home overlooking the Pacific. Understandably: the draughty Edwardian semi of a lowly law lecturer with political ambition could hardly compete with the swimming pool, the sun-drenched terrace and, a short walk away, the rolling Pacific breakers. But that was then, a lifetime ago. Now, Ryder thought, Margo was happier, more settled ... or was that resigned? They lived in what the glossy magazines in dentists' waiting rooms would describe as a beautiful home. Margo ran her own business, in good years earned considerably more than he did, was sought as an after-dinner speaker ...

"Nothing," Margo said. "Nothing on TV at all. As usual. Just football. Though there's a late night movie ..."

"We'll have something recorded. Or a DVD. If you want to watch ..."

"No. It's okay. Not really in the mood."

She replaced the television guide on the coffee table and turned to gaze at the flames fluttering in the grate. Artificial coals, and gas, of course, but effective. And only the second or third time that autumn the fire had been on since the weather, now cooler, had been unseasonably mild. The glow lent lustre to Margo's still glorious red hair, the feature that had caught Ryder's attention all those years ago when, an exchange scholar at the University of California San Diego, he first set eyes on her. Ryder was reminded, not without pride, that his wife was still beautiful. Apart from the hair it was her skin, firm, faintly freckled, falling away from the crest of a slightly snub, slightly mischievous but nevertheless dainty nose ... a nose Ryder had wanted to kiss the moment he saw it across a table in a grad-school seminar. And wanted to kiss again, now, except that he was comfortable, his legs splayed before him on the sofa extender, no risk of any pressure on the knee.

It had begun to trouble him during the afternoon, though nothing like as alarmingly as on the FCO stairs, while he was traipsing dutifully round the constituency party Autumn Fair. This time, though, it was more painful: the knee was both there, because it was aching, and at the same time not there, because anything happening below it ... putting his foot on the ground, walking ... was taking place without him, in spite of him. It was all very strange. He wondered if he should tell Margo. But it was probably nothing, one of those things that would go away. Ever since he turned 40 there had been minor aches and irritants, all of which cleared themselves up, together with a twinge of back pain. The Harley Street physiotherapist, recommended by his consultant, and who made a lucrative living pummelling, it seemed, most of his parliamentary colleagues, gave him a lecture on posture and told him at his age to expect the body to creak.

That was all very well, but the uncertainty in his step had made the Autumn Fair even more of a strain than usual. Small talk, chatting to the party faithful, remembering names, was exhausting at the best of times. And expensive, too. As MP you were expected to spend on every stall: cakes, jams ... the house was full of pots and jars, most of which were binned as their contents passed their taste-by date ... but worse were the trinkets, the knick-knacks, all those crocheted mats, toilet roll holders, unwanted china cats, superfluous jubilee mugs and other royalist paraphernalia. Particularly the last: to spurn anything to do with monarchy was equivalent to crossing Niagara Falls on a tightrope. It was an act of folly, of extreme danger, and would be remembered when the time came to select or reselect a parliamentary candidate. At least the retirement homes around the constituency welcomed the royalist tat and other white elephantitis he so generously distributed among them: it went down well with residents, they said. As for the cost of these unwanted purchases, there used to be a time when you could waltz it onto expenses. Not any more. A duck house had done for that.

Ryder was conscious Margo was watching him.

"So," she said, pouring herself more wine and passing the bottle to her husband, "what sort of week was it?"

This was the ritual, the Saturday night routine: if there was nothing decent on the television, which there rarely was, then it was catch-up time, the only opportunity in the week to compare notes, swap busy lives, touch base, as Margo put it. It seemed to suit them. Ryder sometimes wondered if their relationship wasn't stronger because, at least while the house was in session, and at other times too, they were together only at weekends. And that, in practice, meant Saturday evenings: the rest of the weekend was taken up if not with constituency work then with FCO business. And Margo was always planning her next pitch, or phoning, texting, making sure everything was in place, nothing going wrong, with whichever event she was organising.

"Where do I start?" said Ryder, shifting on the sofa, taking care not to disturb the knee. "I mean ... it's very odd. Irregular, almost."

He told her about the meeting with Pemberton and his theory about scouting. Margo was amused: she said as he couldn't change a light bulb properly, or operate a television remote, he'd be a pretty useless scout. She was less amused that someone had dug into her background to drag her into proceedings. Politics, she insisted, was her husband's preserve, not hers, and while prepared at times to play the dutiful wife, posing for the obligatory happy family photo for an election leaflet, she drew the line at further involvement. Besides, she found British politics stuffy, small town, certainly no comparison with growing up in a staunchly Republican household, debating the grander issues, as she saw them, of congress or the presidency, and turning out at primaries to share in the razzamatazz so noticeably lacking at British elections. So there was no way, she said, that either she, or for that matter her family, however distant, would be pawns in whatever crazy game the prime minister had in mind.

"But you don't have to be," Ryder objected. "I mean ... as I said ... it's just a sort of scouting expedition. Intelligence gathering."

"Oh, come on," Margo snapped. "I mean ... anyway ... we hardly know them. They're up there ... in Edinburgh, in their own little world ... we're down here. When did we last have anything to do with them?"

It was true, Ryder realised. Apart from Christmas cards there was little contact. Margo followed on Facebook, in desultory fashion, two or three of her cousins, including Duncan Buchlyvie, now an MSP, who had been one of the few of the Edinburgh contingent to come out to California for the wedding. Here, after countless bourbons, he had denounced

American whiskey as grossly inferior to anything produced in Scotland, danced a furious jig, kilt twirling, sporran thrashing, and, to the amusement of the mainly Californian guests, passed out beneath the Pacific sun. Tim and Margo had been to Duncan's wedding, a couple of years later, where they met up with the rest of the Buchlyvies. Even here they felt themselves outsiders, invited out of duty, at the meal placed as far from the wedding pair as possible, on a ragtag table with a man who did the gardening for Duncan's parents and his dinner lady wife, a couple of clients of Duncan's father's law firm, and a handful of other people whose function they never fathomed. Most of the male Buchlyvies were lawyers, involved in the family practice, mainly in conveyancing or else advocacy in the lower courts. Despite his own legal background Ryder had found them dull, dour. Even their wives, Margo said, had already donned the mantle of parochial Edinburgh respectability, and their conversation revolved round private schools and afternoon tea at Jenners. Only Duncan Buchlyvie, in fairness to him, showed any spark, any vitality, and both Margo and Tim agreed he was probably the best of a wearisome bunch. Well-meaning resolutions to keep in touch had, of course, faded: young families, careers and, in the case of both Tim and Duncan, the graft of placing a foot on the electoral ladder, took their toll. Including on Duncan's first marriage. He was on wife number two, Margo learned from Facebook. She wondered what had happened to wife number one, whose name or features she could no longer recall. Perhaps he'd had an affair. He always had a bit of a glint in his eye.

Suddenly she was curious. Curious about this family of hers of whose existence Tim and, indirectly, the prime minister, had reminded her. Despite her reservations about being used, exploited, it might be interesting to pay a visit, catch up with Duncan Buchlyvie, check out this new wife.

"As it happens," Margo said slowly, "I'm up at St Andrews the week after next."

"You are ...?"

"Yeah. The Confederation of Scottish Industry ..."

"Didn't know they had one."

"It's new. Newish. Set up in anticipation of independence ..."

"Right."

"They're taking over St Andrews early next year to showcase Scottish industry. Arabs, Indians, Chinese ... they're all invited. Pretty high power. Anyway ... we're doing the conference arrangements ..."

"But that's great, hun ..."

"Yeah, well. I'm going up there to look over a couple of things. I guess we could ... "

"Go up together and I could stop off in Edinburgh. Then it doesn't look fishy if I go by myself."

"I'm having no part in this political espionage. And if you get to talk to anyone ... any of the Buchlyvies ... I don't want them used."

"No one's talking about using anyone, hun. It would just be a chat. A little chat between ... family, friends, like-minded people. And all off the record. Anyway, I don't know what there is to say that hasn't been said already. It's all been raked over umpteen times. I reckon the PM's grasping at straws."

"He's grasping at you, Tim Ryder. And you need to be careful."

***

A phone was ringing but Ryder wasn't bothered because he knew one of his assistants would answer it. He wondered if it was the PM wanting to find out about Scotland. The next thing he knew he was being shaken, violently. Pemberton had hold of him, was jerking him to and fro, but there was nothing to report ...

"Wake up. Wake up, for god's sake ..."

"Gerroff," Ryder mumbled."Whayer doing?"

"It's the police. It's Alistair. They want to talk to you. Now," Margo said, thrusting the phone at him.

"What ...?" Ryder attempted to sit up in bed. "What is it?"

"Talk," Margo instructed, slamming the phone into his hand. "Put it on speaker so I can hear. And say something."

Ryder peered bleary-eyed at the phone and pressed the red speaker button. "Hello ...?"

"Inspector Kinsey here. Merseyside police. Am I talking to Tim Ryder MP?"

"Yes ... but ..."

"Sorry to disturb you, sir, at this time in the morning. But we've picked up your son ... causing a nuisance ..."

"What?"

"He's been drinking and ..."

"Is he okay? I mean ... not harmed?" Margo interrupted.

"Nothing that a decent night's sleep won't cure. And I imagine he'll have a thick head until well into the following day."

"Where is he?" Ryder wanted to know.

"Northaven police station. We'll put him in a car and bring him over. We've given him a talking to but I'm not sure how much he's taken in. Apart from rather a lot to drink. Given the circumstances ... I mean, bearing in mind your position ... it's not our intention to take this matter further. But ..."

"That's very decent of you, inspector."

"Of course I would remind you, sir, that underage drinking is a serious matter ..."

"Quite. Absolutely."

"Something this force is determined to curb. Therefore it might not be possible to be so lenient in the future ..."

"No. I understand entirely. You've been very reasonable. We're very grateful."

"So I think we can leave the matter in your hands. If you need any support ... we do have a specially trained officer ..."

"No. That'll be fine. I'm sure we can manage it from here. Again, thank you, inspector."

"Thank you," chimed in Margo.

"All in the line of duty, sir ... madam. Goodnight." And the phone clicked off.

"Bloody hell," Ryder said, casting aside the duvet and getting out of bed, flinging the phone on top of it. "What's he been up to? I mean ... did you know he was going to be out all night?"

"He said he was visiting with friends. Be back by midnight."

"Well, he wasn't, was he? Crying out loud. I'm going to put the kettle on."

Grabbing a dressing gown, Ryder stalked from the bedroom and down the stairs to the kitchen. He was conscious his knee had not enjoyed being woken in the middle of the night: his leg felt fluffy, feathery, but it would pass. Besides, he had other things to think about. Entering the kitchen he had barely filled the kettle and switched it on when the door from what they still called the granny flat opened and Marie-France stood blinking in the harsh fluorescent light.

"It's okay," Ryder said, his heart sinking, unable to cope with Marie-France at this early hour. "All under control. You go back to bed."

"Plees ... I 'ear noise in ze kitchen. Somezing 'appen."

Marie-France had been with the Ryders ever since they moved in, shortly after Tim won the Northaven seat. She had been an au pair, slipped seamlessly into the role of nanny after Alistair was born, and then, as he was growing up, and the Ryders spent more and more time away, reinvented herself as housekeeper. Her baking and, in the summer, her salads, were legendary; likewise her girth, and also her cleaning, though for the wrong reasons. Once a year she went back to her parents' farm in the Auvergne, where Margo and Tim half-hoped she would stay; but every year she returned, plumper than ever, grumbling about her brothers who wanted her to marry an elderly goat farmer, so his land might eventually become theirs, and proclaiming the Ryders to be her true family and the former granny flat her home.

Marie-France had her uses but not, Ryder felt, glancing at the kitchen clock, at 2.30 in the morning.

"Look. It's alright. Please ... just go back to bed."

"It ees Alistair. I not 'ear 'im come 'ome. It ees ze boy, non?"

No need of a guard dog with Marie-France around, Ryder thought, taking a teapot to scald it and add the loose leaf tea. Still thinks the British national drink is made by dangling a teabag over a glass of lukewarm water, but otherwise doesn't miss a trick.

"Alistair's been out on the town and is a bit worse for wear. The police are bringing him back ..."

"Ze police ... but zat ees terrible. Poor boy ... it ees not good for 'im just now. 'Is A level ... 'e ees under much pressure. All ze work ... ze school ..."

"That's no excuse for going out, getting drunk and coming back in a police car. Besides, he's under age. And I've my position to think of. Er ... thank you,

Marie-France," Ryder rescued the teapot about to fall into French hands. "I'll make it, if you don't mind. It's no trouble. You ... er ... as I say. You go back to bed."

Muttering, Marie-France returned to the flat, clattering the door shut behind her. Ryder finished making the tea, took two mugs, added milk, cursing to himself when the carton slipped through his fingers, splashing white droplets onto the work-surface. He put the mugs with the pot onto a tray and carried it to the lounge where Margo was waiting. He installed himself on the sofa, again stretching his legs on the extender. Margo stood by the window, staring into the night, before she came to sit down.

"You've forgotten the strainer."

"Sorry."

"You know I can't stand tea leaves."

"I'll get it."

"It's okay. I'll manage."

She poured the tea. They drank in silence.

Headlights, sweeping the lounge, bathing it briefly in a yellow glow. Tyres, crunching over gravel.

"That'll be them," Margo said, standing up, striding to the door. Tim hauled himself from the sofa and followed. Entering the hall they found Marie-France already at the front door, unbolting it, pulling it back, stepping out onto the porch.

"Mon petit," she said, seeing Alistair helped from the police car, and flinging open her arms to give him a huge hug. "Mon pauvre petit."

"Didn't know he was French. Speaks good English, your boy, doesn't he?" a constable, not much older than Alistair, addressed Marie-France.

Margo emerged from the house. "I'm his mother," she said frostily. "That'll do Marie-France. We can take it from here."

Reluctantly she released the boy who stood,

swaying slightly, blinking at his surroundings.

"Had a bit to drink," he said.

"For Christ's sake ... we can see that," Ryder exploded. "Most of it's over your shirt ... your trousers. What in hell's name ...?"

"Hey ... now's not the time." Margo laid a restraining hand on her husband's arm. Then, to Alistair: "Come on. Let's get you inside."

The two women took him and steered him into the house. "Not feeling too good," he mumbled, as they manoeuvred him past his father on the porch. "Think I might be going to ..."

"Downstairs bathroom," Margo instructed. "Quick."

The young constable was watching proceedings with interest.

"Thank you, officer," Ryder said. "And your colleague as well. I don't think we need detain you any longer. I ... that is, we ... can of course count on your discretion in this matter."

"You what?" the policeman said.

"Your ... I mean ... none of this goes any further."

"No. We just ... like ... make our report and that's an end of it."

"That's alright, then. Good night, officer."

"Good night to you, sir."

The man raised a hand in half-hearted salute and got back into the car. Ryder watched it reverse over the gravel, turn in front of the double garage, and make its way down the drive to the road where it halted before turning right to head back into town. Ryder shivered. The air was cold and damp. Decidedly autumnal. He looked up at the sky where clusters of stars glinted through gaps in the cloud. From beyond the coast road, silent at that time in the morning, and on the other side of the sandhills, he could hear the sea. And smell it. It wasn't a bad spot, he thought. Just a pity he spent so little time here. He shivered again, conscious his limbs were tingling, twitching, especially his leg. Yes, it was decidedly chilly.

Returning inside, shutting the night behind him, he was aware of the sound of retching emanating from the downstairs bathroom. Retching, and clucking, in French, and the more assertive tones of his wife.

"Bloody hell," he muttered, shaking himself. "Bloody hell."

**

Ryder was in his study, attempting to get his head round a Scotland office report on the financial implications of devolution, when he heard Alistair get up and cross the landing to the bathroom. He glanced at his watch. Almost three o'clock. The lad had been flat out for pretty well 12 hours. Alright for some, Ryder thought. When he eventually got to bed, when the house was at last quiet, he had hardly slept. He wondered if, despite the assurances of the police, there would be any comeback. Then he found himself going over in his mind what he would say to Alistair. He rose early, cursing there was no newspaper, but when it turned up he found he was too tired to take it in. Margo suggested he went for a walk by the sea, clear his head, but Ryder was not in the mood.

It struck him he went to the beach less often than in the past. At one time it had been a regular weekend feature, especially when Alistair was little. Father and son, out of the house, across the coast road where once a railway ran, then through the sandhills to the beach. There they would dig a sand car, place Alistair proudly in it, tiny hands clutching a driftwood steering wheel, or, when he was a little older, build dams to stem the streams trickling into the sea. Toy boats, sand-sculpted harbours, much splashing, shouting, then frenzied excitement as the dam burst and the waters rushed to the waves beyond. As Alistair was growing up they would walk, miles, along the margin of the sea, the wind in their faces, talking, as fathers and sons do. Then there came a time when the boy discovered electronics, games, music, girls, and Ryder found himself striding out alone. Margo rarely accompanied him. This was no beach, she said. This was a glorified mudflat, bleak, windswept, which made her ears ache, and which bore as much resemblance to the warm golden sands of her own childhood by the Pacific as paste to pearl. With a tremor Ryder realised he had hardly been on the beach at all that year. Was it pressure of work? Or was there something else going on? The knee, for instance? Had there been some message passing subconsciously, and perhaps for some time, from knee to brain that exercise of this nature was best avoided? He really ought to go and see Ellie, at her surgery, get her to take a look. But when?

As he reached for his desk diary ... safer, he found, than any electronic equivalent, at least in his hands ... he heard Alistair leave the bathroom. He pushed back his chair and went onto the landing.

"Hi, dad." Hangdog, hungover. Nothing recalcitrant, Ryder noted. That was good.

"How are you feeling?"

"Shit. And parched. Throat like ... like ..."

"Yeah. I know. Bottom of a budgie's cage."

"Something like that. Look. I'm sorry. I mean ... I don't know ..."

Ryder looked at his son. He was going to wipe the floor with him, lay down the law, ground him. He was going to tell him he needed to remember who his father was, that with a general election round the corner he couldn't afford to put a foot wrong. Supposing the press got wind of this ... they'd had a field-day when Blair's son was found in a gutter in Leicester Square. And so on.

But, looking at Alistair, Ryder suddenly saw himself. The sixth-former he once was, all those years ago, though it seemed like yesterday. Mistakes to be made, life to be learned. There are things no amount of telling off will alter, Ryder realised. The best lessons are those you discover for yourself.

Below, he heard Margo open the door from the lounge and enter the hall.

"Come on," he said. "Let's stick the kettle on. And see if Marie-France has done any baking."

***

That evening, after Alistair had retired to bed, and Margo had installed herself in the lounge, hunched over a spreadsheet on her laptop, and displaying one of her unwritten "Do not disturb" notices, Ryder wandered into the kitchen. Here he found Marie-France bustling about with much purpose but, he thought, little effect.

"Marie-France," he began, sitting at one of the stools next to the breakfast bar. "I've been thinking ... something you said."

The woman looked at him, almost with pity, Ryder thought, as she turned to pull open a cupboard, peer inside, and close it again.

"Yes. It's something you said last night ... this morning ... whenever. About Alistair. You said he was under a lot of pressure."

"C'est vrai. Oui," Marie-France said, moving to the next cupboard.

"But ... A levels. Everyone's under pressure. I remember when I did mine ... head down, get on with it. I know he's got his Oxford interview next month ..."

"Alistair does not wish to go to Oxford."

"I'm sorry ...? Of course he wants to go. He must."

Marie-France shrugged. Again, that look of pity. She opened another cupboard.

"For god's sake ... will you stop opening and shutting cupboard doors. I can't think."

"But I look for ze ..."

"I don't give a ... "

He caught another of Marie-France's looks, this time tinged with reproach.

"Okay, okay. Sorry. We're all very tired after last night. But ..."

"Alistair ... 'e want ... 'e want a gap year. Go away."

"A gap year? That's ridiculous. He never said. And he'll walk into Oxford."

Marie-France sighed. She turned her large brown eyes to him ... bovine, Ryder thought: he could see her on a lush French field, grazing ... and placed her bulk on a stool opposite him.

"Monsieur Ryder ... you pardon what I say. You ... and madame ... are clever people. I zink too ... good people. But ... you not understand. 'Ere ... 'ere 'e ees ... ah ... stifled. 'Ere 'e ees not 'imself. 'E ees your son ..."

"Of course he's my son."

"But you are a man of importance. Everyone know. And 'e ... 'e ees in your shadow. At school zey say Tory boy ..."

"Nonsense. He never said."

"Because ... 'e not want to worry you. Cause trouble."

"That's not causing trouble ..."

"Alistair ees like you. 'E work 'ard, try to please. But keep zings ... ah ... bottled. But now 'e say ... ça suffit. Now ... I please myself. Zat ees why 'e need to get away."

"Have you been putting ideas into his head? I mean

..."

"Non. I 'ave not. You should not say ..."

"Okay. Fine ... sorry."

"You ask what ees ze problem. I say what ees ze problem."

"Yes. Indeed. Quite right, Marie-France. I'm grateful. I shall need to find time to speak to him ..."

"Find time ... find time. You speak as if 'e ees one of your ... your people. Your constituents. You now make for 'im an appointment. Mon dieu ... 'e ees your son."

Glaring, Marie-France flopped from the stool and flounced across the kitchen. For the second time in less than twenty-four hours the door to her flat banged shut.

"Everything okay?" Margo's concern drifted from the lounge.

"Yeah. Fine, hun. No worries."

Manchester. October 2014.

It was a total waste of time. In that sense, Ryder reflected, it was like most business meetings: convened for appearance while the real decisions were made elsewhere. It was the grand old Duke of York syndrome: meetings existed to march everyone to the top of the nearest agenda-layered hill and march them down again. But they served their purpose. They kept the foot soldiers occupied. Fooled them into believing they had something to contribute. And kept them off the dole. At least, that was the idea.

Ryder sighed and, reaching for the bottle of sparkling water in front of him, twisted the top. For some reason it took effort to open it, but eventually the cap yielded and the contents, angered by his actions, gave a loud, gaseous hiss. Earnest eyes turned briefly upon him. He tried to pour the water as quietly as possible, but his hand was shaking, and the liquid fizzed and frothed into the glass. Again, Ryder had the vague feeling he was interrupting something, disturbing the studied concentration round the table. Damn it ... someone had to take a lead, be first to break out the water. After all, that was why it was there. To be drunk. Or was it? Perhaps it was a test, designed by some bright-spark management guru to gauge leadership skills. Who would be the first to go for the water, to introduce a new element into proceedings? Who, and how many, would then follow? Even as the question crossed his mind, he saw from the corner of his eye Jack Merryman, who had taken Bolling Valley at the last election, lean forward and reach for one of the bottles. Interesting. Ryder picked up his glass and drank. The liquid effervesced in his mouth, tingling on his teeth, his tongue, and, swallowing, he wondered if he would need to stifle a belch. Replacing the glass on the table, and choking back an unwanted exhalation, he noticed the label on the bottle. Buxton Water. At least it was local. Or localish. Presumably this was why they were meeting at the Midland Hotel in Manchester, rather than Westminster. Northwest MPs supporting the northwest economy. Fine in theory, but whatever they had to say to each other, which appeared to be little, could just as easily have been said in a parliamentary committee room, and probably at much less cost. Though today doubtless the taxpayer, rather than the party, was picking up the tab.

The purpose of the meeting was to find common ground on which the region's Tory MPs could present a united front at the forthcoming election. Unity is strength, someone said, but it seemed there was little of either. The only item on which they seemed able to agree was disagreement which, as their chairman, Sir Wesley Blenhesket, who'd been in parliament before most of them were born, reminded them, was no way to represent themselves, or the region, at an election. A couple of those round the table wanted to know why regionalism was suddenly so important. This was Lib Dem policy, they said, and they wanted nothing to do with it: it smacked of the European Union, had never been in any Tory manifesto, and would suggest the party was trying to impose an additional tier of government which, in an age of austerity, would not sit well with voters. Blenhesket, a former chief whip, removed over whispered suggestions of tax dodging and who had never forgiven the party hierarchy for their treatment of him, said if the newly independent Scots made a go of it then regionalism would be back on the agenda. He should know, he said, since the vast Lake District constituency he had the honour to represent looked out across the Solway to Scotland and would be among the first to feel the effect.

Merryman piped up and told them the issues in his rural, lowland constituency were not the same as in Blenhesket's upland national park. Ayesha Farani, lazily twisting an elegant bangle round an elegant wrist, said the needs of rural communities were irrelevant to the clutch of once prosperous mill-towns she represented, now locked into post-industrial decline.

"Too true," Ryder heard himself speak. "And the same applies to my constituency. Coastal resorts, dormitory towns, are a separate category again. But," he went on, unsure whether moved by inspiration or desperation to get the meeting over, "there is something."

He paused. The room was his. Everyone was looking. He had their attention, he was in charge. Even Blenhesket was attentive. A rare moment, he realised with a sudden thrill, for a humble parliamentary under-secretary of state, a pawn of floundering ministers and wily civil servants, and whose opinion counted generally for naught. It was an occasion to enjoy.

"Well?" said Blenhesket, inquisitively. "What is it?"

Ryder leaned forward, panning slowly round the table to take in the attendant faces. "Tourism ..." he began.

Derision and scorn greeted his opening.

"Come on," someone scoffed. "We were expecting a great revelation ..."

Ryder held up his hands for silence.

"Hear me out," he spoke over the hubbub. "Obvious, yes ... but none of you had the wit to mention it. Look. This region's got some great attractions. Mountains ... stupendous scenery," he said, nodding towards Blenhesket. "Some wonderful stately homes ... half-timbered buildings ... and industrial heritage. Something for everyone."

"We do all that already," Merryman said. "We're

awash with tourist brochures ..."

"Individual towns, yes. Councils ... but there's no co-ordination. We need to launch this as a package. Right across the region. We've a story to tell ... and we're not telling it."

"You might have a point," Blenhesket nodded in encouragement.

"And not just across the region. We need to sell this abroad ..."

"Scotland ..." a voice said, to laughter.

"Scotland, yes. But across the Atlantic. How much marketing goes on in the USA, for example? Why should Americans fly in to Heathrow to gawp at Buckingham Palace and the changing of the guard? Why not encourage them to fly in to Manchester ... take in the sights ..."

"Satanic mills," someone muttered.

"Coronation Street ..."

"Look," Ryder continued. "If we can show voters we're on their side ... doing our best to bring jobs to the region ... and dollars, euros ..."

"We don't want the euro ..."

"You know what I mean. Anyway, that's my suggestion, for what it's worth. If you can come up with anything better ... fine. But ..." Ryder checked his watch, pushed back his chair, and stood up ... "you're going to have to excuse me. I need to be off. Somewhere else to be. Sorry."

"What's she called?" Merryman asked, to laughter. "Hope she's worth it."

Blenhesket frowned. "Not our Tim," he said firmly. "And we'll have less of that. Some decorum, please. Now ... back to the matter in hand."

Ryder grinned at Merryman. Then, sweeping up his papers, and stuffing them in his briefcase, he turned from the table and headed for the door.

"Good luck," he said. "Hope you reach some sort of agreement."

With that, he was gone.

***

Outside the Midland Hotel the doorman hailed Ryder a cab.

"Moss Side," Ryder said, leaning through the window to the driver. "Raby Street medical centre."

The driver gave him a quizzical look. Moss Side was an unlikely destination for a smart-suited gent stepping from the grandeur of the Midland Hotel. True, the area had gone up in the world since the drug-dealing and shootings that had earned the city the name Gunchester. But ... the Midland Hotel to Moss Side. It was champagne to chips. On the other hand, a medical centre. Very likely the bloke had some sort of problem he wanted sorting on the quiet, out of sight of his regular quack. And his missus. The driver made a mental note of the surgery name. In his line of work he got asked all sorts of things. Dodgy doctors was one of them.

"Okay," the driver said. "You're on. Raby Street it is."

Once in the cab Ryder checked his phone. There were no messages. That was good. Ellie had promised to see him when her morning surgery was over. She would text him, she said, if there were any emergencies, any delays. The last thing Ryder wanted was to share a germ-filled waiting room with out-of-work alcoholics, sallow-faced methadone-users, pallid and pregnant teenagers and querulous, quarrelling kids. At least now, at this time in the morning, there would be few people around and Ryder would be able to walk straight through into Ellie's office.

He had known Ellie from the first week at university. They had met at the freshers' ball, discovered they were both reading law, and things had gone from there. They explored the campus together, shared the same lectures and seminars, moved in the same circle of friends. At the end of the first year Ellie decided law was not for her and, on the strength of strong science A levels, and a nudge from her surgeon father, switched to medicine. She wanted to help people, she said, and didn't feel she could do so from behind statutes designed to obfuscate, rather than enlighten. Ryder, disappointed they would no longer be taking classes together, nevertheless supported her decision and stoutly, if not rashly, declared he would be her very first patient when she eventually qualified. Her defection to medicine was tempered by the fact that, in the second year, they had already agreed to share a house with four other lawyers. In the third year Ryder and Ellie moved into a squalid bedsit, much to the horror of the surgeon father who turned up, unexpectedly, one weekend. There they took a leaf out of Ellie's medical books and studied the human body, anatomy, and the physiology of the heart, greedily, wildly, passionately, while Ryder flung himself into his finals, producing a sparkling dissertation on public international law. The ensuing first class degree, was, he always held, the product of the sex that nourished him through that glorious final year.

The dissertation, however, was their undoing. Because of its excellence, Ryder's tutors, anxious, as all academics are, to recreate themselves, to set a bright student on their own bookish path, urged him to take up a scholarship in the USA. Once in a lifetime opportunity, they told him. Things like that don't grow on trees. Who knows where it might lead?

At first Ryder refused. He would not leave Ellie. He

41

would find a post-graduate course in this country ... not professional training to become a solicitor, or barrister: his future, if any, was as an academic lawyer ... or, if worse came to worst, he would get a job. It was Ellie, however, who persuaded him. He would be away just twelve months, she reminded him, and the time would soon pass. Perhaps he could come back at Christmas. What she refrained from saying was that she was tired, exhausted, that she was finding their hedonistic existence increasingly difficult to reconcile with the relentless demands of medical study. She needed him, at least temporarily, out of her life.

When, not at the end of one year, but at the end of two, Ryder returned to Britain with a red-haired American beauty on his arm, Ellie was neither surprised nor, slightly to her amazement, unduly bothered. She was enjoying medicine too much, could see herself in a few years' time in general practice, contrary to the wishes of her father, in the type of run-down inner city surgery where she had spent part of her training, helping where the need was greatest. She had moved on from the bedsit days: so too, obviously, had Ryder. Their reunion was amicable, alcoholic: Ellie tolerated Margo as an inevitable part of Ryder's future, Margo tolerated Ellie as an inevitable part of his past. When, later, the newly qualified medical practitioner put her brass plate on the wall outside the Raby Street medical centre Ryder, true to his word, became her first patient. He remained on her books until his election, whereupon it was suggested that, if he knew what was best, he would take the private health care that was on offer and, with it, the Harley Street consultant. Somewhat reluctantly, but as a new MP feeling he should toe the line, he acquiesced. Ellie was understanding: as she said, her frenetic, frantic Moss Side practice might have been alright for a struggling law lecturer but was hardly the place for an up-and-coming parliamentarian. Nevertheless, on the rare occasions when Ryder felt under the weather, and required talk, rather than medication, it was to Ellie that he returned. Unofficially, of course. And it was also a convenient, and at least semi-legitimate way, of keeping in touch.

"Here we are," a voice said. "For you, squire, eight pound seventy. And no worries. I'm sure they're good in there. Used to sorting out gentlemen such as yourself ... if you know what I mean."

***

The first thing Ryder noticed when he stepped from the cab ... no tip for the driver because of his insinuating tone and, besides, he wasn't a constituent ... was blackened brickwork round the surgery entrance. Frowning, he swept into reception where he found Ellie talking to a nurse.

"Hi, Tim," she flashed him one of her radiant smiles. "With you in a minute."

Ryder didn't know whether to be relieved or disappointed. Greeting Ellie was always something of an ordeal. He never knew whether to play it cool, stick with polite pleasantries that avoided physical contact, or whether, for old times' sake, to take her into his arms, give her a huge hug, and plant a lingering kiss on her lips. He lusted invariably after the latter, but succumbed generally to the former. This time the decision was taken from him: neither pleasantry nor passion seemed appropriate under the inquisitive eyes of the nurse.

Ryder bit his lip. Ellie was looking ... what? Lived-in came to mind, a little scuffed, chipped ... perhaps, so too, did he ... but she still exuded that earnest vitality he recalled from their student days: she was still good-looking, still eminently beddable. Damn it, he thought, with a savagery that surprised him, why can't we tell people what we think? Why can't we let it out? I fancy you something rotten and I want to shag the hide off you. Why not? Why not say it? Would society, civilisation, collapse? The world end? No. It might be a better place for a spot of raw honesty. On the other hand, copulating couples on every street corner ...

A tremor, a frisson, went through him. Both Ellie and the nurse must have seen, sensed it: the nurse, pointing at something in the notes she was holding, stopped and both women stared at Ryder.

"I think we're done," Ellie said, pushing the papers back at the nurse. "If you want we can talk again tomorrow."

The nurse, a starchy, older woman, frowned, as if to suggest she felt there was more to say, and fixed Ryder with a disapproving stare. Then she gathered the papers and, moving behind the reception desk, began ostentatiously to file them.

"Okay," Ellie said, again bathing Ryder in the luminescence of one of her smiles, and motioning him to follow her to her room. "I'm all yours."

For a second Ryder wondered if this was a come-on. Was she telling him ...? He felt the colour rise to his face. But no. There was no suggestion, no suggestiveness, in her voice. Of course not. Their relationship was professional, doctor-patient, clinical, antiseptic. As it should be.

He wondered if Ellie had noticed him blush. To hide his discomfort he began talking, the first thing that sprang to mind.

"Outside. A bit of mess ..."

"The riots. Last summer. Kids ... well, not all kids ... from Salford thought it would be fun to stir things up in

Moss Side. Set fire to a wheelie bin ... but round here they weren't having it. The blaze was out long before the fire brigade turned up. People round here might not have much ... but they've got their pride. A sense of community. And no one from outside was going to mess with that, still less take it from them."

They had reached Ellie's room, which was much as Ryder remembered it. Ellie positioned herself at her desk, nudging the computer into life, before swivelling to face her visitor who sat down opposite her.

"It's been a long time," she said.

It had. Well over a quarter of a century since those days and nights of lust and licence in that awful bedsit.

As if reading his mind, Ellie said: "Since you were last here. You've obviously been looking after yourself. You seem in good shape."

There it was once more. A coded message. Good shape ... surely, she was trying to tell him something. Again, why couldn't people just speak their minds? Perhaps if he ...

"Okay. So what's troubling you, Tim? I mean ... it's got to be something to bring you to the wilds of Moss Side."

The moment had passed. If, indeed, there had been any moment. The charge, the tension, Ryder had felt, or thought he felt, had gone. He exhaled, deeply, and felt himself unwind for the first time since entering the building.

"Why is it doctors always ask a patient what's troubling them? What's the matter ... how they're feeling? If they're ill the patient wants the doctor to tell them ... not the other way round."

Ellie laughed. "It's because we're professionals. Unlike politicians, we talk to people first, and listen, before offering remedies we have no idea will work."

"Ouch," said Ryder. "You said that as if you mean

it."

"I do. I work in the health service. Or what's left of it. Too many so-called cures for too few so-called ills. It's a mess, Tim, and your lot are to blame."

"Wow. I wasn't expecting a full-frontal ..."

"Sorry. I didn't mean to. And I know it's not your area. But it's not every day I get someone in government ..."

"A junior someone ..."

"Someone in government sitting in my surgery."

"You know we have to be rigorous in seeking efficiency savings to deliver maximum benefit to stakeholders ..."

"If you knew how hollow that sounded. How empty. My god, Tim, you used to have beliefs. Not soundbites. Look. Sorry. Let's leave it. Let's talk about you. I mean ... you're here for a reason. Not to listen to me going on about the health service. Or the government. So ...?"

Ryder, happy to avoid a fight with Ellie, of all people, relaxed. Even though she seemed more brittle, more fractious, than in the past, Ryder knew he could open up to her more than to anyone else. Even Margo. Especially Margo. There was a bond between Ellie and him, always had been, always would be. Words were almost redundant, meaning conveyed by glance, by gesture, by intuition. Nevertheless Ryder spoke, told her about the weakness in the knee, how long it lasted, how often it came, when he first noticed it. Ellie listened, thoughtfully, asked about old sporting injuries ... there were none ... and made notes.

"Right," she said, motioning towards the examination couch. "I shouldn't really be doing this ... I mean, you're not my patient. But, well ... for old times' sake. Come on ... up you go."

Ryder rose from the chair and crossed to the couch. Perching on the side, he was about to swing his legs horizontal.

"Hold on. You need to remove your trousers."

Ryder felt his colour rise, and Ellie laughed.

"It's not as if I haven't seen ..."

"No, no," Ryder stammered, standing, and fiddling to undo his belt. "Of course not. I mean ..."

"I can hardly examine your knee through a layer of expensive tailored suit."

It was Ryder's turn to laugh.

"It's not that expensive. I'm not a banker, you know."

"No. A politician. And in the eyes of the public you both score pretty well zilch."

"I hope I score a bit more than zilch with you," Ryder heard himself say, immediately cursing the corniness of the quip.

"Depends what I find. Come on, lie down."

A moment of panic as Ryder wondered whether he'd put on a clean pair of boxers that morning. Either way, too late to worry. The panic abated as Ellie began gently to feel round his knee, both knees. It was good to have her fingers manipulating his flesh, and Ryder felt a mildly erotic, faintly guilty thrill. What would he do if he began to feel aroused? She would surely notice ... but now she was asking if he felt any sensation, any pain, and the danger passed.

"No," he told her. "No pain. Not at the moment. Or very little. It's just ... when it comes ... a sort of stabbing. Then a dullness. And it comes and goes. Most times there's nothing ... but it's one of those things that if you think about it you imagine it's there. And it seems to be happening more often."

Ellie nodded. "I can't find anything ... but it doesn't mean there isn't anything there. It's possibly just a touch of gout ..."

"Gout? I thought that went out with ... with the Hanoverians."

"Hardly. If anything, it's making a comeback. Too much good living. In your case, perhaps, dining out ... no doubt at the taxpayers' expense ..."

"I should be so lucky ..."

"It's the wine that does it. Or the beer. Uric acid in the blood. How much are you drinking these days, Tim?"

"Well ... more than government guidelines. Ironic, I suppose. But always in moderation."

"They all say that. And, please, do get up. I suppose while I'm about it there's no harm in checking weight ... blood pressure."

Ryder raised himself from the couch and swung his legs to the ground.

"Of course, it could just be a trapped nerve, particularly as it seems to be one knee only. You could perhaps do with some painkillers ... for when it happens again. It's quite likely."

Ellie checked his weight. He could do with losing a bit, she told him, or at least keep it in check. He should also try and take more exercise. Ryder said he was off exercise, these days never felt like it. Ellie, with Ryder now at her desk, taking his blood pressure, told him not to be silly and to join a gym.

"You've got one, I believe, at the House of Commons," she said. "Use it."

Ryder told her he didn't care for it because it was sweaty, too hearty and macho. Ellie laughed, called him a wimp, and, removing the rubber cuff from his arm, told him his blood pressure was only slightly up and it was nothing to worry about.

"However," she went on, "I think you ought to get yourself a blood test."

"What do I want a blood test for?"

"To check for one or two things."

"Such as?"

"For a start ... diabetes."

"Crying out loud. I haven't got anything like that. It's my knee."

"Could be related. Anyway, it needs to be ruled out."

"Or in. So what you're saying is ..."

"What I'm saying is nothing. But you need to look at all eventualities. So you need to get yourself a blood test ..."

"Can't you do it?"

"No way. I've done far more than I should already. You need to go back to whoever you see in London ... tell him what you've told me ... I assume it's a him ... and I imagine he'll say the same."

"I haven't time for all this ..."

"Ah, I forgot. Tim Ryder doesn't do health. Or, rather, sickness."

"Quite right. You know clinics and surgeries and hospitals ... simply the smell of them ... give me the willies. That's why I like to come back to you. At least it's familiar. And you're the only doctor I trust."

"I'm flattered. And, by the way, you can put your trousers back on."

Ryder smiled. "Like old times. Casting off our kit."

"I think we're a bit past that. Don't you?"

It was on the tip of Ryder's tongue to say no, he didn't think so. Far from it. Unfinished business, and all that. But there was a finality in Ellie's tone that stopped him. Instead he said lamely: "I haven't had lunch. Perhaps we could go for a bite to eat ..."

"Sorry. We've a practice meeting this afternoon and I need to prepare. About managing the GP budget. The GP budget, for god's sake. Do you know ... I came into medicine to heal the sick. Not run a business. It's wrong, Tim. All wrong. Why can't you people see that?"

Ryder, pulling on his trousers, had no answer. Nor

did he wish to attempt one. No man in a state of semi-nudity, he realised, displaying perhaps yesterday's boxer shorts, and still revealing an unedifying expanse of hairy thigh, was in any position to engage in serious discussion on this or any other topic. He tugged his trousers to full mast and pulled up the zip.

"Perhaps another time," he said. "Lunch."

"Another time. I'd like that."

A few moments later, waiting in reception, again under the stern eye of the nurse whom he had encountered when he arrived, he rang for a taxi to take him to Piccadilly station. His mind ran over the conversation with Ellie. Did she mean it ... mean she would like to have lunch with him? Or was she just being polite? The old rapport, the old affection, Ryder felt, was still there; they had laughed, joked, but it had been tempered. Health service reform: that's what had done it. It was almost as if she held him personally responsible. Then, when he had tried to explain, she accused him of insincerity, said he was talking in soundbites. Perhaps she was right. Perhaps he was the one that had changed ... not her.

Edinburgh. November 2014.

It was, at Ryder's behest, a languid journey to Edinburgh. For her part Margo had been impatient to reach the Scottish capital and then press on to St Andrews, reminding her husband that for her this was a business trip and that time was money. Ryder, however, as usual, wished to savour his escape from London. Even towards the start of the journey he insisted, to Margo's irritation, on pottering along the motorway at no more than 65 mph so he could take in the lush fields, with their sturdy farmhouses and ancient stone walls, which flanked the M6 beyond Preston. Besides, he said, it wouldn't look good to be done for speeding. Chance would be a fine thing, Margo sulked.

It seemed to Ryder, as they drove on in silence, that the further north they travelled the more the motorway became lost in the countryside, an irrelevancy beneath the timelessness of the cloud swirling above the Lune gorge, shrouding the Shap fells beyond. It was the rawness, the roughness of the landscape that appealed. It was untameable: neither the adjacent railway, now demure, maiden-auntish, nor its usurper, the motorway, loud and brash, could be said to have corrupted these wild, relentless hillsides. Despite man's markers there was an honest openness in this terrain which, Ryder realised with a shock, was absent from his own existence, absent from the spin, the half-truths, the muddle masquerading as mastery which were the politician's stock-in-trade. Suddenly he wanted this landscape to embrace him, envelop him. To take him.

He prodded the window control of the Range Rover. The glass slid away, and a blast of clean, crisp air, laced with rain, assailed his nostrils. Margo, dozing, came round with a start.

"What are you doing?" she said. "Shut that

window."

"Hun ... feel it," Ryder exulted, inhaling deeply. "Drink it. Fill your lungs ... let it in."

"All you'll be letting in is the stench from that truck in front of us. And I'm getting wet. For the love of god ... shut that window. And pay attention where you're going."

Ryder, content, closed the window. Those few moments, he felt, had put him in touch with something. He wasn't sure what, perhaps, briefly, his inner self, but he felt it was beneficial. Cathartic. And he felt invigorated. Stronger. That's what it was: strength. There was a force in this landscape that was immutable. Whatever might befall ... economic collapse, civil disobedience, riot, terrorist atrocity, or even the unlikely event of a Labour government ... those fells would outlast them all. Everything else, in comparison, was of scant significance. Including himself.

They stopped for coffee at Tebay services. Margo had a slice of lemon cake which seemed to improve her mood. Ryder, mindful of Ellie's strictures about his weight, declined, telling himself that cake was a post-meridian decadence and that, if mid-morning sustenance were really needed, a digestive or a fig roll should suffice. He was annoyed, though, when halfway through his coffee the cup, as he was replacing it, clipped the side of the saucer, landed unevenly and tipped over, spilling its contents onto his trousers and falling to the floor with a clatter. People looked round, albeit momentarily, and Ryder scowled at them.

"The handle was damp," he told Margo, as she passed him the paper serviettes she had collected with her cake. "No damage ... it's only coffee."

"Butterfingers," she said, leaving him still dabbing at his trousers as she went to visit the farmshop.

Ryder, sticky and uncomfortable, took out his phone

and checked his messages ... no strident call to return to Westminster for a late-night division, no FCO flap about drought in South Sudan or rising sea levels along the coast of Ghana.

When Margo returned she declared herself pleasantly surprised.

"These motorway places are sure improving."

"Ah, well," Ryder began. "It's to do with our initiative on ..."

"The government can't take credit for what's on offer in the farmshop. Sure, I know there's an election coming up and you guys'll grab hold of anything, but the Conservative Party isn't that desperate ... is it?"

Ryder grinned, weakly. He said nothing to Margo but it struck him that, perhaps indirectly, the government could indeed take some of the credit. Indirectly, in that this was Blenhesket country. Although Sir Wesley Blenhesket's constituency began the other side of Shap it was almost certain that produce from the sprawling Blenhesket estates would be on sale in any farmshop in the area. If, to get what he wanted, there were backs to scratch, arms to twist and, quite likely, palms to grease, then Blenhesket was the man. That was how he operated at Westminster, at least in his heyday. Even now, behind the scenes, his influence was huge, his patronage much sought. Not a man to be crossed, Ryder realised.

A voice cut in on his thoughts. Margo was talking. "We'll stop on the way back. Stock up. Get some stuff for the freezer. Don't let me forget. And don't you go sailing past when we get here."

"Hun ... come on," Ryder pretended to look hurt. "Would I do a thing like that?"

"Yeah. You sure would. And you know it."

***

It was late afternoon by the time they reached Edinburgh. Ryder, revelling in the vastness of the countryside, had insisted on leaving the motorway at Moffat to take the cross-country route. Margo told him the M74 and then the M8 would be quicker, but Ryder would have none of it. On the moors, near the source of the Tweed, they were caught in a deluge that reduced visibility to nil and left no alternative but to pull to the side of the road and wait.

"This would have been hell on the motorway," Ryder said. "All this rain. The spray."

"It's hell here," Margo snapped. "At least on the motorway we could probably have kept going."

They sat without speaking as the rain hammered on the roof of the Range Rover and water sheeted down the windows. It reminded Ryder of the time he'd been behind a waterfall and gazed out through the cascading torrent. Everyone had been given outlandish macs and hats and wellies and ended up looking like Paddington Bear. The noise was deafening. Where was it? Niagara, most likely.

To try and take Margo's mind off the weather Ryder told her what he had learned about Alistair not wishing to go to Oxford.

"That's just Marie-France talking," Margo said. "Stirring things. Have you spoken to Alistair?"

Ryder said he hadn't. He'd thought about it but decided it would be best to let things take their course. Too much pressure and Alistair might turn against the idea completely.

"You may be right," Margo said. "Anyway I guess I'll be able to sound him out when I take him down for his interview. Try and get him in the right frame of mind. But if he's absolutely set against it, then I guess there's not much we can do. And what exactly does he mean by a gap year?"

"Search me," Ryder said. "That's something else you can talk about."

"Gee, thanks. I sure get all the fun."

When the rain abated, and they were able to move again, they found they had lost so much time that they pitched into Edinburgh as rush hour was starting. Partly with the satnav and partly ... probably more, Ryder thought ... with luck, they managed to skirt the city centre, eventually to join the traffic heading homewards across the Dean Bridge. Shortly afterwards Ryder turned down a side street and a metallic voice told him he had reached his destination.

"It's okay for you," Margo said. "You've arrived. I've got to find my way out of here."

"Easy," Ryder said, moving to the back of the Range Rover to remove his bag, and waving an arm in the direction of the Queensferry Road they had just left. "Out of here, follow signs for the Forth Bridge, and there you are. More or less."

Margo, shifting herself into position behind the wheel, grunted. She adjusted the seat and mirrors, reset the satnav and, lowering the window, called to her husband on the pavement.

"See you tomorrow night. And try and fix up so we can meet Duncan for a drink."

"No worries, hun. And enjoy St Andrews. Oh ... and you might need to stop at a petrol station and fill up. Diesel, remember."

Margo arched a despairing eyebrow and put her foot to the accelerator. The Range Rover lurched away to disappear into the dusk of an Edinburgh rush hour.

***

Ryder's appointment with Duncan Buchlyvie was not

until 11am. Buchlyvie had been surprised to receive the phone call, had registered Ryder's name only when he said he was Margo's husband, but then apologised immediately. He said he wasn't with it because he'd been up half the night with his three-month-old son, and told Ryder to come to the parliament where he would be delighted to renew their acquaintance. It struck Ryder that Buchlyvie expressed no curiosity why his ... what? cousin-in-law? was there such a thing? ... should suddenly ring up and want to see him. Too tired to think straight, probably, which could work to his advantage. If the man were suffering sleepless nights then his guard would be down, and he would perhaps reveal more than he otherwise might. This scouting business, as the PM put it, seemed something of a doddle, with the added advantage of a couple of days away from Westminster, enjoying the comfort of a solid, if faintly old-fashioned hotel ... if the internet were to be believed ... away from the bustle of the city centre.

The reality, however, was different. On the first evening, after he had checked in, he discovered the Wi-Fi would not function. The manager was sorry, it had gone down before and they were working on it, but for the meantime there was an internet cafe not far away. Ryder couldn't be bothered to walk into the city to find some place that could very well be closed: instead he watched in his room a limpid documentary on alcoholism among orchestral percussion players. An odd topic, he thought, but then most documentary themes had surely been done to death: presumably producers were scratching for anything, however batty. He waited for the headlines on the ten o'clock news ... a volcano erupting on some island or other, a busload of tourists, mainly German, blown up in Sri Lanka ... nothing, therefore, to trouble her majesty's government

... and then, tired after the long drive, took himself to bed.

Around midnight he was woken by slamming doors, giggling, and voices and footsteps on the corridor outside his room. Wrapping a dressing gown round him he went to investigate. He was taken aback to find four young women, wearing next to nothing, and reeking of perfume, gathered round a mobile phone apparently attempting to ring a taxi.

"Do you mind ..." Ryder began.

"No ... we fucking don't," one said, to gales of laughter.

"Might I remind you this is a hotel and ..."

"Might I fucking remind you," another said, mimicking Ryder's received pronunciation, "that we've paid for our fucking rooms and so we can do what we fucking like."

"I don't think that sort of language is helpful ..."

"Hey," a third said, rather more reasonably, "chill ... okay? If ... like ... we can get a ride we'll be ... like ... out of here. Won't we, girls?"

"Yeah ... girls' night out," the others roared. "You coming, gramps?"

"I don't think so," Ryder said, and shut the door.

A few moments later the giggling receded and, with the final crash of a distant fire door, all fell quiet. Ryder slept fitfully, was conscious of a taxi returning some time before dawn, and disgorging its now more subdued passengers, and, when sleep finally evaded him, repaired in grim mood for breakfast. Of his nocturnal nemesis there was no sign. He wondered if he should bang on their doors, wake them, give them a taste of their own medicine. That would be churlish, and probably serve no purpose. His temper was not improved when the breakfast arrived and he found the orange juice watery, the bacon salty and the toast soggy.

"Breakfast chef ... go home. Latvia. Mother sick. She die," the waiter told him in tones that suggested he might be a countryman of the departed chef. "I cook. Learn. Is not easy."

"Indeed not," Ryder agreed, pushing aside a sausage drowning in grease. "Not easy at all."

He consoled himself with the thought that, if those women put in an appearance for breakfast, there was a fair chance that, given the probable amount of alcohol they had consumed just a few hours ago, they would gag on the hotel's full Scottish or, rather, half Baltic breakfast. As long as they didn't throw up in the corridor outside his room. But then the likelihood of that lot making it down to breakfast was remote. This was the generation that turned night into day, day into night. He wondered if Alistair would succumb to this inversion of the natural order, whether at Oxford or on the gap year he seemed to want. Perhaps he ought to have spoken to his son about it, not leave it to Margo. But these days, for the most part, she seemed closer to him than he did.

To clear his head Ryder determined to walk to the parliament and his appointment with Duncan Buchlyvie. The exercise would do him good: it would get the circulation going, remove the twitching in his knee with which he had woken up that morning, presumably after sitting in the car for several hours the previous day. The twitching was a recent phenomenon. Like everything to do with his knee, it came and went, but of late it was more coming than wenting. Was there such a word in English? he wondered. If there wasn't, there ought to be. He'd noticed the twitching that night Alistair had been brought home by the police, but that was probably a result of standing around in the chill nocturnal air. He'd been shivering all over, he remembered, when he came in. Anyway, a stroll to the parliament would do him good. And hadn't Ellie told him to be more active, not give in to this peculiar phobia about exercise? He had studied a street plan in the hotel and calculated it would take perhaps an hour to wander into the city, down Princes Street, through the gardens, then up and along the Royal Mile to Holyrood. The previous day's rain had moved on, it was breezy but not cold, and Ryder welcomed the chance to renew his acquaintance with a city that had undoubtedly changed since he and Margo attended Duncan's wedding.

Leaving the hotel, he followed the Queensferry Road to the Dean Bridge. Here he crossed to look down into the surging Water of Leith and into the village, straggling but spruce, which gave the bridge its name. He wondered how much property would cost down there, how it would compare with London. Or Manchester. He'd no idea. Musing, he turned away, to cross back over the road, and as he did so there was a brief pain in his knee, which seemed to seize, to contract, before he lost all sensation in it. For a moment he thought the other knee had gone the same way: his legs were about to buckle, collapse, and he heard himself cry out as he grabbed the parapet for support. He could feel the sweat on his forehead, though the day was crisp: it was like the time on the FCO stairs, only worse. His mind raced: perhaps he had turned too quickly, somehow sprained something. He could understand twisting one knee, being caught off-balance, though not both, not at the same time. But he was imagining things: his other knee was fine, just a slight tingling, the leg planted firmly on the ground. However the other one, of which he thought increasingly as his gouty leg, his gammy leg, was a different matter. There was nothing: no twitching ... at least, if there was, he couldn't feel it ... no sensation. This is what it must be like to have just one leg. An emptiness, where there should be substance. But why? Why should it go like that? Something must have triggered it. Something he'd eaten. That breakfast, surely ... greasy, swimming in fat. That couldn't have done him any good. What was it Ellie had said? Too much uric acid. Was there uric acid in toast and sausage and bacon? Somehow Ryder didn't think so. But there had to be a reason.

He leaned back against the side of the bridge, on the narrow pavement. He might have fallen, he realised with horror. Fallen forwards. Cars and buses were passing just a couple of feet from where he was standing ... had he collapsed into the road the result could have been fatal. He rested his hand which, like his forehead, was clammy, sticky, on the parapet. The stonework was cool and reassuring and Ryder was seized with an urge to bend, kneel, place his forehead where his hand now lay, to absorb the cold, numb the brain, make everything go away. This was ludicrous, he realised: trying to prevent his collapse and, at the same time, to will it, to sink to the stone and its chill reassurance.

He looked round. A woman, with a child in a buggy, was approaching along the pavement. He should stop them, ask for help. He was about to call out when he registered the fear on the woman's face: what is this creature, this maniac, lolling on the bridge, barring my way, threatening my child? Before he could speak, the woman had spotted a gap in the traffic and darted to the relative security of the opposite side of the road. Without a further glance at Ryder she put her head down and fled, the wheels of the buggy twirling and twisting to align themselves with the direction of travel. The child squealed in excitement at such fun, until sight and sound were obscured by a passing bus.

He needed to get off the bridge. He wanted to sit, to take the weight from his legs, at any rate his one good leg. If he could hail a passing cab ... but there was none in sight. Besides, what driver would stop on a narrow, busy road for a wild and anguished soul from whom young mothers fled? There was nowhere on the bridge to sit: the parapet was too high and, if he attempted anything, he would finish in the water below. However, at the end of the bridge, on the city side, were steps. The road rose and the pavement, it appeared, was tiered. If he could manoeuvre himself along the bridge, supporting himself on the side, then he could sit on the steps, perhaps massage his leg, get the blood flowing, or whatever it was. So what if he were to perch there like some old wino ... a wino with a briefcase and half-decent overcoat: the beggars he ignored in London came in all shapes and sizes. Fortunately, in Edinburgh, no-one knew him. The likelihood of a parliamentary under-secretary being recognised in the Scottish capital was slim. For the first time in an uneventful political career Ryder was glad he had never climbed beyond the lower rungs of the ministerial ladder.

He set off, clinging to the parapet as if his life depended on it which, he realised, given the propinquity of the traffic, it probably did. What was going on? What was happening? Ellie had spoken of gout, but surely this was not the same thing. He racked his brain to recall what exactly she had said, but he couldn't remember. He hadn't taken it in: as she knew, Tim Ryder did not do illness, did not speak its language, did not know its meaning. Apart from the odd cold, the occasional twinge here and there, which had cleared themselves up, and that back trouble, he'd never suffered serious illness. But this was different. Perhaps it was arthritis, rheumatism. Or wasn't there something called rheumatoid arthritis? Ellie hadn't mentioned these ... but she'd told him to have a blood test. He'd done nothing about it. Perhaps if he had they might have discovered something, got him sorted. And he wouldn't be lumbering like some drunk across a bridge miles away from home. He'd have that blood test done first thing. As soon as he was back in London. The very first thing.

All the same, something was happening in his knee. Sensation, a degree of control, was returning: he could feel the pavement beneath both feet and manage a couple of paces without grasping for support. By the time he reached the end of the bridge he was able to totter across the road leading up from Dean Village and, hauling himself between a row of bollards aligned to the steps, collapse onto them.

How long he sat there, how long he had been on the bridge, he couldn't tell. Only when he looked at his watch he realised there were just 15 minutes before his meeting with Duncan Buchlyvie. With a grimace he hauled himself to his feet, feeling to his relief the pain ebbing, an element of normality returning, and looked for a passing taxi. The third one at which he waved was free and slid to a halt on the opposite side of the road. Summoning his flagging energy, he lumbered into the carriageway, causing a cyclist to swerve, narrowly avoiding a delivery van, and crabbed across the road.

"Ye all right?" the driver asked, as he approached.

"Yes," Ryder said, opening the rear door. "Just take me to Holyrood ... the parliament."

***

It was airport security. At least, on a smaller scale. Belt off, coins out, briefcase, coat, jacket onto a tray: yawning jaws of an x-ray machine. Then the metal detector. State-of-the art, no doubt: strip me naked, check for weapons. Could suss out my knee, too, Ryder thought, find out what's going on. But strength was returning, though slowly. They probably wouldn't find anything.

As Ryder, aware he was dragging his leg, shuffled forward behind a queue of elderly Japanese tourists, he was overcome with the sinking feeling that afflicted him in the face of all security, that, contrary to basic British justice, you are guilty until proven innocent, a terrorist until laid bare, exposed, to the satisfaction of officialdom, as presenting no risk, no threat. Security was all very well, Ryder told himself, now propping himself against the table where his jacket and coat lay squashed in an undersized tray, and fumbling to remove his belt, but did it have to be so demeaning? So undignified? It was moments like this he questioned who was winning the so-called war on terror: a timid and nervous western civilisation, with its wealth and apparent power, or the shadowy successors to Osama bin Laden? Besides, how many Britons were killed each year as a result of terrorism? A handful, half a dozen, perhaps. Whereas on the roads ... it was ludicrous. Out of all proportion. All that expenditure to protect a nation brain-washed with fear. As he stepped beneath the metal detector he wondered briefly if the machine could read thoughts. In this day and age he wouldn't be surprised. Yet this was seditious, lefty thinking, with no place in the mind of a right and righteous Tory MP. His role was not to question, but to accept, to approve. To go along with whatever policies, however half-baked, his political masters, the Pembertons of this world, cooked up. Sometimes it was difficult. Very difficult. Those were the moments he yearned for a more balanced, a more one-nation approach of an earlier, pre-Thatcher party. Had he been around in the 1980s he might even have been a social democrat. But that belonged to a different age.

Called on from beneath the metal detector he was conscious he was sweating again. Not just his brow, but his hands, his fingers. Trying to put his belt back round his trousers he was aware it was refusing to go through the loops: his fingers slipped from the smooth leather; he had no purchase, no pulling power. This was ridiculous. He'd had no difficulty that morning in the hotel bedroom. Or had he? He couldn't remember. The hotel, that dreadful breakfast, seemed a lifetime ago. But why wouldn't the belt ... ah, another loop. Good. He must concentrate, focus. He was obviously shaken by the events of the morning and, although his knees, his legs, were slowly recovering, he still wasn't right. And, if anyone noticed him, struggling with his belt, and bathed in sweat, then they would be suspicious. Wasn't sweating a sign of nerves, anxiety, something these people were trained to watch out for? Good ... another loop. Just one to go. Come on ... come on. Got it.

Somehow he did up the belt and, remembering he had a tissue in one of his jacket pockets, he reached in to find it and wipe his fingers, dab his brow. He felt calmer, more collected. Pulling on his jacket, and putting his coat over his arm, he limped to an enquiry desk.

"I've a meeting with Duncan Buchlyvie at ... er ... about now. I think I might be a few minutes late."

The young man on reception flashed Ryder a wide smile. "Mr Ryder, is it? Mr Buchlyvie's rung down with his apologies to say he's caught in a meeting. He'll be with you as soon as he can and in the meantime you're to wait in the cafeteria ... over there. I'm sure he'll not be long."

Ryder was delighted. He could sit down, gather himself ... have a coffee. He thanked the man, and asked to be directed to the gents. A quick wash and brush-up would not go amiss.

"By the exit. Just near security. You can't miss it."

***

Some twenty minutes later, still wearied, and worried, but fortified by a respectable Americano and a shortbread biscuit ... concerns about weight could take second place, Ryder thought, and he probably needed the sugar ... he was feeling more composed as Duncan Buchlyvie bounded into the cafeteria and, looking round, picked out his visitor at once.

"Unforgivable," he gushed. "Unpardonable ... to keep a distinguished member of her majesty's government waiting like this. Before we know it, we'll have a diplomatic incident on our hands. Gunboats up the Forth, and all that. That is, if her majesty's government can afford gunboats these days. So ... how are you?"

Despite his concern over his knee, Ryder couldn't help but smile. This was the Duncan Buchlyvie he remembered: larger-than-life, the showman, the entertainer. True, he was plumper than Ryder recalled, and shorter: somehow fleshier, jowlier, altogether rounder. He was like a little rubber ball to be thrown against a wall, where it would change shape and bounce off at an unexpected angle. Yes, that was Duncan Buchlyvie. Impossible not to like him, despite his tendency to grab the limelight.

"I'm fine," Ryder lied, hauling himself with difficulty to his feet and extending a hand, which Buchlyvie took, squeezed a shade too hard for comfort and, for good measure, began pumping up and down.

"And how's that lassie of yours, that fragrant and delectable US cousin of mine, the fair Margo?" he enquired.

"Still fragrant and delectable," Ryder replied, managing to extricate a sore hand from the Scotsman's grasp, "but now US and British. Joint nationality."

"Aye, that's wise. Still has a wee bolt-hole when England, severed from the Scots, gives up the ghost. Of course, we could always find her a Scottish passport."

Ryder was about say this wouldn't be necessary, since England was not about to give up the ghost, when Buchlyvie was off on another tack.

"But now you'll be wanting a tour of this fine building of ours. Before we get down to business. I'm assuming it's business that's bringing you here."

Buchlyvie's eyes narrowed and for an instant he looked hard at Ryder. The man would not be the pushover he hoped he might be. Behind the banter was a flintiness, a don't-mess-with-me toughness, that made Ryder wonder briefly if he had been spirited from genteel Edinburgh to the barren and dispossessed streets of Trainspotting.

"Well ..." Ryder began, caught momentarily off-guard. "I mean ... business and pleasure. Always good to see you, of course. And this isn't an official visit. No way. If it had been ..."

"Och, in our line it's always official. Whether it's labelled official or not. There's no such thing as an unofficial visit. Like football. No such thing as a friendly match."

Ryder felt himself blushing. The meeting, like the entire morning, was rapidly unravelling. He needed to draw in the threads, bring them together, but Buchlyvie was speaking again.

"So ... we'll start with the committee rooms. Give you a feel for the place. Then look at the debating chamber. And you'll be getting out your notebook, for you'll be wanting to jot down ideas for the time you see sense and build an English parliament that's fit for purpose, fit for the 21st century."

It was on the tip of Ryder's tongue to say he could do without the tour, that he would rather go straight to Buchlyvie's office, where he could sit, not put undue strain on the leg which had now adopted its familiar dull ache, but his host was off, striding through the cafeteria, waving a cheery greeting at an acquaintance, and talking the whole time. Ryder struggled to keep up, and caught but snippets of commentary.

"Committee rooms ... what you'll see ... all glass ... openness, transparency ... nothing behind closed doors ... at least, that's the idea ... believe that, you'll believe anything ... " and a guffaw rattled the pictures lining the walls. By the time they reached the debating chamber Ryder was exhausted: too many corridors, too many steps; his leg was quivering uncontrollably, and with every pace he feared it would give way. Nausea overwhelmed him, as he found himself before a Piranesi drawing, of varnished wood rather than carved stone, an image of slopes and ramps, curves and angles, of raked roof beams and bowed lecterns, illuminated by pale, dusty sunlight shafting past a ceiling spiked gunmetal grey. There was no repose in this chamber, nowhere for the eye to rest: the room was heaving, quaking, shifting shape, constantly reinventing itself, and Ryder felt sick.

"Got to get out. Need fresh air," he mumbled at Buchlyvie who, in full spate, was telling him the interpreting booths were largely for the benefit of the one MSP who insisted on speaking Gaelic which no one else could understand. Another guffaw shook the chamber which, in response, metamorphosed yet again before Ryder's disbelieving eyes.

"I feel sick," he said, and this time Buchlyvie heard him.

"Christ," he said. "You look as if you've seen Margaret Thatcher. Let's get you to a ..."

"Fresh air," Ryder whispered. "Want fresh air."

A few moments later he found himself perched on a low stone wall in the parliament gardens. He had no idea how Buchlyvie led him there: faces, voices enquiring if he needed first aid, paramedics, doors opening, and finally fresh, cool air, at which Ryder gulped greedily. He felt better almost at once, secure in the knowledge that he could take the weight from his leg, that he was not required to move, to walk. At least, not for the time being. He would have been happy to stay on that spot for ever.

"You fair gave us a fright," Buchlyvie said, the jester gone from his voice. "What ...?"

"Food poisoning," Ryder said quickly, aware his whole body was trembling. "I had a bit of turn on the way over here. Something I ate ... this morning, I imagine, at breakfast, in the hotel."

"Hardly a good advertisement for Scottish tourism," Buchlyvie growled. "I hope you'll report it."

"Hardly worth it. I think the place is aware of its shortcomings."

Buchlyvie asked the name of the hotel. When Ryder told him he said he knew it: it was close to his home. He wanted to know how long he was staying. Ryder said he was heading back the following day with Margo who would join him that evening. It struck him, as he spoke, that if his legs were playing up he might not be able to drive.

"Margo?" Buchlyvie flung open his arms. "But you didn't say. That's fantastic."

"I was about to ... tell you, I mean. I thought we might meet for a drink ..."

"I'll hear of no such thing. You'll come over. Meet Fran ... the bairns. She'll rustle something up ... she's used to me appearing with folk to be fed. And if you're not in the mood for eating ... if your stomach's still off ... then we'll understand. Or you can just have a wee bite."

Ryder said Margo would be delighted, that she had said she hoped they could meet up.

"Aye, and cast an eye over the new love of my life. I know what these women are like," Buchlyvie said. "And perhaps, while the womenfolk are weighing each other up, we can have our wee chat. I'm not sure you're up for it at the moment. The best thing now is to get you back to your hotel ... if you're sure, that is, you don't want to see a nurse, or someone. If not, I suppose the best thing is to rest, wait for Margo ... and, as long as you're up to it, we'll see you, say, around seven thirty. Here ..." and he handed Ryder a card with an address. "So you know where to find us."

As Buchlyvie escorted him to a taxi, with his visitor leaning on him for support, he commented that Ryder was having difficulty walking.

"It's nothing," Ryder said. "I think I must have pulled a muscle when I had that sudden turn on the bridge."

Thirty minutes later Ryder was back in the hotel, where the manager greeted him with the news that the Wi-Fi was working and the problems of the morning had been resolved by importing a proper breakfast chef from a neighbouring establishment. Ryder waved him aside, took the lift to the floor where his room was and, flinging himself onto the bed, fell asleep within seconds.

***

The taxi driver was astonished.

"It's no but round the corner. Ravelston ... it's there,

man, you can all but see it. Just across the Queensferry Road."

Ryder thrust a ten pound note at the driver. "For your trouble," he said, bundling Margo into the back of the vehicle and climbing in alongside her. The cabbie muttered something incomprehensible but pocketed the money.

"What was that about?" Margo asked, as the taxi set off. "I mean ... if it's that close, why aren't we walking?"

"How was I to know it's just along the road?" Ryder fibbed. "Besides ... I thought it might rain. I know what you're like about not wanting to get indoor shoes wet."

"Money to burn," Margo grumbled. "I think you might have checked."

Indeed, Ryder had checked, using the map in the hotel, and realised that Duncan Buchlyvie's home was, at the very most, a ten minute walk away. Despite the fact that his knee was much recovered, that he could stand without feeling he was about to keel over, he was unwilling to subject his leg to avoidable stress. He refrained from mentioning to Margo his ... what was it? his turn, his do, on the Dean Bridge, telling her merely that he'd had a stomach upset, had been forced to break off his meeting with Duncan, but now appeared to have slept off whatever it was that was troubling him.

The evening with the Buchlyvies began in congenial and convivial style. Both Tim and Margo took immediately to Fran, Duncan's second wife, who, they learned, had been a postgraduate researcher at the parliament where they met. Despite being half Duncan's age she seemed to have his measure: there was an easy division of labour in the home, with Duncan providing a rich vegetable soup as starter and Fran a choice of fish pie ... her speciality, she told them ... and, in case their guests were not fish-eaters, a vegetarian casserole. Anything left over, she assured them, would be frozen. Child-care, too, seemed similarly egalitarian: Duncan and Fran flitted to and fro to put their toddler, Rowena, to bed, while Jamie, just a few months old, spluttered and gurgled in a carry cot.

"The wee one never sleeps," Duncan said. "He's the one responsible for keeping us up all night. If I can't concentrate on my work, can't do my job, and the business of parliament grinds to a halt, then we know who is to blame."

He gave a mighty guffaw and the child, in appreciation either of the witticism or of its place in politics, thrashed its little legs and arms against the side of the cot.

Over the meal, which Ryder, not having eaten since breakfast, devoured with enthusiasm, sweeping aside any suggestion from Margo that his stomach might still be off and he should take things easy, the talk turned naturally to politics. At once Buchlyvie became earnest, all trace of casual bonhomie, of flippancy, erased. Scottish nationalism, independence, Ryder noted, were too serious to be treated with anything other than absolute attention and respect.

"Look," Buchlyvie said, leaning back and wiping a morsel of fish from his chin, "this referendum decision is the most significant event in Scottish history. It means at long last we can be ourselves."

"Be ourselves," Ryder repeated, trying to suppress a sneer, "and what does that mean? You sound like some teenager ..." and he suddenly thought of Alistair ... "trying to break from parental control."

"In some respects that's exactly what it is," Fran chipped in. "For centuries we've been prevented from growing up, finding our own way ..."

"That's nonsense," Ryder interrupted. "You've been part of one of the most successful empires ... perhaps the most successful ... the world has ever seen. You've shared in its progress, its prosperity ..."

"And Scots have played a huge, possibly disproportionate, part in that development. It's time now to tap into that creative potential, to make it work for Scotland."

"Romantic claptrap, Duncan, and you know it," Ryder scoffed, catching a cautioning look from Margo. "You need a sound economic base ..."

"Which we have," Fran put in quietly. "Or will have. It's all been carefully costed. The key is energy ..."

"Come off it ..." Ryder dropped his knife and fork to the plate with a clatter. "North Sea oil ... I mean ... way past its sell-by-date."

A mischievous grin played round Buchlyvie's lips. "Who said anything about oil?"

Fran picked up the thread. "What you don't understand ... never understood ... is that this country of ours is surrounded for the most part by sea."

"I seem to remember something about that in geography."

"The coastline of the Highlands alone is longer than that of France ... and Argyll and Bute isn't far behind. And that's just for starters. The potential for wave power ... clean, cheap energy ... is unlimited."

"There isn't the technology ... at least, it's not economically viable."

"That's where you're wrong," Buchlyvie joined the debate. "And that's where the British government ... and now, you English, since you'll be on your own ... have gone wrong. Abject failure to invest in alternative energy. Which is what we've been doing over the past few years ... working with our universities, our shipyards. Perhaps you haven't heard of the sea snake ... harnessing wave power ..."

"Yes, but all this electricity ... you need to sell it,"

Ryder taunted. "No good producing it if you haven't the markets."

"There's England, for a start. And ..."

"We've got nuclear. A new generation of plants ..."

"Thanks to the Chinese, the French. And, in the long term, how reliable do you think they'll be? I mean, as partners. They're in it for one thing, one thing alone ... themselves. And when it all goes pear-shaped, like the banks, the poor old taxpayer will be there to bale them out. That's all Westminster is, these days. A giant insurance company."

Ryder shrugged. "We're entirely confident ..."

"There are huge markets in the EU. The Benelux countries, Germany ... especially Germany, desperate to fill the gap after it pulled the plug on nuclear, and to replace unreliable Russian energy ... are welcoming us with open arms. What's more ..."

"So you swap dependency on the UK for dependency on the EU. I don't recall that being flagged up when you were debating this so-called independence of yours."

"It was always there. You people south of the border never bothered listening because you didn't think it would happen. Anyway, we're not talking dependency. We're talking partnership."

"Partnership? In what? The EU? For pity's sake ... it's falling apart ... it's had it. And do you really want the hassle of applying for membership as a separate country and having to take on board the euro?"

Buchlyvie sat bolt upright. "If you people in Westminster looked over the parapet occasionally you'd realise the EU is changing. Not falling apart ... adapting. Forget about southern Europe ... that's history. We'll be forging a new, smaller, tighter and, dare I say it, nordic EU. Scotland is determined to be a part of it ... where we belong."

"It'll never work. The writing's on the wall ..."

"You could be right. It might end in failure. But ... and this is the difference between your country and ours ... we're prepared to give it a go. We're prepared to embrace change. What we're doing is ... we're articulating a narrative. Our own narrative."

Ryder smiled to himself. Articulating a narrative: if Ellie were here she'd jump down Duncan's throat, accuse him of speaking in soundbites. She'd have relished the evening ... got stuck in to a degree, Ryder realised, that Margo hadn't. Apart from disapproving looks she had contributed nothing. The penalty of being an outsider, at any rate born an outsider. Difficult to get a handle on someone else's politics. Anyway, she'd never much cared for the Westminster scene.

Buchlyvie was still in full flow. "Of course, the trouble with you ... the English ... is you don't have a narrative. At least, it stopped in 1945. What was it that US secretary of state ... Dean Acheson ... said? Lost an empire, not yet found a role. How right. I mean ... what's England for? What does it do? Where's it going? Do you know?"

"Well," Ryder began, "we play a crucial role in international peace-keeping ..."

"Aye ... and you've privatised schools and hospitals to pay for it ..."

"That's entirely different."

"Look," Buchlyvie said. "It's simple. Where do you see England in twenty years' time? I'll tell you where I see Scotland. A major player in a prosperous, nordic EU. A world leader in renewable energy, with an educated workforce enjoying a high standard of living. And England?"

"I would hope ... in twenty years' time ... well, I mean ... it depends ..."

"I'll tell you where England will be in twenty years'

time. Adrift off the shores of Europe, rudderless, isolated, a heritage centre, a theme park of castles and stately homes, manufacturing nothing, counting for nothing, socially and economically moribund. And why? Because you lack vision. Too focussed on the past to look to the future. That's what you need. Vision. And decent leadership."

A leaden silence descended on the table. The only discernible sound was a gentle cooing from Jamie's cot. Margo cleared her throat, as if to say something, but it was Fran who spoke first.

"I'll be taking these things away now, if we're all finished, and fetching the dessert."

As she stood up, to collect the plates, Ryder's mobile began ringing.

"Sorry," he said, in fact grateful for the interruption, and reaching into his pocket. "Ought to have switched it off."

He glanced at the screen to see who was calling. Blenhesket. Ryder frowned.

"Sorry," he said again, standing up. "I need to take this."

Ryder had reached the doorway by the time he was connected. "Sir Wesley ..." he began.

"I don't know what you're doing ... but drop it. Find a computer and get on to YouTube. Do a search for your name and see what comes up. Then ring me back and tell me what the hell's going on. I might add the PM's livid."

"I'm not with you ..."

"Just do it." The phone went dead.

Ryder turned towards the faces watching him from round the table. He realised the hand holding his phone was shaking. "I need ..." his voice trailed off.

"What is it, honey?" Margo said, standing up. "What's the matter?"

"Can I get YouTube on this thing?" Ryder asked, waving the phone at Margo. "I'm sure I ought to be able ..."

"YouTube ...? What do you want YouTube for?"

Ryder poked desperately at the phone. "It's Blenhesket. Something's cropped up. Something I need to see ..."

"Give it to me," Margo said, then, to Duncan and Fran: "He's hopeless with technology."

"If it's YouTube you're after," Duncan said, "use my laptop. Faster ... better quality. Half a second ..."

He left the room and returned almost immediately with the laptop already open. "Just need to get in," he said, sweeping the cutlery aside, placing the machine on the table and deftly tapping the keys. "There ... now wait for it to fire up. Do you want me to ...?"

Ryder nodded, glumly.

"Okay. What are we looking for?"

"Something about me. On YouTube. Blenhesket said if you put in my name ... and search ... something will come up."

Buchlyvie rubbed his chin, watching the screen, as the others positioned themselves behind him. "Right. Here we go. Let's see what we get."

He inserted the words Tim Ryder and clicked search. At once a list of titles appeared. The second one down read: "Tory MP drunk in street".

"What the ...?" said Ryder, as Margo gasped.

Buchlyvie opened the clip. At once a grainy image of Ryder, sitting on steps, then staggering to his feet, played out before them. The camera, wobbling, followed Ryder lurching across a road and apparently falling into a taxi. It was all over in less than a minute.

"Christ," Buchlyvie said. "It's had over three thousand hits ... and it's only been up half an hour."

Ryder groaned. "It's a fabrication ... pack of lies. I

wasn't drunk ... no way. My god ... I mean ..."

"Calm down," Buchlyvie said. "What you'll be needing is a stiff drink."

***

The rest of the evening, at least for Ryder, passed in a blur. The first thing he did was ring Blenhesket who accepted without demur the tale about food poisoning.

"We can work with that," he told Ryder. "Damage limitation. It could be worse. Leave it with me."

Ryder wanted to know how the clip had appeared on YouTube, who had shot it. Blenhesket said no one was sure, or was saying, but as far as they could gather it was a freelance reporter who had covered the last party conference, when Ryder gave a speech, had recognised him on the street, and then filmed the incident on his phone. That accounted, Blenhesket said, for the poor quality.

"Of course," he went on, "the bugger then offered it to the Sun which put it on its website ... that's how it then got onto YouTube ... and they're running a story in tomorrow's first editions."

"Christ," Ryder said.

"They wanted to take the line you were out clubbing all night with a group of women from your hotel ..."

"What ...?"

"Apparently they got hold of these women ... girls ... don't ask me how ... who said you bought drinks for them ..."

"I never ... that's crap. I'll sue them ..."

"No need. The story won't stand. The porter at the hotel said he never saw you all night ... saw these females go out by themselves and come back by themselves. There's no record of you at the club you're supposed to have visited with them. We've traced them

... spoken to them ... lawyers have ... and it's going no further."

"But the YouTube film ..."

"Not much we can do about that. And the Sun's still taking the line you were drunk."

"But ..."

"We'll give them a statement about the food poisoning. Even the Sun ... in this enlightened post-Murdoch age ... will be obliged to print that. And it's not going on the front page. You can thank some overpaid premier league striker caught *in flagrante* with a supermodel not his wife. Never had much time for football, myself ... but it obviously has its uses."

"What about the PM?" Ryder wanted to know. "You said ..."

"Furious, by all accounts. At least when the balloon went up. Charging up and down, shouting about bringing the party into disrepute before an election, and so on. Completely lost his rag, apparently. Some poor secretary woman in tears ..."

"I suppose that means I've no alternative but ..."

"Don't be so stupid," Blenhesket rasped into the phone. "No one ever resigned over food poisoning. At least, not on my watch. Besides ..." and Ryder thought he detected a note of cunning ... "we might be able to make this work for us."

"What do you mean ... make this work ...?"

"Later. For the moment ... you need a decent night's sleep. Then, tomorrow, next few days, a low profile. Stay at home. You're ill ... food poisoning, remember? And no talking to the press. I'll be in touch."

The phone clicked off. Ryder, ashen-faced, collapsed into an armchair. Duncan placed a generous measure of whisky next to him as Margo came to him, taking his hand in hers.

"It'll be okay, honey. It'll be okay. I know it will."

The evening that had begun so auspiciously was ruined. The whisky, with which Duncan Buchlyvie plied his guest in an effort to cheer him, served only to render Ryder maudlin and morose. At a suitable moment, and to everyone's unspoken relief, Margo rang for a cab to take them back to the hotel. Doorstep farewells were muted: regrets for spoiling a wonderful evening, insistence that no apologies were needed, an invitation to return under more favourable circumstances, and the requisite avowals to keep in touch.

As the Ryders' taxi drew to a halt outside the hotel a shadowy figure jumped from a parked car and began taking pictures. Ryder, befuddled from the drink, and dazzled by the flash photography, stepped clumsily from the cab, raising his arm to shield his face from the glare.

A voice, from behind the camera, called out to him. "Drinking again, Mr Ryder? Clubbing? Anything you want to say?"

Margo stepped towards the photographer, still invisible behind the searing flash, and for a second Ryder thought she was about to hit him.

"My husband has not been drinking. He has not been to any club. He is suffering ... as he has done all day ... from a severe bout of food poisoning. And I'll thank you ..."

"If he's ill, why isn't he in bed ...?"

"Why aren't you in yours? It's late."

"I've a job to do ..."

"So have I. To look after my husband. Goodnight."

Turning from the camera, she seized Ryder, frozen like a frightened rabbit, and swept him into the hotel.

They left the following morning, before the city was

awake. Margo had checked them out of the hotel the night before and their departure went unnoticed, for which Ryder was glad. The press, presumably, had its story, and no longer needed to stake out the hotel. Besides, as Margo told him, to try and lift his spirits, no paparazzo would be on the street at that time in the morning. Reporters, she said, kept the same hours as liquor stores: they were out and about only when drink was available. And that, she guessed, was not the case in a city still coming round after the night before.

They made good time back to Northaven, using the motorway, avoiding cross-country routes. Margo drove: Ryder said he didn't feel up to it. They broke their journey at Tebay where Ryder instructed Margo to bring him copies of the morning papers. While she spent what seemed like an eternity in the farmshop he skulked in the Range Rover, slumped in his seat, head down, fearful some tattooed and beer-bellied lorry-driver would recognise him, and feverishly leafed through the tabloids. There it was, the Sun, page five, the lead story: a blurred and almost unrecognisable picture of him lifted from the YouTube clip beneath the words Ryder Comes A Cropper. He read on:

Shoppers in the genteel city of Edinburgh were shocked to see a government minister staggering across one of the busiest roads in the Scottish capital.

Eagle-eyed freelance reporter Jason Hackley caught on camera under-secretary of state Tim Ryder, 47, as he diced with death lurching between cars and buses to reach a waiting taxi.

Mother-of-three Moira Lenzie, 34, said: "My first thought was the man was drunk or on drugs. He was all over the place. I really thought he was going to fall over in the middle of the road."

A spokesperson from the foreign and

commonwealth office, where Mr Ryder is in charge of monitoring climate change, said he was suffering from food poisoning.

"Mr Ryder was suddenly taken ill. There is no question he had been drinking," the spokesperson said.

Last night Mr Ryder was unavailable for comment. It is not known if the Northaven Tory MP was in Scotland on official government business or on a private visit.

One of the other tabloids reported the story, using a picture taken outside the hotel and showing an angry Margo looking as if she were about to lash out, while Ryder stood helplessly in the background. The headline read: Ryder's Feisty Filly. When Margo returned to the Range Rover, laden with bags, Ryder thrust the papers at her.

"Could be worse," she said. "And I guess I rather like that feisty filly business."

Ryder groaned.

"Say, though, honey," she furrowed her brow as she stowed the shopping, "I've been thinking. How come, if you had this food poisoning bug, you managed to pack away so much at Duncan's last night? I mean ... if that had been my stomach ..."

Ryder shut his eyes. Now was not the time for explanations.

"One of those things, I expect. Just sort of ... came and went. And please ... if you're done with the shopping, can we get moving? I just want to get back home."

Northaven. November 2014.

For what seemed like the umpteenth time Ryder leaned back on his study chair as far as it would go and rolled his eyes towards the ceiling.

"I've told you, Alistair ..."

"You could at least have rung. Warned us we were going to have half the world's press on our doorstep ..."

"I think that's a slight exaggeration. And anyway ..."

"That's what it felt like. You weren't here, so you don't know. And then, when I get to school, everyone waving copies of the paper at me ... wanting to know what it felt like to be the son of a page three pin-up ..."

"It wasn't page three ..."

"Someone pissed out of his mind in the middle of the morning ..."

"I wasn't pissed ..."

"Whatever. But that's what everyone said. Sending me links to that thing on YouTube ... as if I hadn't already seen it."

"Look. I know it's sometimes tough ..."

"I never asked for this. You've got your life ... I've got mine. I don't want to get caught up in whatever it is you do ... and what do you do? I mean ... being an MP? Just shouting at each other and jeering and voting the way you're told ..."

"It's not like that ..."

"Yeah, well ... whatever. But I don't give a shit. Because that's your life. Not mine. I just want to ... to be me. And ..."

"I think, Alistair, that's we all want. Deep down. To be ourselves. To be our own person. And sometimes that's not as simple as ..."

"I suppose that's what you were doing on that street in Edinburgh. Being your own person ..."

"Oh, for god's sake. Don't be so stupid."

"They're saying you'll be out at the next election. That no one wants a piss-artist as an MP ..."

"They're saying ... who's saying?"

"Marie-France said she'd heard ..."

"Tittle-tattle ... idle chatter. And you shouldn't be so hooked on what other people say or think ..."

The desk telephone shrilled into life, making them both jump. Ryder grabbed the receiver.

"Yes ...?"

"Sandhills FM ... your local station ..."

"Bugger off. I've nothing to say."

He slammed the receiver back onto its cradle and turned back to his son. Alistair, however, had gone.

**

Ryder spent most of the day in his study. There seemed little point in going downstairs. Margo was quiet and brooding, bent over her laptop, presumably writing up her findings on her visit to St Andrews. Alistair, he felt, was avoiding him, holed up in his room, listening to music, and saying he had a series of free periods which meant he didn't need to go to school. As for Marie-France, rattling around in the kitchen, Ryder had no desire to subject himself to her questioning and, worse, to the silent reproach he would inevitably read in her eyes. He knew that, in her mind, he had brought shame on himself, on his family and, by implication, on her. Damn it ... it was nothing to do with the woman. It was nothing to do with anybody. It was just ... a mess.

He wondered whether he ought to tell Margo the food poisoning story was just a ploy. That, while crossing the bridge, he'd had a flare-up of something he'd had before. But what? It all sounded so silly, unreal. And it probably wasn't anything. After all, Ellie had given him an examination and found nothing. He thought he should ring her at the surgery, tell her what happened. What really happened. But all she'd want to know was whether he'd had the blood test which, of course, he hadn't. Too busy. Or too worried ... too worried lest they found something? But what? Diabetes? Thousands of people had diabetes and led perfectly ordinary lives. No, there was nothing to be worried about. He would arrange for the blood test as soon as he was back in London. And then, perhaps, that would be the time to tell Margo. If, of course, there was anything to tell. Which there wouldn't be.

It occurred to him, to be on the safe side, he could test his hypothesis now, prove his legs were in good working order. He'd no pain, just a bit of a twitch now and again, and he could flex his muscles, twiddle his feet. He stood up, crossed to the study door, closed it and, kicking off his slippers, stood on the carpet by his desk. Slowly, keeping his back straight, he dropped to the floor in a squatting position. It was a long time since he'd done anything like that: exercise was not his thing. He began to bring himself upright, feeling his knees, his upper legs, take the strain. He reached out to steady himself on the desk. But no, he could do it. He didn't need support ... the knees, the legs, were fine. There he was, standing ... standing from a crouching position, using his gammy knee, his wonky leg, with no trouble at all. Apart from the fact he was sweating. Profusely. Yes, it was an effort. But he was out of condition. Ellie had said as much, told him he was overweight. That's what it was. Perhaps he needed to overcome his stupid, irrational dread of the gym. He needed a fitness regime, building up, a personal trainer to take him in hand. He might get some lithe and nubile female ... but no, that was not the point. With an election coming up he ought to look his best, toned up, fit, especially if there were stories circulating that he was some sort of alcoholic. That's right. That's what he'd do. He could beat this. Yes ... and he flopped gratefully onto his chair.

"Honey ..." the door to the study pushed open. "Say ... you okay? You look ... sort of ... all washed up."

Ryder nodded. "It's the heating. Must be turned up a bit high. It's getting rather stuffy in here."

"You shouldn't have had the door shut. You don't normally. Anyways ... look. I've been thinking."

She paused, waiting for him to speak, waiting for him to invite her to share her thoughts. Ryder said nothing.

"I've been thinking ... with all this newspaper business ... and an election next year ... what you need is a bit of serious R & R."

Ryder waved his arm dismissively.

"So ... I've been online ... booked for us to go out to La Jolla for Christmas ..."

"What ...?"

"I've been in touch with my folks. They're so looking forward to it ..."

"Hold on ..."

"Come on, honey ... when was the last time we went out and visited with them at Christmas? Years ago ... when Alistair was nine ... ten. They bought him a ..."

"I can't. No way. And you can't just spring this on me. Out of the blue. I mean ... I need ..."

"I knew it ... just knew that's what you'd say. That's why I went and did it. My god, Tim ... you Brits ... you hate change. You're so stupid, stubborn. All of you. Well ... I'll tell you this. I'm going. You please yourself whether you come or not."

"Hun ... you don't understand. It's not ..."

Margo turned from him, sweeping from the room, slamming the door behind her. Ryder made to follow, explain, make amends, but his knees, his legs, both of them ... flaccid, fluid, everything in flux, the room too, and he fell back.

"Margo ..." but his voice bounced back, muffled, dulled, from the books and files lining the study. A few moments later, from below, he caught the click of the front door ... opening, shutting ... then footsteps, receding quickly down the gravel drive.

"Margo," he groaned. "Margo."

***

He was still in his chair, slumped over the desk, when the phone, inches from his ear, jangled. It startled him. His brain was numb, he'd been asleep, head on his papers, no idea how long ... he twisted himself to a sitting position and fumbled for the receiver.

"Hello ...?"

"Blenhesket. You sound a long way off. You alright? Still shaking off that food poisoning ...?"

"What ...? Yes ... getting over it."

"Good. Now listen. I've sent you an email ... text of a press release, a statement, from you ... concerning ..."

"I haven't made any statements. You told me ..."

"You have now. Or you will have, once the embargo's lifted. I've taken the line ... or, rather, you have ... that you were the victim of over-zealous reporting ... an invasion of privacy that could happen to any of your constituents, at any time ... and that you feel strongly the press should be reined in."

Ryder, the receiver clasped to his ear, shook his head. He told Blenhesket he'd rather drop the whole thing, put it behind him. There was no point, he said, in raking it up, bringing it again to public attention.

"Nonsense," Blenhesket snorted. "This is a splendid opportunity to get you out there ... get you known ... a champion of the ordinary man and woman. It plays well with voters and it's just what the party needs."

Ryder told him it wasn't what he needed. He was perfectly well known in his constituency without seeking further unwanted notice from a dodgy YouTube clip.

Blenhesket would have none of it. "It's what we were saying the other week at that meeting in Manchester. We need to work together ... create a united front. This is a perfect opportunity. We get behind you ... back you up ... on the side of the electorate against the power of the press. So ... I need you in London tomorrow."

"I can't. I'm not up to it. Still feeling groggy."

An irritated grunt met his words.

"We can postpone this 24 hours. But no longer. So I want you here the day after next ... and we'll give this to the media in time to get you on the Today programme the morning after that."

"What?"

"You heard. At least it gives you a bit more time to prepare ... work out the line you're going to take."

A sudden thought occurred to Ryder. "I'm going to need clearance. I mean ... has this been okayed with number 10? I wouldn't want ..."

A throaty, sardonic, almost sinister laugh, Ryder thought, greeted his enquiry. "Play your cards right and no one will bat an eyelid. Least of all the PM."

A dozen questions tripped to Ryder's tongue but none would form.

"Excellent, then, that's settled. You just make sure you're ready. There's a lot at stake ... a lot."

The phone went dead. Typical Blenhesket, Ryder thought, replacing the receiver. Why waste time on formalities when you can simply hang up?

***

His back ached, from being curled for too long round the desk, and his head was fuzzy from its rude awakening by Blenhesket's call. His legs, though, and his knees felt firmer: they were part of him once more. The feeling that they were about to drop off, that whatever held his limbs together had turned to paste, had receded. He was able therefore to make his way across the study, along the corridor and down the stairs to the lounge, where he found Margo apparently engrossed in a book.

"You went for a walk," he began. "Where ...?"

"Out. Just out," she said, curling up into herself on the chair, almost recoiling from him. Ryder thought she had been crying: there was a redness, a puffiness round her eyes.

"Hun ... look. I'm sorry," he said, dropping into his usual place on the sofa. "It was all a bit ..."

"I don't want to talk about it."

"I do. I need to."

She looked across at him, fleetingly, over her book. He was right: she had been crying.

"It's just that ..."

The book snapped shut. "I don't know why you can't put yourself out just for once. It's not as if we go every year. They make us very welcome ... love to see us ..."

"Hun ... any other year. But with the election ..."

"Election ... election. You've one of the safest seats in the country."

"I know ... but ... this election's different. Unknown territory. The coalition ... the economic crisis. I need to bone up on this financial stuff."

"You can do that over there."

"But I can't. It's a constant round of parties and drinks ... very pleasant, don't get me wrong ... but exhausting. Those pushy senior vice president types in sales and marketing ... their wives dripping jewellery, checking out each other's nose jobs ..."

"Last time you were lapping it up. The centre of attention ... especially from the wives."

"It's my lil' ol' British accent ... my olde worlde English charm that does it. I'm actually no more than a performing monkey ..."

"Oh, come on. They're not bad people."

"No ... no. Sorry. I know they're not. But ... I don't think I can face it. I mean ... the socialising. Standing around. Then there's the journey. It's just that ... right now ... I'm not ... I'm not up to it."

"Well, clearly. The food poisoning ... all these crazy newspaper reports ... they're bound to have an effect. That's why you need to get away."

"It's not that. It's ... I mean ... I've been having a spot of trouble ... with the old joints."

Margo frowned, arching an eyebrow.

"The knees. One in particular. Sometimes a bit wobbly. I mean ... nothing to worry about. Ellie said ..."

As soon as he mentioned her name Ryder knew he had made a mistake. Margo tossed back her head, drawing a sharp breath: her body tensed, bristled, and it struck Ryder how noble, how elegant, how desirable she looked when she was angry. All the same, he had blundered: the chill, the frostiness he felt when he entered the lounge, and which he had managed slowly to dispel, had returned, and Ryder cursed his clumsiness.

"I see. You have something wrong ... and you go to her. She's not even your proper doctor. But you tell her first ... not me."

"I didn't want to worry you. I mean ... it's really nothing."

"Wait. You say it's your knees. That business in Edinburgh ... you falling about in the street ... is that anything to do with it?"

Ryder nodded glumly.

"But you said food poisoning. You know ... I thought it didn't add up when you ate so much that night at Duncan's. But what ...?"

Ryder told her about the numbness, the lack of feeling in his legs, the sensation that sometimes his lower limbs no longer belonged to him. He was worried about falling, he said, and wanted to get himself sorted before committing to going away.

"But honey," Margo said, "there are excellent physicians in San Diego. Probably far better than over here. We could get you an appointment. It's another reason for going."

Ryder said that he would see his man in London, that he was going to have a blood test, and that it was all under control. It was probably just gout, he told Margo, and he'd soon be as right as rain.

"Good," she said. "In that case, if it's under control, there's nothing to stop you spending Christmas with your in-laws."

Ryder pursed his lips.

"Come on, honey," Margo suddenly changed tack, "you know you'll enjoy it when you get there. And we don't have to go to all those parties. I agree they're a bit over the top. You can find time to hide away with your boring old papers ... and we can go for some invigorating walks by the sea."

"If my knees ..."

"Your knees will be fine. If not, we'll just take it easy. Rest ... relax. Mind you ... you've got a point. You could sure do with more exercise. Okay, I've had mine today ... I've had a walk. But I could always use more ..."

Her tongue licked lazily at her upper lip and her gaze drifted to the open door and the stairs beyond.

Ryder grinned.

"Alistair ...?"

"Listening to music. Headphones. He's out of it."

Ryder nodded. Hand-in-hand she led him upstairs. The dull pain in Ryder's knees had vanished, replaced by an aching, a yearning, more urgent, more intense, elsewhere in his body.

***

Later, lying lazily on the bed, after they'd made love ... why, Ryder pondered, was daytime love-making invariably more satisfying than at night: something to do with a denial of the Protestant work-ethic, perhaps ... he realised he'd agreed to go to California at Christmas without being aware he said he would. He didn't care. The sex had been good, better than for some time: possibly the thought of more of the same on the beaches round La Jolla, as years ago when they were courting, helped trigger his acquiescence. True, it would not be summer when they were there, but winters in southern California were mild ... often wet, but sometimes not unlike early spring days in England. Certainly, if they were going to cavort by the Pacific in December, there would be few people about to disturb them. He felt a thrill of furtive anticipation.

His only irritation was that Alistair would not be with them. Ryder couldn't decide whether this was a good or a bad thing. On the one hand, it might present an opportunity to spend time with him, to talk. On the other hand, if Alistair were sulky and moody ... teenagerish ... then this might ruin the trip. Margo had begged her son to go: a real family holiday, she said, and without him her Christmas would not be complete. Alistair, however, had refused, saying he wanted to stay at home to study and promising to go out in the summer, after his A levels, to visit his grandparents. Margo grudgingly agreed. On balance, Ryder felt, it was probably best to let him stay in Northaven with Marie-France. She never returned at Christmas to her relations in the Auvergne: her excuse was always the difficulty of travel, the risk of snow, cancelled connections. In reality, Ryder knew, the prospect of spending the so-called festive season with avaricious brothers intent on marrying her to an elderly neighbour was more than she could contemplate. Alistair would therefore be well fed, looked after in every way ... and Marie-France would have no truck with drunken teenage parties. She would be mortified, Ryder knew, if the home were trashed while she was in charge.

Nevertheless he felt a degree of resentment. Alistair was not accompanying them so he could get on with his course work, prepare for his examinations. For some reason it was fine for her son to stay behind to work, but when her husband suggested the very same thing, to do in effect his own course work and prepare for the election, the request fell on deaf ears. Typical mother-son relationship, Ryder thought. It's no wonder men had affairs when their sons replaced them in their wives' affections, and an image of Ellie floated into his mind.

Not that he could complain. The sex with Margo had been exhilarating. Nourishing. And very welcome.

London. November 2014.

No announcement. No apology. Not even the standard, gabbled message, stating the obvious, that they would be underway as soon as they received permission to proceed. In the meantime, as the minutes ticked by, Ryder's train from Northaven remained stuck outside the tunnel into which it should have dived long ago, beneath the streets of Liverpool, to take him to Moorfields station to change for the Lime Street service.

Looking at his watch for the umpteenth time, he cursed. It was just his luck Margo was in Leeds that day, seeing a client, and had been unable to take him into the city. It was at moments like this he wished Marie-France could drive. He'd offered to pay for lessons, but she refused, claiming she would never get used to traffic on the wrong side of the road. They ought to have made it a condition of service: nanny, good with children, able to drive. Sod the cooking.

Ryder frowned, and consulted his watch again. He always allowed plenty of time when using public transport, but this was cutting it fine. He'd a meeting with Blenhesket at two, and if he missed the London train, had to catch the following one, he would never make it. That would put the cat among the parliamentary pigeons. Blenhesket, who seemed to think he was doing Ryder a favour by getting him on the Today programme, and wanted to brief him about what to say, would not be best pleased. Blenhesket was used to getting his own way and would not accept that trains might be delayed or cancelled. He'd tell him he should have come the previous day, as he wanted, and that Ryder should not have hung around in Northaven when he was required in London.

Damn this commuting, Ryder thought. Damn this

to-ing and fro-ing between Westminster and home. And damn the job. What was the point of it? Did it serve any purpose? Did he serve any purpose? After all, what was he? A constituency MP whose in-tray was brimming with complaints about holes in the road or hospital cleanliness or Saturday-night town-centre yobbishness, matters not for him but for the council, the hospital trust or the police commissioner. Then there were the people wanting to know what he was doing about UFOs, demanding that electricity be generated from treadmills in prisons, that ancient Greek be compulsory in primary schools. Cranks and nutters, the lot of them: occupational hazards on a par with judging vegetable shows or attending nativity plays. As under-secretary of state at the FCO he was equally hamstrung ... responsible for matters for which he had no responsibility: global warming, hurricanes in the Caribbean, tsunami in the South Pacific, volcanoes, earthquakes and other dubious acts of god. He remembered the constituent who wrote to him about reintroducing village stocks: he was the one in the stocks, day in, day out, as all and sundry, Blenhesket and the prime minister included, pelted him with their stupid ideas and expected him to do something about it. Christ ... was it worth it?

The train shuddered, as if in sympathy with his plight, and began to move. Ryder caught the eye of a pony-tailed, leather-jacketed man of about his age, with a ring in his ear, who grinned broadly and said in grating scouse: "Bring back British Rail". Ryder looked away, out of the window, but at that moment the train plunged into the tunnel, and he caught in the glass a brief reflection of the pony-tailed one looking at his mobile. Ryder grasped his briefcase, ready to get up and make a swift exit as soon as the train drew into Moorfields station, but to his horror it ran past the platform, which seemed strangely deserted, and into the tunnel beyond. He looked round in panic. "Bomb scare," the scouser informed him, raising his voice above the rush of the train in the tunnel. "They closed the station. Me daughter texted me."

Confusion gripped Ryder. Where was the train taking him? Where would it stop? When? He'd never make that meeting now. He'd have to ring ... apologise ... but, surely, the phone wouldn't function in the tunnel. On the other hand the scouser ... with that revolting pony-tail ... his phone worked. He got a text message. But perhaps it came before the train went into the tunnel. And, anyway, even if he could get a signal, he'd never hear above the din. But the train was slowing ... lights ... people ... Central, Liverpool Central. Surely, that was alright. He could make it to Lime Street if he ran. Glancing at his watch, he realised he might just have time.

As the train stopped Ryder was waiting, coiled behind the doors, to spring as soon as they opened. Leaping onto the platform, he felt a twinge in his knees, but there was no time to worry about that now. He scythed his way through the subterranean gloom to the escalators and, barging past harassed mothers, burdened with buggies and wailing children, he reached the top and catapulted himself onto the station concourse. Following the flow he circumnavigated the barriers, flashing his ticket at a surprised official standing by an open gate, and raced along a short shopping mall, vaguely registering a food shop and a bakery, and emerged onto a street. Momentarily disorientated, he looked up and down the road and saw to his relief, at one end, the Adelphi Hotel. Here was salvation. Beyond the Adelphi, to the left, lay Lime Street. A blue sign, by a pedestrian crossing, indicated the station was four minutes' walk away. He checked his watch again. Five minutes to make that train. Ignoring the protest from his lower limbs, he set off at a gallop.

He was flagging by the time the arc of the station roof came into view. Immediately he was faced with a dilemma. The direct line to the concourse was via steps. The gentler, but slightly circuitous route, was along a pavement, rising, but without steps, with a left turn at the top to the station's sliding doors. Ryder chose the former and regretted the decision at once. The steps were high, their shiny metal rail ill-aligned to offer assistance, and he was panting, aching in every inch of his body, as he barged through the narrow entrance. Glaring at the statue of Ken Dodd, tickling stick raised, greeting arrivals at Lime Street, he lunged towards the ticket barrier as it was about to close.

"Just in time, sir. But you need to board the train here. It's ready for departure."

Ryder mumbled an acknowledgement. Summoning his remaining energy he headed towards the waiting Pendolino. For some reason, for which later he could offer no explanation ... perhaps, as a first class ticket holder, something inside him said he should board at a first class door ... he ignored the first carriage, the second, the third. A shout, from a distance, urged him to get on now, he was delaying the departure, they would have to close the doors and leave him behind. An image of Blenhesket, ruddy-faced, choleric, fulminating, flashed into his mind and, gripped by fear, Ryder flung himself at the nearest aperture. As he did, his foot caught on the carriage step and he fell headlong into the vestibule. The last thing he recalled was the door sliding shut behind him.

***

96

He had but the vaguest recollection of reaching his seat in first class. He became aware of his surroundings only as the train was slowing, passing between the lattice girders of the Runcorn bridge, with its flickering glimpses of the sluggish Mersey, and preparing for its first stop.

"There you are, Mr Ryder," a faintly familiar female voice said. "We were worried about you."

Ryder turned, following the sound. For a moment he couldn't place her: what was this woman doing, looking down at him, concerned and anxious, and then he realised. The carriage attendant, the one who always looked out for him ... the MI5 mole ... what was her name? He squinted at the badge pinned to her uniform: Eileen ... of course, that was it.

"You took a bit of a tumble, Mr Ryder. We were worried ... but it seems there's no harm. A bit of a bruise, probably ... but you'll be okay."

Ryder wanted to know what had happened. Eileen told him she had seen him on the platform and realised he was heading for first class. She assumed he had joined the train lower down, because it was about to leave, but was concerned when he failed to take his seat. She thought he might be talking to someone, one of his constituents, but when there was still no sign of him she went to look. She found him, she said, propped in a seat in standard class and being looked after by two students. They had found him, dazed and disorientated, and made him sit down. Someone had gone to find the train manager, someone else had given him something from a hip flask. By the time Eileen arrived he was recovering and able, with the help of one of the students, to be assisted to his place in first class.

"Those carriage steps are lethal, Mr Ryder. You're not the first person to trip over. Especially when you're in a rush. And perhaps you weren't thinking. I mean ...

all that stuff in the papers. A lot on your mind, I'm sure."

"That was a pack of lies ..."

"Exactly what I said. I said Mr Ryder's not like that. I know Mr Ryder, I said, and he's always polite and decent. Not like some of my regulars, I can tell you. It's all the fault of the press. Say anything, they would, just to sell a few papers. They want taking in hand."

Ryder shut his eyes. That was precisely the view, presumably, that Blenhesket would want him to adopt on the Today programme. Why had he agreed to go on air ... be grilled on one of the most widely listened to programmes on the radio? It occurred to him that someone like Eileen would make a better job of it: her indignation was genuine, heartfelt; people would sit up, take note, relish her common-sense, matter-of-fact opinions, whereas he was just another dull old grey politician, rent-a-quote, droning on about ... about what? He'd no idea what he was going to say. He hadn't given it a moment's thought: his mind was on Christmas and the trip to California. He realised he'd been relying on Blenhesket to steer him in the right direction, but he needed to bring something to their meeting, barely two hours away, otherwise he would look foolish, ill-prepared. Which, of course, he was.

"Thank you," he said to Eileen, ignoring his aching, still trembling legs. "I'm feeling much better. I wonder if you could bring me some water ... just water ... and then I need to do some work ... get my head round a couple of things."

"Certainly, Mr Ryder. I'm glad you're feeling better ... though you perhaps ought to get yourself checked over. By a doctor. You've had a bump on the head and you can't take any chances. Promise me you'll ...?"

Ryder nodded, reluctantly. As Eileen turned away, he had an afterthought.

"Those students ... who sorted me out. Would you ... I mean, if it's no trouble ... could you find them ... get them coffee, drinks, a snack ... whatever they want. With my compliments. I'll settle up with you later."

Eileen beamed her approval. If only, Ryder thought, it were so easy to charm and to woo voters. Anyone, in fact. It probably wouldn't be as straightforward the following morning in the Today studio.

***

Mercifully the meeting with Blenhesket was swift. Sir Wesley was in a no-nonsense mood and appeared impatient to get away to another appointment. He seemed not to notice Ryder's slightly dishevelled appearance, or the bruise he could feel on his forehead, but barked his instructions, reminding the younger man that as the innocent victim in what was clearly a gross abuse of press freedom, he should go on the offensive, demand a thorough review of journalistic ethics ... if that wasn't a contradiction ... and suggest that, if newspapers and other news media proved unable to clean up their act, then the government would do it for them.

"But remember," he continued, "the object is sympathy. Winning the punters over. God knows most of the people in this party come across as upper class twits lining the pockets of their city cronies while the economy ... and ordinary people ... go to wrack and ruin. In six months we've an election to win. The fight has got to start now ... and you're part of it."

Ryder nodded, but before he could gather himself and ask how he was part of it, Blenhesket had thumped him on the back, wished him luck, and ushered him from his office.

As Ryder made his way to the FCO, he tried to

focus on what Blenhesket had said. He was aware he hadn't taken much in. Blenhesket's rant was just another affront to add to those he had already suffered that day: the undignified dash to the station, the ignominy of falling in the carriage, the possibility that a member of the public ... a journalist, perhaps ... recognised him as he was being led, wilting and groggy, through the train. Damn it. And now his head, his whole body ached: all he wanted to do was go to bed. He resisted the urge, however, to return to his flat. There was too much to do. His in-tray, he knew, would be bulging: a report, he remembered, demanding action, on the Lord's Resistance Army and child sex-slavery in the Democratic Republic of Congo, another on the dumping of toxic waste by a British firm into the seas off the Ivory Coast. Yet what in reality, what, short of sending in a regiment or deploying a frigate, could he do? Those days had long gone. He was powerless, he could do nothing, apart from pen a bland response which no one would read, or give a feeble statement in parliament to the handful of MPs who would bother to attend. Gesture politics, that's all it was, Ryder thought grimly, as he hauled himself up the stairs at the FCO. In fact, the whole place, the whole vast edifice, was gesture: a impotent gesture to a long forgotten past.

Of more immediate, and certainly of more relevant, personal concern, were the Today programme and the need to concoct something on his Scottish trip for the PM. Pemberton was all too well aware, thanks to the YouTube fiasco, that he'd been to the Scottish capital. He would expect results. Indeed, it was astonishing someone from number 10 hadn't messaged him already demanding to know what he'd found out. But perhaps ... hell ... he was suddenly persona non grata with the PM. Blenhesket had said Pemberton was livid about the video clip. Perhaps he'd given up on him. Dropped him.

Thank god there wouldn't be a government reshuffle before the election, otherwise he'd be out. The thought of it, the shame, the ignominy, brought him to a sudden stop. He was shaking, felt clammy, but this was nothing physical, occasioned by his knees. At least, he didn't think so. This was in his mind, for his political future was at stake. He leaned for support against a door frame, which was solid and reassuring, and for a second closed his eyes. Get a grip, he told himself. And then: what would it matter if I were fired? Minister for paperclips: wasn't that how someone in his position once described himself?

Moving away along the corridor towards his office ... fortunately no one was about to observe him communing with a door ... it occurred to him he ought to follow the advice from Eileen on the train and get himself checked out. He'd had a bump, could feel the bruise, and one couldn't be too sure with these things. All the same, apart from that, and the general weariness in his limbs, normal these days, he felt fine. At least, more or less. Besides, Blenhesket hadn't noticed anything ... perhaps because of the poor lighting in his room ... and he'd have been the first to have said if he had. He obviously didn't look too bad, despite everything. This was encouraging. All the same, if he had a check-up ... not at some ghastly A&E department, hopelessly underfunded, he reminded himself, by the coalition of which he was a part, but with his consultant ... then he could get that blood test done. Kill two birds, and all that. Though killing, in the context of doctors, was unfortunate. He gave an involuntary shudder. Nevertheless he groped in his pocket for his mobile, found it had been switched off, cursed, and, ignoring the waiting messages, ran down his list of contacts. Eventually he found what he was looking for and, after failing twice for some reason to hit the desired key ...

the design of these phones was not helpful to fingers that refused to bend as they should ... he succeeded in ringing the number.

A Harley Street receptionist told him Mr Henderson had already left but if it was urgent he could be seen by another consultant. Ryder said he would prefer to see his own doctor and it would wait until the following day. He was given a half past nine appointment which, he calculated, would give him ample time to leave the BBC after his Today programme interview and make his way there.

As he walked into his outer office a phone was ringing. A young man, crisply suited, picked up the call.

"Excuse me ..." he said, as Ryder stalked past, head down, intent on the solitude and relative tranquillity of his own office, "it's for you. A Mr Duncan, calling about a book from the library. Sounded foreign ..."

Ryder glared at the man, who took a step back. Dulwich College and Cambridge ... he remembered this, though not the name ... an intern, a protégé of Miller, the foreign secretary, and deputy leader of the party, who had insisted he find him something to do. Another incompetent who in twenty years' time would doubtless be in the cabinet.

"I'll take it in there," Ryder growled. "Put it through. And make sure I'm not disturbed."

Shutting his door behind him, he eased himself into a shabby leather chair, inherited from a predecessor, for there was no money to replace furniture, and which creaked as it tilted back beneath his weight. Ryder felt immediately more relaxed, more secure, and picked up the phone.

"There you are," purred a familiar voice. "At last. Been trying to get you all day. Find out how you are. Your French maid said you were back in London."

Despite himself, Ryder laughed. "Hello, Duncan,"

he said. "And before you start getting the wrong idea ... Marie-France is not a French maid. I mean ... not in that sense. French she may be ... a maid of sorts ... but definitely not a French maid. Besides, you haven't seen her."

"Oh," Duncan said, sounding disappointed. "I thought I might have caught you in some indiscretion."

"There's been quite enough indiscretion ... not of my making ... over the past couple of days without manufacturing any more. That's all we need: Junior minister in French maid romp. And concocted video footage to match. Christ ... I hope this line's not tapped. Or it'll be all over tomorrow's tabloids."

"Bound to be tapped, my wee laddie. Bound to be. Security and surveillance ... the only growth industry you people south of the border have. Of course, it helps massage your appalling employment figures."

Again, Ryder laughed. Duncan Buchlyvie was good for him: mildly irreverent, iconoclastic, the antithesis of most of those he worked with in Westminster, with their animal earnestness, their beady and furtive intent. But Buchlyvie could be serious, too, and was not afraid of ... what was that cliché? ... thinking out of the box, projecting, looking ahead, in contrast to the short-termism, the single-parliamentitis, that blighted Ryder's political life. Perhaps he ought to pack it all in and get himself elected to Holyrood.

Buchlyvie was asking how he was, whether he'd recovered from his food poisoning, and whether he was likely to return to Edinburgh. "Where your film career started," he reminded him, and roared with mirth down the phone.

Ryder told him he would be on the Today programme the following morning to talk about his film career, as Buchlyvie put it, and to demand an end to press harassment of ordinary citizens.

"You're hardly an ordinary citizen," Buchlyvie said. "But I'll make a point of listening. May as well, while we've still got the Beeb."

"What do you mean?"

"Think about it. An independent Scotland will need a national broadcaster with a more Scottish focus ... a Scottish Broadcasting Corporation, if you like. Of course, we'll probably have a couple of English newsreaders, like the Beeb does now with its token Scots and Welsh, just to appease the minorities."

"Well," Ryder said. "I suppose if you're going down your independence path a separate broadcasting organisation makes sense."

"Aye ... and that'll not be the only separate organisation. I tell you, as long as we retain the trappings of our colonial past there's no way we can build a new identity for Scotland. Border controls, for example ... if you're not in Schengen we'll want to see your passport ... and Scots, of course, will have their own. I've seen some of the designs for our new passport ... real works of art. None of that 'dieu et mon droit' nonsense all over them, either."

"What ...?"

"Scotland will be a republic. You can keep your royals. Privatise them, for all I care ... raise some cash. The Scots don't want them ..."

"Hold on ... that's ridiculous. There's no evidence ..."

"Opinion polls show strong republican feelings among the young. Okay ... I'm perhaps getting a wee bit ahead of myself. But it makes sense. Monarchy ... and certainly not an English monarch, actually of German descent ... has no place in a Scottish democracy in the twenty-first century."

"Why am I hearing all this only now?"

"Because you haven't been listening. It's been on the cards ever since we opened this whole independence debate. But, as I've said before, you English so love your own navels you haven't the wit to look in anyone else's. And that's something else you might say if you're talking tomorrow on the radio about the press. Newspapers ... the media ... shouldn't be so insular, so London-biased. They need to get out and about ... find what's going on elsewhere, report it. Tell people not what they want to know but what they need to know. And that's why we want a strong and independent SBC."

"That's all very well, but ..."

"Sorry ... I've got to go. I'm being called for a debate. We'll keep in touch, Tim ... and give that bonny wife of yours a big kiss from me. See you."

Ryder stared at the phone in disbelief as Buchlyvie ended the call. He dropped the receiver back in its place and leaned back in his chair, which groaned in sympathy. That business with the monarchy ... that would need watching. It was certainly something Pemberton should know about ... pass on to the palace. Though on second thoughts it was probably common knowledge in royal circles. The general impression at Westminster was that the crown was generally far better informed, through its lingering influence and patronage, than the average government minister. Indeed, courtiers were probably already plotting a royal charm offensive in Scotland: more visits to Balmoral and photo opportunities with flag-waving children bribed with an afternoon off school. Anyway, that was certainly something with which to feed Pemberton. And, Ryder congratulated himself, he hadn't actually had to do anything, pose awkward or leading questions, for Duncan to spill the beans. A successful bit of scouting, if ever there was one, and all from the dubious comfort of a hand-me-down government chair.

Nevertheless Pemberton's report would have to wait.

The priority was preparation for the Today programme. Frowning, Ryder leaned forward and prised open his laptop, the cover of which was stiff, awkward, and for which, fumbling, he needed two hands. He prodded it into action. While it was stirring itself, he went to the door of his office, yanked it open and, spying the intern with his feet on a desk, texting furiously, he demanded a pot of tea and a fresh prawn sandwich.

Dulwich College and Cambridge, or whatever his name was, could make himself useful ... perhaps for the first time, Ryder thought, returning to his desk, in a probably pampered, privileged existence.

***

The car arrived at a quarter to eight to take him to Broadcasting House. It was ridiculous: his flat was barely three streets away ... cross Great Titchfield Street, cross Great Portland Street, and he was there. But Ryder didn't entirely trust his knees, especially after the previous day and the dash through Liverpool and the episode on the train, and he wanted no repeat of the Dean Bridge fiasco. Anyway, the assistant from the Today programme had insisted. You are our guest, she had told him, and it's not our policy to make government ministers walk the streets to reach us. Walking the streets sounded faintly immoral, but perhaps not at eight in the morning, and Ryder wondered where in human hierarchy the cut-off came for a car not to be dispatched. An opposition backbencher, for instance: would he or she enjoy courtesy cushions or would it be the underground to Oxford Circus and then shanks's pony to Portland Place? Whatever ... Ryder was grateful he wouldn't arrive flustered and harassed, for he needed to be alert. The Today programme was known for being confrontational and government ministers were legitimate prey. Ryder had no wish to be cast to the listening lions.

The studio had the muted, airless feel of all enclosed spaces. It was probably the nearest anyone came, Ryder thought, to being buried alive. Turn out the lights, cut the sound, and that's what it was: an oversize coffin where, he realised, given a mauling by one of the presenters, a name, a reputation might well be interred, never again to see the light of fame or fortune. Shelagh O'Malley, however, did not look the mauling type. A relative newcomer to the Today programme, she gave him a reassuring smile as he took his seat. Or perhaps that was the ritual, like the dance performed by stoat or weasel to mesmerise its quarry, to create a false sense of security. He must not succumb to such wiles; he must focus, but already his mind was elsewhere, on the debate preceding his interview, an acrimonious discussion between a dietician and a spokesperson for academies defending their right to peddle junk food in their schools. Of course, Ryder reasoned to himself, it was wrong that academies enjoyed a freedom denied to schools that clung to the local authorities. It was all very well granting autonomy to academies, or at any rate, given central government controls, the illusion of autonomy, but no one ever proposed they should enrich themselves by making already fat children fatter. Or ruining their teeth. And then there was the question of ...

" ... with us under-secretary of state in the foreign and ..."

Christ ... that was him. He was on ...

"Mr Ryder ... good morning."

His throat felt like old leather and his lips as cracked and parched as a dried-up river bed. "Good morning," he croaked, his voice remote, dislocated, as if in a distant call centre. "Good morning."

"Mr Ryder ... let's get straight to the point. Images of you ... shall we say in a distressed state ... were published on the internet without your knowledge. Why, when you're apparently so upset about what is, according to you, a clear invasion of your privacy, have you not taken legal action against the perpetrators?"

"Well ..."

"Surely, rather than pursuing justice in the media, you should be pursuing justice in the courts."

"That's easier said than done. It's very difficult ..."

"The Human Rights Act, article eight, says everyone has a right to respect for private and family life. There's nothing difficult about that."

"Indeed not. A right to a private life, enshrined in law, is vital to protect the individual in situations where ..."

"Then why is your party committed ... and has been since before the last general election ... to repealing the Human Rights Act, including article eight which you say is so vital?"

What was the woman on about? Panic seized him as he performed a rapid search and find in the dustier areas of his brain and recalled that the home secretary, only recently, had indeed said the act was not fit for purpose. But he wasn't here to talk about the Human Rights Act. He was here to ... to ... beneath the table he clenched his fists, digging his nails deep into the fleshier parts of his palms. He took a deep breath.

"We believe ... er ... we should retain the spirit of the act ... but there are certain anomalies ... terrorists, for example, exploiting it, turning it to their advantage ... at the expense of law-abiding citizens for whom the act was intended. And it is precisely those law-abiding citizens who require protection from the prying eyes of newspaper paparazzi and from the editors and other unscrupulous people who publish these pictures."

"But the Human Rights Act already offers protection, redress, as well as ..."

"Clearly the Human Rights Act is not doing its job. And, despite the fine words in the wake of the Leveson enquiry the other year ... if you recall, into telephone tapping and other abuses by the press ... the situation has barely changed. Ordinary people, going about their ordinary business, are still victims of press intrusion ... can find their good names dragged through the mud. And it's got to stop."

"And how would you propose to do that, Mr Ryder?"

"Journalists like to tell us they belong to a profession. Other professionals ... doctors, lawyers ... are licensed ... declared fit to practise. I'm suggesting there should be licensing for journalists ... and anyone who transgresses against their professional ethical code should have their right to practise ... their right to report ... revoked."

"Isn't this just an overreaction on your part following the reports about you that appeared in the press?"

"Not at all. Indeed, I would go further than simply licensing and registering reporters. If the industry ... this so-called profession ... cannot abide by existing regulation, then it must be subjected to the same sort of constraints as broadcast media. If you look at Ofcom ..."

"Which, of course, has the ultimate sanction of withdrawing a broadcaster's licence. Are you saying the same should apply to newspapers ... that they should be licensed in some way, with the threat ultimately of closing down a publication?"

"As I said, if the industry cannot adhere to existing guidelines, it must be policed in such a way that ..."

"Surely, this is censorship. Are you not concerned this would have a detrimental effect on free speech? Are you and your party opposed to free speech?"

"As you well know, there's no such thing as free speech. You broadcasters are constrained by Ofcom, by laws on racial and other discrimination ..."

"Given that these days, Mr Ryder, we are all citizen journalists ... carrying cameras with us in our mobile phones ... how are you going to prevent someone who is not a licensed journalist filming me or anyone else in a compromising or embarrassing situation and publishing the pictures ... the footage ... on the internet? These people fall way beyond the scope of your licensing proposal."

"What we need is a long, hard look at the whole question of privacy and, possibly, introduction of a privacy act ... which, of course, at the moment we don't have ... which will look at exactly such scenarios. In the Irish Republic ..."

"So is this government policy? Will we be reading about the licensing of journalists and editors ... a privacy bill ... in the manifesto your party puts to the country at the general election?"

"I'm not one of those drawing up the manifesto. But, yes ... I'm sure the party will be talking about the whole issue of privacy in the run-up to the election and in the parliament beyond that."

"Mr Ryder ... I'm afraid we need to leave it there. Thank you for joining us this morning. No doubt we'll be hearing a lot more about privacy over the coming weeks. Now, with the time coming up to ..."

Ryder leaned back in his seat, bemused. That was it. All over, and just as he was starting to enjoy it. That was the trick, of course: as soon as they feel you getting the upper hand they cut you off, so they can sink their teeth into the next victim. Well ... he hadn't done too badly. He hoped Margo had been listening, and Alistair ... but he'd be on his way to school. Perhaps just as well. The last thing he'd want would be for his father sounding off on prime-time radio. It ought to have gone down well with constituents, though. That was what Blenhesket wanted. He'd certainly have been listening ... probably preparing the post mortem even now. But there'd be nothing to be post-mortemish about. It was good ... he'd said what he wanted to say. He wondered if Ellie had picked it up, in her car, on the way to the surgery. She'd be impressed. Her tame minister ... that's probably how she saw him ... broadcasting to the nation.

Shelagh O'Malley was looking at him, a half-smile on her face, and indicating he should leave. Someone else, behind a glass panel, the girl, the young woman, who had escorted him from the car through Broadcasting House, was waving and pointing to the door. Typical, Ryder thought, trying to make as little noise as possible as he slunk from the studio: a guest one moment, a fugitive the next. What was it Franklin said? Guests, like fish, begin to smell after three days. Only in the case of broadcast media it was three minutes.

The girl was by the door as he came out.

"That was fine, Mr Ryder. Thank you for coming."

"My pleasure. Any time."

"You know ... my boyfriend is a great admirer of yours. He's very impressed."

"Oh, yes ...?" said Ryder, only half-listening, still preening himself on a job well done.

"He works with you in your office. An intern. Clive Smalley-Smythe."

"I don't think I ..." Ryder began, and then corrected himself. "Of course. Dulwich College and Cambridge."

"How clever of you to remember," the girl beamed.

"That's where we met. Cambridge. Actually it was me who got Clive the internship. Well, sort of. More your boss, the foreign secretary, Jeremy Miller ... I'm his god-daughter. Jeremy's a great friend of our family."

Ryder was on the point of saying he supposed it was Miller who got the girl into the BBC but thought better of it. But that was what it was all about. The establishment. Looking after its own. Old school ties and Bullingdon clubs. Okay, that was Oxford. But it was the same thing. Suddenly the ex-comprehensive, redbrick university boy felt very much an outsider. And his legs had begun to tremble.

***

The consultant, despite his elegant rooms, the rich carpets, the plush seating, the subtle lighting, posed largely the same questions, performed largely the same examinations, that Ellie had conducted in her far less salubrious Moss Side surgery. Ryder felt almost disappointed: considering the amount of taxpayer money underpinning his private health care he felt somehow entitled to more.

True, Mr Graham Henderson was more thorough than Ellie. Having checked Ryder's head, peered into his eyes, asked him, almost as a joke, his patient thought, to hold up a number of fingers, and suggested various symptoms, none of which applied, he dismissed the fall on the train.

"You've been lucky," he said. "It could have been worse."

However, after listening to Ryder's concerns about the debility particularly in his lower limbs, he spent considerable time gently manipulating the area round his joints, particularly the feet and knees, as well as his fingers and hands. He made him wiggle his toes, rotate his feet, and clench his fists, and he wrote careful notes, with a fountain pen, as his patient described the tingling in his arms and legs, the sudden pain, or sometimes lack of sensation, and asked whether he had noticed any stiffness in his joints. Ryder said he hadn't, rather a weakness, but mentioned his occasional clumsiness ... tripping on the train, sometimes dropping things ... as well as feeling generally out of condition.

"Sweating? Breathlessness?" Henderson probed.

Ryder nodded, recalling his moment of panic on the Dean Bridge or his dash to Lime Street station on the previous day.

The consultant eased himself back into his chair, the leather of which ... hand-stitched, Ryder noticed, and clearly not government issue ... shaped itself gracefully to his contour.

"I think, Mr Ryder, I would like you to return at your earliest convenience for a blood test. Nothing to eat or drink during the previous twelve hours ... just water. I'm also, if you have no objection, going to refer you to a good friend of mine, a consultant neurologist. I think it might be useful if he were to undertake an examination. Two minds are better than one, as it were."

"Why ... I mean ... why a consultant neurologist? Have you found something?"

"Early days, Mr Ryder. Early days. We don't want to jump to conclusions. But I detect a slight lack of response ... not quite what I would expect to find ... in the muscular tissue in certain areas. That's why I would like Mr Meakin to take a look. Perhaps carry out one or two tests."

"Tests ...?"

"Merely exploratory. That's all. Now ... my secretary will contact you when we have a date for Mr Meakin ... and in the meantime, if you would care to ring to let us know when you might be calling in for your blood test ... I think perhaps sooner, rather than later ... this would be helpful."

"Helpful ...?"

"To give us an idea what we might be dealing with. Then we can take things from there."

Ryder swallowed hard. His throat hurt: it was dry, he could do with a glass of water. Or perhaps something stronger. But it was still early. He'd gone straight from Broadcasting House to Harley Street and, besides, he'd been summoned to a late-morning meeting with Blenhesket. It wouldn't do to go along reeking of alcohol. Certainly not at that time of day.

"Thank you, Mr Ryder," Henderson was saying. "We'll be in touch."

***

Sir Wesley Blenhesket was in conspiratorial mood, enhanced by the perpetual gloom that reigned in his room. Why did he never fully open the curtains, or turn on additional lights? The one table lamp, that pooled its rays onto whatever document lay on the desk, meant its reader remained behind it, tenebral, suggested rather than realised. A hologram, Ryder thought: the real Blenhesket was probably miles away, tramping his estates in Cumbria, exhorting his tenants to ever greater effort.

"What I'm telling you," a voice emerged from the shadows, "remains within these four walls. Is that understood?"

Ryder nodded, unsure whether a gesture, something unsaid, would register as a response in the semi-darkness. Presumably it did, for Blenhesket carried on, in hushed, earnest tones.

"There are those of us in this party who believe it's

moving too far from the core values of one-nation conservatism. We're too closely aligned to business ... banks, large corporations that sweep up government contracts, are often registered abroad, and pay less tax than the average household ... none of which plays well in the country. And with an election coming up ... you don't need me to tell you we've an enormous presentational problem. Accordingly ..." and the voice dropped to a whisper, so that Ryder had to lean forward, straining his ears ... "some of us are in the process of establishing a small group to help bring the party back to its senses. We call ourselves Tory Trust ..."

"Not another one," Ryder interrupted. "This party's got more groups than a pop festival. I mean ... there's Miller and his thatcherites ..."

"This is different. Most of them are single issue groups ... anti-Europe, pro-nuclear, church and country, whatever ... but you're right. We're riven with so many factions we've no idea what we stand for ... what our core values are. Nor has the electorate. That's where Tory Trust comes in. To halt the increasing influence of the right and, at the same time, regain the trust of voters. Ultimately, make ourselves re-electable ... and without having to rely on the Lib Dems. Not that that'll be a problem after next May ... the way they're going there won't be enough of them to fill a phone box. Anyway, some of us think you're the right sort of person to play a key role in our group."

"I've always tried to steer clear of ginger groups," Ryder said. "I always thought it gave me more room for manoeuvre."

"That's precisely why we need you on board. Because you're not linked to any particular faction. Honest broker, and all that. But let me tell you ... Tory Trust is growing. We're collecting names ... we've

115

backbenchers, for instance, who'll defy the whips and vote against the next round of cuts ... social services, housing, policing, and so on ... that Pemberton's hellbent on making before going to the country. Political lunacy, of course ... the triumph of principle over pragmatism. Some of these backbenchers have slim majorities ... unless they make a stand they're out. In that respect they've nothing to lose. But at least this way we'll be sending a clear message to voters that there are people in this increasingly toxic party who care ... that we're not all city types in it for what we can get out of it."

"Yes ... but I'm in government. If I step out of line ..."

"You're useful where you are. And, by the way, you're not the only member of government who's with us. But we need people like you ... on what I might call the social democratic wing of the party ... and in safe seats ... to be floating ideas in line with what the public wants. Like you did this morning."

"Ah ... how did it come over?"

"Fine. As I knew it would. Which doesn't mean to say you won't have ruffled a few feathers in Downing Street. But, given our aims, that's no bad thing."

A chilling thought struck Ryder. Blenhesket had set the whole thing up ... the surreptitious filming, the YouTube release, the management of his rage against the popular press ... as a sort of test, an initiation. But that was nonsense. Blenhesket couldn't have known he'd be struck down with whatever it was on the Dean Bridge ... it was mere misfortune, sheer chance. No one could have known. Unless, for some reason, perhaps to do with this crazy Tory Trust idea, he was having him followed, and a photographer, hired by Blenhesket, had got lucky. Or ... and Ryder could feel his head start to spin ... had Blenhesket's henchman slipped something into the breakfast at the hotel, so that the food poisoning he concocted as a convenient excuse was in fact the explanation? But no, this was ludicrous ... conspiracy theory gone mad, the stuff of throwaway airport thriller or tawdry TV drama. All the same, he was confused: he needed to know more, at the same time wanted to know less ... this was toxic, potentially lethal. He had to get out, find fresh air, clear his brain. An image of the Shap fells, in their mist-shrouded majesty, their purity, their raw integrity, rose before him, and he wished he were there.

Blenhesket was talking, questioning, with the same quiet urgency as before. "So," Ryder heard him say, "are you with us? Can we count on you?"

Ryder summoned his concentration and looked firmly at the spot behind the lamp whence the voice came.

"Sir Wesley," he said, "I need time ... time to think. This is ... what you're asking is a decision not to be taken lightly."

A nod, a flicker of acknowledgment, emanated from the shadows. At least, Ryder thought it did. Encouraged, he carried on.

"I'm grateful for the confidences you've shared with me this morning. I shan't betray them, you have my word, however I decide. What I need, though, is to think about my loyalties ..."

"Your loyalty is to this party ... not the party hijacked by the right but the party of Disraeli and his successors ... his true successors. Beyond that ... your loyalty is to the people of this country we claim to represent."

"No. With respect, Sir Wesley ..." and Ryder heard his voice, as if from afar, estranged, yet profoundly his own ... "my loyalty is to my conscience, my principles. 'To thine own self be true', and all that. If I can't be loyal to myself, then my loyalty to others is a sham. My loyalty, first and foremost, is to me."

***

Ryder could feel himself nodding off. Days like this were no help: off early to the BBC while most people were still eating their breakfast, or sitting in their cars on their way to work, then Harley Street, followed by a cloak-and-dagger meeting with Blenhesket at the house. And now the second reading of the Overseas Aid (Official Development Assistance Target) Bill. It was all he could to keep his eyes open, but he knew he must. Commons cameras were everywhere.

The purpose of the bill was straightforward: to ensure that the government spend nought point seven percent of gross national income on overseas aid, and that independent checks be in place to guarantee appropriate distribution of the funds. It was a private members' bill and Ryder was in the house to watch the interests of his department. The chamber was sparsely populated which allowed him to feign engagement while his mind ranged over the implications of Blenhesket's words. It was a bit like fishing. Someone once told Ryder that if you sat in a chair, patently idle, you would be branded a loafer. Place a fishing rod in that same person's hand or, in this case, parliamentary papers, and all would be forgiven. A thin line between dreamer and doer. Fishing line, as it were.

Ryder smiled to himself, but his amusement was brief, and even briefer his ability to focus on the Blenhesket question. The debate was proving pointed, acrimonious; the dozen or so members of his own party present in the chamber apparently united in their insistence that, given the need for austerity, the aid budget was too generous.

118

One of those he noted, with surprise, was his northern colleague Ayesha Farani. Ryder, turning round, caught a flash of expensive bangle as she condemned the quarter of a billion pounds destined each year for India, a country, she angrily informed the house, that could afford to finance a Mars probe while millions of its citizens were starving. How would such views go down in the deindustrialised northern mill-town she represented, Ryder wondered, with its second and third generation families from the Indian subcontinent? What was she playing at?

Ryder shook his head to dispel his drowsiness and try and make sense of what he was hearing. This debate, he told himself, should not be happening. Overseas aid should not be called into question ... indeed, there was a strong case for it to be increased. Alright, perhaps not to a rapidly developing country such as India, though even here he was assured the aid went to areas where there was greatest need. No, the premise on which his parliamentary colleagues were basing their argument was flawed. There was no need to sacrifice funding such as this on the altar of austerity. If the government had the courage to square up to the city ... tackle tax avoidance, slash bonuses, redistribute wealth, force banks to put the country, not themselves, first ... and then recognise that a fiscally floundering nation could no longer afford foreign wars, a round-the-clock nuclear deterrent, then billions would be available not just for overseas aid but also for schools, hospitals, social services, jobs ... in other words, for people. It was this moral bankruptcy, rather than any looming monetary bankruptcy, which rebalancing would fix, that irked Ryder. It was so simple: why couldn't the Pembertons of this world, and their acolytes, see it?

Anger seized him and, though not down to

119

contribute to the debate, he felt he should try to catch the speaker's eye and intervene. He was about to rise, signal his intent, but fatigue, a torpor, had possessed him, permeating his body and reaching every extremity, each toe and finger. For a moment he was unable to move. As if from afar he watched himself, willed himself to act, but in vain, while words, debated words, passed him like strangers on a street. He was powerless, surrendered to stupor, to somnolence. Only when his stomach rumbled, loudly, insistently, did he stir himself, come to, cast off his lethargy, recalling crossly that he'd had nothing to eat that day, barring two slices of swiftly swallowed toast. He needed to eat, sugar probably, for energy: that would pick him up, get him going.

A lull in the debate, hijacked by a Labour backbencher pointing out the need for clean water and claiming subsequent wars would be fought over access to such sources, enabled him to rise, groggily, from the comfort of the green leather bench and slip unnoticed from the chamber. He made his way slowly, battling weariness, to the tea room where, having collected a cheese sandwich, a slice of ginger cake, a bar of chocolate and a pot of Earl Grey, he flopped at a table where Jack Merryman, whom he'd last seen in Manchester at Blenhesket's brainstorming morning, was engrossed in committee papers.

"My god," Merryman said, surveying the tray. "I can tell you're not on a diet. I'd be like Miss Piggy if I ate that lot."

"Bit peckish," Ryder grunted, biting into his sandwich.

"You know," Merryman continued, flinging his papers to the table, "I've been here two and a half years and I still can't make head or tail of this lot. It's double Dutch."

"Occupational hazard," Ryder replied, through a mouthful of bread and cheese. "You'd think party conferences ... standing orders, amendments, motions about motions, and whatnot ... would prepare us for this bullshit. But they don't."

Merryman smiled weakly, unsure whether Ryder was joking or not. He changed the subject.

"You're looking a bit frazzled. The aftermath of that YouTube business, I suppose ... which was really pretty mean. You're right to go on the warpath ... clear your name."

Ryder snorted. If he was looking frazzled, he said, it was because of the debate going on in the house. Ayesha Farani, of all people, slagging off overseas aid to India.

"Ah ... Little Miss Bling," Merryman grinned. "All that jewellery. But she couldn't care less what she comes out with. Other fish to fry, so I hear."

Ryder looked puzzled.

"Yeah ... rumour has it she's not standing again. She's got herself shacked up with some big-time party donor ... getting married in the summer, apparently ... and so it's not in her interests to see his squillions ... her squillions ... squandered on the undeserving poor in the third world. He'll want to make his donations work for him ... not someone else. A knighthood, at least. Christ ... that'll mean it'll be Lady Ayesha. We'll all have to scrape and bow. At least with that jewellery we'll hear her coming and can get out of the way."

Ryder laughed. Merryman was a decent sort, no airs and graces. Was he a Blenhesket boy, Ryder wondered. Probably not. His Bolling Valley seat was safe enough, and he'd worked diligently since his election to earn a reputation as a conscientious, hard-working MP. He'd probably nothing to gain by throwing in his lot with Blenhesket and, quite likely, a considerable amount to lose.

Tipping sugar into the Earl Grey ... not something he would normally do, but today he felt excused ... Ryder looked round the tea room. He'd discovered a new game: spot the blenhesketite. Which of those people, munching salads, toying with their jacket potatoes, sipping tea or coffee, were plotting against the prime minister to wrest the party from the right, from Pemberton's public school cronies?

From the corner of his eye Ryder noticed the door to the tea room open and, as if on cue, the prime minister strode in. The chatter, the hubbub, was immediately hushed, as conversation faltered: one or two people stood up, someone pushed forward, arm outstretched. To all this Pemberton was impervious. Disdainfully sweeping his gaze over the tables, his eye met Ryder's and, emitting a yelp of anguish, suppressed rage ... no one could agree later how to describe it ... he bore down on his victim.

Ryder hauled himself to his feet. "Prime minister ..."

"You ... you ..." Pemberton was choking with fury, barely able to enunciate. "You fool ... moron."

A sepulchral silence fell on the tea room. Ryder, knowing everyone was watching, and fearing the PM was about to strike him, stepped back. Spittle, foam, flecked Pemberton's lower lip and chin. The image of a rabid dog sprang to mind.

"No one ... no one ... except for me ... determines the policy of this party. Still less a nobody ... a nonentity ... like you, Tom Ryder ... on a radio programme. The press ... regulating the press ... like some mickey-mouse community radio ... it's not on. We need them ... need the press ... hell, we've an election to win ... while you ... you, you fool ... play into the hands of the goddam BBC ... plebs, socialist plebs, the lot of them ... and say we'll shut down newspapers the moment ... the moment

Pippa Middleton's bum is splashed over the centre pages. We need these people on side, you oaf ... on message, do you hear?"

Pemberton was swaying, rocking on his heels, and Ryder wondered if he had been drinking. There was no smell of alcohol, though. From the other side of the tea room someone coughed, clearing his throat, rather too loudly. As if from nowhere two people, one of whom Ryder knew as a party whip, the other a parliamentary private secretary, appeared at Pemberton's side.

"Prime minister ..." one of them said quietly.

"Fuck off," Pemberton retorted.

"Prime minister," the other said, producing a mobile phone. "A call for you. You can't take it here ... confidential. I think outside ..."

"Who ...?" Pemberton began.

"Not here. As I said ... outside."

A scowl darkened the prime ministerial countenance. Then, as if remembering his office, his dignity, he appeared to collect himself.

"Very good. Lay on," he commanded and, looking neither left nor right, acknowledging no one, as MPs of all shades shrank from him, he sailed from the room. One of the whips closed the door behind him. At once the place erupted in chatter and speculation.

"Christ," Merryman addressed Ryder. "He's lost it. I mean ... did you see? He was foaming at the mouth. I know all prime ministers eventually go barmy ... if they weren't already, before taking office ... but this ... well ..."

Ryder wasn't listening. He was fumbling with his phone ... again, why did the buttons have to be so tiny, so fiddly ... to ring Blenhesket. No one, not even a prime minister, could slate him like that in public and expect to get away with it. When he got through to Blenhesket, he was to the point.

"I've thought. I'm with you. You can count me in."

He rang off, sat down, mopped his brow. He was shaking. His whole body. Yet somehow, at that particular moment, it didn't seem to matter.

La Jolla. December 2014.

Boorish and fretful: this was Margo's verdict on her husband when she took him aside on the third day after their arrival in California.

"You're spoiling things. You need to chill. After all, it's Christmas."

"I don't see what that's got to do with it," Ryder grumped, and immediately apologised. "Sorry, hun. It's just that ..."

His voice trailed away. He gazed morosely at the rain falling steadily on the neat lawns and dainty flower beds, the droplets flicking from the Santa sleigh and the two grinning elves that flashed their seasonal tidings to passers-by on the road above. It had been a mistake to agree to come. The journey, with a nine-hour delay at Chicago, because of snow, which meant they missed their onward flight to San Diego, had been especially tiring. He was still jet-lagged, while the constant drizzle, and the need to make polite conversation with Jim and Grace Murchison, his in-laws, did nothing to sweeten his mood. Anyone who went away at Christmas, especially in the northern hemisphere, must want his head examining, Ryder thought.

It was his weariness, the lethargy, that troubled him most. He slept well, the exhaustion saw to that, but when he woke he was as if made of soggy papier-mâché, as if he had absorbed the dampness that dripped dull and drear from the skies outside. If they had to go anywhere at this time of year, they should have gone south, instead of to the halfway house of a southern Californian winter, neither cold nor hot, just muggily warm. A few days lounging by a pool, the sun beating down, would have dried him out, filled him with vitamin, invigorated him. But somehow this argument didn't convince him. Moreover, the aching tiredness was making him clumsy, careless. On the previous day a cut-glass whisky tumbler ... his father-in-law's cherished Waterford ... had slipped through his fingers and smashed on the parquet floor. Jim Murchison had been dismissive of the accident, but later Ryder overheard Grace ask her husband how much Tim had drunk. She thought his speech was slurred, and said he didn't look well.

The curious thing was that, throughout the earlier part of December, he'd been fine. At any rate, if he hadn't, he'd been too busy to notice. There was the usual grind, of course, of constituency correspondence: the curse of the internet, since any illiterate fool with two fingers and a keyboard could now complain or cajole, lobby or lambast, and all too frequently did. More demanding, and requiring supreme concentration at mind-numbing meetings with so-called experts and advisers, was the position paper on global warming. Of this Ryder was both wickedly pleased and bitterly ashamed. The document was a study, an object lesson, in high intent, low cunning and little else. No one of any worth or influence would read it, still less act upon it, for in essence it said nothing, or at best purveyed platitudes long since pricked. It would enable, though, the government to claim it was doing something, listening, consulting, indeed governing, whereas it was doing no such thing. The report was but a staging post on the way to the next review, the next royal commission, which themselves were markers to a another report, another paper, which in turn ... and so on. This was government: a fairground ride of dazzle and din, ever revolving, going nowhere, operated by shady, shadowy figures accountable only to each other. It was futile ... and his role in it a sham.

At least he was able to draw cruel comfort from the report compiled for Pemberton on the Scottish situation. The prime minister, he knew, would ignore it: Jeremy Miller, the foreign secretary, had told Ryder that as far as Downing Street was concerned he was an unperson, airbrushed from the canvas Pemberton was painting of a party in its pomp following its inevitable landslide victory in May. Ryder didn't care and sent the report to spite Pemberton, to remind him that the so-called moron was still around despite the unprecedented and humiliating scene in the tea room ... humiliating, it was whispered at Westminster, more for the prime minister than for Ryder. The report was a way of getting back at Pemberton, to irritate him, and Ryder felt better as soon as he had sent it. To complete the round of activity he contributed comment pieces to the broadsheets outlining his proposals for press reform: the publications in question paid tolerably well, and Ryder knew the articles would further rile Downing Street.

Then, given the season, there was the round of Christmas parties at Westminster, hosted by penny-pinching government departments and, more lavishly, by several of the embassies. It was almost a relief, and certainly kinder to his liver, to return to his constituency. Here, attending the annual Conservative Club Christmas dinner, applauding school nativity plays and trying not to sing out of tune at the civic carol service, he felt almost sprightly. Of weakness, debility, there was barely a trace. Perhaps, on reflection, it was less the whirl of work and play that made him forget whatever was ailing him, and more the warm, rich wines from the embassy drinks cabinets, even the local Con Club sauvignon blanc, that had anaesthetised him, pickled him, rendered him immune to pain. Perhaps there was something to be said, after all, for becoming an alcoholic. He wouldn't be the first at Westminster.

Amid the flurry and fuss of those dark December

days he had remembered to have the blood test. The result came back as inconclusive. The consultant, Mr Henderson, refused to draw any inference from the result, requesting merely that his patient return for another test. Ryder was concerned and rang Ellie in Manchester.

"What's it mean ... inconclusive? Have they found something and for some reason aren't saying?"

"More like it they've gone and lost the sample. I have to say since you and your political cronies privatised the NHS path labs it's become a nightmare. Samples mislabelled, lost. You've no idea."

Same old Ellie, Ryder thought. Always wanting a pop at government health policy and holding me responsible.

"Yes, but seriously ... what does it actually mean?" he pressed. "Because they want me back for another."

"Well ... it depends. Perhaps they didn't find what they were looking for. And now they want to test for something else. It's routine ... a process of elimination. That way they'll get to the bottom of it. But, really, you need to ring your Mr Henderson, or whatever his name is. I can't give an opinion. And, if you don't mind, I've a surgery full of people all coughing and barking and spreading germs over each other like there's no tomorrow. Which there won't be, unless I can get to them. Let me know what happens with the next lot of tests. And ... Merry Christmas."

With that, Ellie had hung up, leaving Ryder little the wiser. Nevertheless, with some apprehension, he returned for a second blood test, hoping the seasonal spirit coursing through his veins would be sufficiently diluted not to skew the findings. He was told the result would be sent to the consultant neurologist, Mr Meakin, who would see him in the new year on his return from his annual lecture tour of South Africa.

Ryder was unsure whether to be pleased or concerned. Putting it off until after Christmas, forgetting about it, had its attractions. On the other hand, if there were something wrong, the sooner they knew what it was and could do something about it, the better.

But Christmas had come, or almost, and with it the feeling that he was inhabiting someone else's body, that nothing seemed quite to fit, to belong: it was like renting, rather than owning. Of course, it was the weather, after that dreadful journey, the delay, the anxious hours at the airport, that exacerbated his general apathy. But it wasn't going away. Margo again told Ryder that if he was worried he should seek a specialist in San Diego, get some sort of diagnosis then and there. Even though it was holiday time, there would surely be someone who would see him. This was the USA, she reminded her husband. The country didn't get where it had by people taking time off for holidays. This was a nation of go-getters, she said primly, with thinly veiled criticism of her adopted homeland on the other side of the Atlantic.

Ryder sighed. "I'm sure I'm in very good hands in London. Anyway, that first test didn't come up with anything. That's got to be good, hasn't it?"

Margo looked at him with a mix of pity and despair.

"I sure hope so, honey," she said. "I sure hope so."

***

The day out was at Grace Murchison's insistence.

"You can all go. I sure don't want you tomorrow under my feet. You too, Margo. You'll only be interfering, spoiling my plans ..."

"Mom ... that's not fair ..."

"Go visit the zoo ... the Birch aquarium ... and leave the caterers to me."

"What caterers?" Ryder asked, immediately feeling obtuse, and wondering if he ought to be able to answer his own query.

Grace turned to him, looking faintly exasperated. "Our party ... our soirée ... tomorrow. You don't seriously believe I'm going to be decorating this house ... preparing food, setting it out ... drinks ... for over a hundred people ... then clearing up afterwards? That's why we have catering companies. Surely you got catering companies in England? Besides, the folk who come to our home ... don't forget this is the high spot of the Republican Party Christmas fundraising ... expect nothing but the best. As I say ... we provide the dishes, they provide the dollars."

"Sure," Jim said. "Because, as Tim knows, they are the best ... the crême de la crême. You take Max Deutscher ... as fine an attorney general as this state has ever seen. Ran a good campaign in the congressional elections the other year and only narrowly missed out. An outstanding young man ... tipped as a future governor and one day perhaps as president. You two'll get on just swell. Then there's ..."

"Tim doesn't want a roll-call of the great and the good of the grand old party in southern California," Grace said. "But they'll all be here. It's tradition. And that's why I call in the professionals. Under my supervision, of course. So I know that when I pop out to get my hair done everything's just about wrapped up."

"I can't leave you with this ..." Margo began.

"Of course you can. You go enjoy yourselves. At the zoo. You haven't been since you were a kid," she reminded Margo. "You used to love it. The elephants. I don't think you'd ever set eyes anything so big or lumbering. Apart from your father, of course."

"Hey ... that'll do," Jim grumbled good-naturedly.

130

"Big I might be ... lumbering, no way. At least, not in those days. Not when I was younger ... in my prime."

"I guess you've never visited the San Diego zoo, Tim," Grace said, addressing her son-in-law. "If not, you sure missed out. It's huge. They've got everything ... you want to see it, it's there."

Ryder was about to say he saw enough animal antics on the floor of the House of Commons without paying to see more, but thought better of it. The Murchisons would not get the humour. They'd think he was being awkward, stuffy, a party-pooper. British, in other words. Ryder suddenly wished he were back home, where he could relax, be himself, share a joke with friends. Ellie, for instance.

Instead he said: "It sounds wonderful. I'd love to go. But I think, if you don't mind, I'll stick around here. I've some work to do ..."

"Hey, lighten up," Jim said. "It's Christmas ..."

"And the zoo'll have something seasonal, I guess. Lights, and carols," Grace added.

"I'm sure the animals will appreciate that," Ryder said, immediately biting his tongue. "I mean ..."

"Oh, well ... that's fine if you don't wish to go," Grace said tartly. "I get the message."

"Mom ... Tim's tired. You know he's been under a lot of pressure lately ... and the journey didn't help ..."

"If Tim doesn't wish to go I guess we can find something for him to do. He can help hang mistletoe ..."

"Hanging's not my scene," Ryder said. "Neither mistletoe nor people. I'll see how I feel tomorrow."

***

The following morning dawned dry and bright. Perfect, for the time of year, as Ryder admitted to himself, for a

131

day out. He was half-tempted to go: it was, after all, a long while since he'd been to a zoo. It was Chester, probably, in the first year of university. Ellie must have gone too but, strangely, he'd no recollection of her. Perhaps it was the very early days, before they'd become an item, inseparable. The only thing he could recall with any clarity was the monkey house, with the chimps crappng everywhere, over everything and each other, then eating their own excrement. At least they knew where their food had come from, Ryder thought, which was more than most humans. Including the guests at the Murchisons' Christmas extravaganza ... Ryder refused to call it a party ... who would be fed, watered and waited on by an army of caterers. The advance guard had already occupied the house, bearing tables, chairs and boxes of kitchen equipment, and including a generator to illuminate the lanterns and lamps, the snowflakes and icicles, even now being strung incongruously round the perimeter of the property. On the terrace someone was unpacking a nativity scene, setting out the figures, testing the wiring. Baby Jesus sported a twinkling halo, and a warm glow issued from the crib. Ryder secretly hoped it contained real hay which might catch fire if the power were left on too long. The wise men, whose gifts similarly glinted and glittered, wore the same look of frozen jollity as the Santa on his sleigh, apparently directing operations from the front lawn. No wonder: these gift bearers, Santas, wise men, all came probably from the same Chinese or Taiwanese factory. Come to think of it, Santa's elves looked like Baby Jesus. Or should that be the other way round?

It was ghastly, Ryder told himself, and yet the caterers and their associates had barely begun. Grace Murchison seemed in her element, bustling about, giving orders, issuing instructions ... no, the Christmas tree could not go there; yes, the serving tables could be placed here. Activity, febrile, frantic, was in the air. It dripped from the walls of every room, gasped from every cushion plumped, rose from every carpet hoovered, glinted from every wine glass polished ... and Ryder knew he would do no work that day. Instead, he needed to escape, flee ... but not in the company of his wife and father-in-law. Not today. It was out of the question.

He'd checked on-line: the San Diego zoo was enormous, comprising canyons, and trails marked as steep terrain, which would involve hours of walking. Or rather, shuffling. Standing and shuffling from one cage, one area, to the next. It would be like the constituency Autumn Fair, only worse: doing the rounds, walking slowly, stopping, unable to get into his stride. Then, if he had to be on his feet all evening, making conversation at the extravaganza, he couldn't afford to overdo things. He needed to take it easy, and the zoo, because of its size, would be anything but easy. He simply couldn't face it. Besides, if there was some sort of seizure, a repeat of the Dean Bridge episode, he'd probably need a wheelchair, worse, an ambulance. People would look: sod's law dictated that someone would recognise him, even thousands of miles from home, and before he knew it he'd be facebooked or tweeted into the pages of the tabloid press. He'd been there before, a few weeks previously, and he'd no desire to return.

"I think, if you don't mind," he said, "I'll leave you to it. Even if I can't get any work done ... these people have rather taken over, haven't they? ... there are one or two things I need to get my head round. I'll probably just take a stroll into the village ... down to the cove, perhaps along the beach ... blow away the cobwebs."

"You can blow away the cobwebs at the zoo," Grace

said. "It's not as if you'll be indoors."

Shielding his mouth, such that only Margo could see it, Ryder gave an ostentatious yawn. He knew she would correctly interpret his meaning.

She nodded, her nostrils flaring slightly, reminding him of the newspaper caption: Ryder's Feisty Filly. Today she looked the part, a true thoroughbred, and he suddenly wanted her ... not at the zoo, not gazing at creatures that gazed back, baleful, reproachful, but upstairs, in the guest room with the wide windows and the view through the pines to the ocean beyond ... that's what would blow away the cobwebs. It was on the tip of his tongue to suggest they did just that, stay in, make love ... but today there would be no privacy. No doubt some wight would requisition the bedroom to festoon from its balcony the neon Joyeux Noël he could see being unloaded from one of the trucks. Besides, Margo was giving her verdict: "I guess we'll leave Tim to his own devices. It'll be better that way. As I told you, he's pretty worn out ... a lot on his plate at the moment."

Jim and Grace Murchison exchanged glances.

"Okay ... if that's what you want," Grace said. "Tim's our guest. He can please himself. Just so long as he doesn't wander off and forget to come back for our little soirée."

Ryder, dragging himself back to reality, effected a wan smile. "Now ... would I do a thing like that?"

***

They gave him a lift into La Jolla and dropped him at the corner of Prospect and Girard, before doubling back to join the feeder to the freeway that would take them past the Old Town and the airport and bring them some thirty minutes later to the zoo.

Ryder was grateful for the lift. Admittedly, in setting

out for a walk, it seemed silly to start with a car ... a snippet of schoolboy French sprang to mind, *se promener en voiture*, which had always struck him as contradictory ... but it enabled him to get where he wished to be, close to the cove and the sea, without much effort, which would leave him in a better state to tackle the coast path back to the Murchison home. Or, if exhaustion set in, his legs refused to cooperate, he could go back into town and pick up a cab. For the moment, though, he felt fine, buoyed by the prospect of sea air, the ocean stretching boundless before him, and solitude.

He was glad to be alone. Had he gone to the zoo, traipsing round looking at animals, he would not have been able to go at his own pace, rest when and where he wanted, sit and, above all, think. Walking by oneself, for this reason, was infinitely preferable to tagging along with other people. Only when Alistair was little, on the beach at Northaven, striding out along the sands, had he ever enjoyed the walking company of anyone else.

Alistair. How was he getting along with Marie-France in charge? There would be no wild parties, of that he was assured. But what was the boy doing? Studying, perhaps, though Margo had said the trip to Oxford, and especially the interview at the university, had not gone well. Alistair had said little about the experience, but Margo thought he had deliberately not impressed. When she enquired what had happened at the interview, the sort of things he had been asked, Alistair had not been forthcoming. We talked about this and that, was all he would say. He seemed relieved, Margo said, when they got in the car to return home. He'd done his duty, done what his parents wanted, and nothing more. Still, Ryder thought, surveying the tall, swaying pines above him as he descended Girard

Avenue, and taking in the expanse of ocean as it opened before him, there was more to life than Oxford. The place was overrated, a snake pit of snobbery and privilege that had nurtured Pemberton and his cronies ... Alistair was probably better off out of it. Besides, a decent redbrick had done him no harm. Quite the contrary. And if he hadn't gone to Manchester he'd never have met Ellie. Just as if he hadn't studied here, in La Jolla, at UCSD, he'd never have met Margo. It was a strange world, full of chance and coincidence. Only a fool would attempt to plan it ... and of fools there was no lack.

Including himself. For what was he trying to do, beneath this pale blue Californian sky, if not plan the next phase, the next half ... no, less, that point had likely already been passed ... of his shapeless, senseless, life? It was wrong, of course, to wallow in self-pity. No doubt the vast majority of the country would give its eye tooth to be in his position: comfortable, indeed, more than comfortable; well-paid, secure in his job, more so than most of his parliamentary colleagues, to say nothing of the workforce at large; and possessed, as an MP, as a junior minister, of at least a passing prestige that invested him, at the very minimum, with a pretence of power.

A pretence. That's what it was. That was the trouble. A show, a sham. What real influence could he bring to bear on things that mattered? Come to think of it, what did matter? He'd spent too long in parliament, cushioned, cocooned, inflating the trivial, ignoring the rest, to have any idea what mattered any more. Jobs, security, family, health: round and round they went, spinning, spun, on a merry-go-round of incentivisation, pathfinders, roll-outs, empowerment, and other meaningless initiatives designed, apparently, in the words of party managers, to engage with future visioning. What, in plain English, was that supposed to mean? It was futile, all utterly futile.

He had reached the top of the steps leading down to the cove. Following the line of the coast, as it stretched into a blurred infinity, he breathed the damp, tangy air, inhaling deeply, swelling his lungs. He felt immediately calmer, somehow cleansed, and at the same time elated. He'd known that moment before, recently ... when, where? Ah ... the trip to Edinburgh, the fells, passing through the Lune Gorge, Shap ... one of those moments, however fleeting, that whisper of sublimity, of eternity, that set all else in petty, puling perspective. Perhaps in previous times religion fulfilled that function, Ryder thought, seeking to uplift, to elevate. Not any more.

On impulse, and ignoring the voice that told him he might later regret such exertion, he began to descend to the beach, holding the rail for support. Not that he needed it. He felt in robust form, better than he'd felt since arriving in California. Clearly he was over the jet-lag, had put the tribulations of the journey behind him. Moreover there was no trace of tremor, of weakness, in any of his limbs. The holiday, if Christmas with in-laws could be so termed, was beginning to prove its worth.

Looking over the cove, as he descended the steps, he saw it was deserted, save at the far end for a man and his dog who seemed to be investigating rock pools. The dog was running round, wagging its tail, sniffing at every excitement it could find, while its owner, equally occupied, poked with a stick, perhaps a piece of driftwood, at holes and crevices in the rocks. Everyone else, Ryder thought, would be at home, preparing, like Grace Murchison, for the Christmas festivities, though presumably not in such lavish and extravagant style.

The sand was soft and, where it had been washed by the tide, smooth and clean. It was not like the beach in

Northaven, Ryder realised almost with a shock. There, as the tide ebbed, it left tiny undulations in the sand, wavelets, a reminder to tread warily, for this was trespass on Neptune's domain. Indeed, the ridges of this sand-sculpted sea could, at particular times, after a certain kind of tide, be hard, harsh on the soles of bare feet, causing their possessor to pause, to seek the more supple surface of a sandbank raised as the waters scurried and swirled in their rush to the sea beyond. But here, in the cove, along the margin of the gently lapping ocean, Ryder thought he had never seen sand as fine and as delicate as this. He had to know it, feel it, be part of it, be one with the ageless and mysterious processes that had formed it. Slowly he bent down, removing first one shoe, then another, and attempting, without much success, to roll up his trousers. Then, leaving his shoes, his socks, on the beach behind him, he stepped forward, onto the sea-kissed sand, feeling its caress, cold and clammy, first in his toes, then his feet, then throughout his body, as it chilled him, calmed him, called him.

He took one step, two, three, welcoming the embrace of the shifting, shapeless substance beneath his feet, watching as the sea teased him, toyed with him, running at him, lapping at his feet, retreating, reforming, coming at him again. Somewhere in the distance a dog barked, urgently, nervously. Ryder ignored it. He didn't care. In that moment he had found himself, reached an awareness, a decision. Elated, exhilarated, devoid of ache or pain, he turned to face the ocean. For a moment he paused and then, as the sea itself seemed to stand still, he waded into the waiting waters.

***

"I got lost."

"What do you mean ... got lost? And look at you ... anyone would think you've been shipwrecked ... washed ashore on some desert island ..."

"Hardly ..."

"Why didn't you ring? We've been worried sick."

Ryder blinked dejectedly at the faces attending him on his return to the Murchison home. He could almost see himself reflected in their gaze, and the image was not flattering: shoes caked in mud, trousers with a tell-tale tide-mark, coat creased and crumpled. And exhaustion weeping from every pore.

"I'm sorry. I didn't have my phone. I forgot it. I didn't think ..."

"Didn't think. Didn't think. Sometimes ... sometimes you can be so stupid. You know that? Stupid. And selfish. All the time it's you. You you you."

Margo burst into tears.

"Hun ..."

"Leave me alone. I'm going up. To get ready. And you need to get yourself cleaned up. You're a mess. Unless, of course, you're going to skulk all evening on your desert island. You'd probably be happier there."

Ryder moved towards his wife but Jim Murchison checked him.

"You sure look as if you could use a drink. And I don't think Grace'll be too pleased if you trample all over her freshly cleaned carpets in those shoes."

"I sure as hell won't. You can take them off right now. Anyways, they look as if all they're fit for is the garbage. And is that seaweed? Oh my god ... on my carpet ..."

"Come on," Jim said. "We're best off out of here. And I guess I could use a drink, too."

***

Some thirty minutes later, fortified by rye on the rocks, Ryder made his way back to the guest wing where he and Margo shared the largest and most sumptuous of the rooms. It would not be out of place, Ryder believed, in the most upmarket of five-star hotels and, indeed, would put many to shame. The en-suite bathroom was probably greater in area than many British homes and boasted not only a sauna but also a steam room. The only thing missing, Ryder felt, was its own swimming pool. A rest room in every sense of the word and, lest people were tempted too long to tarry in its welcome embrace, the main bedroom was equipped with a second, and separate toilet cubicle.

When Ryder entered, warily, he found Margo before a mirror, surrounded by an arc of lights that might have come from a Hollywood dressing room. She was drying her hair, flicking her head this way and that as she bobbed the dryer deftly over her radiant red curls. The noise from the blower masked his entrance and she was unaware of his presence. For a moment he stood and watched, fascinated. Then, perhaps sensing she was no longer alone, she span round, killing the dryer as she did so. Ryder took a pace towards her.

"Hun ... look. I'm sorry."

"Uh huh," Margo offered, turning back to her dressing table and starting the dryer again.

"I'm sorry," Ryder raised his voice over the racket. "I mean ... you were right. I should have come to the zoo. It would have been better. Except ..."

He paused, wondering if she'd taken any of this in.

"Where did you get to?" Margo flared, flinging the dryer aside, and turning to face him. "I mean ... what have you been doing all day?"

"I ... I went to the cove. Down to the beach. And then ... then I just fancied a paddle. In the sea."

"A paddle? In December? Are you crazy?"

"Perhaps. I don't know. But it seemed right. It was ... I had to. A sort of ... washing away of the past."

"Oh, for god's sake. I mean ..."

"I was going to come back along the coast walk ... then, halfway, head back into town. But I lost my bearings. I mean ... I knew the direction. Roughly. But I ended up at that park."

"Mount Soledad."

"I thought I could cut across ... but somehow I just kept going round and round. Then it came on to rain."

"We were worried. We all were. We thought when we got back we'd find you here. That you'd been back hours. But no ... no sign. No word ..."

"Sorry."

"They were going to phone the police department."

"Hell. Really?"

"We didn't know what had happened. You might have had one of your turns ... collapsed somewhere ..."

"Actually ... I feel just fine. I mean ... a bit achy, tired, after all that walking. But ... you were wondering what was happening. Well ... I can tell you something has happened. I've ..."

"I don't want to know. Not now. Guests will be arriving in an hour ..."

"It's important ..."

"It's more important you get in that steam room. Give yourself a good session. You look as if you need it. Then we can talk, if there's time, before we go downstairs."

"Hun ..."

"You've got to promise me you'll be on your best behaviour. You know how much this means, for Mom in particular. I don't want anything spoiling it. Promise?"

For a moment Ryder was back in school, quailing

beneath a teacher demanding the highest standards. It was almost funny, and Ryder was about to say so when a look from Margo stopped him. She was entirely serious, in no mood either for wit, or analogy, or both. On any other day she might have accepted his pathetic attempt at humour, rewarded him with a faint smile. Not, however, today.

"Promise," Ryder said meekly. "Promise. Scout's honour."

***

The steam room was just what he needed. He turned the temperature as high as he could bear it and sat there, sweat running, breathing the scented steam ... a herbal essence he couldn't identify ... deep into his lungs. The warmth seemed to permeate his whole body, soothing it, relaxing it, and at the same time expelling any impurity, any disease or ailment, that might be lurking there. He'd toyed with the idea of a steam room at home but felt he would not get value from it: he spent too much time away, in London, and when he was there to enjoy it no doubt it would be occupied by Alistair. Teenagers were like that: they were squatters, moving uninvited into parts of your life where they had little right to be, until they drifted off, at your expense, to live it up at university. Rather, of course, as he had done, though in his day taxpayers had footed the bill. Ryder frowned, blinking away a droplet of sweat that had run into his eye: what was Alistair going to do? Oxford didn't seem likely, given what Margo had said, and he didn't seem over-enthusiastic about anywhere else. He would have to sound out his son over this gap year business, try and find out what he wanted. Gross hypocrisy, of course, given that he himself, that very day, having realised what he no longer wished to do, had no idea what in fact he did wish to do. Perhaps they could both do a gap year. Sort themselves out, get their heads straight. That would be good: the father-and-son bonding that had gone badly astray, sacrificed to a life of public service. If ...

A thump on the door of the steam room broke his train of thought. Through the mist, through the condensation trickling down the inside of the door, he made out Margo's form. She was saying something, unclear over the hiss of the steam and the whirr of the pump, but Ryder gathered he'd just twenty minutes to get out of there, get himself dressed, and go down to greet the first guests. Reluctantly he called an acknowledgment and pressed the button to turn off the steam.

Stepping out, and wrapping himself in a soft, white bathrobe ... he fully expected to see the motif Waldorf Astoria woven into its fabric ... he returned to the bedroom where he found Margo, standing proud in a long, flowing evening dress, made of some silky, satiny material, that he couldn't recall seeing before.

"Wow," he said. "You look ..."

"A present from the folks. It's nice someone thinks of me occasionally. It would never occur to you to buy anything like this."

Ryder smarted at the rebuke.

"It needs doing up. At the back. But be careful."

She turned, presenting him with a triangular parchment of flesh he wanted to explore. The nape, in particular, yearning for the kiss he longed to plant upon it, and which he knew from experience would ... but no. This was not the occasion. Reluctantly he drew on the zip, inhaling her fragrance, her femininity. He wondered if perhaps, later, they might ...

She turned to face him. "You need to dry yourself off. I've put out a shirt ... and a choice of ties."

Ryder sighed. "Do I have to wear a tie?"

"Of course you do. This is a formal event."

"I thought it was a party."

"Both. Get a move on."

"Look, hun," he began, removing the bathrobe and starting to towel himself down, feeling vulnerable in his nudity, but wondering if ... and half-hoping ... she would notice he was aroused. "While I was out today ... I was thinking."

"Glad to hear it," Margo said, turning to sit in front of the mirror, where she began to fiddle with a necklace.

"I've decided ... I'm going to pack it in. Not stand at the election ..."

"What ...?" Margo twisted to face him. "What do you mean? Not stand ...?"

"Exactly that. I've had enough. It's all ... a waste of time."

"That's crazy. I mean ... you can't. You're a political animal ... as much, more, as any of the people who'll be arriving on this doorstep in just a couple of minutes. Politics ... it's in you like ... like ... jam in a doughnut. What would you do instead?"

"I don't know. I'm sure there are companies that would want me on the board ... political consultant, that sort of thing. If push came to shove I could mug up on corporate law ..."

"You never wanted to be a lawyer ..."

"It would give me time with Alistair. And with you."

"Oh, sure. Great. Alistair will just love you for that. Especially as this fall he'll be off to school ... college ... at least, we hope he is."

"Whatever. But my mind's made up."

"This is no way the time to be talking about something like this. And will you please get some clothes on? Look ... we can go into this tomorrow.

When we're all a bit calmer, more relaxed."

"I'm perfectly relaxed. About the whole thing. It just ... sort of ... feels right."

"It doesn't feel right to me. In fact, it stinks. This midlife crisis of yours ..."

"It's not a midlife crisis ..."

"It sure as hell sounds like it to me. This, and everything else that's been going on ... these turns, these attacks of yours. Psychosomatic, if you ask me. So, before you do something rash ... something you'll regret, you and I are going to sit down and have a serious talk ... but not now," Margo added, raising a cautionary hand to her husband, about to speak.

Ryder knew there was no point pursuing the matter. He changed tack. "Seen my deodorant?" he asked.

**

The soirée, as Grace Murchison termed it, was in full swing when Ryder, on a third glass of punch, and valiantly trying to explain to a mother and daughter in real estate why it was wrong to say Scotland was part of England, spotted his father-in-law bearing down on him. He was with a trim, athletic looking man, whom he steered skilfully round the conversing couples, acknowledging with a brief nod any passing greeting, and avoiding the waitresses with their trays of drinks and canapés. A basket-ball player, Ryder thought, his heart sinking. Or baseball. Or, heaven forbid, another real estate agent. And one who worked out.

Jim Murchison was diplomacy itself. "Excuse me," he said to the two women, "but I wonder if I could persuade you to trade this piece of fine English real estate for a fresh glass of punch. There's a new bowl out there and it's just begging to be sampled. Of course ... I don't want to break up your little party but I know the attorney general is anxious to meet our illustrious English visitor."

The women, rising to the occasion, and grateful to escape Ryder's exegesis on the constitutional settlement of the British Isles, said how much they'd enjoyed listening to him but understood that two important public figures might like to join together to discuss the issues of the day.

"All this brilliant talk and you've quite worn us out, Mr Ryder," the older one said. "I think a visit to the punch bar is just what we need."

When the women left Jim Murchison introduced Max Deutscher.

"And now I'm going to leave you two boys to it," he said. "I guess you've a lot you can talk about and, besides, I'll be in Grace's bad books if I don't look after our guests."

Max Deutscher smiled as Jim moved away to mingle. "Quite a guy, your pa-in-law. And Grace, too. The Republican Party in this corner of the world sure owes them a hell of a lot. And do call me Max. I know some of you Brits sometimes like to stand on ceremony."

Ryder managed a faint smile. The last thing he wanted was talk. He'd had quite enough with the women in real estate, who seemed to know very little, and now someone else had come along who looked as if he might know too much. Besides, he'd had to raise his voice above the babble in the room to make himself understood: the two Americans seemed to have difficulty with his British accent and his throat felt harsh and rough. Reason enough to keep taking the punch: to lubricate his vocal cords. And now his head was aching from the chatter, the laughter, around him.

But apart from the effort of conversation he was worn out: he'd been on his feet far too long that day and his knees ... not just his knees, but his entire body ... felt it was slipping away from him. It was the old business, the lethargy, the weariness, this alternation of good days and bad days, of normal functionality punctuated with pain and encumbered with clumsiness. It had been going on too long ... but neither the consultant nor, indeed, Ellie, had come up with anything. Just more tests. He frowned. There was a gremlin, or demon, within him, and something he had done or said had roused it, angered it. It was a cunning thing that possessed him, striking him down, rendering him gauche, maladroit: it was a shape-shifter, able for weeks on end to lie low, evade detection. After all, the medical examinations, the tests, had shown nothing. And yet, damn it, here it was, making itself known. He needed to sit down, desperately, but the few chairs in the room were already occupied by women of uncertain age whose smooth but pallid skin spoke of face lifts and other surgery. Looking round he noticed Margo, smiling in the company of a silky, smartly dressed middle-aged man. That was the one she'd been through high school with, Ryder recalled. Childhood sweetheart, and all that. Now something big in petroleum, or oil ... executive vice president, whatever that meant. And recently divorced, according to Margo. Ryder felt a pang of jealousy, downed the last of his punch, which suddenly tasted sickly, sweet, and moved towards them, but stumbled, to be caught deftly by Deutscher.

"Steady on," the American said, holding on to his arm. "I guess it's that punch ... got quite a kick, they tell me."

Ryder shook himself free, muttering his thanks, and looked to where Margo and the oilman had been. There was no sign of them, and Ryder wondered if he had imagined it. Surely not ... the punch was certainly potent, and he'd already had a couple of ryes, but he couldn't be mistaken that he'd seen his wife. With that man. Or could he?

Deutscher was talking, and seemed to be saying he'd followed Ryder's career with interest. Ryder couldn't hear properly: everyone around seemed to be shouting. It was a characteristic of Americans, Ryder reflected, to make a lot of noise: probably something to do with the wide open spaces into which they were born. All the same, it was irritating. So, still needing to sit down, and abandoning any hope of finding Margo, he suggested they go somewhere quieter where they could talk.

"Sure thing," Deutscher said. "Lead on."

Ryder knew exactly where he could find the peace he craved. He led Deutscher through the various reception rooms, full of gowned and glamorous women with their sveltely suited men, through the glittering hallway, resplendent beneath its sparkling chandelier, and paused at a door half-hidden by a gigantic Christmas tree.

"Strictly speaking it's out of bounds," Ryder said, turning to Deutscher, and pushing open the door. "But I don't think Jim will mind."

The study, or snug, as it was known, was modest in comparison with the other rooms in the house, but it was here Jim Murchison was able to hide, managing his investments, playing the markets, and building his stamp collection which, he would hint with a twinkle in his eye, comprised a not insubstantial portion of his assets.

"Ah ..." Ryder said, spotting the drinks table. "Scotch?"

"Thank you, no. I don't," Deutscher said. "But, please ... don't mind me."

Ryder needed no second bidding. He took the decanter, poured himself a generous measure, and flopped into an armchair.

"That's better," he said, feeling instantly more relaxed, the headache banished. All he wanted now was for Deutscher to go away so he could enjoy his whisky, then close his eyes, shut out the world and succumb to sleep. The American, however, had other ideas.

"You know ... Jim Murchison talks a lot about you. Proud of you, he is. Says you're a man of integrity ..."

"He does ...?"

"An honest politician at a time when most people are in it for what they can get out of it. I guess that's quite a compliment."

Ryder sipped thoughtfully at his drink. If Deutscher were to be believed, that was quite a revelation. He'd always imagined his father-in-law regarded him as a failure, never quite good enough for his daughter.

"Anyway," Deutscher continued. "I'm glad we're alone. I guess here we can talk freely. Some of the things we might be saying as sure as hell wouldn't find favour with many of the folks out there."

What did he mean? And why was he so keen on there being just the two of them? Ryder, feeling uncomfortable, wondered if he'd missed something earlier in the conversation. It was a bad sign the man didn't drink. Too serious by half. And it was supposed to be a party. The sooner he could get rid of him, the better. Ryder felt like a spectator, a witness to something in which he was apparently involved but which meant nothing to him. Wasn't death supposed to be like this, when you rose from your body to look down on your own lifeless form? Or perhaps his detachment was a result of too much punch.

"Listen," Deutscher leaned forward, lowering his voice, which became urgent, conspiratorial, "I've been studying what's going on in your country ... your Conservative Party. What's happening over there with

149

you guys has already happened here. It's got to be stopped. And it can be. Now. Before they take over completely."

Take over ...? The man was talking in riddles. Aliens, extraterrestrials. The Americans were big on that sort of crap. Why had he allowed himself to be closeted with this madman in his father-in-law's study? He wondered if Jim Murchison kept a gun in his desk.

"The point is," Deutscher was saying, bent forward in the chair, his hands cupped, like claws, ready to pounce, "this party has been hijacked. Infiltrated. It's a warning."

Ryder's heart missed a beat. That was it, then. The party, Grace's soirée. All those wealthy and eminent republicans ... hostages to some terrorist outfit. Those caterers ... the baby Jesus ... dodgy wiring to electrocute the guests, blow them sky-high. Or else poison them ... the food, the drink. Of course, the punch. Ryder half-rose, conscious his head was beginning to pound once more. He needed to get out there, tell them, do what he could. But Deutscher ... was that his real name? ... was still talking. Not about punch, but about tea. Yet there wasn't any, at least not that Ryder had seen. It wasn't a tea party, it was a ... and suddenly he realised. The Tea Party. Fool that he was ... and he fell back into his seat, with a grunt of exasperation.

"Say ... you okay?" Deutscher asked, breaking off his monologue.

"Fine," Ryder replied. "It's just ... sorry. It's been a long day. Look ... if you don't mind ..."

"Sure ... you want to get back to the party. I'm monopolising you. But I just want to say ... people like us need to fight the far right together ... stand united ..."

Ryder groaned and, spying the decanter, lifted himself from the chair. With trembling hand he poured himself another large measure. Unwise, he knew, given the amount he'd drunk already. On the other hand, if he was to put up with this fellow much longer, he'd need it.

"The way I see it is this. In England ... as I remember from grad school ... your party was built on one-nation toryism. For a hundred years it was the natural party of government. But now, while you might not have a Tea Party by name, you have a Tea Party in spirit, a party dominated not by wealth creators but by wealth consumers ... banks, international corporations moving their tax liabilities overseas, private companies sweeping up public assets ..."

"There's certainly some truth in that," Ryder began, finding it an effort to speak, and aware he was slurring his words.

"Yeah ... and what do we have to show for it? Unemployment, recession, and a shrinking GDP both here and in your country. That's what we're up against, Tim, and that's where people like you and me come in. We need to fight for traditional, core values ... bring our two great parties closer to the centre again where they belong. You with me?"

Ryder shut his eyes. Briefly, to focus. It was Blenhesket all over again. Of course, the man was correct. The far right was an evil. Its tentacles were everywhere, contaminating political debate, polarising opinion where consensus was needed. But this was a storm that had to blow itself out, whatever damage it left in its wake.

"Of course, I guess you're wondering why I'm saying all this."

Ryder nodded, and took a mouthful of whisky. The alcohol slammed into the back of his brain, which exacerbated the headache. He should lay off the drink. He'd had too much. And too much exertion during the day. Altogether too much.

"Look. You've an election coming up next year, okay? If you let your party drift to the right, if you fail to reach out to everyone, rich and poor, young and old, black, white, hispanic ..."

"No hispanic. Irish ... or Polish," Ryder corrected him, annoyed at being lectured.

"Okay ... whatever ... but if you don't create that one-nation feeling you'll lose, like Romney two years ago. You'll scare off your average Joes ... be seen as the party of the dollars, not the doers. In the long term, that can't be good. And that's why we have to rid ourselves of these right-wing hijackers, get ourselves back to the centre ... your party, my party. Otherwise the party's over."

"The party is over," Ryder said, draining the last of his whisky, instantly regretting it, and levering himself to a standing position. The room was churning, in slow motion, and Deutscher seemed everywhere at once.

"The party is over," he repeated, summoning every ounce of clarity and cohesion left in his body. "For me, at least. I've decided ... enough's enough. I mean ... don't get me wrong. You're right. Absolutely right. But what can one person do ... your average Joe, as you say? Nothing. And that's why I'm quitting. You carry on ... but don't count on me. And now ... if you'll excuse me ..."

He started forward, to where he believed the door to be, but Deutscher, or several Deutschers, loomed before him.

"You quit ... and you betray everything you stand for. Not just your party ... your family. Above all ... you betray yourself. You and I ... we're in a position to do something. Influence people ... make a difference. We can work together ... fight ..."

"Fighting days ... over," Ryder lurched towards Deutscher, pushing him aside. "Can't you see? They've shafted us. Bastards have shafted us."

He swung past Deutscher, reaching the door, pulling it open. As he stepped out from the study he collided with the frame, smashing his arm against it.

"Told you," he said. "The bastards have shafted us ... good and proper."

***

Ryder had no recollection of making it back to the bedroom. The first thing he knew was Margo, shaking him. He couldn't tell what she was saying, nor was he interested. He was aware of someone removing his clothes, which made him giggle, and the next thing he remembered was throwing up into a toilet. Then he was back in bed, which was fine, because all he wanted was to be left alone, for everybody, everything, to go away.

He slept fitfully, waking every so often drenched in sweat. He remembered Margo coming in, removing her dress, saying the party had finished. What party? The place was overrun with terrorists, who were holding everyone hostage, including Blenhesket, and Ryder knew he had to rescue them. The task was hopeless, since he was horribly outnumbered, but he wouldn't quit. If he could only get the gun in Jim Murchison's study ... then he'd show them, put everything right. But it was the right that was the problem. He tried to tell them, to warn them, but he had no voice. He called, shouted, roared, did everything he could to make them listen, but no sound came: I'm not a quitter. I'll not betray you. I'm on your side. But no one heard. Except in his own drink-dappled mind.

***

The following morning Ryder showed no inclination to

leave his bed. He was ill: apart from the hangover he was feverish, with a throat which he said seemed gummed up, and he wanted nothing to eat. Margo and Grace Murchison decided to call the family doctor, despite Ryder's protestations.

"I don't want anyone," he wheezed. "Leave me alone. I'll be fine."

Dr Hayter was a bluff, no-nonsense medic of the old school who took Ryder's temperature and peered down his throat and felt round his neck. After hearing of Ryder's jaunt in the ocean he declared he had probably caught a chill and, as long as he kept warm, he'd be as right as rain for Christmas Day. He thought there might be a touch of laryngitis brought on by the chill and, when Ryder said he'd done a lot of talking, and had to raise his voice over the chatter at the party, the doctor nodded and said it certainly wouldn't have helped. He prescribed something to reduce the fever, and asked if the Murchisons had a humidifier to moisten the air which would ease the throat. He told Ryder to take plenty of fluids ... not alcohol, he reminded him, arching an eyebrow ... and to rest his voice as much as possible.

"Difficult, I'm sure, Mr Ryder, for a politician," Hayter said, with a twinkle in his eye, "but you're here on vacation and can relax. So ... no speeches."

When the doctor left Margo stayed for a few moments with her husband. Ryder was racked with remorse. He apologised for his behaviour on the previous evening, saying he had no idea what came over him. He hoped he hadn't spoiled the party and wondered how the Murchisons had taken it.

Margo said her parents had hardly noticed. They were too busy playing host and hostess at the soirée which, to their delight, had raised almost twenty thousand dollars. Everyone understood, Margo said,

154

that Tim was stressed and tired, and would be susceptible to coughs or colds or other ailments that were going round. She added, though, they thought he was drinking too much and should go easy on the alcohol.

"I couldn't talk," Ryder said in a whisper. "My throat was ... is ... giving me hell. I had to drink or it would have seized up completely."

"You could have drunk water," Margo pointed out.

"What ... at a party? I don't remember anyone offering water."

"You could ... okay, never mind. You just rest, honey. That's what you need right now. Doctor's orders. Oh ... and when you're recovered ... when you can speak ... you'd better give Max Deutscher a ring. To thank him. He's the one who came to find me ... he was most discreet ... to tell me you weren't well. That's when I found you here."

"I've let you down, hun, haven't I ...? And myself. It's a sort of ... betrayal. A betrayal of ..."

"Ssssh. No more talk. Rest."

***

By the time Christmas came Ryder was up and about, although still feeling tired and lethargic. It was that gremlin, sapping his energy, and Ryder wanted it to go away. His throat, however, still troubled him, and sometimes it was awkward swallowing. Margo had bought him some lozenges, which helped, though they seemed to quell his appetite. His stomach was awash with fruity flavours that would not sit well, Ryder imagined, with Christmas dinner. Perhaps he would have a small portion, to be polite.

On Christmas morning, after they had risen late, following attendance at midnight communion to humour their hosts, Ryder had given Margo a pendant with an emerald set in finely worked white gold. The London jeweller, from whom he had bought it in early summer, assured him it was a new piece made to a traditional design. Ryder didn't care. He paid the asking price, without haggling, content in the knowledge that the Christmas present problem was solved for another year. All he had to do was hide it and then remember where he had put it. When Margo opened the parcel, tastefully wrapped by Marie-France, she gave a squeal of delight ... perhaps overdone, Ryder thought, for the benefit of her parents ... and insisted on wearing the pendant at once, even though, as she admitted, the colour fought with the top she was wearing. In return, Margo presented Ryder with a Manchester University tie ... his old one, she reminded him, had gravy stains down it and wasn't fit to be seen ... and a pair of university cufflinks.

"Well," he said, admiring the crest with its familiar sun motif, "I certainly shan't be short of cufflinks."

"I could say the same about pendants," Margo said, with a faint sniff. "I suppose I should be grateful last year's was a ruby."

"Was it?" Ryder queried. "I thought ... ah ..."

"It's a good job I like pendants. And at least you make the effort ... don't leave Christmas shopping to your office manager."

"You might get something more original if I did," Ryder said glumly. "I'm not much good in the present-buying stakes. Sorry, hun."

Seeing Ryder's downcast face, Margo burst out laughing. "It's lovely. Honestly ... it is. I really like it. And even if you're shit at present-buying I still love you."

She got up, crossed to where Ryder was sitting, and kissed him.

"Okay, you two love-birds," Jim Murchison chipped in. "Eggnog time. It'll perk you up, Tim ... do you good, medication or no medication. Grace ... you find me that cinnamon I asked for?"

"Sure I got you that cinnamon. Nutmeg, too. But nothing for me. I've the turkey to attend to."

***

By late afternoon, by the time the festive table was laid, and the bird about to be offered for carving, Ryder was pleasantly relaxed. He'd enjoyed the eggnog, and accepted another, and declined an invitation to accompany Margo and her father on a walk. He wasn't up to it, he told them, which was true. While they were out Ryder, having dutifully enquired of Grace if he could assist in the kitchen, and having been shooed away, settled himself in front of the television and promptly fell asleep. When he awoke, on the return of Jim and Margo, and shortly before the meal was to be served, he was feeling better: the alcohol had dulled the ache in his body, inducing warmth and wellbeing, and even the huskiness in his voice was less evident. Nevertheless, when the time came to carve the turkey, he declined: there was little grip in his hands and he had no wish to risk fumbling with the carving knife or have it slip through his fingers. He told his hosts that the days when Brits carved up American possessions were long gone.

Jim Murchison was laying slices of turkey onto the plates when the the phone rang.

"Darn it," Grace said, rising from the table to answer the call. "Who can that be at this time? Some folks just never think."

"It could be Alistair," Margo said. "We couldn't get him earlier ... perhaps he's returning the call to wish us a merry Christmas."

Grace lifted the handset. "The Murchison residence," she intoned. Then, moments later: "He is. Just one moment."

Turning to her son-in-law she said: "Tim ... it's for you." Then, in a whisper, "I couldn't get the name. It's not a good line. Blanket, something like that. Definitely British."

Ryder frowned and, taking the phone, lumbered to his feet.

"Sorry about this," he croaked. "I'll take it out here. And that's enough meat for me ... thanks."

He left the room, shutting the door behind him. For a moment he thought it might be Ellie, indeed hoped it would be Ellie, to exchange season's greetings. But that was stupid. There was no way she knew, could have got hold of, the Murchisons' number. Besides, if she wanted to ring him, she'd have used his mobile. Except it was switched off. Puzzled, he put the handset to his ear.

The turkey was served, and the vegetables about to be passed round, when Ryder reappeared in the doorway. He was ashen, swaying slightly, and shaking. Margo, shocked, leaped to her feet.

"Honey ... what ...?"

"That was Blenhesket. It's Pemberton. A stroke. Collapsed, face down, into his Christmas dinner. There's an emergency meeting of the parliamentary party. I've got to go back to London. Now."

London. December 2014.

The meeting in committee room 14 at the Palace of Westminster had already begun by the time Ryder sidled in. He caught Blenhesket's eye as he entered, and across the packed room the older man gave him a curt nod. Ryder was unable to determine whether this was an expression of disapproval or merely an acknowledgement of his presence. Either way, he didn't much care. He wanted the meeting to be over as quickly as possible so he could go to his flat and sleep.

He slumped onto a seat by the wall and found himself next to Jack Merryman, who turned to greet him.

"Christ," Merryman muttered. "You look awful."

"Thanks," Ryder rasped. "I've got this throat bug. Something I picked up over there. And the journey didn't help. Three days on the move. San Diego to San Francisco, Tokyo, Paris, then here. The only available flights. Ridiculous. Don't ask me what day, what time of day it is. I haven't a clue."

Ryder tried to force his wearied brain to concentrate on the meeting. He knew that Pemberton, on medical advice, had stepped down both as party leader and PM. Doctors had ordered complete rest which meant Pemberton's political career was over. The need now was to appoint a new leader, and new prime minister, and to confirm the mechanism and timing to bring this about. All were adamant that the deputy prime minister, a Liberal Democrat, should not be allowed to lead the government for a moment longer than necessary. There was a risk the junior coalition partner might exploit its position, allow its leader to assume a gravitas that could garner votes at the forthcoming election.

"God knows what they might do," ran the tea room talk. "Sign us up for the euro, or some such nonsense."

"Or Schengen ... even more blasted foreigners pitching up over here ..."

"Abolish Trident, leaving us at the mercy of any lunatic middle east jihadist dictator ..."

Ryder, struggling to keep his eyes open, was overcome with a desperate urge to remove his shoes. His feet, he felt, were trying to tell him something. Probably that they'd been incarcerated in the same shoes for the best part of three days and craved liberation. It struck him that, while he'd managed to take off his shoes on the Tokyo-Paris stretch of the journey ... he remembered this because he'd had to scrabble awkwardly under the seat in front to retrieve his footwear as the plane was landing at Charles de Gaulle ... he probably hadn't removed his socks since leaving San Diego. It would not, therefore, be a good idea to take off his shoes now. Not, at least, if he wished to remain on speaking terms with Merryman and others around him.

This, of course, was the issue. What did it matter if he stank the place out? Why should he bother what his colleagues thought? Had he not resolved to pack it in, to step down at the next election? In which case, what was he doing back at Westminster? Why hadn't he stayed in La Jolla, with Margo, with his in-laws, enjoyed Christmas, seen in the new year, as planned? This was precisely the point Margo made when he declared his intention to return to London.

"What are you going back for?" she berated him. "You've no reason. Let them know you're not going to stand. I mean, if you're serious, you've got to tell them some time. Now's as good as any."

When Ryder prevaricated, saying it was his duty to go back, a pivotal moment for party and country, of huge historical significance, and he wanted to share in it, she accused him of insincerity.

"You tell me one thing one day, another the next. I don't know what to believe. Like these spasms, these aches and pains you say you get. One moment you're in agony, can't move ... next you're striding along the beach, leaping about in the ocean. And now you want to ruin a wonderful Christmas, with my folks, whom I hardly see, and go charging halfway round the world to join a bunch of people you say you no longer want to be with. It doesn't make sense. I mean ... I don't understand you any more."

Ryder said he couldn't help what was going on with his body, but it was all perfectly genuine, which was why he'd been to his doctor.

"Yes ... and to Ellie as well. A convenient excuse to go see her. Perhaps that's why you're slinking back to England."

Ryder, biting his tongue, said if that was what she thought there was no point in discussing the matter further.

"While you're about it, get her to check you into a rehab centre. For alcoholics. I think that's your problem, Tim Ryder. Washed out all the time ... it's the drink. The amount you've stashed away this vacation ... don't think we haven't noticed. I mean, my folks ... they're worried ... so am I. That's where Alistair gets it from ... when the police bring my son home in the back of a cruiser it's because of you."

Something tightened inside Ryder. For the first time in his life he had wanted to lash out, strike her, anything to silence her. She was so wrong, so very wrong. But Margo, with a disdainful toss of her head, had turned her back, retreating, renouncing him ... consigning him to a part of her, it occurred to Ryder, that belonged to a more certain past. Then she had spun round and glared at him.

"Go on, just go. Back to your political family. Your

real family ... you care more about them than you do about us. At least when you're there you can drink yourself stupid and nobody'll care ... nobody'll notice. You'll like that. So go. Just get out of my sight."

Someone, or something, was pulling at Ryder's sleeve. He flapped a hand in the direction of whatever it was to swat it, make it go away.

"You're snoring," Merryman breathed into his ear. "And you need to give your approval ... now."

"Approval ...? What for?"

"Just do it ... a show of hands. Here ..."

He felt Merryman guide his arm upward and, looking round, he saw a forest of hands that might have belonged to children vying for teacher's attention.

"Against?" a voice said.

Arms, including Ryder's, thumped back onto desks.

"Abstentions?"

No one moved.

"Nem con," the voice intoned, sonorously, to a buzz of excitement, as chairs were pushed back and the MPs made to leave the room.

"What was that about?" Ryder asked Merryman. "I mean ... sorry ... I was out of it."

"We noticed. Or, rather, heard," Merryman said, giving a malicious grin. "But don't worry. You've just agreed to set wheels in motion to have a new leader ... a new PM ... in place in the new year. Done and dusted by the time the house returns in January. Exciting ... or what?"

***

The statue of Margaret Thatcher was, Ryder thought, out of proportion. It dominated the members' lobby and he invariably grimaced when he saw it. Seemingly larger than life, the Iron Lady ... a pity the statue was of bronze, Ryder reminded himself ... was wagging a warning finger at anyone fool enough to linger in her presence. At the same time she looked about to launch into a lecture that would brook no contradiction. Ryder shuddered. Churchill, on the other hand, glowering in an opposite corner, was sombre, brooding, altogether more solid and reliable, and as Ryder checked to see if there were any messages for him ... there were none ... he looked up at the old man and winked.

He was about to leave the lobby when he felt a hand on his elbow. He turned, half expecting to find Margaret Thatcher about to give him a dressing-down for not changing his socks for three days, but it was Blenhesket.

"Tim," he said, drawing him aside out of earshot of other MPs. "Glad I've caught you. There are things we need to discuss."

"I don't think ..." Ryder began.

"God, you sound rough. But I know you've had a difficult trip and I appreciate the efforts you've made to get here. But you'll understand ..." and Blenhesket lowered his voice "... that given the circumstances we need to make our views known. There'll not be another opportunity like it in this parliament or the next. What I'm saying is ..." and Blenhesket almost breathed the words "... we can't let Miller have a clear run at the leadership. We ... that is Tory Trust ... need to flex our muscles."

"Muscles," Ryder repeated vaguely, involuntarily attempting to flex his own but finding little response. He felt limp, ragged. It was all that travel.

"Look. I know you're exhausted. But we've a meeting arranged for later today ..."

"No way. I can hardly keep my eyes open. I need to get to bed ... sleep. Catch up."

Blenhesket pursed his lips and looked hard at Ryder.

"Alright. Perhaps ... I suppose at this stage we can do without you. We can set the ball rolling ... agree tactics ... and you can come in later. But we shall need to talk. Soon."

"Yes, yes," Ryder said, thinking of his bed, wondering whether he'd bothered to make it when he last crawled out of it, and whether he'd need the electric blanket to air the sheets. "Yes. We'll talk tomorrow."

"Keep your phone on. We're going to have to act fast if we're to get what we want ... whom we want. Remember, as I said, there's a lot hanging on this. We won't get another chance."

"Indeed not," Ryder agreed. "Act fast. Essential."

"Good. Glad you're on the same wavelength. Until tomorrow."

Releasing his grip on Ryder's elbow, Blenhesket flashed a faint smile and strode off across the lobby. The man's in his element, Ryder thought, machiavellian, manoeuvring and manipulating, turning a crisis into a crusade. But a crusade for what ... for whom? Ryder didn't know and didn't care. He was too tired. The Iron Lady, still gazing disapprovingly upon him, could survive on a couple of hours' sleep. Tim Ryder, however, was no Margaret Thatcher.

***

The building, in which Ryder's cramped but adequate flat straddled the third floor, dated from late Victorian, early Edwardian times, and was rumoured to have been occupied by ladies of doubtful provenance installed there by wealthy city gents who visited after work. There was no evidence, no proof, that this had ever been the case: presumably the gentlemen concerned were careful to cover their tracks. Nevertheless Ryder enjoyed the faintly naughty, faintly degenerate impression the place gave off, and every time he put his key in the lock and entered the dark, airless hall, he received a frisson of anticipation, of illicit tryst and lustful liaison, as if he were stepping back in time. He'd thought of bringing Ellie here, allowing both the building and himself to relive a more passionate past, but he had never summoned the courage, never dared ask. He often wondered why. Perhaps it was refusal he feared, the risk of spoiling a friendship with a request that would make him look weak and foolish. Besides, affairs were ... for whom? Adventurous souls ... buccaneering types, rantipoles, more confident of their own sexuality than he was even in middle age. And then there was all the conniving, the lies, the secrets. To say nothing of Margo, who deserved better of him. Much better. Margo, who would join him in London, in the tiny bachelor flat, to go to a show, an exhibition, or sometimes shopping. Ellie and Margo sharing, albeit at different times, the same bed ... it was wrong. A betrayal of both women. All the same, he cursed himself for his sensibilities, his prudishness. Sometimes he felt he was missing out on experiences which others seemed to take in their stride, that as a result he was letting himself down ... as well as the honour, however dubious, of the flat's previous occupants who must be in despair at the tortured morality of their successor. Perhaps, Ryder told himself at such moments, he should have been a vicar. His belief in god was weak but these days it was acceptable to look on the deity as a bartered, bespoke being, all things to all men, if less so to women. Yes, he'd have found a place in today's confused and crumbling church.

Given the antecedents of the flat, and its squashed, slightly squalid state, it was a matter of wonder to Ryder that, on the day after the meeting at Westminster, his tiny sitting room was graced, if that was the correct word, by no less a grandee than Sir Wesley Blenhesket. Ryder had been roused from a deep, jet-lagged sleep by the doorbell which he mistakenly took to be the alarm clock. He couldn't work out, when he extended an arm from the warmth of his bed to strike the offending timepiece, why the ringing persisted. The clock had to be the culprit, he told himself, realising even in his befuddled mind that if his mobile phone had an alarm he had no idea how it worked. Only when the ringing became more strident, more angry, did he realise that it must be someone standing on the street at the front door. He staggered out of bed, wondering why the flat was so cold, and recalling he hadn't adjusted the heating, and pressed the button by the intercom. Immediately, despite distortion, he recognised Blenhesket's tones.

Ryder cleared his throat. "What on earth ...? I mean ... how did you know where ...?"

"I know everything. Let me in," Blenhesket snapped.

Ryder released the front door to admit his visitor. Panicking, he lurched back to the bedroom to pull on trousers and a jumper. Slippers would have been useful, but he could find only one. Cursing, he pulled the door shut on the disorder in the bedroom and was about to make his way to the kitchen to sort the heating when there was a rap at the door. He opened it and Blenhesket stepped into the narrow hall.

"Bloody hell," he said. "It's colder in here than it is outside. And that's saying something."

"I'll get the kettle on. If you'd just like to go through ... you might have to shift some stuff to sit down. Haven't had time ..."

"Quite understandable. And coffee would be fine," Blenhesket said, glancing round and, Ryder thought, wrinkling his nose. Clearly, the place would strike cold and musty. Why hadn't he got the heating on?

When Ryder returned, bearing a cafetière and a plate of digestives past their sell-by date, and having fiddled with the heating switch in the kitchen, he was relieved to hear the clunk of radiators as they warmed to water passing through them. He found Blenhesket still in his coat and standing at the window, staring down.

"You've a pub across there. Looks quite decent. Ever go?"

Ryder said he'd been a few times, but was hardly a regular: he was generally too busy, or too tired, to bother. It also tended to be noisy, he added, especially at weekday lunchtimes, though it was reasonably comfortable. It struck him Blenhesket might prefer the pub, since it would be warmer than the flat, but when he suggested it, and said they could perhaps have something to eat, his visitor snorted.

"What I've got to say is not for the ears of drinkers ... at least not yet. Sit down."

It was strange, Ryder felt, to be told to sit down in his own flat. Nevertheless he obeyed. Sir Wesley Blenhesket was not the sort of person to be crossed, even in a matter as trivial as taking a seat.

"You may recall," Blenhesket began, pushing a couple of reports from the sofa and settling back into it, "that Tory Trust held a meeting yesterday immediately after the one you attended in the house."

Ryder nodded.

"The purpose of the meeting was to choose a candidate, acceptable to those of us who see ourselves as more traditional, one-nation conservatives, to challenge the more obvious, right-wing, contenders for party leader and, ultimately, PM. Accordingly we want you to be that candidate. What do you say?"

***

Some time later Ryder was conscious that Blenhesket was ringing for a cab to take him back to Westminster. The intervening discussion, if such it was ... Ryder recalled more of a monologue, akin to the prosecution setting out the facts of a case, the outcome of which in this instance was in no doubt ... passed in a blur. He remembered thinking he wished he had found his other slipper: how many people invited to present themselves for the highest office in the land had found themselves curling their toes into a shabby, tea-stained, wine-tasted rug? Of course, the whole idea was out of the question. The suggestion that he, a nobody, a nonentity, who had never risen beyond under-secretary of state, could leapfrog cabinet ministers, all of whom would expect the succession to pass to them, was a non-starter. Blenhesket was out of his mind. The arch-plotter, the arch-fixer, had lost it: this was a piece of political mischief too far.

All the same, it was not without its merits. If he were going to quit parliament at the next election he could at least go out on a high, be remembered ... what was it? ... as a stalking horse to whomever the party apparatchiks fielded as their preferred candidate. Most likely his boss, the current deputy leader and foreign secretary, Jeremy Miller. It would certainly be one in the eye for Miller, revenge for dumping the departmental rubbish on him: global warming, hosting tedious receptions for dodgy dictators to flog them a second-hand frigate ... one careful owner ... or a squadron of clapped-out aircraft. As well as foisting on him the sinecured sons of Dulwich College and Cambridge. Yes, running for party leader would ensure his place in history: true, as a footnote in the memoires of the great and the good, or in donnish tomes destined to be unread, unreviewed even in the more serious literary journals, but a footnote nevertheless. This, of course, was all a simple ex-comprehensive boy could ever hope to become: a footnote in someone else's story.

Somehow Blenhesket was now at the door, still wearing his coat, saying he would go down and wait for his taxi outside. The longer he waited, the less the tip, he told Ryder with satisfaction.

Then: "I'm waiting for your call. As soon as you've made yours. I want to know. At once. Understood?"

Ryder nodded, as Blenhesket turned, swept along the landing and, without looking back, disappeared with a clatter down the stairs.

For a moment Ryder stood motionless at the door. Then, conscious of cold air round his feet, he stepped back, shut the door, and kicked the draught excluder, a snake bought years ago at a fund-raising function, and known as Sammy, behind the gap. What was that about phone calls? As soon as you've made yours? What was Blenhesket on about? What did he expect him to do?

Ryder flopped back wearily onto the sofa recently occupied by his visitor. His mind was churning, his thoughts racing. Surely, this was all a dream. He would wake any moment, cramped and cross, in a cattle-class airline seat somewhere over the Pacific, with a lip-sticked smile bending over him, bearing fake concern and a tray, and enquiring if he had ordered the vegetarian option. He'd no recollection of ordering anything, hadn't been offered a choice, and because it was airline food he probably couldn't tell the difference anyway. Of course, if he were prime minister, he could legislate for improvements to in-flight catering, and demand greater legroom all round. There again, though, if he were PM, he wouldn't be in cattle-class, but up front, behind those curtains, being served exotic foods and exquisite wines, as in those ridiculously mendacious airline advertisements, which never revealed the snaking queues for check-in and security, or the clatter and chatter of airport so-called lounges. Yes, if he were PM ...

He was woken by the buzzing of his phone. He rose, feeling stiff and headachy, and traced the sound to the pocket of the jacket he had been wearing the previous day and which he had flung over a chair. He fished for the phone and sank back onto the sofa as he tried to see who was calling.

"Hello ...?" he coughed, to clear his throat.

"Jack Merryman here. Listen ... we're all agog. We've just seen Sir Wesley come back but he swept past ... said nothing. So ...?"

"Ah ... so you're one of Blenhesket's gang. Well, well. I wouldn't have thought you needed ..."

"What have you decided? I mean ..."

"Decided? Oh, I see. Er ... I don't know. That is ..."

"What are you saying ... you don't know?"

"I haven't ... I can't ... I need to speak to my wife ..."

Of course. That's what it was. That was what Blenhesket meant when he said he should make a call before then ringing him. Margo ... he must have said, told him he needed to consult her ... but he'd no recollection of so doing. It was as if one of those mists had rolled in from the Irish Sea, blotting out the Northaven beach, shrouding everything, his mind, his thoughts, in swirling, curling doubt.

Merryman grunted, sounded impatient.

"Jack. While you're there. Tell me ... this sounds stupid ... why me?"

"What do you mean ... why you? Surely Sir Wesley explained."

"Yes ... yes. Of course. But ... I'd like to hear it from ... from someone else."

"Well ... obviously ... we need someone who can

170

bring the party ... and the country ... back to its senses. The Old Etonians and their cronies in the city have been milking this country for too long. If we're going to stand any chance of being re-elected we've got to appeal to ordinary voters ... show we care ..."

"I know all that. But why me, for god's sake?"

"I'm not detecting any hesitation, am I? Any doubts? I mean, if so, then ..."

"No. I mean ... I just need to know. Be absolutely clear that ... that I'm the right person ... that you've made the right choice."

"For Christ's sake, Tim, this is the chance of a lifetime. There are people in this party who'd sell their sisters into slavery for an opportunity like this. And of course you're the right person."

"But I'm an unknown ... in the country and, for the most part, in the party. At least in the higher echelons. I mean ... I'm hardly a household name."

"Exactly. And that's why we're backing you. Because anyone with the support of the higher echelons, as you put it, anyone currently in the cabinet, is toxic. A Pemberton mark two, tainted by the failure of our economic policy, hamstrung by u-turns and broken promises, and a Tory toff to boot ... it's a gift to UKIP, as well as the Labour Party. Put it this way ... no one's going to turn out and vote for more of the same ... if these days they can be bothered to turn out at all."

"You still haven't answered my question."

"Why you? Look ... it stands to reason. The very fact that you're an unknown ... no disrespect, quite the contrary ... is an enormous advantage. It means ..."

"But I've never had cabinet responsibility ... never got beyond FCO bag carrier."

"Does that matter? You've had more experience of government than, say, Blair when he took over. And how long did that silver-tongued pseud go on for? Ten years."

"I wouldn't want to see myself as a Tony Blair. Anything but."

"Nobody's asking you to. The point is, because no one knows you, we can reinvent this party. And you're the man to do it. Sir Wesley has been singing your praises ... an independent mind, he says ..."

"I don't know where he gets that from."

"He was impressed by the way you handled that food poisoning business ... the YouTube thing ... and especially that interview on the Today programme."

"It was Blenhesket who set it all up. My inclination was to drop it."

"Ah ... the old fox was testing you. But you came out with flying colours ... got your points across exactly as you wanted. There was no doubt in that interview whose side you were on ... Mr and Mrs Three-Bed Semi. And were you aware, by the way, we were up two points in a poll in the Daily Mail just a couple of days later?"

"Coincidence."

"Maybe ... but Sir Wesley didn't think so. Clear evidence, he said, of the Ryder factor. Someone who can resonate with the electorate ... speak their language."

"Surely there must be others in Tory Trust who'd be more suitable."

"There isn't. We're not a large group ... but when the rest of them, as well as a good few ministers, realise they're facing unemployment in May unless the party changes its tune, they'll come round to our way of thinking ... and back you. You mark my words."

"Your words ... I hear the words of Blenhesket. What's in it for him, I wonder?"

Merryman was silent before replying.

"Revenge. The way the party dropped him as chief

172

whip after those allegations ... never proven, of course ... of tax fiddling. I mean ... I know it was before my time ... but it seems they just wanted rid of him. Face no longer fitted. And I don't think he's ever forgiven them."

"That was a long time ago."

"I know. I might be wrong. I also think, for what it's worth, he's doing it for you. I suspect he sees in you what he himself once was ... or might have been. He wants to see his protégé succeed in a way he never did. At any rate, though he might not show it, I'm sure he's fond of you. Very fond, in fact."

***

After Ryder had spoken to Merryman and attempted to digest what he had said ... he mind was still whirling; things were happening too quickly and his body had not caught up with itself after its peregrination halfway round the world ... he realised he should ring Margo. It was too early, though. Lunchtime in London ... early hours of the morning in La Jolla. It occurred to him he hadn't even rung her to say he'd got back safely. He'd tried to text her from the airport in Tokyo but the phone slipped from one network to another. Ridiculous, of course: didn't they manufacture the wretched things in Japan? If they worked anywhere then it ought to be where they were made. Though perhaps these days it was Thailand. Or Indonesia. It was so difficult to keep up with the changes in the world. And it didn't help that, when trying to text, his already tired and jet-lagged fingers refused to cooperate. They kept sliding from the keys so that if any message had been sent it would resemble wartime code ... or perhaps the vowelless lol-laden emoticoned textese adopted by Alistair and his ilk ... rather than a sensible communication in English. At any rate, there'd been no reply from Margo, which suggested either she had received nothing or she was sulking after he'd walked out in the middle of Christmas family festivities. No, the small hours of the morning were not the right time to ring ... not even with news as eventful as this.

He needed, though, to speak to someone. He hesitated a moment before selecting Ellie's number and pressing connect. There was a chance there would be no reply. He couldn't remember the last time he had rung her on her mobile and the number might have changed. Usually he spoke to her at the surgery but something told him she wouldn't be there. He listened. The number was ringing.

"Tim," a familiar voice said. "Is that you?"

"It is," Ryder replied, feeling himself relax. "You're not working this Christmas, then?"

"I'm sorry. You're going to have to speak up. There's a lot going on."

Down the phone Ryder could hear shouting, laughter, children's voices.

"Are you ... you're not by yourself, then?"

A pause. "No. I'm at Simon's."

"Simon's?"

"Simon's my ... I've been seeing Simon for the last six months. I'm spending Christmas ..."

"Christ."

"I was going to tell you, Tim. Not that it's anything to do with you."

"No. Of course. Quite."

"Simon's a surgeon. Divorced. We're probably going to ..."

"That's wonderful. I mean ... congratulations. Wow."

"Are you alright, Tim? You sound ..."

"Fine. Never felt better."

"You sure?"

"Positive. I just wanted to say ... well ... a belated merry Christmas. And a happy new year. Which I'm sure it will be. Especially now."

"Thanks. The same to you and Margo."

"Thanks. So ... all the best. And ... enjoy your party, or whatever it is."

"We shall. Bye."

"Bye."

Ryder clicked the phone off, hurling it to the sofa. He was shaking, riven with rage. She'd no right ... how could she? A surgeon ... he could see it all ... rolling in money, a huge Victorian house, kids at private school. A ready-made happy family. It was all wrong. Ellie was untouchable, inviolate ... there'd been no one after him, so he told himself ... there couldn't be. She wasn't the marrying type: a modern-day nun, married to her work, her vocation, renouncing carnal pleasures, lust, liaisons. And if he couldn't have her then no one should. But what was he saying? This was folly ... no, call it by its proper name. Jealousy. That was it: he was sick with jealousy ... at the back of his mind there'd always been the thought if something happened to Margo, or something happened between them, he could go back to Ellie, pick up where they left off. Puerile, perhaps; pathetic, certainly. But he'd always told himself ... stupidly, senselessly, that somehow she'd keep herself for him ... be waiting for him. And now ...

Snap out of it, he told himself angrily. You've no right. You don't own her ... never have. You're happily married, a fine wife, whom you love, a son. You've everything going for you ... especially now ... in a couple of weeks you could be prime minister, hobnobbing with presidents, heads of state, sending troops into battle, determining the direction of one of the leading nations of the world. All this you could have. But invariably it's the things you can't have ... the

175

simple things, the things you might once have had but lost, thrown away ... that you want most. And not the things. The people.

Ryder collapsed back onto the sofa. He needed a drink. Desperately. There was too much going on, thoughts and emotions vying for attention, crying for release, but they were constrained in the confines of the flat, suddenly cloying, claustrophobic. He had to get out. In his mind's eye the pub, the one Blenhesket had spotted, beckoned. Forcing himself to his feet, still trembling, uncoordinated, he shuffled through to the bedroom, extracted shoes and socks, sat awkwardly on the bed to put them on, then crossed to the hall, where he grabbed a coat. Minutes later he was in the Wig and Whistle with his first pint in front of him.

***

Two hours and double the number of pints later Ryder was regretting his decision to decamp to the pub. He had eaten nothing, bar a packet of plain crisps, for the pub served no food in the days after Christmas because its customary clientele ... the software designers, the music publishers, the architects who had established themselves in basement offices round about ... were at home with their spouses and children. A staff shortage contributed to the absence of food: a notice behind the optics appealed urgently for kitchen staff, and when Ryder enquired why it was difficult to recruit, with unemployment at nine percent and rising, he was told if he wanted a job no experience was necessary and he could start at once. He declined, reflecting that his rumpled state, the result of jet-lag and hasty dressing, marked him among the nine percent. He might yet join them, he realised, swell their ranks, if he left parliament in May with no firm idea of what to do.

But now the beer was taking its toll, leaving him dull and despondent, and still no clearer ... indeed, less so ... about where he stood in respect either of Blenhesket's preposterous proposal or of what he perceived as Ellie's betrayal. Thinking like this, of course, was a nonsense, and deep down he knew it: the proposal was as sincere as Ellie's happiness was hers, hers alone, to determine, and he had no right to question either. All the same, try as he might, he was unable to shake off the impression that he was somehow a victim, a pawn, in power games, shifting loyalties and changing allegiances, that lay beyond his control. Impotent ... that's what he was, and he despised himself for it. At the same time, as he exchanged the glow of the Wig and Whistle for the gloom of an early evening street, weaving his way across it to fumble with the key to the door of the former gentlemen's chambers, he knew he must act, reach a decision. From the brace of matters exercising him, demanding resolution, he told himself if he couldn't have one, then he must seize the other.

The flat had warmed up and, to retain the heat, he drew the curtains, shutting out the evening, shutting out a city abandoned in that uneasy, post-Christmas no-man's-land, waiting for the familiar and almost welcome hostilities of targets and deadlines, reports and meetings, office intrigue and gossip, to extract their toll once again in the new year. It was the moment to shut out all else, to reach inwards, deep into himself ... and to contact Margo in La Jolla.

He retrieved his mobile from the sofa where he had flung it and, stabbing with his finger, switched it on. He found the number, pressed connect. He wondered where she would be ... still in the bedroom, or downstairs in the breakfast room. If here, she might not have her phone with her. He had no desire to ring the

Murchison home and speak, however briefly, to Jim or Grace. It was Margo he wanted.

"Tim ... hi."

Her voice took him by surprise. He half-expected her to be angry, resentful: they had not parted on the easiest of terms when she realised he was set on returning to London. But here she was, friendly, affable, and Ryder felt a surge of relief.

"Hun ... I ... it's good to hear you. I didn't know ... I mean, the time difference ... wasn't sure. I didn't want to wake you in the middle of the night. How are things?"

"You okay? You sound ... weird. Slurry. You've been drinking, haven't you?"

"No. I mean ... no. It's just my throat. Still a bit rough. And I've not got over the journey. A nightmare. Took days ..."

"You should have rung. We've been worried."

"Sorry. I know. But it's been one thing after another."

"You made it for your meeting ...?"

"Just about. But that's why I'm ringing. It's ... I mean ... crying out loud ... how do you fancy being ... in your parlance ... first lady?"

"Excuse me ...?"

"Wife of the prime minister."

"What?"

"I've been asked ... that is, there's a group ..."

"You have. You've been drinking. I can hear it in your voice. You're not clear ... and, no, it's not the phone ..."

"I'm serious. You've got to believe me."

"This is a wind-up. I guess if you think this is funny ..."

"No," Ryder screeched down the phone. "Okay ... I've had couple of pints ... but this isn't a wind-up. I'm

178

deadly serious."

Something in Ryder's tone told Margo her husband was in earnest.

"Wait. You're not telling me ..."

"There are people at Westminster ... Blenhesket's the prime mover ... who want me to stand for party leader, against the old guard, and if elected ... Downing Street here we come. Of course, I don't stand a cat's chance in ..."

"I thought you were through with politics. You told me ..."

"That was before all this. I mean, yes ... I was fed up, ready for out. But this is an opportunity ... I don't know ... to make a difference. And even if I'm not elected ... as I said, there's only a slim chance ... then at least for a few days I can have my say. Reach out to the nation. And bow out in a blaze of glory."

Ryder heard Margo tell someone ... presumably one of her parents ... that it was Tim and he'd been asked to go for party leader and possibly prime minister and that she didn't think he was bullshitting.

"I'm not bullshitting," Ryder raised his voice. "Straight up. Someone's got to do it. And they want me. Though I'm not sure why. But, hun ..." and Ryder spoke more quietly, "I've not said I shall. Not without speaking to you. I mean ... if you don't want me to ... if you'd rather I just got out in May, no fuss, as we said ..."

"But we hadn't. Not in so many words. You quitting politics ... it's crazy. Politics is your whole life ... it's you. You'd be lost without it. If this election business makes you see sense ... makes you see where you need to be ... then so be it."

"So ... you think I should go for it? I mean ... you don't mind?"

"Honey ... I want what's best for you. For us. And of

late ... okay, I guess it's been pretty difficult. That video ... in Edinburgh ... those peculiar aches and pains. But get them sorted and ... okay ... you go for it. I think you'd make a wonderful prime minister."

"I don't know about that ... "

"On one condition."

"On one condition what?"

"That you tell Alistair before it goes public. Tell him in person. I think you owe him that. You know how touchy he is about your political life."

"I'll get back home first thing tomorrow. And in the meantime ... I can ring Blenhesket with your blessing."

"With my blessing, honey. Go for it."

***

Blenhesket received the news with a satisfied grunt. He told Ryder to come to his office the following day to check and sign papers and approve the candidate statement, as well as press releases, he had prepared. When Ryder expressed surprise that Blenhesket had gone to so much trouble without knowing whether he would accept, the older man permitted himself a growl of amusement.

"Never doubted it for one moment, my lad. Never doubted it all."

Northaven. December 2014.

It was late afternoon by the time Ryder managed to extricate himself from the campaign preparations begun by Blenhesket. Sir Wesley was reluctant to let Ryder out of his sight, claiming there was too much to do, that the candidate couldn't afford even for a night to leave the capital to return to Northaven, but Ryder insisted. Blenhesket wanted Merryman to accompany him, ostensibly to discuss strategy, but in all probability to keep an eye on him, to guard him, though from whom, or from what, was unclear. Perhaps Blenhesket imagined that, if word got out too soon that Ryder was to mount an outside challenge to any of the big names that put themselves forward, then they would attempt to turn him, promising cabinet honours in a revised government under Miller, or whoever proved to be victorious. Merryman, Ryder noted, was fast becoming another Blenhesket, revelling in the cloak-and-dagger elements of the campaign. He would make a good government whip, Ryder thought, just like his mentor, and could well prove useful later.

Not now, though, on the journey to Northaven, which Ryder took alone, enjoying the luxury of a first class carriage all to himself. No one appeared to be travelling: the entire nation was at home, comatose after Christmas, bracing itself for the bogus bonhomie of new year. Either that, or recession and austerity meant people were staying at home, not travelling or, at best, were squashed into the straitjacketed seats of standard class. As the train sped north out of Euston, Ryder watched for the lineside pub, the Windermere, his marker, his signpost, that he was heading home, away from the strictures of the capital towards a kinder, gentler, less deceitful world. There it was ... and with a thrill he registered, for the first time, the wording set high on the Windermere's walls: Take Courage. It was a message, a glad omen: a brewery slogan, maybe, but one he found apt and uplifting. Shortly afterwards he slipped into a deep sleep, to be woken only by the announcement that the train was approaching Lime Street station.

He arrived home shortly before nine o'clock. The house was in darkness and, as Ryder let himself in, it struck him as airless and musty, almost uninhabited. Dumping his briefcase in the hall, and switching on lights, he walked through to the kitchen, his joints protesting at the end of a wearisome day, to make himself a cup of tea and find something to eat. As he filled the kettle, finding it inexplicably awkward, difficult to hold the heavier it became, the door from Marie-France's flat was thrust open and Alistair emerged, dishevelled but radiant. Light, warmth and an aroma of alcohol pursued him, and behind him stood Marie-France, awkwardly smoothing her trousers.

"Dad ... it's you," Alistair intoned, the radiance fading from his face. "Mum said you were back ... but I didn't know ..."

"I left a message ... on your mobile," Ryder said. "Saying I was coming. Which you obviously didn't pick up. What have you been up to?"

"Watching a DVD. I mean ... it's Christmas."

Marie-France came forward. "Alistair and I ... we 'ave looked after each other very well zees 'oliday. Two lonely 'earts ... we watch ze television in my flat where it ees warm ... cosy."

She giggled, and Ryder frowned.

"You've been drinking. Both of you ..."

"Monsieur Ryder ... it ees ze season of kindness and goodwill to all 'uman being. You not ... you not grudge us fine French wine ... to keep out ze English cold. And Alistair ..."

"I suspect Alistair's had quite enough," Ryder said sharply, recalling Margo's reproach that her son's underage drinking was a result of the poor example he set. "Besides ... he and I need words. But now's not the time. I think we might wait until morning. Over breakfast will do. But I mean ... over breakfast. I need to be away again pretty sharpish. So no lie-in ... understood?"

"What's this about?" Alistair mumbled.

"I said ... it'll do tomorrow."

"It's not about you and mum, is it?" For the first time that evening Alistair looked concerned. "I mean ... is this why you left her and came back? Is there ...?"

"It's nothing like that. Nothing like that at all. It's ... something entirely unrelated I need to run past you. But I need your brain in gear. That's why we'll talk when ... frankly, when you're sober."

"I'm not ..."

"You are. And that's why I suggest you take yourself to your room, now, no more drink ... Christmas or no Christmas ... so you've a clear head in the morning. And, no, it's not about your drinking we need to talk. Though, come to think about it ..."

"We're in the middle of a DVD."

"If it's a DVD it'll wait. Pause it, or whatever you do."

"Dad ..."

"Away with you. Now."

Alistair opened his mouth, as if about to speak, but immediately closed it. Perhaps something in Ryder's voice told him further protest would be pointless. Exchanging a quick glance with Marie-France, he brushed past Ryder, scowling, resentful, and slammed the door behind him.

Ryder turned to Marie-France, surprised at the rancour in his words as they came tumbling out. "I leave you here *in loco parentis* ... in charge ... and what do I find? The boy's drunk ... if not completely, then well on the way. I tell you ... it's got to stop. Right this minute. There's to be no more of this ... this carousing. Is that understood?"

The woman stared at Ryder. Again, he was struck by her huge, brown eyes, deep and placid, betraying nothing. Had she understood anything he had said?

"You'll appreciate ... with Alistair growing up ... about to go away to university ..." was that a response, fleeting, flickered? "... we might well have to discuss your position. It would be a pity if anything untoward ... uncalled for ... were to colour those discussions. Do I make myself clear?"

No, Ryder told himself, irritated, you are not making yourself clear. Why not just tell her when Alistair leaves home a live-in nanny is superfluous? As, indeed, if he were honest, he should have done years ago, when Alistair left primary school. They could have got by very nicely with a home help a couple of times a week, and at a fraction of the cost. Instead ...

Marie-France was still looking at him, almost coquettishly, Ryder thought with a jolt. But no, that was impossible. It was his imagination. The woman did not do coquettish. She was incapable of it. He frowned.

"Well ...?" he said.

"Monsieur ..." and she gave an enormous shrug, of pantomimic proportion, which infuriated Ryder. "Monsieur ... 'e know best."

Giving Ryder a nod, an almost teasing, playful smile on her lips, she turned from him and retired to her flat, gently closing the door behind her.

Ryder reached across to the kettle, to switch it on. But his hand was shaking, and he needed to sit, take the weight off his feet. He'd never seen Marie-France like this. There was something almost defiant in her demeanour, a strength, an awareness, he'd not noticed before. It was unsettling, disturbing. Something was going on, something was not right, but Ryder didn't know what, couldn't put his finger on anything. He should ring Margo, talk to her, tell her. But tell her what? There was nothing to tell ... a look, an impression, that was all. Nothing specific. Margo would think he'd been drinking again, was making it up. Damn it. He needed her. Here. This minute. Now.

***

The egg was all over the kitchen floor. At least, that was the way it seemed to Ryder, on all fours, furiously trying to encourage yoke and broken eggshell to remain on the cloth for long enough to squeeze into a bowl. Most of it, he found, oozed back onto the floor, some of it onto his trousers. He ought to call Marie-France: the kitchen, after all, was her domain, and she'd know about clearing up broken egg. But he didn't want her. What he had to say was between Alistair and himself. It was nothing to do with Marie-France: nothing at all. But, he thought, as he flicked the cloth underneath the fridge to extract more of the sullen, sticky mess, there must be easier ways of cleaning up. And what to do with the remains? Perhaps he should strain them, toss them into a frying pan, eggshell and all, beat them to a pulp and make an omelette. Waste not, want not: there were people all over the world who would welcome the contents of that bowl, and who wouldn't give a monkey's about the cleanliness of the floor.

How the egg had slipped from his fingers was a puzzle. He'd already taken one, entirely successfully, for the fry-up he was preparing for himself and Alistair. But the second one ... it had jumped, that was the only word for it. Like the sausage, in the café, when he was a small child. It was one of his earliest memories. He had knocked a sausage from his plate and his grandmother, his dear, forgiving grandmother, told him it had jumped. How he laughed! He laughed so much it hurt, but he couldn't stop, and soon the whole place was laughing with him. It was one of the most joyous moments of his life. Even now he could recall the wonder, the delight, that people were laughing on account of something he'd done. Not in any spiteful, vindictive way, but innocently, genuinely, wholesomely. It must be very rewarding, he thought, to be a comedian and make people laugh. Not at you, as in the case of politicians, but with you. Though, judging by the amusement cartoonists and others drew from his profession, perhaps politics was the next best thing.

"Oh ..." Alistair halted in the doorway, unaccustomed to seeing his father engaged in anything as domestic as cleaning. Ryder lifted himself to a kneeling position and, surveying a streaky but otherwise eggless floor, explained what had happened.

"You can keep your breakfast," Alistair said. "I'm off that shit. It's not good for you."

"You used to like my cooked breakfasts," Ryder pouted, stretching out a hand to support himself on the work surface to assume a standing position. He ached, and his body was filled with a dullness that made movement a chore. And his breathing was tight: all that unaccustomed exertion. Ellie was right: he was out of condition. If he couldn't even clean a floor without feeling the effects then he really ought to try and get into shape. Especially with this leadership election in the offing.

"Juice. That's all I have in the mornings," Alistair said, pushing past his father to wrench the fridge door open, and casting a disdainful glance at the frying pan. "I mean ... look. It's gross. Burned pig meat."

It was true. Ryder had forgotten about the bacon while dealing with the egg. Now it was dark brown, crisp, and starting to smoulder.

"I like it like that," Ryder lied. "It'll be fine with an egg. And there's mushrooms in the fridge. I'll throw in some more butter ..."

"So what do you want to talk about? Why've you got me out of bed at the crack of dawn?"

"Hardly. It's ..."

Alistair, clutching his juice, seated himself at the table. "It's not my usual hour. I'm a student, remember? Or have you forgotten? I mean ... do you know who I am?"

"For god's sake ..."

Whatever small appetite Ryder still possessed after dealing with the egg evaporated. He turned the gas off below the burned bacon and, standing in front of the cooker, faced his son.

"I want you to be the first to know ... that is, after your mother, people in Westminster. I want you to know before you find out second-hand on the tele, the radio. The point is ... they want me to run for party leader ..."

"What ...?" Alistair choked on a mouthful of juice.

"Which might mean ... if I'm successful ... that you're talking to the next prime minister of Great Britain."

"No shit."

"That's it. That's what I wanted to say. To let you know before ..."

"That's wank."

"Please ... I don't think language like that ..."

"It sucks. I mean ... you can't. It's stupid. And what about me? If you're ... like ... prime minister ... there'll be people following me round the whole time. Like I'm a terrorist risk. In case some fundamentalist loonies try

187

and kidnap me. I mean ... no way."

"I don't see why it should affect you."

"Of course it'll affect me. Where've you been for the past ten years? I mean ... you blind, or something? All the time at school ... everything I say, do. Tory boy ... that's what they call me. Any time I open my trap it's ... don't listen to him. He's just saying what his old man would say. I'm just ... just a clone. And I tell you something else. I'm not living in London ... Downing Street. No way."

"You wouldn't have to. You finish you schooling here ..."

"You should have packed me off to boarding school. With the other posh Tory MPs' kids. Then I'd have been out of the way ..."

"We wanted you to have a normal education ..."

"Yeah ... great. You've a warped idea of normal. I mean ... you can't be normal. Not when you're dad's the MP. No way. And now ... why can't you think of us, for once in your life?"

"What do you mean?"

"Instead of putting yourself first ... like ... you the MP, the minister, the prime minister ..."

"It might not come to that. In fact, it's highly unlikely."

"Yeah ... that's what you say. But it's all about you. You never think about us ... mum, me ..."

"That's not true. I'm thinking about you now. It's why I'm here."

"That's crap. You're here because ... because you want to make it look as if you care. But you don't. You only care about yourself. Typical politician. All show."

"That's not fair."

"It fucking is. So I tell you. Fuck you and your stupid plans. Fuck you."

***

The laptop was open, the page blank, as Ryder watched the backs of the homes adjoining the railway, some with twinkling Christmas lights in their festive windows, give way to barren factories, abandoned for the holidays, and then to equally desolate fields. Liverpool was several miles behind him, the train leaning to the curve on the Weaver Junction flyover, but still the words would not come. It was the speech he knew he would need to make to his parliamentary peers in the leadership election but the approach, the angle he knew he must find, remained elusive. And his thoughts kept returning to Alistair.

Quite possibly the boy was right. Growing up, an only child, in a house with two career parents, often away from home, couldn't have been easy. Leaving him in the care of a live-in nanny was perhaps a mistake, especially as he grew older. As Alistair said, boarding school might well have made better sense. That way he wouldn't have stood out. At least, not in the same way. Perhaps, in fact, Margo and he should never have had a child. If they'd been honest they might have realised they weren't cut out to make the sacrifices that parenting ... good parenting ... demanded. They'd put themselves first, not Alistair. And now, if elected party leader, and became prime minister, he'd be parent to an entire nation. Was he up to it? If he couldn't be a decent father to his son, how could he be a decent father to the nation? Perhaps this whole leadership business was a mistake. A gross error of judgment. He should never have consented, never have allowed himself to be bounced into accepting the nomination. He should have stuck to his original plan to quit parliament, quit politics ... try and become the father to Alistair he'd failed to be over the past few years. Not that Alistair

189

would need him. He'd be leaving home, off to university, if he applied himself. Not that he seemed bothered about uni. But perhaps if he thought his parents were there for him, hadn't abandoned him, he might show more interest.

Ryder sighed, and looked out of the train window. A horse stood in a field, swaddled in blankets to keep out the cold. It was okay for horses. They didn't have to think about issues such as this. But he could sort it. There and then. The laptop. A quick email to Blenhesket, tell him he'd had second thoughts ...

"Ah ... Mr Ryder ..."

Startled, he looked up to see Eileen, the carriage attendant, standing by his seat.

"Mr Ryder ... they said ... further down the train ... you were on board."

"I ... yes," Ryder cleared his throat. "Back to London. No rest for the wicked."

"Yes. I suppose ... so much to do."

"Quite."

"Especially now. And I just wanted to say ... on behalf of us all, on the train ... good luck. We're right behind you."

"I'm sorry ...?"

Eileen seemed taken aback. "This ... whatever it is ... leadership thing. And then prime minister. I mean ..."

"What?"

She hesitated. "That's right, isn't it? It was being tweeted. Someone said at the station it was trending ..."

"Oh, Jesus. It's not supposed ... look. It's speculation. You know how people get the wrong end of the stick. I mean ... yes, okay. There's been talk. But I don't think ..."

Eileen's face fell. She began gnawing at her lips, as if engaged in debate, wanting to speak, but unable. She ran her hands down her uniform, looked up and down the aisle of the lightly loaded coach, and sat down opposite Ryder.

"I hope you don't mind," she mumbled. "We're not really supposed to. But ..."

It was too late to object. She was there, peering at him nervously over the laptop. Damn it. He needed time to think. This was supposed to be under wraps. And ...

The woman was talking. "Now I'm all confused. But ... if you are going to be prime minister ... then we're with you. Everybody said ... he's the man for the job. If anyone can sort this country out, this is the person to do do it. That is ..."

"Come on," Ryder forced a smile. "You hardly know me. You see me at the end of a week in Westminster ... knackered, burned out ..."

"Yes. And it's the real you we see. I know, tired ... but soldiering on. The rest of them ... " and Eileen lowered her voice ... "all we ever see is what they want us to see. And they treat us like dirt. But you're different. You're ... sort of ... real. And we need a real person to run this country. Know what I mean?"

Beneath the table their knees briefly touched. Ryder winced, and shrank back in his seat.

"Mr Ryder ... it's all going pear-shaped. The country. It's these bankers and the rest of them. The energy companies. What they're doing ... they're taking our country away from us. We want someone ... you ... to give it us back."

"That's a tall order. A very tall order. I'm not sure ..."

"Please, Mr Ryder. Don't let us down."

Eileen fixed Ryder with a gaze that was long and hard. He blanched, feeling trapped, unable to move. He suddenly felt tired ... his default position these days ... and he shut his eyes.

The cat was out of the bag. The press, someone, had

got hold of his candidacy. It had been leaked ... Blenhesket, possibly, deeming the time was ripe to show their hand, rattle their foes, build support in the country at large. Already, if Eileen's imprecations were anything to go by, it was having an effect.

Christ. If he backed out now, sent that email to Blenhesket, he'd play straight into the hands of the Millers of this world, the toffs, the crème of the self-styled crème, and the bastards would have it all their own way. Again. He owed it to himself ... no, to the Eileens out there, the millions of decent, hard-working people shafted at every twist and turn by the establishment, by the government. He could change that. And he wasn't alone. Tory Trust ... that man Deutscher ... people were beginning to talk, to realise things could ... should ... be different. And he could make that difference. He would ...

"Tea, milk, no sugar," Eileen said, abruptly rising from the seat, as if realising she'd outstayed her welcome, perhaps said too much. Again she ran her hands over the skirt of her uniform, smoothing it out, and before Ryder could protest, to say all he wanted was water, she was away, off down the aisle, to bring not just tea but also as likely as not, biscuits and other unwanted snacks.

Ryder leaned back, inhaling as deeply as he could, though his breathing was raspy ... he still hadn't shaken off that throat infection, despite the lozenges and cough sweets, and perhaps now he was sickening for a cold ... and closing his eyes, attempting to make sense of the moment. The blackness that welcomed him, shutting out the carriage, the train, at once gave way to eyes, the woman's eyes that had bored into his, imploring, pleading, behind them thousands, tens of thousands more, and accompanied by a chorus of voices: Please, Mr Ryder. Don't let us down. Don't let us down. Don't let us ...

The train rattled over points, the carriage swayed, and Ryder was jolted back to the present. Tea and, indeed, crisps and biscuits were before him, but of these he had no need. He felt remarkably refreshed, revitalised. Perhaps for the first time in his life he felt he knew where he was going, what he needed to do. And it felt good.

London. January 2015.

The new year, for Ryder, passed quietly, studiously: the reading he had told Margo he needed to do to prepare for the general election now assumed a particular urgency. He had no time to be tired: much of the lethargy, the inertia, that characterised his sojourn in La Jolla, dissipated in a frenzy of activity. He gave interviews to the broadsheets, provided a belated Christmas present to TV news editors happy to fill their bulletins with something other than seasonal sales and snow warnings, and waited patiently at the end of a phone for calls from regional and local radio stations that squeezed him between inane banter and second-rate pop songs.

The interviews, he realised, even those at the serious end of the media spectrum, treated him in the main as something as a joke. The real contest, the pundits had decided, was between Jeremy Miller and the chancellor, Henry Sandringham. The clear favourite was Miller who, it was said, would make a decent, if unadventurous, prime minister, rather in the Pemberton mould, someone who would take the country into a general election on a "steady-as-she-goes" ticket and with a hint of better times to come. There was some support for Sandringham, mainly from the right-wing press, who saw in him a champion of the square mile and of the bankers and brokers who, they steadfastly believed, were the sole generators of the nation's wealth. However, beyond the city of London and its apologists in the press, enthusiasm for Sandringham was muted. He was burdened by broken promises of prosperity that never came, all too apparent in the empty high street shops once occupied by household names, in the boarded-up libraries, in the sporadic riots unchecked by over-stretched police required to slash numbers ... all in the name of austerity that delivered successive quarters of zero or, at best, fragile growth, while partner countries, or competitors, depending on the point of view, were registering solid and consistent, if not yet spectacular, growth.

Ryder, on the other hand, was an unknown quantity. Interviewers were more interested in probing his background, rather than his beliefs, his personality rather than his policies. Both Miller and Sandringham were well-documented: private money, public schools, Oxbridge; Miller, the family publishing house and then parliament; Sandringham, merchant banking, a flirtation with academia and, likewise, parliament. The public knew them, indeed, all too well: they were perceived, not entirely accurately, as upper-class huntin' shootin' fishin' types who could tell you in a trice the price of a bottle of Bollinger but not of a pint of milk. Because of this familiarity, and also of the need for novelty, the column writers and interviewers had little choice but to question them on policy, to try and establish how a Miller government might differ from a Sandringham government, and which of the two might ultimately be more beneficial to the country. In fact, Ryder thought, reading the various interviews, there was little to choose between them. Both represented the past, a past discredited, no longer fit for purpose, which was where Ryder believed them to be vulnerable.

Not that any of this passed his lips during his own interviews. Besides, the media were far more interested in getting to know him as a curiosity, as a minor celebrity granted his five minutes of fame, rather than understanding him as a politician, a future prime minister. Ryder wasn't going to win this ballot: it was between the heavyweights, those with cabinet experience and, reading between the lines, those with a divine right, certainly a privileged, natural right, to rule.

Ryder was an interloper, the joker in the pack, the provider of light relief: less a stalking horse, as one commentator put it, but a pantomime horse. Therefore the journalists were going for human interest, concentrating on his marriage to an American beauty ... one of the tabloids produced a picture of Margo shopping in La Jolla ... or else showing shots of his home in Northaven, as well as desolate scenes of his seaside constituency battened down and boarded up for winter. They also wanted to talk about rumours of riotous living in Edinburgh.

All this, as Blenhesket, relishing the campaign, told him, was to the good. Ryder could keep his powder dry, reserve the serious business for later, then take his rivals by surprise, in effect ambushing them. In the meantime, if the public were warming to him as something of an underdog, valiantly engaged in a contest he had no hope of winning, but inspired by a sense of duty to offer choice, then so be it. The British, Blenhesket said, rubbing his hands with delight, liked an underdog. Popular approval would then feed back via constituency chairmen to MPs: a word here, a suggestion there, that if this Ryder chap were going down well in the country he might be worth a punt in the leadership ballot. After all, with a general election coming up, a new incumbent enjoying good ratings ... honeymoon period barely over ... would work well for the party as a whole. It might even preserve some of those marginals tipped to go the other way ... save the party's bacon, as it were. Oh, yes, Blenhesket said, a twinkle in his eye, things couldn't be better. You wait and see. The bigwigs won't know what hit them.

The hustings had been arranged for the Monday after new year. On the previous Friday morning, as Ryder was working on his speech, he had received a call from a private clinic in west London. He was told that as a result of the blood tests Mr Meakin would like to see him at his earliest convenience.

"What's this about?" Ryder asked, his head elsewhere, creaking with training and employment figures. "Who's this Meakin fellow?"

A female voice explained that Mr Meakin was the consultant neurologist to whom he had been referred. Mr Meakin would make time to see him on Monday morning ...

"Out of the question," Ryder snapped. "Don't you people read the papers? I mean ..."

The voice, slightly flustered, apologised and said if it were inconvenient then perhaps Mr Ryder would like to suggest another time.

"I can't. Not at the moment. I'm up to my ..."

"Mr Meakin has asked me to impress on you the importance of a visit."

"Why?" Ryder queried, relinquishing the statistics swirling in his head, and homing in on the urgency in the woman's voice. "Have those tests come up with something?"

"That's not for me to say. But I understand Mr Meakin would like to undertake a further, exploratory examination."

"Christ."

"I'm looking at Mr Meakin's diary. Should we say ... if that would be better ... the following day ... the Tuesday?"

"Crying out loud. I ... I ... fine, yes. Tuesday. Whatever."

"Excellent. Perhaps ... 10.30?"

"10.30 it is. But wait ... where are you? I don't think I know ... I mean, perhaps somewhere ..."

The voice gave Ryder an address which he scribbled down. He thanked the woman, rather brusquely, he thought afterwards, and rang off. He found himself shaking, trembling. It was as if the gremlin, this creature that had invaded his body, were trying to tell him something. But, apart from the odd difficulty with the hands, with his grip, the gremlin hadn't been any trouble over the past week or so. It was just that throat infection he couldn't throw off, and the tiredness, and he couldn't lay those at the gremlin's door. All the same there was an urgency about this appointment that unsettled him. But doctors, hospitals, clinics: they always had this effect. Though not Ellie. With her ... but that was in the past. Now she had this surgeon fellow. Damn the man. Damn the whole medical profession. He needed a drink. What time was it? Too early. Sun not yet over the yardarm, and all that crap. Though in northern climes, at the start of January, it was doubtful if the sun ever rose above the yardarm. Anyway, what was a yardarm? Did ships still have them? Oh, what the hell. A whisky would help make sense of those figures on youth and employment. At least it wouldn't make any less sense. On the other hand ...

An idea was forming as Ryder steered himself, slightly unsteadily, round the clutter in his flat to the drinks cabinet where he poured himself a whisky. Downing it in one, he realised that for the hustings he had no need of numbers and percentages, figures and statistics. They were all bogus, anyway ... compiled by PR people paid lavishly to lie. No ... he would adopt a different approach, make them sit up, take note. He would ...

With trembling hand Ryder poured himself another whisky and made his way back with it to the sofa. Sweeping aside the notes he had begun, he seized a fresh pad and, ignoring the numbness in his fingers as they closed round his pen, began writing fast and feverishly.

***

On the morning of the hustings the telephone roused Ryder from troubled sleep. Words, phrases, pitchforked at him by fiery, fiendish blenheskets, warning of everlasting putrefaction in the Lords should he not include such wisdom in his speech, racked him until, towards dawn, as exhaustion set in, the demons took flight and granted him brief repose. Ryder was relieved to find the call was not from Blenhesket, with yet more amendments to the text he insisted his protégé deliver, but from Margo, phoning from California, to say because her mother was much recovered she'd arranged a flight which would return her to Heathrow on Tuesday morning.

"Recovered ...?" Ryder mumbled, blinking into the grey light in the room.

"The virus. Worn out, I guess, after the party. All that arranging."

"Ah ... of course."

A vague recollection this was the reason Margo had stayed longer in La Jolla than planned stirred in Ryder's brain. He shuffled himself to a sitting position in the bed.

"Anyway, I don't think I could stand another weekend," Margo told him. "I guess after a while, much as I love them, the folks get a bit much. It's Pop ... always wanting to drag me out somewhere when I'd rather just stay home. We're just back from the Petersons ..."

"The whosits?" Ryder asked, still bleary.

"The Petersons. You remember ... I went through high school with Randy. He made a fortune in oil ..."

The smoothie. And loaded, Ryder remembered, with a stab of envy, as an image of Margo at the Murchisons' party, talking to the creature, flashed across his mind.

"Bored out of my brains," Margo continued. "At school, I guess, he used to be fun. But now ... it's all barrels and markets and trends. I'll be glad to be back. I can't stand another evening like that. So ... I don't know if you want to show up at the airport. It's a 7.30 arrival."

"On Tuesday. Hell. I don't know. I mean ... I've an appointment with a quack a bit later on ..."

"What appointment?"

"These blood tests ... you know. They want to see me."

"Why? What's happened?"

"I don't know. They just said something about further tests ... an examination. It's probably ... I don't think these blood tests are too reliable these days. A bit of a check-up, maybe. At any rate it won't do any harm."

"I said you should have got yourself looked at when you were over here."

"Yeah, well ..."

"You got a cold, or something? You sound ... sort of ... husky."

"No, no ... fine. Just ... I'm not up yet. Need something to wet my whistle."

"Sorry, honey. Hope I didn't wake you."

"You did ... but no matter. I need to be up and doing."

"I know. And that's also why I'm ringing. To wish you luck. It is today, isn't it? It's so difficult to keep up."

"Kicks off in a couple of hours. Of course, I've as much chance of making it as ... as frog spawn, but it'll be fun. And it'll give me a chance to get a few things off my chest."

"Be careful. Don't go putting people's backs up."

"Why not? It's about time they heard a few home

truths."

"I'm not sure. But whatever ... we're proud of you. The folks here are all rooting for you. I mean ... a British prime minister in the family. So ... yeah ..."

"Thanks, hun."

"And don't worry about the airport on Tuesday. If you can't make it, fine. I'll get a cab."

"Can't wait to have you back. Love you."

"Love you. And ... good luck."

***

They were in Blenhesket's sepulchral, sequestered office ... was he in perpetual mourning for ambition blighted, life unfulfilled, Ryder wondered ... for a final, pre-hustings briefing. The older man seemed tense, edgy, which paradoxically rendered the candidate calmer. It was as if any nervousness Ryder might have felt were automatically vested in Blenhesket. They were a good team, Ryder thought. It was a pity this effort would be wasted.

Blenhesket, having approved, with amendments, the final draft of the speech Ryder would give, went over the mechanics of the morning. It had been decided the candidates would address their fellow MPs in reverse alphabetical order, thus Sandringham, Ryder and Miller. Blenhesket had pressed for lots to be drawn, on the grounds of impartiality, but the returning officer ... a millerite or, as Sir Wesley disparagingly preferred, a millerlite ... had decreed otherwise. This, he told Ryder, was patently unfair, since he would be squeezed in the middle while Miller, the favourite, would have the last word. Blenhesket went over, for the umpteenth time, the length of time the candidates should speak, then reminded him about the ensuing question and answer session. Voting, by STV, would take place after lunch and a result declared as soon as possible, certainly no later than tea time.

"Wonderful, isn't it," Ryder said, "that we elect a leader by single transferable vote, while any mention of anything so revolutionary for a general election would give them all apoplexy."

"That's the way it is ... how they like it," Blenhesket shrugged. "One rule for us, another for the country."

"Precisely," Ryder said. "And that's got to change."

"Yes, but STV will work in your favour. I'm relying on the second preference votes. I can't see many millerlites giving their second choice to Sandringham, or vice versa. There's no love lost between the two factions. You've got to pick up enough second choices to come sailing down the middle."

"I know. But if they stick to form ... I mean, half of them haven't a clue how STV works ... and just vote for their own man, then I'm scuppered."

"That's why you've got to go in there and charm the pants off them. We know you won't get enough first choices ... at least, you're very unlikely to beat Miller ... but if he doesn't hit the quota on the first round then we've got him on the second. That is, of course, if the second choices come up trumps. At any rate that's the theory."

Ryder nodded, and asked if Blenhesket had any water.

"I've got something stronger if you want it," Blenhesket replied, "but I'm not sure that would be wise."

"I don't want anything stronger. It's just my throat ... a bit dry. I don't want to croak at them."

Blenhesket leaned down, pulled open a drawer in his desk, and produced a bottle of water.

"Here," he said. "But not too much. You don't want to be excusing yourself to dash off to the gents when you're supposed to be taking questions. Anyway I expect if you need it they'll have water on the table."

Managing a faint smile at Blenhesket's pleasantry, Ryder took the bottle and attempted to open it. The top was stiff, refusing to turn, and his fingers slipped uselessly over the plastic.

"What's the matter?" Blenhesket asked, peering through the gloom at the struggling Ryder.

"I think ... it's ... can't get a grip. My fingers ... a bit sweaty. Nerves, probably."

"Give it here," Blenhesket said, taking the bottle and twisting the top open immediately, before handing it back. "You need to watch that, you know. You got a handkerchief ... tissues ... just in case? But, for god's sake, any sign of nerves and you're done for. They'll eat you alive. Remember Blair and those pictures of that sweat-soaked shirt?"

Ryder took a swig of water which was warm, lacking sparkle. Nevertheless it slipped down readily, easing the constriction in his throat.

"There's something bothering me," Blenhesket said, as Ryder made a determined effort to replace the cap on the bottle. "I hear ... that is, the millerlites are putting it about ... you're having some sort of medical treatment."

"Medical treatment ...? Not at all."

"There's talk of seeing a consultant ... a neurologist, or something."

"For god's sake ... I mean ... as it happens, yes, I've an appointment ... tomorrow, as a matter of fact ... purely routine ... with a consultant in ... in ... the west end somewhere. Simply to follow up on some blood tests. That's all."

"You're sure ..."

"Of course I'm sure. Bloody hell ... half the parliamentary party's trotting off to some consultant or other. So what? It's just a few twinges ... nothing that a bit of massage, physiotherapy, whatever, won't sort out. For pity's sake ..."

"As long as that's all ..."

"Of course it is. But ... where's this come from? I mean ... how does anyone know I'm seeing a consultant? I've never mentioned it ... told anyone. Why should I ...?"

"Facebook ...?"

"Don't be stupid ... sorry, I mean ... I don't use Facebook. And it's certainly not on the constituency blog ... anywhere like that. The only thing I can think of ..."

He paused. The Scottish tones of Duncan Buchlyvie rang in his ears: Bound to be tapped, my wee laddie. Security and surveillance ... the only growth industry you people south of the border have.

"Christ. It's the phone. It's been hacked. The bastards have been listening in. God knows what else they've heard ..."

Blenhesket sighed. "It's the way of the world, I'm afraid. The times we live in. But cheer up. Two can play that game."

He passed a sheet of paper across the table.

"You might like to cast your eye over this before you address the troops. It's the gist of Miller's speech. Entirely predictable, simply more of the same ... cuts, cuts and more cuts. But it's good to know ... don't you think?"

**

The room was a blur of faces as Ryder, clutching his speech, made as dignified an entrance as last-minute nerves would permit. His heart was pounding, his breathing was erratic, and at that moment he wished he were as far from Westminster as possible. Someone began a slow hand-clap, others briefly joined in, only to be silenced by a stern female voice reminding them this was not the Labour Party and it wasn't how things were done. Ryder thought he recognised the cultured tones of Ayesha Farani, which was surprising, since he would not have put her down as a natural supporter. On the other hand, if she were, that was a good sign. Probably, though, he was mistaken.

The returning officer, a florid old-school Tory by the name of Timmins, who represented one of the smaller cathedral towns, motioned to Ryder to sit as he laboriously went through procedure, largely familiar from Blenhesket's briefing: a speech, with a three minute warning, questions, ditto, nothing *ad hominem*, purely policy. Ryder took the opportunity to pour himself some water, clutching the jug as firmly as he could and holding it well above the glass to avoid any contact and a give-away clink. He hoped his audience would be concentrating on Timmins and not notice his trembling hand as he slopped water into the glass. He had replaced the jug, taken a sip, when Timmins, reminding him of the gravity of the occasion, invited him now to address the assembled parliamentary party.

Ryder turned to thank him and, attempting to stand, realised he was quivering in every limb. Nerves. It was the school play all over again. Waiting in the wings, listening for the cue, wondering why on earth he'd allowed himself to be cajoled, bullied, into stepping onto a stage. It was ridiculous. He was used to public speaking: addressing party meetings, even the chamber of the House of Commons, he took in his stride. But this was different. He was acting a part, taking a role, just like the school play, and the old emotions came flooding back. But now he was on his feet and, although his stomach was churning, and he felt hot and clammy, and the room was swaying, he heard himself speak.

"Ladies and gentlemen," he began, in a squeak more befitting a kindergarten child than a future prime minister.

Someone cackled and, during the amusement that rippled round the room, Ryder cleared his throat, swallowed hard, and started again.

"Ladies and gentleman," and this time, rather to his astonishment, his voice rang clear and commanding. "Battered, betrayed. This is the state of Britain today. And we are the ones who have battered and betrayed her ... and have lost the trust of the people."

A gasp greeted Ryder's words, surprise, shock, and cries of "rubbish" and "nonsense" rose simultaneously from several throats. Timmins half-lifted himself from his seat, to quell the unrest, but Ryder had already raised an imperious hand and was speaking again, over the hubbub, in a voice even firmer than before.

"Unless this party ... that is, those of us in this room ... engage with the people ... listen to them ... act upon the good sense that abounds in every home, every workplace, in the land, then we shall lose the forthcoming election. Lose it hands down. And deservedly so."

Ryder paused to survey his audience. Self-interest ... fear of losing a seat, the salary and perks attached to it, to say nothing of the ghastliness of joining the unemployed, the so-called shirkers and skivers much mocked by the Department for Work and Pensions and its henchmen at the Daily Mail ... was a strong card to play. Suddenly he had their attention. They had fallen quiet ... and Ryder, more confident, beginning to enjoy himself, allowed himself an inward smile.

"We cannot," he continued, deliberately lowering his voice, and assuming a more intimate, more earnest tone, "we cannot continue battering, betraying this country in the way we are doing ... in the way, too, governments before ours have done. And what do I mean by battered and betrayed? Well ... look around you."

As if inviting them so to do, Ryder swept his gaze round the room. He caught a glimpse of Blenhesket, pale, panicked, turning to mutter at Merryman next to him. This was not the plan, not the proposition, parcelled and packaged by Blenhesket, to be delivered to the electoral college. Too true it wasn't, Ryder thought savagely. This was the speech he wanted to give, the speech of a lifetime, his own words, his own ideas. A triumph of heart over head, sincerity over expediency. He drew a deep breath, and carried on.

"The welfare state, the bedrock of this country for over sixty years, has been systematically dismantled, vandalised, one might say. Many of us in this room, and many more outside it, have cause to be grateful for the foresight of Beveridge and others who created in this country something that became the envy of the world. Indeed, many nations, the USA included, still struggle to achieve in health care what you and I for too long have taken for granted. But, sadly, not any more. Equality of provision, equality of opportunity, have given way to inequality of choice, inequality of profit. Governments, and our own is no exception, have vied to outdo each other in battering at this bedrock, breaking it up, selling off the pieces, sometimes not even to the highest bidder, often to overseas investors, even, if you please, to companies unashamedly owned and operated by agencies of our partner nations. It is little wonder, ladies and gentlemen, the British public feels betrayed. It is, as someone told me only a few days ago, time to give this country back to its people."

Ryder halted. His throat required relief. He reached for the water and, lifting the glass to his lips, was

207

encouraged to find his hand steady. The room before him was taut and tense: a spring waiting to uncoil. But not yet. The key had to be turned still more, twisted ever tighter. From the corner of his eye Ryder noted with satisfaction Blenhesket sitting upright, staring at him. Of his previous, panicked look there was no sign: in its place curiosity, enquiry.

Refreshed, Ryder returned to his narrative. "The consequences of this betrayal are enormous. The all-important social contract between government and governed, between the state and its citizens, is weakened. The trust that needs to exist in any successfully functioning democracy between the institutions of the state and the people, in whose name such institutions are established and whom they should serve, has been eroded. It is little wonder that we, the politicians, are held in low esteem, that elections, both at national and particularly at local level, are increasingly regarded as irrelevant, a distraction for the chattering classes. It is a tragedy that more people vote in television reality shows ... a contradiction in terms if ever there was one ... than in elections which could determine the direction of the nation. Of course, a conspiracy theorist might argue this is a deliberate and cynical ploy: alienate the voters, disengage them, so a political elite, largely unencumbered by the checks and controls of the ballot box, can buffer up to the bankers, cosy up to corporations poised to profit from outsourcing ... what we used to call by its now discredited name of privatisation ... in sectors such as health, education, transport, law and order, to name but some. I, however ..."

"Rubbish," someone shouted, as other voices were raised, some approving, some disapproving. Timmins lumbered to his feet to protest at unbecoming, non-parliamentary language but Ryder, relishing the opportunity to assert his authority, with a sweep of his hand brushed the babble aside and, adopting an air of Churchillian gravitas, growled: "I, however, do not subscribe to idle conspiracy theories. The position in which we find ourselves is a result not of conspiracy but of cock-up. And ..."

A rumble of dissent reverberated round the room. Thunder rolling from far-off fells ... and suddenly Ryder wondered why he was not out there, in the mountains, breathing fresh, clean air, away from all this, the posturing, the histrionics. But no. He knew what he was doing when he let his name go forward: an opportunity to get things off his chest, a last hurrah before quitting parliament for a more honest, more wholesome existence. And now it was time to appeal once again to self-interest. Time, too, to reach out to those who, Ryder marvelled, despite the increasingly fractious mood of the meeting, were nodding in quiet and thoughtful agreement. Again he raised his hand for silence.

"Let me spell it out. If we persist on our present path, giving to our city friends, while taking from those we brand as scroungers, we render ourselves unelectable. Instead of working against the vast majority of people in this country, we should work with them ... listen to them, respect them. And what do these good people tell us? They tell us, in opinion poll after opinion poll, that the two things which give them most pride in this country are the national health service and the military. That's right, not the royal family or the BBC, not green fields or the white cliffs of Dover, but hospitals and soldiers. Tamper with these ... and you tamper at your peril. The public, ladies and gentlemen, does not want choice in the health service. It does not want to be directed to a hospital in a neighbouring town where the treatment may or may not be better, more cost-effective, or otherwise. It does not want dubious consortia to be making money out of a service which should be run on a not-for-profit basis. If money is to be made from the health service, and not at the cost of staff cuts or closed wards, then the public tells us these profits should be put back into the service, not into the pockets of so-called investors or their shareholders. What people want is an efficient, freely available, easily accessible, readily understandable health service operating on its own doorstep. And, if we are to win the forthcoming election, we need to take this on board, listening to the public, admitting we made mistakes, and setting about righting these wrongs."

"Hear hear," someone ventured, to be shushed by those around. Ryder allowed himself a moment's satisfaction. His audience, for the most part, was attentive and engaged and, while there were some whose minds he knew he would never capture, there were others more obviously open to persuasion. It was these to whom he must reach out. He swallowed, and carried on.

"I mentioned a minute ago the military. The public is justifiably proud of the achievements of our forces fighting in some of the most hostile and challenging parts of the world. What people are less happy about is the loss of British life sustained in places where, frankly, this country has little reason to be. Therefore ..."

A gasp, part astonishment, part rage, released itself into the room. "Shame," someone bellowed. "Support our heroes ..." another. An elderly backbencher, usually more visible than vocal, stood and pushed his way to the exit, declaring he wouldn't listen a moment longer to any more left-wing Guardian drivel. Someone told him to be quiet, to stay, because Ryder was talking sense, the future of the party ...

"Future?" the man barked, apoplectic. "There's no future if you support this Judas."

Timmins was on his feet, perspiration on his brow, and blinking anxiously into the room, as if fearing insurrection. "Hear him out. Please hear him out," he pleaded, as Ryder seized the moment to gulp some water. Over the rim of the glass he stole a glance at Blenhesket. His mentor was leaning forward in his seat, brow knotted in concentration. It was difficult to know what he was thinking. Merryman, next to him, was bobbing up and down, looking round, attempting to catch the eye, Ryder thought, of potential supporters.

"Please ..." Timmins called. "Mr Ryder has just a few minutes remaining ..."

"Good ..." someone said, to ribaldry, drowning the calls that Ryder be allowed to proceed.

"Please ... remember who we are," Timmins persevered. "Please afford the candidate the courtesy of listening to what he has to say. It's the least we can do."

"Even that's too much," another voice piped up.

"Enough," Timmins snapped, his patience at an end. "We've a serious task to perform and we're not helping ourselves. Mr Ryder ... I apologise for the interruption. Please continue."

An expectant, sultry silence descended on the room. Ryder suddenly felt limp, languorous, as if the three minute warning, if that was what it was, had opened a tap, drained him of his energy and élan. He grasped the table for support, feeling he might keel over, and the contact with the cool, smooth, polished wood, firm and solid, restored his sense of purpose. He gave a discreet cough, and began speaking: his voice was strained, less resonant than before, lacking conviction, but he hoped in the aftermath of the upset and excitement no one would notice.

"Thank you, Mr Chairman. Perhaps I should be the

one to apologise, since mine were the words that offended. All the same, I stand by them. Let me reiterate. To regain public trust, to make ourselves electable, we must be open to the views of the people. If they tell us they do not want British lives squandered in costly military escapades we cannot win, and involving no direct threat to this nation, then we should not allow ourselves to become so embroiled. Eighteen months ago parliament made a brave, indeed noble, decision not to invade Syria. That was as it should be. But, if truth were told, if we were honest with ourselves and with the public, we would admit there is no money for such adventures. Austerity is but a front to conceal the unpalatable realisation that this country can no longer pay its way ..."

Jeering, scornful laughter greeted this assertion, and Ryder strained to raise his voice over the din.

"The sooner we acknowledge this, the better. Honesty, ladies and gentlemen, is the key to our re-election. Honesty and trust ... and these I would place at the heart of any government it were my honour and privilege to lead. Thank you."

He nodded briefly towards the audience before before dropping back onto his chair. His voice had become raucous, like a chorus of frogs, and his throat felt stiff and sore. The room in front of him erupted into a cacophony of isolated but enthusiastic applause, heckling, catcalls and animated chatter. He registered the words "twat" and "arsehole" but Ryder, draining the last of the water in his glass and pouring himself a fresh measure, didn't care. He'd given food for thought, made the party think about where it stood, its relationship with the electorate, and established a case for honesty and openness in the context of a new social contract. At least, he hoped he had. He gazed at his unused notes. There were probably things on those pages he'd meant to say, but hadn't, things which might have been better phrased, more nuanced, but that was in the past. By leaving the notes on the table, by not clutching them in a tremulous hand, his audience had been spared any manifestation of insecurity, of nerves. Surely it was better like that.

Timmins was calling the meeting to order before the Q&A session when Ryder realised Blenhesket was on his feet, waving his arm for attention.

"Yes, Sir Wesley," Timmins enquired.

"I think it might be sensible to take a short break. Some of us are ... shall we say ... a little emotional and could perhaps do with a change of scenery. Perhaps even a breath of fresh air."

There was general approval for Blenhesket's suggestion. Timmins said it was highly irregular and contrary to agreed procedure for conducting the hustings. He said he would need to consult the candidates to see if they agreed. Ryder, grateful for the opportunity to gather his flagging strength, accepted at once. Timmins, muttering, left the room to find Miller. A couple of minutes later he returned. Miller had no objection, while Sandringham was nowhere to be seen. Timmins frowned.

"I'm bending the rules," he said. "But okay. You've got fifteen minutes."

***

The remainder of the session, when it resumed, passed in a haze. Ryder, seated, heard himself as if from a distance explain that his lack of experience was no obstacle, since most of the present cabinet had never served in government following thirteen years in opposition; that austerity should be tempered by investment in infrastructure, jobs, to get the country moving; that it had been a mistake to sell off the post office and to let the east coast mainline, returning over two hundred million pounds a year to the taxpayer, fall back into private hands; that even partial withdrawal from the EU would threaten trade, employment, weaken Britain's influence in the world, and accordingly, if he decided not to cancel the in-out referendum on the EU, he would campaign vigorously to remain in; that ... and then he heard Timmins telling him time was up and thanking him for sharing his views with the meeting. Applause, polite rather than sincere, stippled the room.

Ryder smiled wanly and, gathering his unused notes and his remaining energy, left the room with as much aplomb as he could summon. Moving towards the door, he looked across at Blenhesket, who was observing his progress. The knight's eyes were hooded, cowled, like a bird of prey, giving nothing away, but Ryder thought he saw a faint smile glimmer on his lips. Excellent. He hadn't disgraced himself in that quarter. At any rate, not entirely.

Leaving the hustings, Ryder encountered Miller waiting his turn on the corridor outside.

"Dead meat, Ryder," the foreign secretary drawled. "If you think when I'm PM you'll be anywhere other than on the back benches you've another think coming."

Bastard, Ryder thought. It isn't over yet.

***

In fact, as Ryder well knew, it probably was. Over, that is. Miller, while not especially popular, was nevertheless the man to beat, the face of current conservatism, the candidate to ensure the party performed no u-turns and expose itself to opposition taunts of vacillation. That's what his colleagues would go for, Ryder reasoned, settling into one of the armchairs in the D room of the commons library. Better to save face now and to worry about losing the election later: typical political short-termism. Where was the survival instinct in his fellow MPs, the will to win the next election? Had they given up already? Surely not.

Ryder sighed, and gazed round the book-lined room in which he found himself. There was great comfort in books, especially the ancient, leather-bound tomes that faced him, ranged along the partition forming the speaker's corridor. They gave perspective, in that the scraps and squabbles of which they surely spoke, should anyone disturb their slumber, were now paragraphed and paged, catalogued and classified, and rendered harmless, thus offering a cautious reminder that life goes on and that nothing, ultimately, matters. Perhaps this, Ryder reflected, was what directed his tired steps to this quietest of rooms at the end of the suite comprising the library. Otherwise he had no explanation what he was doing there.

All he knew, on leaving the hustings, and following his spat with Miller, was he wanted to get away, to be by himself. He'd had enough of people, at least for the time being: all those peering, leering faces, hectoring, heckling voices ... one could only take so much. He thought he might go to the flat, lie down: if he rang for a taxi he could be there in a quarter of an hour. After all, return home was what the candidate did on the day of a general election, in those desolate hours between close of poll and the count getting underway, when there was suddenly nothing left to do, nothing that would sway the vote, bring out the electors, excite the media: three weeks of frenzied activity guillotined, the fevered body now a lifeless corpse at the mercy of agents beyond its control. Limbo, that's where he was ... in that halfway house, that holding area for souls awaiting a declaration of an electoral afterlife. God the divine returning officer, with a mayoral chain round his neck, the shoulders of his jacket frayed by the chafing of the weight of civic honour: I, God, the returning officer for the Conservative Party constituency, hereby give notice that the total number of votes given ...

"Wake up. It's over. Come on ..."

How long he'd been daydreaming in that library armchair he'd no idea. But now Blenhesket was leaning over him, Merryman in the background.

"They said we'd find you here. Time to stir yourself."

"Over ...?" Ryder croaked, his throat tense and dry. "You mean ...?"

Blenhesket guffawed. "Give them a chance. Miller's only just finished spouting his nonsense about cutting spending and keeping a tight rein on government departments and sticking to this crazy promise of an in-out referendum on Europe ... exactly the line we knew he'd take."

"Pretty tedious, if you ask me," Merryman put in. "A bit of an anticlimax after all your fireworks."

"I have to say you had me worried," Blenhesket wagged an admonitory finger. "Going off message like that ... after I'd prepared ..."

"But it worked. And at least no one's in any doubt what you stand for ... what we stand for," Merryman corrected himself.

"Come on," Blenhesket said. "Lunch ..."

"I don't want any lunch," Ryder said. "I think I'd just rather ... I mean ... I'm not sure I want to go and mingle."

"That's exactly what you want to do. Go and show yourself ... show them you're not afraid of entering the lions' den. They're all trooping off to the dining room now ... and if the rank and file needs to fortify itself for casting its vote then I'm sure you do too. Besides ... you need to oil that voice of yours. You sound decidedly wheezy. You're not going down with something, are you?"

Blenhesket stared hard at Ryder, as if he were an ailing herdwick on one of his estate farms, and to which perhaps a vet should be summoned.

"I'm fine," Ryder fibbed, easing himself reluctantly from the depths of his chair, and wondering if he could conjure appetite from the pit of his stomach. "But you're right. A spot of lunch would do me good."

***

The votes were cast, the count was underway, and most of the MPs had returned to their offices, or to one of the commons bars, to await the result in more comfortable surroundings. Ryder, feeling better after his nap in the library, and having managed for lunch a portion of fish pie and a glass of chablis, which seemed to steady him, had installed himself in a corner, nervously watching, while Blenhesket roamed the room, studying the voting slips, phone in hand, occasionally punching presumably numbers into the machine. From time to time he turned to Ryder, nodding his head, a satisfied look on his face, before devoting himself once more to his scrutineering. Miller was standing in another corner with his coterie: his lieutenants prowled the room on the same mission as Blenhesket. Sandringham had looked in at the start but promptly disappeared, leaving his campaign manager to represent him.

The room was stuffy, overheated, in contrast to the world beyond where, Ryder observed, looking out through the windows, snow had begun to fall. London looked its best beneath a blanket of winter, Ryder felt. It blotted out much of the dreariness of the older parts of the city, with their beaten, hangdog air, their remorseful reminder of better times. It was a magic wand which, touching the drab and doleful streets, lent them lustre and sudden sparkle. Illusion, of course, and, like all illusion, false: already those snowflakes, fluttering past the window, were baiting buses, teasing trains, hobbling the hopes of commuters anxious for early escape from the snow-snarled city. The usual chaos, too, at airports ... but Margo was flying in tomorrow, Ryder recalled with a start. Hadn't he promised to meet her? But what if the plane were diverted? The flight cancelled? He ought to ring her, warn her to check ... but she'd do that as a matter of course. No way Margo would arrive at an airport without making sure beforehand the flight was on time. That was Margo. Efficient, organised. Ryder wished he had a fraction of her management skills.

Something was happening at the table where the count was taking place. Or, in fact, not taking place, for the counting appeared to have ceased. The tellers were checking their notes, their calculations. They conferred with Timmins who, having jotted something on a piece of paper, beckoned Blenhesket and the two other campaign managers. They exchanged muttered words and then Blenhesket, having recorded the result in his phone, and looking pleased, marched across to Ryder.

"As I thought," he said. "No-one reached the quota on round one. Miller's well in the lead with ... let me see ... 141. You got 96 ..."

"For god's sake," Ryder said. "That's hopeless. Almost 50 down ..."

"Yes, but you were second. Sandringham's out of it. He was last ... just 60. I think he knew the game was up. That's why he kept a low profile. Anyway ... now we wait and see what happens in round two when we carve up the leftover votes. Patience, my boy ...

patience. Not long now."

"I need the gents," Ryder said, standing up, mindful of a knotted stomach, and feeling queasy, and now regretting the fish pie. Nerves. This was worse than any general election when the result, if not the tally of votes, was a foregone conclusion. Northaven was one of the safest seats in the country, while the outcome of the first election he fought, in a rotten borough and Labour fiefdom in Stoke-on-Trent where they might just as well have weighed the votes, rather than count them, was equally clear-cut. This, though, was different. There was an unfamiliar edge to this contest, one of Donald Rumsfeld's known unknowns, and Ryder was uncomfortable. He wanted it to be over.

"Just you come straight back," Blenhesket ordered. "No lingering ... no quick cigarette to calm you down."

"I don't smoke," Ryder said truculently.

"I know you don't. Lighten up. I'm joking. But, as I said, don't linger. They're starting round two now."

Making his way to the toilet Ryder met several MPs who, alerted that the count was entering its final phase, were returning to share in the melodrama of the declaration. One or two, clearly millerites, scowled and said nothing as Ryder slunk past; others grinned and wished him luck. These were people he hardly knew, parliamentary colleagues, members of the same party, yes, but acquaintances, rather than friends, who now addressed him with easy familiarity. One even called him "Tim" and patted him on the shoulder. What was this? What did they want? Already fishing for favour and preferment? Was this what it was all about?

Entering the toilets Ryder made straight for a cubicle and locked the door. He wanted to throw up but, despite his waves of nausea, the fish pie refused to oblige. Ryder didn't know whether to be glad or not. He'd no wish to return to the count reeking of vomit, though this might be preferable to a heaving stomach redolent of a cross-channel ferry in a gale. But this was nonsense, he told himself. He wasn't at sea, he was on dry land. Any queasiness was a result of the stress. It was all in the mind. Get a grip, make it go away. He took a deep breath and felt better at once. All the same, the retching had exacerbated the dryness in his throat. Flushing away the few drops of spittle and bile he had coughed into the toilet bowl, he left the cubicle, crossed to a basin, wrestled with the cold tap to turn it on and, cupping his hands beneath the flow, bent and slurped lustily. Water dribbled through his fingers, clasped imperfectly as tremulous hands rose to expectant mouth, and this he repeated several times, assuaging his thirst and extinguishing, he hoped, the fever, imagined or otherwise, in his stomach. Bloated, from the as yet undigested cold water washing around in his insides, but otherwise satisfied, he was debating whether to return to the cubicle for a pee when Merryman burst in.

"Got you," he said. "Come on ... they're not far off. Christ ... what have you been doing? Having a water fight?"

Merryman gazed in wonder at Ryder's damp and darkened jacket.

"Wanted a drink."

"I'm not sure your suit did. It's all down your front. If you wanted a drink why didn't use the fountain?"

"Bugger," Ryder said. "Didn't think. Other things on my mind."

"Fair enough, I suppose. But we need to get you cleaned up. You're on in a couple of minutes. Either way, whatever happens, you need to say something. And look presentable."

Merryman crossed to a paper towel dispenser and grabbed a handful of sheets.

"But I haven't a clue what I'm going to say. I've

nothing prepared."

"Excellent," Merryman said, starting to dab at Ryder's lapel. "Improvise. You're good at that, if this morning's performance is anything to go by. All the better for being spontaneous. From the heart, and all that. That's what's going to win you this election."

"You think so? But ..."

"Wait and see. Okay. That's the best I can do. Now ... get moving."

Minutes later they were back at the count, where a buzz of excited voices greeted them. Ryder, still with butterflies in his stomach, but grateful for the walk from the gents which enabled him to compose himself, saw Blenhesket with Timmins and Miller's campaign manager. The latter looked grim. Sir Wesley, on the other hand, was a lesson in diplomacy, his features betraying nothing.

"Ah," Timmins said, seeing Ryder had entered the room, and lifting his voice over the chatter. "If the candidates would care to approach the table ..."

Ryder and Miller moved forward as Timmins raised his arms for silence. He cleared his throat and began speaking.

"In the matter of the ballot conducted according to the rules and regulations approved by the parliamentary ..."

"Get on with it," someone called.

Timmins peered round the room to trace the culprit but, failing, cleared his throat once more and continued.

"The votes in this second round having been redistributed I shall read the results in alphabetical order according to surname."

He paused, conscious everyone was watching him, savouring his moment in the limelight. Ryder was briefly reminded of one of those courtroom dramas when the jury foreman is about to speak. Suspenseful silence ... verdict, and the public gallery erupts in vociferous response.

"Miller, Jeremy," Timmins intoned. "One hundred and forty ..."

A mighty roar from several dozen throats drowned the rest of Timmins' words. Blenhesket, grinning from ear to ear, swung round to Ryder, arm extended, to shake the victor's hand.

"Congratulations," he enthused, and Ryder thought he detected a tear in Sir Wesley's eye. "Congratulations. I knew we could do it. I knew it."

"There must be some mistake ..." Ryder countered.

"Miller, Jeremy," Timmins repeated, over the uproar. "One hundred and forty four votes. Ryder, Tim ..." and his voice rose to a screech ... "one hundred and fifty ..."

He could get no further. No one cared about the final digit: the psephologically-minded would have time later to rake over the figures. For the moment the room was filled with isolated whistling, jeering, but mainly applause, hurrahs, cries of "Well done!" and "You show 'em, Tim!" Suddenly Ryder was besieged by supporters and well-wishers, jostling and pushing, all trying to shake his hand, slap him on the back. He'd won ... he'd actually won, against all the odds, having displaced the favourite, the front-runner. What had he let himself in for? His mind was racing, ears furred, eyes fogged ... and through the blur a figure, looming, menacing, hand outstretched.

"A fair fight," Miller said, between clenched teeth. "Now we need to move on. Party first, personality second. I'm sure you agree."

"No," Ryder replied, rallying, taking the outstretched hand but squaring up to Miller. "Country first. People first. That's the way from now on."

Miller gave a half-smile, withdrew his hand, and turned away. Meanwhile Timmins had managed to quell the excitement and was calling for quiet so their new leader ... their new prime minister ... could say a few words.

Ryder cleared his throat, which was again rough and dry, and holding up his hand, waited for silence. They were not in the house now, where the ability to speak over braying benches was required of any government minister. He would show them who was boss. It was as simple as that.

"Ladies and gentlemen," he began, when he knew he commanded their attention. "I thank you for your support ... for the confidence you have placed in me today."

Someone made a comment audible only to the rear of the room, and there was brief laughter. A pair of millerites made a show of leaving, rattling at the door as they did so, and then leaving it open. All eyes, though, were on Ryder.

"You may recall, in the days of Margaret Thatcher, there was much talk of wets. They were the people in the party who, out of step with the ideology of the day, remained faithful to the tenets of one-nation conservatism. Now some of you, no doubt, will have noticed these darker patches on my jacket and tie ... caused by over-zealous efforts a few minutes ago to slake my thirst. This, ladies and gentlemen, clearly singles me out as a wet ... a wet who will not dry up until ..."

A guffaw. A snort, a grunt, of amusement. The tension in the room snapped. It was as if the collective breath, stilled, was suddenly released in an exhalation of relief.

"... who will not dry up," Ryder continued, straining his voice, "until we have won the next election resoundingly on firm Conservative principles."

Noisy approval greeted his words. Cheers, applause,

echoed round the room as Blenhesket moved forward and pulled Ryder to one side.

"I've the BBC on the line. Then there's the rest of them ... tearing themselves apart to get at you. Come. We've work to do. And before you go in front of the cameras we need to get you a fresh jacket. Then ..."

"First things first. I need to ring Margo ... and Alistair. I need to tell them before they hear about it from elsewhere. After that ... I could do with the loo."

Blenhesket scowled. "Hurry up, then. As I said ..."

Ryder cut him off. "Relax. We've come a long way. I know there's work to be done ... a lot. But let's savour the moment. Okay?"

Blenhesket nodded, curtly, and turned away to speak to someone else.

Ryder dug in his pocket to find his phone to ring Margo. As he was fumbling with the keypad he glanced out of the window. It was still snowing. Hard. He wondered if that were an omen.

Somewhere. January 2015.

When the earth beneath your feet shivers and strains, and an abyss, black, unfathomable, cracks open before you, you run. You run for your life. To safety. Security. Home. And Ryder ran. Except ... he was in that abyss. In the darkest place he'd ever been, ever imagined. The dark was absolute, such that no eye could accustom itself to it. A place where no light shone, nor would ever shine; where no sun, no moon, held even the slightest sway. A place from which there was no escape, salvation; no hiding from the gremlin he now knew beyond all doubt to dwell there. From far away, but this was surely his imagination, voices, faintly familiar, but deadened, dull; perhaps, too, a ghostly hand on his; but no, he was alone, in this place beyond human help, beyond succour. And running. Running still. From himself. From the questions echoing from the sides of his unseen tomb: Why me? What have I ever done? Are there not others more deserving? How long ...? But answers came not. Just silence, stretching through the darkness to the nothingness beyond. Then Ryder realised he should stop running, for flight was futile. Realised, too, that the light he sought, to dispel the cimmerian blackness into which he had been so cruelly pitched, flickered frail and feeble within him. Of the abyss there would be no leaving, no humbling of the gremlin, but now Ryder could make out shapes, contours, discern features, faces, and from these he drew strength, found fortitude. And could face the world again.

London. February 2015.

The atmosphere in the study ... the same room in number 10 in which Pemberton had once received Ryder ... was of shocked disbelief. Blenhesket was staring at him, agape; Merryman, whom Ryder had appointed as parliamentary private secretary, was looking down, nervously fiddling with his fingers; while Sir Marcus Price-Loxley, the cabinet secretary, who had joined them at Ryder's request, sat unmoving, studiously contemplating the wall.

Blenhesket was the first to break the silence. "I ... I ... this is ... good god. I don't know what to say. I mean ... I'm so sorry."

"I think that must be a first," Ryder purred. "Sir Wesley is stuck for words. Sir Marcus ... I believe that should be noted."

The mandarin inclined his head, almost imperceptibly, by way of acknowledgement, but said nothing.

"This is just ... so unexpected," Blenhesket ploughed on. "But surely ... I mean ... you must have known ..."

"It was confirmed last week," Ryder replied calmly. "I've known for something like ten days."

"But why didn't you say?"

Ryder reached for the teacup next to him on the table and raised it cautiously to his lips. Try not to spill any of the liquid, he told himself. But the cup was wide, from a set he'd asked Margo to buy. Wide, and reasonably light, with a large handle, so he'd have no difficulty, at least not yet, holding it.

"I needed to come to terms with it. Get my head round it. Talk it through ... with myself, with the family."

"Christ. I ...bloody hell, Tim." Blenhesket leaned back in his chair and ran his fingers through his thinning hair.

"Forgive me," Merryman said, his voice quavering. "I've not really come across MND before. I've heard of it, of course, and the person who springs to mind is Stephen Hawking, but ..."

"Basically, in a nutshell," Ryder cut in, "you watch yourself die. And there's no cure."

"Jesus," Merryman flinched.

Ryder replaced the teacup, annoyed at the tell-tale rattle indicating his failure to replace it cleanly on the saucer.

"It's a wasting disease. It weakens the muscles, as I know only too well, so that eventually ... well, it's probably a wheelchair, having to be fed, like a baby. That sort of thing. But ..." and Ryder gave an involuntary sniff, jerking back his head, "... it doesn't affect the brain. The brain is ... it's a prisoner trapped in a body rotting round it. All the time watching, waiting ... but powerless."

"Surely, in this day and age, there's something ... some drug ..." Merryman ventured.

"There is. It slows things down ... the deterioration. But I don't think for very long. And it affects people in different ways. In the end, though ..." Ryder shrugged.

"I take it," Blenhesket said slowly, "there's no chance they've got it wrong. It's something else, perhaps."

"They've done all the tests. I've had needles stuck in me to monitor nerve activity. I've been wired up to pads which put out some sort of impulse to measure signals ... electrical signals in the nerves. I didn't know the nerves had electrical signals. In my case, they probably don't. Or very little. Actually, I'm becoming quite an expert."

Price-Loxley cleared his throat. "I have to say, prime minister, you seem remarkably sanguine. I'm sure, if this were me, I'd not be so disposed. Quite the contrary. It goes without saying you have my deepest sympathy, my support and, I might add, my admiration for your courage in the face of ... of such adversity."

Ryder smiled. "What choice do I have, Sir Marcus? I can assure you over the past week I've thought long and hard about this. Harder than I've thought about anything in my whole life. In fact, if I'm honest, I've thought about nothing else."

"Understandably," Price-Loxley said gravely.

"I've no doubt, during this period, you found me wanting. Diffident, distant ... you wondered if I was coping, and you put it down to the pressures of a new job ..." the cabinet secretary discreetly tilted his head "... but all the while I was trying to grapple with what is ... let's not beat about the bush ... a death sentence ..."

"For god's sake ..." Merryman shook his head.

"And when you haven't much time ... I don't know how long, they can't or won't say ... it means certain decisions have to be made."

"Ah," Blenhesket said pensively. "Obviously, we have to think ..."

"I'm not resigning, if that's what you're saying."

"I wasn't. I mean ..."

"Of course you were. It's the first thing Margo said after she'd got over her shock. Wanted me to throw in the towel ... to use the time I have left to do what I want, while I still can. Go on a world cruise ... a safari ... something like that. Of course, if I were to chuck it in I'd become probably the shortest-serving prime minister in British history. It's one way to be remembered, I suppose ... as an answer in a pub quiz. Like Spencer Percival, the only PM to be assassinated."

Price-Loxley smiled appreciatively at the reference.

"So I'm following Margo's advice. I'm going to do what I want to do and while I can. And doing what I want means staying here, in this job, to complete the task you good people ... not you, Sir Marcus, obviously ... mandated me to do. Namely ... to get this country going again. Also this party of ours."

"Good on you," Merryman said.

"So," Ryder concluded, "in the midst of death we are, so to speak, in life. And to be absolutely clear ... I intend to carry on as long as I can. Jack's already mentioned Stephen Hawking ... if it comes to it I can conduct operations from a computer strapped to a wheelchair."

"Wait a moment," Blenhesket said. "There's a huge difference between launching theories about the origins of the universe and running a country. I'm not sure ..."

"Put like that," Ryder said, "I imagine, in comparison, running a country is rather a doddle. Somewhat smaller scale, at any rate."

Blenhesket forced a smile. "I think we need to be sensible about this. We are, after all, entering uncharted waters. Sir Marcus, what are your views?"

The cabinet secretary clasped his hands together, as if about to pray, and reflected for a moment. "The chief whip is, of course, quite right to say we are entering uncharted waters. The idea of a prime minister with disabilities ... disabilities, as I understand it, which become progressively more restricting ... is, I think, something new. Apart from Roosevelt, I cannot recall any leader with a serious disability. But wait ... "

"A four-term president," Ryder put in. "I don't think being confined to a wheelchair held Roosevelt back ... do you?"

"Not at all. And I seem to remember there was also someone ... Lenin something-or-other ... in one of the South American countries ... Ecuador, I believe. A paraplegic ... stepped down a year or two ago. Did a lot for the disabled ... nominated, I think, for the Nobel peace prize. Very popular, apparently."

"This could work to our advantage," Blenhesket said, almost licking his lips. "A sympathy vote."

"For god's sake," Merryman rounded on him. "You can't capitalise on something like this. It's obscene. I thought we were trying to get away from the image of the nasty party."

"When you've been in politics as long as I have ..."

"I think, gentlemen," Price-Loxley soothed, "and returning to the matter in hand, it would be unwise to commit to any particular course of action at this stage. The prime minister, in my opinion, is entirely capable, at least for the moment and, I suspect, for the foreseeable future, of fulfilling his duties ..."

"Absolutely," Merryman confirmed.

"But the situation will clearly need to be reviewed in light of the progression ... or non-progression, since I understand this disease chooses its own rhythm ... and action then be taken accordingly."

"That seems sensible," Ryder said. "So ... business as usual."

"With respect ... not quite," Price-Loxley hesitated. "I think the cabinet should be informed at the earliest opportunity, and parliament immediately afterwards. If not, you run the risk of the press getting wind of it ... they watch your every move ... and then, apart from the gossip and speculation, there's a run on the pound, and the financial markets, with all the uncertainty that creates. That's the last thing anyone wants."

"Sir Marcus is right," Blenhesket growled. "We've got to be able to manage this ... make it work for us. Fine ... I know what you're going to say ..." he held up an admonitory hand to Merryman ... "but if we're trying to tell things as they are, win trust, we have to be up front with parliament ... and with the electorate. We're way ahead in the opinion polls ... brand Ryder has seen to that ... and we want nothing, no cover-ups, no economies with the truth, to dent that. I believe if we're open and honest ... explain the situation ... we can build further on this goodwill."

Blenhesket leaned back in his armchair. Ryder looked round the study, as if inviting further comment. None came.

"Very good," he said. "I'll inform the cabinet at the next meeting and make a statement to the house the same day."

He reached out for the tea. His throat, with what felt like an almost permanent lump, which made swallowing sometimes awkward ... the neurologist, Mr Meakin, had warned him of this ... needed lubrication. But Ryder had only to touch the cup to realise the tea had gone cold. Like life itself. His life. But it could still be drunk. Picking up the cup, he gulped its contents.

"Thank you, gentlemen," he said. "I think that will do for today."

***

The news was received round the cabinet table with more interest, Ryder felt, than strictly proper. True, the right noises were made ... a tragedy, prime minister, we feel for you, prime minister ... but looking behind the eyes that surveyed him, seeing a freak, a man facing the gallows, Ryder could discern calculation: How's he going to cope? How long can he hang in? When's he going to go? Some of them had immediately marked him a lame duck, including inevitably Miller, whom Ryder had retained as foreign secretary. Keep your friends close, but your enemies closer, Blenhesket had reminded him, and Ryder acted on the advice. Indeed, he'd made few cabinet changes. One face missing was that of the chancellor, Henry Sandringham, who, tired of the taunts that his stewardship had left the nation in worse financial shape than when he found it, and bruised by his third place in the leadership ballot, had retired to the back benches. He would leave parliament in May, it was whispered, to return to banking, where blunders would be blunted by broad and bountiful bonuses. Ryder had replaced him, to some surprise, but to public approval, with Vic Roper, a Lib Dem, whose views on the economy were contiguous with his own. It was a bold move, demonstrating to the country a certain magnanimity in that he bore no animosity to his hapless coalition partners, while signalling to members of his own party that preferment was not to be taken for granted. At the same time it neatly wrong-footed the Lib Dems, who were left wondering whether their political future, if such there remained, rested not as they imagined with Labour but with a continuing coalition with a more centrist, less nasty, Conservative Party. If this was the stroke that would split the Lib Dems, putting them out of the misery in which they had wallowed during the previous four years, so be it. He'd be doing them a favour.

Curiously, Ryder realised, rousing himself from his reverie, it was a Lib Dem who was now speaking.

"I should like," Vic Roper was saying, "to congratulate the prime minister on the excellent opinion poll results ... ten points up, with personal ratings higher than any previous prime minister at this stage in an administration."

There was a murmur of approval round the table.

"This is a clear indication we've got the country, and the press, behind us. They can see that boosting public spending is working in the USA, and in Japan, and it can work here, too. Even if we're increasing public debt."

"Absolutely," Ryder broke in. "And that's why we

need to cash in on this goodwill and get things moving. Break with the policies of the past."

He shot a glance at Miller, apparently immersed in the papers before him.

"I mean," he went on, savouring the moment, "you'll have seen the report that certain of our northern cities have been forced to make budget cuts equivalent to a week's worth of military expenditure. That's scandalous. That's why we need to rein in the military, to spend this money in town halls, to create jobs and protect services."

Miller looked up, about to speak, but Ryder held up his hand.

"Therefore, in this spirit, I've asked the chancellor to draw up legislation to curb bankers' bonuses and, at the same time, to examine the case for retaining bail-out banks in state hands."

"Come off it," Miller could restrain himself no longer. "There's no mandate for this whatsoever. You can't just ..."

"I can and I will," Ryder said. "Look. This ludicrous idea that the state is incapable of running anything has got to stop. The public has got the message, even if we haven't, that private doesn't necessarily mean better. Local authority schools perform just as well as privately sponsored academies, often better, and are more accountable. We've already had to take back into public ownership train companies that have defaulted on their franchise. Hospital deaths ... remember those, a couple of years back? ... were the result of outsourcing, short-term contracts and cost-cutting. Privatised, profit-based cheeseparing ... and the public knows it."

Someone at the table cleared his throat, as a prelude to speaking, but Ryder was in full flow.

"I tell you this. A government that franchises huge chunks of its core business ... policing, prisons, health,

233

education ... to private contractors has lost its purpose. It's no longer a government, but a regulator ... an insurance company to pay out when the private sector screws up. No wonder fewer and fewer people bother to vote. That sort of government has lost respect. It's an irrelevancy. It's passed its responsibilities to directors and shareholders of shady little companies out for a fast buck at taxpayers' expense. Government needs to be hands-on, not hands-off; less dignified, to speak with Bagehot, and more efficient. It can't cower behind franchises and outsourcing but must do the job the voters elect it to do, namely govern. And I'm going to see it does."

Ryder sat back, satisfied. Let them put that in their pipes and smoke it. It's what the public wanted to hear, why he was riding high in the polls. Suddenly people beyond Westminster, beyond the Guardian readers, the chattering classes, were beginning to take an interest in politics, because suddenly politics was taking an interest in them. Austerity had been found wanting, its dogmas and rigidities disgraced; in its place a more flexible, more responsive era, less corporate and more human. For the first time in years the nation was more relaxed, at ease with itself, and Ryder knew he could take the credit.

True, in Conservative clubs in some of the smarter shire counties, the prime minister was castigated as a damn socialist, hell-bent on dismantling the legacy of the sainted Margaret. Disgruntled members returned party cards, sliced neatly in two, and cancelled annual subscriptions. Treasurers fretted that party backers were restless, that donations were down, with monies, it was whispered, redirected to UKIP. Ryder was concerned, of course, but if this was the price to pay for returning the party to core values, gaining the confidence of the nation, and winning an election, then he didn't care.

Nor did he care about the inevitable speculation in which his ministers, watching him from around the coffin-shaped table in the cabinet room, would indulge following the revelation about his illness. Let them plot and plan all they wished. The time for machination and manoeuvre would come in due course, after the election was won and his weak and wasted frame was able no longer to endure the exigencies of the highest office in the land. At that point he'd be beyond caring ... beyond caring about most things, in fact. Except probably death. Yes ... he might still care about that.

***

"The prime minister ..."

The speaker's voice, calm and authoritative, brought some semblance of order to a restless house assembled to receive Ryder's statement. The chamber was full, some MPs were standing, and the press gallery was packed. A sense of occasion, a feeling something was about to happen, had brought them there, and the atmosphere was tense, expectant. As the house quietened Ryder rose, slightly unsteadily, extending an arm to support himself on the despatch box.

"I am grateful, Mr Speaker," Ryder began, in tones stretched and strained. "I shall be brief in what I have to say, for I have no desire to dwell on a subject of personal consequence to myself while there is much work ... important work ... to be done to meet the challenges that face our nation. Nevertheless, I believe honourable members should be told, indeed as I told the cabinet earlier today, that I have recently been diagnosed with an illness for which ..."

The remainder of the sentence was lost in a collective gasp of surprise, of shock. The MPs turned to each other, questions on every lip.

"Order," the speaker called. "Let the prime minister continue."

Ryder, silent, gazed at the floor, avoiding the eyes he could feel boring into him, and allowed the hubbub to subside. He looked up when the house was quiet and attentive again, and only then began speaking. His voice was low, controlled, and those in his audience who were hard of hearing were forced to bend their ears to the loudspeakers in the back of their seats.

"This is an illness for which there is, as yet, no cure. Motor neurone disease ..." several nodded heads on the opposition benches in front of him suggested that at least some in the chamber had heard of it ... "is a wasting disease that attacks the body but not the mind. My medical team, for whom I have the utmost respect, tells me the disease is in its relatively early stages. I am, however, aware already of a certain loss of control in the lower limbs and hands, also in the throat and neck, and these will undoubtedly become worse. The progression of this disease, though, varies from person to person, and it is almost impossible to predict the rate of physical deterioration. With that in mind, I give notice ..." and here Ryder paused for effect: was he going to say he was about to resign? ... "that I intend to continue in office for as long as I am capable to continue the vital work we have begun. This means ..."

He stopped, aware of a stirring, a swelling, behind him, and turned to find members of his party getting to their feet, some applauding, others waving their order papers, to cries of "Three cheers for Tim Ryder." There were even opposition members doing the same, though not in such numbers, and one or two who had risen to express their support found themselves clawed back to their seat by their neighbours.

"Order," the speaker exhorted. "I must ask honourable members to ..."

But no one was listening. This was Ryder's moment and the whole house knew it. And already, in the world beyond Westminster, the news wires were buzzing.

***

He was exhausted. Something had irked the gremlin which, over the previous weeks, had largely behaved itself. But now his limbs were weak and watery; his throat dry and irresponsive such that, having got through his commons statement, he was beginning to slur his words. Not noticeably, Ryder hoped, but he was conscious he was having to make an effort to enunciate clearly. Sir Marcus Price-Loxley had advised him to lie low after his commons appearance and the press conference and to return to Downing Street to unwind. Ryder agreed, but the major news channels were picketing the place, refusing to leave, unless they could have just five minutes with the PM for their early and late evening bulletins. Eventually Ryder gave way. If these people could help him get his message across, explain it was business as usual, that the changes on the outside did not make him different on the inside, then all well and good. But the interviews had worn him out, leaving him tired and tetchy. He felt slightly sick and hadn't wanted to eat, before Margo persuaded him to accept a boiled egg and soldiers, with which he retired to watch himself on the early evening news programmes. He'd come over well, he thought, and the voxes, with commuters scurrying home from work, elicited nothing but sympathy and goodwill. A UKIP MEP was interviewed who said the prime minister should resign at once because the threat from Brussels was so great you needed to be one hundred percent fit to fight it. Ryder wondered why he didn't say outright you shouldn't have a cripple for prime minister.

Obviously, political correctness ... but had Price-Loxley or anyone else been around Ryder would have been willing to bet that on the next day that MEP would be forced into a grovelling apology. That wasn't what I meant to say; I fully appreciate the outstanding contribution disabled people make to society; think of the paralympics ... and so on and so forth.

Ryder, contemplating with some glee the hole the man had dug for himself, and buoyed by the success of his appearance on the news, poured himself a whisky and retreated to the study, by far his favourite room in Downing Street. He took with him the report he'd commissioned on slashing the defence budget: halving the number of nuclear subs, moving those that were left from Faslane to Barrow ... no point in paying rental to a foreign country to look after what was in effect now the English nuclear deterrent ... and flogging an aircraft carrier, for which there were still no planes, to India. That would show the defence chiefs of staff, he thought ... put them in their place, as well as tell the electorate he meant what he said.

All the same, whether it was the whisky, or the exertions of the day, or the effects of the illness, he was unable to concentrate. On a couple of occasions he caught himself nodding off and, unable to take anything in, he was considering an early night when his mobile rang. He pulled it from his pocket, scattering papers to the floor, and, managing to hit the correct key to take the call, held the phone to his ear.

"I've only just heard. Christ, Tim. I'm mortified. I should have realised ..."

Ellie. Ellie was ringing. She was concerned, still cared about him, despite that ... what was his name? ... that surgeon she was having it off with ...

"I should have thought. I mean, recognised the symptoms."

"Ellie ... please. There was no way ..."

"It never crossed my mind. And it should have. I've seen it before ... I've had three, four patients with MND. But I never thought ..."

"You weren't to know. As you said, it could have been any number of things."

"But it wasn't. And I'm gutted."

"Don't be. Besides, if you had realised, what could you have done?"

"I don't know. Put you in touch with someone. Arranged for tests ... straight away ..."

"And what difference would that have made? None. These things have to take their course."

"Shit, Tim. I'm ... I'm ... I mean, you of all people. Everything going for you. I don't know what to say. Apart from ... I'm so sorry. If there's anything I can do ..."

Ryder shut his eyes. Her voice. He hadn't realised, or else over the years he'd forgotten, how seductive her voice could be. Of course there was something she could do. She could give herself to him, as in the old days, preferably out of doors, beneath a cloudless blue sky, on a balmy summer day. They could make love, languid love, lascivious love, love linked to all the adjectives in any lovers' manual. But they didn't need a manual. They would ...

"Tim. Tim ... are you still there? Tim ...?"

Ryder's eyes jerked open, taking in his surroundings: the study, furniture, fittings. Stop it. Stop it right now. Margo was here, under the same roof ... he had no right to think like that. Anyway, he'd had his chance years ago with Ellie, blown it ...

"Tim ... are you okay?"

With an effort Ryder spoke. "Fine, fine. Just a bit tired. In fact ... very tired."

"It's the nature of the illness. The body's having to

work harder to do things which in the past required no effort. It's bound to leave you exhausted. As if you didn't have enough on your plate ... I mean, prime minister. Who'd have thought it?"

"Do you think I should pack it in? Do you think that would be best?"

A pause. For the first time Ryder noticed the paper on the wall of the study. It was actually rather awful.

"No. No, I don't. I think at long last ... and this isn't just me, it's what I hear from patients, in the surgery ... at long last we have someone in power who understands ... for instance, doing away with Pemberton's ludicrous bedroom tax. A good move. No. I think ... and apologies if this sounds hackneyed ... the country needs you."

"I'm only doing what I think is right. But I'm glad you say I should stick with it. As it happens, I've no intention of quitting. At any rate, not until this thing ... well, you know. Funnily enough, I think it's helping."

"What is?"

"Work. It's giving me purpose ... taking my mind off everything else. In fact, since the diagnosis, and since moving into number 10, I've felt better than I have for months. Years, possibly."

"That's good."

"The consultant seems to think it's halted, at least for the moment, or else moving very slowly. It's like that, apparently."

"Some people live a long time ..."

"Margo said I should put myself first. Do whatever I want. While I still can. But I am doing what I want. You can see that, Ellie, can't you?"

From two hundred miles away, in Manchester, Ryder thought he heard a sniff, as if to fight back tears. It might have been his imagination, or some interference in the signal. All the same he bit his lip and changed the subject.

"Tell me ... you're okay? I mean ... you ... you and Stephen ..."

"It's Simon. And, yes, we're ... well, it's complicated."

Ryder wondered how he might follow this up but nothing suitable came to mind. Instead he said lamely: "Relationships can be tricky."

Another sniff. Faint, but unmistakeable. Ryder drew a breath.

"I'd like to see you. Before ..."

"I'd like that."

"I mean ... if you're in London. You could come to the house ... the commons. You've never been to see me there. Or, better still, I ... that is, Margo and I ... could give you a tour of Downing Street. It's not everyone who gets that, you know."

"That would be lovely."

"Good. That's fixed, then. You let me know when you're coming."

"I will."

The sniffing had given way to silence. Unspoken words hung between them, like a gently swaying jungle bridge of hemp and creeper. Slice through the rope and it would be gone, pitching those on it into an abyss of their own dark dreams.

"Good night, Tim. Look after yourself."

"I shall. And you too. Good night."

The bridge was severed.

"Love you," Ryder breathed into his now pointless phone.

***

For several minutes he remained in the study. It was stupid. He was like a teenager with a crush ... no, not like, he was that teenager, at any rate a middle-aged teenager ... not the head of her majesty's government. What was this hold Ellie had over him? Why was she under his skin like this? He shuddered. And what about Margo ... it was almost betrayal. Wasn't there something in the bible about adultery in the heart being the same as actual adultery? Nonsense, of course ... just another of those guilt-tripping devices employed by the church to put, literally, the fear of god up simple-minded souls ... but if it were so, if adultery in the mind were truly the same as adultery in the flesh, then on judgement day he'd need to ask for sundry and manifold similar offences to be taken into consideration. As if that would help.

Ashamed, feeling almost unclean, he slunk out of the study to find Margo and to make amends ... not with her, but with himself. She was in the flat, as he knew she would be, where he found her watching a rerun of Downton Abbey. She was not adapting well to her first lady role, Ryder realised. She had cut back on her business commitments, after Sir Marcus Price-Loxley had advised her it would be inappropriate to be seen to be involved in corporate hospitality and event management. Tongues would wag, he said, claiming she was exploiting her position as wife of the prime minister. But Margo missed the business world, Ryder knew. She had been a fish out of water when they visited a primary school earlier in the week. She had perched on a tiny chair, trying to read to the children, but how much they understood was questionable. It was one of those worthy but scary schools where the pupils ... Ryder couldn't bring himself to refer to the children as students ... spoke over fifty different languages in their various homes and in which English functioned as an awkward lingua franca. All the same, the children's linguistic prowess put his own ill-remembered French to shame. The little ones grinned enthusiastically as the press snapped away, but Margo looked uncomfortable. At least to her husband it seemed so: the press were merely interested in the pictures and not the person behind them. No doubt she was mentally listing the things the school ought to be doing to promote itself, to get itself noticed, but the sort of budget to which she was accustomed would be unimaginable in that place. No, Margo needed to be doing something, organising something ... and having been advised to back away from her business interests there was little else left. Apart from him.

Of course, she'd been magnificent. When he broke the news of his illness to her she had been devastated, reproaching herself for not having taken better care of him, watched out for him, spotted the signs. But she immediately rallied. Her enforced idleness, she said, was a blessing in disguise, an opportunity to spend time with him, to do things together. Hence the visit to the school and her appearances at other public engagements. It was suggested in some of the gossip columns that the prime ministerial couple was upstaging royalty when it sallied forth to meet the public. It was even said that, should Britain ever become a republic, and in need of a ceremonial presidential figure, then Mrs Ryder would neatly fit the bill ... despite being American. But Ryder knew it was a sham, an act with which his wife was uncomfortable, and performed for him, and him alone, in a private gesture of love and support. For this he was grateful, but mildly sceptical. When she said that, as the illness developed, he would need more and more help, and she would be there for him. Ryder was dubious. Margo had many qualities but patience, and nursing skills, were not obviously among them. When Alistair was little, and had suffered the usual childhood ailments, she had been happy to relinquish the role of nurse to Marie-France.

All the same, Ryder knew he owed Margo much, much more than disloyal and dubious thoughts about Ellie.

"Hun ..." he said, flopping onto the sofa next to his wife.

"Ssssh," she hissed. "It's almost finished. Just a couple more minutes."

Ryder sighed. Since accompanying him to Buckingham Palace, Margo had developed what he felt was an almost morbid fascination with the English upper classes. She had become obsessed with rank, and titles, and was most put out when Ryder told her that if he were ever offered a knighthood he would turn it down. Margo had pulled a face and said she rather fancied being Lady Something-or-other and hoped for her sake he would reconsider.

When the programme finished Ryder tried again.

"I've had Ellie on the phone."

Margo bridled, saying nothing.

"She'd heard the news. She was concerned ... and upset. A bit worried, I think, that when she saw me, whenever it was, she didn't pick up on the MND."

"That's understandable. I never rated her as a physician. I guess that's why she never moved from the back streets of Manchester."

"Ellie's in Manchester because she chooses to be there. I'm sure ..." Ryder checked himself. Anything to avoid a row. "Look. She wanted to know how I was. If there was anything she could do. I said not ... but I told her if she was in London she should tell us. I said we'd lay on a tour of Downing Street ..."

"No way. I mean ... oh my god, Tim ... we've enough people wandering round this place ... supposed to be our home ... without inviting any more."

"We can't help that, I'm afraid. It's the nerve centre of government. All these people have jobs to do."

"I don't see why they have to do it here. And there's no escaping them. The other morning some guy walked straight in, without even knocking, said he was looking for you, and then walked out again. I mean ... come on, Tim ... surely we're entitled to privacy. But some of these people think they own the place."

"I suppose, in a sense, as taxpayers they do."

Margo leaned towards him, landing a punch, part in irritation, part in play, on his arm.

"Ouch," Ryder said, caught unawares. Either the blow was heavier than intended or he was becoming more susceptible to pain. If the muscles in his arm were weakening, if there was less flesh to absorb the shock ...

"Honey ... sorry," Margo said, taken aback. "I didn't mean ..."

"It's okay. Honestly, it is. It's just ... I wasn't expecting ..."

"No. Of course not. I shouldn't have. Sorry."

For a few moments they said nothing. Outside, perhaps in Whitehall, a siren wailed ... a fire engine, an ambulance. Somewhere in the building a door banged, muffled voices, swiftly smothered laughter. Then a telephone ... and what seemed like an age before it was answered.

"I hate this place," Margo said. "It's the pits. It's like ... the other side of the tracks. And then some. I mean ... you're prime minister and first lord of the treasury and whatever else you are and all they can come up with is a dump like this. It's gross ... a couple of poxy little rooms over a store that never shuts. Why? Why do you put up with it? I guess because you're British."

"It's history ..."

"Yeah ... and you know what Henry Ford said about

history. And I think you Brits have got far too much of it for your own good. Always living in the past. Look ... this place wants pulling down ... you need somewhere so if you must live over the store then you can shut it out, not have to listen to it, breathe it, eat it, sleep it, twenty-four seven. And as for bringing people here ... Ellie, for instance ... no way. This place is a disgrace and ..."

The Murchison residence in La Jolla swept into Ryder's mind. He knew where Margo was coming from. Compared with the grandeur of his in-laws' home the Downing Street flat, with its four cramped bedrooms, shabby lounge and inadequate kitchen, with people coming and going day and night, was a rat-hole. He wondered if it would be possible to decamp to La Jolla and run the government, in style and comfort, from there. Margo would be happier, and Grace and Jim had so much space they'd probably never notice. Besides, in the age of the internet, of virtual reality, it ought to be possible. He could fly back once a week for prime minister's questions and ...

Ryder realised Margo was shaking, choking back tears.

"If I must live here ... I want them out. All these people ... strangers ... it's like being in a zoo. A cage ... stared at all the time. I can't take it ..."

This was the second time that evening he'd been exposed to female emotion. He felt inadequate. At least now, however, he could do something about it. He slipped his arm around her.

"Hey, hun ... hun. It's okay. I'll tell them ... give them instructions. To be quiet. And to give us some space. And we'll get this place spruced up. Make it nice ... sort of homely. We'll start with the wallpaper in the study. But whatever you want. You decide."

He squeezed her tighter, as his strength would allow.

"It could be worse. And we know it won't be for ever."

***

Sir Wesley Blenhesket was troubled. He was sitting in Ryder's office in the commons, fiddling with the end of his tie. He looked older, Ryder thought. But then, after barely six weeks in office, they probably all did.

"It's defence spending," Blenhesket said. "I'm hearing that the chiefs of the defence staff are unhappy."

"I hardly expected them to be otherwise," Ryder said.

"Seriously unhappy ..."

"They know the score. Defence spending has got to come down ... the millions we fork out each day in the middle east and elsewhere has got to be redirected where it's going to have most impact ... here, at home, to lift people out of poverty, create jobs. Poll after poll tells us voters are right behind us."

"I'm well aware of that."

"The days of this country playing global policeman ... while the police station itself tumbles down around us ... are over."

"I understand Miller has been having informal talks with the defence chiefs ..."

"For god's sake. That's not his remit."

"He's been sounding them out about our ability to react if our overseas interests were threatened. They say the best training is where the action is ... a theatre of war ... not jumping over ditches here waiting for something to kick off."

"Quite possibly ... but it's a darned sight cheaper. I thought Miller was on side."

Blenhesket pulled a face.

"Then he needs reining in just as much as the military. I mean ... who's in charge of all this? Him or me? Or the generals, for that matter ... or the people behind them, in arms or aerospace, pulling their strings? Come on ... who's in charge?"

"A good question, prime minister. A very good question indeed."

Northaven. February 2015.

The message from the school was short and to the point. Alistair's attendance was slipping, he was behind in his course work, and when he did show up he was withdrawn and uncommunicative. It could be he was worried about his father's illness, which had come as a shock. However, if he continued like this, it was unlikely he would achieve the grades of which he was capable. Would his parents, perhaps Mrs Ryder, given her husband's commitments, please make an appointment as a matter of urgency to speak to the director of studies?

"We should have got him transferred somewhere in London," Margo said. "We should have insisted. Then we could have kept an eye on him. In fact, that's what we might still have to do."

"He won't buy it," Ryder said, peering into the gloom outside the carriage window to try and discover where they were. Long past the Windermere, of course, and the London suburbs ... somewhere in the anonymous, featureless landscape of middle England, as flat and monotonous as the accents of the people who lived there.

They'd left the capital on the Thursday to spend a long weekend in Northaven. Margo had an appointment the following day at Alistair's school. Ryder, apart from a meeting with his constituency chairman, wanted to work quietly on the draft of the March budget that the chancellor, Vic Roper, had prepared. It was to be a budget for expansion, as well as an intelligent, but not overtly popularist, statement of principle on which he could go to the country barely two months later. Public money would be channelled to those areas that would lead directly to growth: green initiatives, such as tidal energy and sustainable transport, as well as life sciences and aerospace which, though relatively strong, would benefit from a boost from the public purse to promote research and development. Investment was crucial, and it had to come from the state: the banks remained obdurate, with lending slack and sluggish. It was time, Ryder felt, to wield the big stick: release your money to support enterprise and industry, backed by government guarantee, or remain indefinitely in part public ownership. He needed to decide whether to slip this into the budget, and if so, how, or whether it would be better to make a separate issue of it, perhaps nearer the election. There would be no opposition from the Labour Party, of that he was sure, and anyway it would be useful to spike their guns lest they loose salvos of their own towards bank nationalisation. No, the opposition would come from his own party, the millerites ...

An insistency in Margo's tone drew him back to the present.

"Honey ... I was saying. Do we tell Alistair?"

"What? Tell him what?"

"Tim ... I know you've things on your mind ..."

"Sorry. Miles away."

"But this is our son I'm talking about and I'd like it if ... okay, forget it. But the point is ... do we tell him I'm going to school tomorrow or not?"

"We do. He's bound to find out sooner or later. After all, we're going to have to talk to him about it. Get him to buck up."

"Why've we had no inkling of this from Marie-France? She's supposed to be looking after him. You'd think she might have said."

"Search me," Ryder shrugged, peering out of the window again. "Perhaps the French treat these things differently. A touch of the old laissez-faire, perhaps."

His forehead touched the glass and he left it there

for some moments, grateful for the cool and the calm it brought, grateful for not having to support the weight that was his head. This was a heavy thing, he was learning, and sometimes the muscles that bore it needed to rest. Besides, he was tired, weary. He knew he ought to be more involved in Alistair's education, but there was so much going on, so much to claim his attention. He was a juggler, trying to keep countless coloured balls of different shapes and sizes in the air, all at the same time, except he was surrounded by other, smaller jugglers, whom he had to keep in play, and who would lob him another ball, sometimes two, and often from unexpected angles, which he was expected, ducking and weaving, to catch. It was a circus, they were clowns, blue balls, red balls, green balls whizzing through the air in all directions, and he was perched on someone's shoulders, who in turn was standing on someone else, but there were people piled on top of him, he could feel them, their feet, great clown boots, crushing his shoulders, bearing down on him ... but it wasn't his shoulders, it was his arm ... squeezed, hurting ... and he woke with a start.

"Honey ... there's a lady ... wants to know if we're being looked after ..."

Ryder roused himself to see Eileen standing next to the table. Out of the corner of his eye, across the aisle, he noticed the SO1 man tense, alert, and Ryder nodded to him to indicate all was well.

"Mr Ryder ... I hope you don't mind. I'm not supposed to be here ... I'm two carriages along. But ..."

"Eileen ... how lovely. Margo ... this is Eileen. She's the reason we're not thrashing up the M1 ... however luxurious the limo you don't get service with a smile in the back of a car."

Eileen blushed. "Only doing my duty ..."

"Besides, I prefer the train. And I don't see why I

251

should alter any more of my habits than I already have just because I'm prime minister. Even if it sometimes makes life difficult for that lot," Ryder motioned towards the protection officer. "And of course ... she's also the reason I'm prime minister."

Margo shot him a puzzled look. Eileen blinked.

"I was having a wobble," Ryder smiled. "In December. It was Alistair. Made me think ... wonder if I was really up for it. If I really should. Eileen came and sat down ..."

Their knees had touched, briefly, beneath the table. Ridiculous the silly things you remember, Ryder thought. Never the big things, the things that matter ... the manifesto pledges, the bills passing through parliament ... but the little things. Magic moments, a touch there, a word here. Perhaps the little things were, in fact, the big things ... the ones that truly counted.

Ryder collected himself and continued.

"You, Eileen ... you said there'd been this tweet. I didn't think it was public knowledge, but it was. And you told me to go for it. If you hadn't ... if you hadn't encouraged me ... I think I'd have let it go."

"So this is the person we have to blame?" Margo put in, good naturedly. "Well, well ... it's always useful to know."

"Please ... I didn't mean anything by it," Eileen said, slightly alarmed. "I mean ... I did. I knew ... we all did ... that Mr Ryder was the right man for the job. And we've been proved right. But I didn't mean to interfere ..."

"I'm glad you did," Ryder said. "Sometimes ... we need that input from outside. To give us a perspective on ourselves we don't have. I think I can find a role for you, Eileen, in a government think tank ..."

"Oh, no, Mr Ryder. I couldn't. I'm very happy where I am."

"I know you are. Please excuse me ... I'm having you on. On the other hand ... if you feel like a change ..."

"Leave the poor lady alone," Margo said. "You're embarrassing her."

"No, no," Eileen said, flustered. "It's alright ... but perhaps I'd better be getting back. I just wanted to say ... this illness of yours ..."

Ryder flicked a dismissive hand.

"We're very sorry. If there's anything we can do ..."

"Mr Ryder's being well looked after," Margo said. "Some of the top people in the country. But thank you, all the same."

Eileen's upper lip quivered and Ryder thought she was about to burst into tears. She controlled herself, however.

"All the best, Mr Ryder. Remember ... we're with you all the way." Then, summoning a half-smile, she was off, scuttling down the aisle, glad, Ryder thought, to be released from the presence of predictable, premature death. As she passed, the SO1 man looked up briefly from his phone, frowning, but quickly went back to his texting. Ryder watched her flight: in so-called primitive societies, he told himself, they do death so much better, for they live with it in a way we don't. Awkwardness in the face of his mortality was something he'd have to get used to. Saying nothing of this to Margo, he leaned back in his seat.

"Amazing. Do you know ... that's the first time she's not plied me with food and drink. And I could murder a bottle of water."

***

Entering the house Ryder was struck, not for the first time, how stale, almost unlived in, it felt. It was as if the place resented his presence, as if he no longer lived there. This, of course, was at least partially true: the suite of rooms ... no, that was too grand ... the set of rooms in Downing Street, which Margo so greatly resented, was now his principal residence. Perhaps the Northaven house, spacious and furnished comfortably, to his taste, or rather to that of Margo, felt abandoned, betrayed, and was shutting him out. But what nonsense. Ascribing feelings to bricks and mortar: was this the effect the job was having on him? Or was it the illness, the intimation of mortality, driving him to anthropomorphism, to find life wherever, and in whatever, he could?

He shook himself, to divest himself of such folly, and made his way to the kitchen, and to the boiler, to wrestle with the heating and get some warmth into the house. He was greeted by Marie-France who emerged, as always when he arrived home, from her flat, splaying light and homeliness through the open door.

"It's cold in here. The whole house ..."

"Ah, monsieur ... when you 'ave been brought up on a farm ... wiz no 'eating ... you do not notice ze cold. You work to keep warm."

"That's all very well," Ryder said, fumbling with the thermostat, "if you're humping great bales of hay round the place or carrying sheep down from the fells, or whatever you do. But if you're doing other work ... studying, for example ... then I'm sorry ... you need to keep warm. Where's Alistair, by the way?"

Marie-France's lips folded into a moue and, motioning with her chin, indicated upstairs. It struck Ryder she had lost weight: her face seemed less puffy, her features better defined. She might almost pass as pretty, he realised with a start, but there was no time to dwell on any transformation.

"Alistair's in his room? Then that's why we need

heat. The place is like a morgue ... though your little flat looks cosy enough."

She shrugged, a gesture Ryder found increasingly irritating. Dumb insolence: wasn't that what the military called it? He could read the minds of his ministers more readily than that of this woman standing before him. She was an enigma ... despite the fact he'd known her probably longer that most of his parliamentary colleagues. Suddenly he felt extremely tired. He needed to sit down, take the weight off his feet, forget the weariness pulling at him, dragging him in a direction he had no wish to go. He shivered. An early night beckoned. With an electric blanket.

Margo came into the kitchen, still wearing her coat.

"You sorted the heating, honey? Ah ... Marie-France. Say ... why's it so cold in here?"

Again, the shrug.

"We turn down ze 'eating. Save money. Alistair and I ... we eat 'ere ... in ze kitchen ... in my flat. Zees 'ouse ... for two it ees too big."

It was on the tip of Ryder's tongue to say there was no need to practise French peasant economies in the home of the British prime minister, but he thought better of it. If she took offence, told the papers ... it didn't bear thinking about. Though if the French took umbrage and EDF backed out of further investment in the nuclear power industry, that would strengthen his hand to go for green. "French turn out British lights": what a resonant headline. He allowed himself a surreptitious smile.

"I need to talk to you about Alistair," Margo was telling Marie-France. "But not now. Tomorrow. We're worried about him, though."

"Alistair ... 'e ees a fine young man. I zink I know 'im better ..."

"We're his parents," Margo cut in. "I'd thank you to

remember that."

"Mais bien sûr, madame. Bien sûr."

A chill silence descended.

"Gotcha," Ryder said, as the heating clonked into life. "Fiddly, that temperature thing. Not designed for fingers like mine. God ... it's coming to something when I can't even adjust the heating. Soon I'm going to need ..."

"Honey, please ... not now," Margo cautioned. "You go settle yourself in the lounge. I'll pour you a drink. And I'll call Alistair. He needs to know what's going on."

Ryder nodded. He looked round to ask Marie-France whether she'd got anything to do him a quick sandwich. But she had vanished, melted away back into her flat. And the door was shut.

**

Ryder slept well. Too well, in fact. He generally did, in Northaven. It was the soporific sea-laced, salt-laden air that hung heavy over the town, particularly along the coast, that lifted lazily over the dunes to deposit itself on the homes, like Ryder's, huddling behind the sandhills protecting them from the westerlies and, in winter, the gales gusting in from the Irish Sea. It was the air, as much as anything, to which the town owed its former prosperity: the gentry, arriving from Liverpool or Manchester to escape the acrid excrescence of thousands of chimneys, both domestic and industrial, bestowed an early cachet, while the coming of the railway opened it to excursionists and wakes-week holidaymakers from the mill-towns of East Lancashire, and beyond. Those days, of course, were gone: the gentry decamped first to the south of France, then further afield, to islands in the Caribbean, while the trippers and the tourists packaged themselves to bars and bodegas in Barcelona or the Balearics. They left behind the now faded elegance of a seaside resort that had reached its apogee in Edwardian England; they left behind, too, the rich and heady sea air, timeless, eternal and, as Ryder knew, sweetly somniferous.

It was ten o'clock on the following morning before he stirred. He was both pleased and annoyed: pleased that he'd slept so long, knowing his body needed the repose, but annoyed that a valuable portion of the day had already been lost. In London he was awake around six: the distant rumble of the city girding itself for the working day, as well as the more immediate buzz and bustle of number 10, were more effective than any alarm clock. Here, in Northaven, he had deemed it unnecessary to set an alarm, imaging he would be awake by dint of habit if not at six then soon after. But here he was, heavy-headed and leaden-limbed through surfeit of sleep, or else because of the gremlin that accompanied him through waking hours, making his way cautiously downstairs in a house he felt instinctively to be empty. Alistair would be at school and Margo, having left later than her son, would now be under the same roof, discussing his academic progress or, as Ryder feared, his lack of it. Of Marie-France there was no trace: she was either keeping her own counsel in her flat or else, with any luck, shopping, selecting something to which she could apply her gallic flair to place steaming and succulent onto the evening table. Like the old days, when Alistair was little. And when life was so much simpler.

While waiting for the water to boil, to make his tea, Ryder rang his constituency chairman. He said he was running behind schedule, couldn't fit in a meeting, but if there was anything urgent then perhaps they could discuss it over the phone. There was something urgent.

A company was seeking planning permission for a casino close to the beach. Older residents were opposed, claiming it would destroy the character of the town. Younger people, and in-comers, were in favour, arguing that any development should be encouraged. Where did Ryder stand on this?

The electric kettle clicked off, steam swirling briefly around the shelves above. Ryder ignored it, staring out instead into the garden at flowerbeds damp and dejected and bearing the stunted traces of the previous autumn's growth. In the past Marie-France had tended the garden, indeed, taken pride in it, but clearly no more. What did she do with her time when they were away?

A cough, a clearing of the throat, reminded Ryder a response was needed to the question of the casino. He sighed, trying to recall party policy on gaming and gambling. He seemed to think it was contradictory.

"Look," Ryder said. "I'm ambivalent. I think, though, if our core vote is against it then so am I. But if you have to say anything ... then right idea, wrong place. I think that covers all bases. And point out anyway that when it comes down to it it's a matter for local planners."

The call ended and Ryder, disgruntled, realised he hadn't made his tea. The day didn't start without tea ... and often didn't finish without whisky ... and no sound decisions could be made on a stomach not lined with tannin. He reboiled the contents of the kettle and, scalding the pot, added the leaves and poured on the water. His hand was unsteady, the grip lacking, but he managed to carry the tray with tea pot, milk and cup up the stairs with minimum spillage. Next time he ought not to fill the pot so full. He settled in the study and, still in his dressing gown, started work on Vic Roper's draft budget. It was good, a clean break with the past, and while Ryder was no economist, whose profession he held in as much esteem as that of pier-end clairvoyants and other soothsayers, he understood this was a clear statement that austerity was over. Roper had shaped a budget modelled on government spending, the easy money policy of the federal reserve, that had seen the USA begin to turn its economy round, boosting jobs and business, and distancing itself from the still largely moribund economies of Europe.

This was the key, Ryder told himself. We need to look beyond our shores, see what others are doing. When the history of late twentieth century, early twenty-first century Britain is written, the verdict will be that we failed to learn from our partners, our competitors. We are mired in our history, our past, convinced that because we once ran an empire on which the sun never set, won world wars, we need no lessons from those we once governed or vanquished. Crass arrogance ... the mindset he needed to change. Roper had made a fine start: in this way Ryder could begin to haul the country away from its smug satisfaction with the past, towards a more realistic and open acceptance of the present. That was the challenge. Yet there were those out there, the Millers, the press barons, the blinkered but burgeoning band of UKIP supporters, who would have it otherwise. And who would howl with rage when he moved to keep the banks under state control, to direct their profits to schools and hospitals, towards people as against faceless, fat-cat shareholders. Whatever the economists might say ... them again: wasn't the country in the mess it was precisely because of economists, because these self-appointed demi-gods failed to see what was coming, failed to warn, to avert? ... whatever they might say, reining in the banks was what ordinary people wanted and understood. All Ryder wanted was courage ... and the right time to strike.

He was still weighing these issues when he heard the front door open and voices, raised and angry, spilled into the house. Margo and Alistair. He stood up, with difficulty, for he was stiff, not having moved for ... how long? He cast a glance at his watch: for over two hours he'd been immersed in the budget, pondering the pros and cons of slipping an announcement about the banks into the chancellor's budget speech. But now, judging by the anger in the voices, there were more pressing matters. He went onto the landing and peered over the balustrade into the hall.

"What's this? What's going on? Why aren't you in school?"

"He's got the rest of the day off ..." Margo began.

"The rest of the year. I'm not going back ... there's no point," Alistair announced.

Ryder began to descend the stairs. "Okay. We need to talk this through."

"Yeah, talk," Alistair sneered. "That's your solution to everything. And that's all we've done all morning ... talk talk talk. And look where it's got us."

"I don't know where it's got us," Ryder said, reasonably. "I wasn't there so I can't say."

"Before there's any more talk," Margo said, "we need to calm down. And you, Tim, need to get some clothes on. I mean ... get out of that dressing gown. And I guess you've not shaved this morning."

Ryder rubbed his chin. It was true. Nor had he showered. He probably looked a wreck. If there were any snappers around, with long-range lenses, their cameras trained on the windows, they'd have a field-day. Fortunately the specialist protection team, on permanent duty outside, would deal with prying paps.

"Okay," he said. "Family conflab ... later."

"Family ..." Alistair's eyes narrowed to slits. "You

don't know the meaning of the word. Neither of you. But it looks good in a manifesto."

Ryder and Margo exchanged glances.

"Let's leave it for the moment," Ryder said. "We'll come back to it another time."

Alistair raised his hands in mock submission. "At last. Somebody says something sensible. I'm off out. That is, if the goons will let me. And, while we're about it, don't think I don't know they follow me around."

"It's for your own good."

"Yeah ... that's the excuse for everything."

"We're actually in a state of not high alert but ..."

"We wouldn't be if you lot ... politicians ... didn't have us fighting wars in places we've no right to be."

"Alistair ..."

A look from Margo silenced him. Let the boy go, she seemed to be saying. He needs space, time to himself. Ryder stepped back as Alistair made for the door, pulled it open and stepped out, admitting a blast of cool, damp air. The door slammed shut behind him.

Ryder was rattled. "I'll go up and have that shower," he said.

***

Shaved, and more suitably attired, Ryder was toying with soup and a roll. It was a comfort to lunch simply and frugally, away from public gaze. Handling food that required cutting, or chewing, was sometimes awkward. Once or twice Margo had needed to chop his meat into bite-sized portions, easily swallowed. The time would come ... not for a while, Ryder fervently hoped ... when everything would need to be liquidised. Like baby food. And perhaps administered via a feeding tube. He shuddered. It didn't bear thinking about. It was a relief, therefore, to banish this spectre and bring himself back to the present ... to Margo, sitting opposite him at the dining table, and to the question of Alistair.

"So," he said. "Where do we go from here?"

Margo frowned, and pushed her soup away. "I don't know," she said. "But we need to take it easy. Not rush things."

The school ... rightly, Margo said ... was concerned about the change in Alistair. Since Christmas he had become increasingly withdrawn, reserved, showing little interest in work or friends. His teachers could offer no explanation, and Alistair spurned all offers of support or guidance. All he would say was he couldn't wait to leave, to get away.

"That's what he's told us," Ryder said. "This gap year business. But it's no reason to give up on his school work."

"If you ask me," Margo said quietly, "he's trying to tell us something. I reckon ... okay, we've not been the best of parents. I mean ... it's not as if we've been here for him. And yet, in a weird sort of way, we have. We've been too much here. I guess you especially."

"I don't follow."

"Honey ... you're a public figure. You're in the paper, on the radio. People talk about you, want to know your views. In this town you're everywhere. And now ... as prime minister ... it's worse. It's national press, national radio and TV. In the nicest possible way there's no escaping you. I guess he feels swamped ... crowded out. He needs space ... his own space ... to grow up. Discover who he is. Not as your son ... but as his own person."

Ryder blinked. "That's a bit heavy, isn't it? I mean ... psychobabble, all that stuff ..."

"It's not psychobabble. It's how I see it. And don't get me wrong ... I'm not blaming you. My career's come first, too. We've both let him down."

"That's ridiculous. He's had everything he could possibly want. And we've always tried to be here at weekends ... be with him."

"Maybe that's not enough. There are things he's wanted that we haven't given. And now ... well ..."

Margo's voice tailed off. Ryder was conscious his soup was getting cold.

"Okay. What are you suggesting?"

"What I'm suggesting ... and the school's behind me ... is that I stay home ... sort of supervise him ... make sure he ..."

"But I need you in London."

"I know you do, honey. It'll be tough. But I think under the circumstances our son needs me more. And it won't be for long. Just to get him through his exams."

"But ..."

"I've made up my mind."

Ryder looked thoughtful, and chewed on his lower lip.

"Does this mean, at long last, we can see the back of Marie-France?"

"I guess it does. If your buddy Blenhesket, or whoever it is, doesn't want me to work, then I've time on my hands to become a good little housewife. And there's not room for two of us in this place."

"I'll speak to her before I go back to London."

"She'll be pretty sore ..."

"She knows it's got to come to an end. And we can afford to be generous. After all, we owe her. Big time."

"I wonder. In some respects I guess she owes us. We gave her the son she never had."

London. March 2015.

The honeymoon period enjoyed by any new leader was over. The press, wary at first of criticising someone terminally ill, had held back, taking time, as Jack Merryman said, to see how far it could go in taking a sick man to task before offending public sensibilities. Soon, though, political journalists, tired of pussy-footing round the illness, adopted the line that a prime minister, whether fit and able or at death's door, was nevertheless a prime minister, that the office should be seen as separate from the person, and that the actions and utterances of that office-holder should be open to scrutiny irrespective of personal issues.

The end of the honeymoon was marked by the European leaders' economic summit in Brussels. Ryder had stumbled, in full view of the cameras, while leaving his limousine to enter the building where the meeting was to be held. He was saved from falling by an aide, who was holding the car door open, but nevertheless the incident was an embarrassment. Within minutes the images had been tweeted round the world, and shortly afterwards a German news website was claiming the British prime minister was drunk as a result of an excess of champagne on the flight to Brussels. The report, headlined "Champagne shame of the British PM" ... "Champagner-Schande des britischen Premierministers" ... included a quotation from an unnamed flight attendant to the effect that Ryder was inebriated before he boarded the plane and, when advised in-flight not to have a second bottle of champagne, he had sworn at the attendant and told him where to go.

Fabrication, of course, and Ryder was furious. Did people not understand he was suffering from a wasting disease, attacking his muscles, rendering him increasingly liable to moments of physical weakness? As for the suggestion of alcohol ... Ryder detected Miller's hand, briefing against him, attempting to confound him, push him out, so he could claim the crown he believed was his. As soon as Ryder learned of the German news story he excused himself from the meeting and contacted Blenhesket in London. Sir Wesley calmly told him he was already engaged on damage limitation. Neither the BBC nor the broadsheets would run the drink story, realising it would not stand up, but the right-wing tabloids were not to be muzzled, saying they would print the rumours about drinking but remind readers about Ryder's illness and let people make up their own minds.

"It's probably the best we can do," Blenhesket told him. "But mark my words, they'll start asking whether you're fit to run the country, let alone represent it at international summits. And, while Miller might have been doing some stirring, you need to remember it was a German rag that printed this stuff in the first place. Don't forget you're hardly the flavour of the month in Berlin."

Blenhesket was right. While the Germans and others were relentlessly pursuing austerity, insisting that cutting public spending was the only way to achieve growth and create jobs, Ryder was intent on an opposite course: to increase spending where it would make the most difference, in education and training, health and welfare, the environment, and infrastructure.

When Ryder returned to his meeting, having spoken to Blenhesket, it was apparent he had been cast in the customary British role of outsider, of trouble-maker. The only half-hearted support he could command was from the southern Europeans, but their views were increasingly irrelevant. The EU, to all intents and purposes, was retrenching to a hard-line, industrial, financial and nordic core. Duncan Buchlyvie, over the meal in his home, had said as much, which was why he wanted Scotland to be part of it. This was where the dwindling wealth of the EU was generated, whose money-makers would not lightly squander their hard-earned riches on bailout after bailout with no perceived return.

Ryder was sympathetic. There was a time when, against party policy, he had argued volubly for the EU, at the same time cautioning that the union remain at 15 members to consolidate its institutions and practices before rushing to encompass weaker and very different economies. Washington, of course, had urged expansion to the east, to gobble up former Soviet satellites and prevent them falling back into the embrace of the Russian bear. One of his predecessors, John Major, had pursued a similar policy but for different reasons: pandering to euro-sceptics in his party, he knew a wider, shallower Europe would be weaker, less sustainable, than a smaller, deeper union. How right, how tragically right, that turned out to be.

But now Ryder, looking round the room at his fellow leaders, fractious, and suspicious, wondered whether the three parts of the United Kingdom ... minus Scotland, after its decision to secede ... had any part to play in a shrunken, nordic Europe. In theory it did: all Ryder's instincts told him this was where his country should be. But the euro-sceptic poison dropped, no, ladled into the ear of the British public by a press dominated by Australians and other non-doms and, more recently, by UKIP, meant the brand was toxic. Whatever the merits of the EU, and there were many, it would remain unacceptable to the public. Yet Britain was too small to go it alone in the global village. The days of splendid isolation were over. Allies, partners, were essential if domestic living standards were to be maintained and, simultaneously, an element of global influence and prestige be maintained.

Ryder frowned, and fiddled with his headphones. The Spanish prime minister was in full flow, but the measured, interpreted English he was hearing bore scant relationship to the animated delivery he was witnessing. Irritated, Ryder cast the headset aside. He had no need to listen to this, no need of EU rant and cant. Instead, an idea was forming. An audacious idea, possibly too ambitious. On the other hand ...

***

The consultant neurologist, Mr Meakin, confirmed Ryder's impression that the disease was on the move.

"In many respects, Mr Ryder, you know your own body better than I do," Meakin told him. "You live with it the whole time. All I can get is a snapshot ... and not necessarily a particularly clear one."

Tests showed Ryder's muscular control was diminishing. His weight, too, was dropping. He tried to make light of it, saying he could afford to shed a few pounds, but the neurologist was unimpressed.

"There are many ways to diet. Most are a waste of time. And this is certainly not a diet I would recommend. To anyone."

He reminded Ryder the disease developed differently in individual cases. Sometimes it would pause, for no discernible reason; at other times it would advance, attacking every muscle tissue it could find. For this reason, perhaps, the gremlin, zapped by the energy generated during the leadership election and adjustment to life in Downing Street, had largely behaved itself in the early part of the year. Ryder had been able to put it to the back of his mind, working round it, allowing for it, accepting the tiredness, the weariness, but ascribing them more to the demands of the job rather than to his illness. Now, however, the gremlin was back. Ryder found he needed to sit far more than before, especially after any exertion, when his breathing became short and sharp. His throat was perpetually dry and tense, his speech often clumsy and strained, his actions lumpen and laboured. Holding ordinary, everyday objects, such as cutlery or a pen, or using a phone or an iPad, was fast becoming an ordeal: grip was ebbing from him, murky and sullen, like the cold grey tides across the cold grey sands beyond his home in Northaven. It was worse when he was tired. The more he struggled to enunciate, to wield knife and fork with any dexterity, the more petulant, the more spiteful the gremlin grew. The tumble from the car in Brussels was a case in point. Ryder was aware he needed to be careful, to allow time for his legs to steady themselves to take his weight, but he had still been caught out. The gremlin had enjoyed its outing to the Belgian capital, and Ryder wondered what he might do to avoid further public humiliation of this kind.

Meakin looked at him with steady, unblinking gaze. "It's probably time," he said slowly, "to consider a stick."

"For god's sake ..." Ryder began.

"A walking stick. Low tech, I know ... but sometimes the old ways, tried and tested, are the best."

"I can't. I mean ... the press would go to town on this. They'd say ..."

"Take it or leave it, Mr Ryder. I can't force you. But with the illness at this stage I believe a stick would offer considerable benefit."

"I'm not sure I wish to be seen ..."

"From what I read the public is sympathetic towards you. Whatever the press might print, people are on your side and would understand."

Ryder leaned back and shut his eyes. A stick. This is what it had come to. A down-and-out, shuffling along a crowded street, stopping for breath, leaning on his stick ... but wait. Didn't Churchill have a stick, a cane? Even as a young man ... those early pictures, photographs, as colonial secretary, or at that siege ... Sidney Street, was it? Surely ...?

Ryder opened his eyes.

"A stick might well be useful. So ..."

Meakin nodded.

"A wise decision. You won't regret it."

***

Vic Roper's budget was received with plaudits and praise from press and public. Ryder had been adamant this should not be an obviously give-away budget, despite the fact that an election was less than two months away. There were none of the crowd-pleasing ploys such as a reduction in fuel duty, or a couple of pence off a pint of beer, ten pence off a bottle of wine. On the other hand restrictions were eased on public sector pay, allowing millions of people to see an increase in salaries for the first time during the coalition government, while employers' national insurance contributions were reduced to encourage them to take on staff. Spending on infrastructure, including railway electrification and up-grading of commuter routes, was boosted, and funds directed towards development of clean, alternative energy.

The budget was accepted as much for what it said as for what it failed to say. Gone, at Ryder's insistence, were the breathless prognoses of such-and-such a percentage growth over the next year, the next two years. Nobody believed forecast figures. Henry Sandringham, the previous chancellor, had been forced so often to revise downwards his predictions on GDP, on borrowing, and such like, that the exercise was altogether discredited. Ryder wanted no promises of future prosperity that could be held against him should he not achieve his aims. Instead, the message he wished Roper to convey at least implicitly in his budget was, he felt, honest and principled: we are doing our best to lift the country from the slough in which we find ourselves; the means we have adopted to bring this about are, we believe, the most appropriate; we are unwilling to commit to any timescale or give guarantees of success because the circumstances in which we are required to operate are complex, poorly understood and, to some extent, beyond our immediate control.

Blenhesket, privy to the budget before its contents were fed to the media and announced in parliament, was horrified. It was a high-risk strategy, he said. A pre-election budget should be stuffed with goodies ... while the admission that success could not be guaranteed, and the fact that no prognoses of prosperity or growth would be given, was sheer folly. Besides, Blenhesket grumped, no one got anywhere in politics through honesty. Quite the contrary, in fact. Ryder had accepted the criticism with good grace. He told Blenhesket to wait and see ... and when reaction to the budget began to manifest itself, and it was apparent Ryder's candour had gone down well, he couldn't resist a sly told-you-so moment at the expense of the older man.

Such a budget would play, Ryder felt, as a prelude to an election manifesto to set the tone for his government. This manifesto, which now demanded his attention, would contain the card he had decided to keep close during the budget: tax-payer controlled banks would remain in state hands, their billions in annual profits to be redirected to the very people who had underwritten and enabled those profits and who had suffered most from the bankers' greed and mismanagement. All the opinion polls confirmed this as a vote-winner, and no Conservative candidate, except those in the safest of colonel-blimpish seats ... were any seats safe after four years of coalition catastrophe? ... would be rash enough to kick against this policy.

And then there was the other idea, the one that had come to him in Brussels. Perhaps that was for later, after the election. If there was a later. That rather depended on the gremlin. Ryder recalled the discussion he'd had with Blenhesket about where power lay in the country. The answer was blindingly obvious. In his case it lay within him. With the gremlin. And it was the gremlin that would have the last word.

***

"And how's that bonny wee cousin of mine?"

They were in the study in Downing Street, where Ryder spent more and more of his time when not in his office in the commons. Opposite him sat Duncan Buchlyvie, as chirpy and as chipper as Ryder remembered him from the ill-fated trip to Edinburgh. The two men had discussed walking sticks, successfully skirting the sensitive issue of illness, and moved to a subject seemingly safer, less emotionally charged.

Ryder explained that Margo preferred to be in Northaven, to keep an eye on Alistair who had been giving them cause for concern.

"Aye ... it's called growing up," Buchlyvie said thoughtfully. "I'll have that to come with my bairns, no doubt. But it can't easy for Alistair. Father in the public eye, and all that. Do you know, when I was his age ... younger ... I was nicking things."

271

Ryder expressed surprise.

"Nothing major, of course. And nothing I needed. Tins of food ... stupid things, like plugs, bits of electrical stuff. You could say it was a cry for attention ... to get back at the old man who was never there, always working. As a strategy it was hopeless, because I was never caught, so he never knew. And then ... things sorted themselves out. As they do. And now we get on rather well. We've earned each other's respect, I suppose."

Ryder, uncomfortable with the turn the conversation was taking, was relieved when a Downing Street staffer appeared with tea and biscuits.

"I'm glad to see you're serving Scottish shortbread," Buchlyvie said, helping himself to two slices as the tea was poured. "Good for exports."

"I thought you could do with the help," Ryder said dryly. "From what I hear ..."

Buchlyvie squirmed. "Aye, well. That's partly why I'm here."

"I didn't think this was solely a social visit. So ...?"

The tea woman exited as smoothly as she had entered. Silence fell. The only sounds came from outside: a pigeon cooing, muted traffic. Ryder slurped his tea, finding it too hot, and spilling some as he replaced the cup. He waited for Buchlyvie to begin. When he did, he was to the point.

"I understand you're planning to move the strategic nuclear deterrent to England and shut down the naval facilities on the Clyde. You realise, I've no doubt, the effect this would have on our economy."

Ryder smiled. "You realise the effect it would have on the economy of the rest of the United Kingdom by keeping it open ... paying, in effect, rental to a foreign nation to house our nuclear fleet."

"Och ... Scotland is hardly foreign."

272

"Of course it is. You've made it so."

"The USA has bases all over the place. Japan, for instance ..."

"This is not the USA. Though, having said that ... never mind. Look. You people campaigned successfully to break with London because you said Scotland would be better off by itself. You argued you had no wish to remain shackled to a country draining Scotland of its wealth and talent because that country was to all intents and purposes bankrupt. Well ... let's work on that assumption. A bankrupt country, one that no longer pays its way in the world, manufactures little, exports even less, one that has put its dwindling financial resources into propping up monolithic and megalomaniacal banks, does not have the luxury of running overseas bases."

Buchlyvie snorted, and shook his head. "I'll not accept that. Even without Scottish wealth the rest of the UK is still one of the richest countries in the world. And there's still the city of London ..."

"I'm only repeating some of the ludicrous claims you were making during your referendum campaign. Anyway, the city's in it for itself, not for the rest of the country. Look at the north-east, for instance. Parts of it even make Glasgow at pub chucking-out time look attractive."

"There's no need to be like that."

"There's every need. You can't have it both ways ... gloating over our financial problems, the libraries and sports centres that have closed, the cuts in social services, care for the young, the elderly, this devastation south of the border ... then boasting that in an independent Scotland this would never happen."

"That's not what we said."

"Of course you did. That's what won you the referendum ... and you know it."

"Nonsense. What we appealed to was ..."

"English gullibility. You thought, with an independent Scotland, there'd be a cosy transition period while we English ... soft, as always ... continued to throw money at you, as we have done for decades, while you got yourselves sorted."

"That's not true."

"Of course it is. But it's not going to happen. We're bankrupt, remember? And anyway ... you brought this referendum, and independence, on yourselves. You've made your bed, as it were, so you can lie in it. We're certainly not tucking you in, still less giving you sheets and blankets. We're not some bloody Oxfam shop."

"I'm not suggesting you are. All I'm saying is ..."

"You're on your own. That's what it comes down to. Besides, I've enough on my hands trying to pull round what's left of the United Kingdom ... Disunited Kingdom, thanks to you ... without increasing overseas aid to a country with, as you're constantly telling us, whisky and North Sea oil."

Buchlyvie sighed. "This isn't getting us anywhere. I've caught you at the wrong moment. You seem a wee bit ... I don't know ... you're not your normal self. But all I would ask is ... think about it. A long term arrangement for the Clyde ..."

"For god's sake, Duncan. You were campaigning for a nuclear-free Scotland. And now you want me to keep weapons of mass destruction in Scottish waters. It doesn't add up. And just as you put Scottish interests first ... so I'm putting mine first. I'm cutting the nuclear fleet ... I'll get rid of the lot eventually. The savings'll go into education ... we've some catching up to do with the Germans and the Scandinavians, to say nothing of the Koreans. And then ..."

"I can't believe I'm hearing this from a Conservative prime minister."

"Nor can many Conservatives. But they're coming round ... fast. Because, to speak with one of my predecessors, there's no alternative. And I'm sorry if you haven't thought through the consequences of independence. All along you knew what you didn't want ... but what you did want was trickier. Pride, patriotism ... that's all very well, but there's no substance. Joining the dots of the past ... that's simple. It's joining the dots of the present that's the hard bit."

"I've never heard so much bollocks in all my life."

Ryder was about to tell Buchlyvie to face facts when he was seized with a spasm of coughing. It was a thin, reedy cough, and as Ryder fought for air his head lolled back onto the chair.

"Christ ..." Buchlyvie stood up.

Ryder gestured he should sit.

"It'll pass," he croaked. "It happens. The lungs ... get blocked. Too much talking."

"Water ...?"

Again Ryder gestured, though to what purpose Buchlyvie was unsure. The coughing had subsided but the breathing was taut, rasping.

"Should I fetch someone ...?"

Ryder shook his head. "Tea ... a sip. But I think ... if you could hold the cup ..."

Buchlyvie, momentarily taken aback, rallied at once. He took Ryder's cup and held it to his lips, tilting it at just the right angle. He was practised: it was like this with his own small children. Then Ryder pulled back, indicating he'd had enough. As Buchlyvie, standing over him, drew the cup away, Ryder looked up.

There were tears in his eyes.

Washington. March 2015.

They were somewhere over the Atlantic when the news came in. British soldiers had been killed in a bomb attack in the middle east. Details were scarce: it was unclear how many were dead and how the attack had happened.

"Damnation," said Ryder. "I ought to be there ... deal with it. At least give a statement. Remind people this is precisely the reason ... to avoid situations like this ... we're getting the troops out of those godforsaken places we've no right to be. Apart from the fact we can't afford it, of course."

"There's nothing you can do about it, honey," Margo said. "I don't think Richard Branson or the rest of the passengers would be very happy if you ordered this airplane to turn round so you could give a press conference in London. I don't think the president, expecting you, would be too impressed, either. Anyway, there's enough press people in the seats behind us for you to brief any time you want."

"I need more information. But it's Miller I'm worried about. He was pretty brassed off not being invited on this trip. But now, if I'm not there, he'll take over the show himself. As foreign secretary it plays into his hands. I should have packed the bugger off to the back benches while I had the chance."

Margo sighed. "If you guys spent as much time worrying about the country as you do about each other you'd have the country sorted in no time."

Ryder ignored her. "The point is he's got a perfect opportunity to argue we ought to be spending more on defence, not cutting back ... beef up the troops, give them extra protection, not expose them to risk."

"The whole purpose of being a soldier, I guess, is exposure to risk. Or have I missed something?" Margo asked.

Ryder was in no mood for banter. "I had a bad feeling about this trip. Perhaps I should have listened to Meakin ... stayed in London. God knows there's enough to do. The election, for one thing."

"Hey ... just take it easy, honey. Relax. You're going to need all your strength when we get there."

***

One of the most significant and, at the same time, unsung reasons for the existence of the president of the USA, Ryder reflected, was so leaders of lesser nations, when facing election in their own tin-pot states, could be photographed alongside the most powerful person in the free world, head of the greatest democracy on earth. Alright, perhaps not the largest: that honour appeared to have passed to India. But who in their right mind would wish to be pictured in a Kolkata slum, unless it was the Mother Teresa vote they were after, when they could be seen on the verdant lawns of the White House, basking in the lustre and luminance of presidential patina?

This, certainly, was one of the reasons for Ryder's Washington visit. Not that he needed the electoral fillip a photograph or press call with the president would bring. Opinion polls continued to indicate Ryder was on target for a resounding victory in May. The country was thirsting for change, desperate for sparkle after the stagnant, brackish waters of a cloacal coalition. Ryder's new conservatism ... in reality there was little new about it, merely a return to forgotten principles ... struck a chord with voters. Opinion was moving against the private sector and the inequalities it engendered. The former state monopolies might not have been perfect but at least their directors didn't suffer from bankitis and pay themselves millions in bonuses while raising prices way over inflation. People were starting to see that the threats from the power chiefs to turn off the lights if they were not allowed to raise tariffs were hardly different from the machinations of the miners in a previous generation. Dictatorship by union had been replaced by dictatorship by board room. No one enunciated this public resentment better than Ryder: he had stolen what little thunder the Labour Party possessed; he had marginalised UKIP, reminding the nation there were more pressing issues than immigration; while the Liberal Democrats, throwing in their lot with the party of Pemberton which was neither liberal nor especially democratic, had lost any integrity they might once have claimed. Politically, short of a strike by petrol tanker drivers, or television camera crews ... the nation needed fuel both for its vehicles and for its leisure hours ... or the lights going out, Ryder was untouchable, and he knew it. Except, of course, for the gremlin. And the gremlin did not play by political rules. The only rules by which it played were its own.

It was because of the gremlin that the neurologist, Mr Meakin, had advised against the trip to Washington. He was concerned about the deterioration in Ryder's health, in particular his difficulties with swallowing, and his occasional breathlessness. If, however, Ryder were adamant he make the journey, then a specialist nurse should accompany him. Purely precautionary, Meakin explained, without going into detail, but Ryder was furious. The press, travelling with them, along with Downing Street staff and officials, would assume he was at death's door. The purpose of the Washington visit ... talks on phased withdrawal from the middle east, the banking crisis, the economic threat from China and elsewhere, as well as a photo-opportunity with the president ... would be lost, buried in eager speculation whether the prime minister was fit to remain in office.

With an election imminent this was the last thing he needed. Besides, he reminded Meakin, hadn't he said his patient probably knew his own body better than anyone else? At the moment he was coping, thank you very much, aware of the limitations the illness imposed but successfully managing them. Moreover he would continue to manage them, just as he would the country it was his privilege to serve.

The neurologist heard him out in silence. Then he told Ryder, quietly but firmly, that unless he consented to a nurse accompanying him on the trip he would have no alternative but to inform the airlines the prime minister was unfit to fly.

"I'm sorry, Mr Ryder," Meakin said, "but I have my reputation to think about. As well as your health and general welfare. Of course, if you require a further opinion you're welcome to seek one. But I assure you the response will be the same. Besides, travelling with a medical professional is hardly out of the ordinary. Royalty, for example ... celebrities, people like that. They all do it."

Ryder, seething, realising he was beaten, glared at the neurologist.

"Discretion," he fumed. "If I'm to go along with this I insist on discretion. You can guarantee that, I hope."

Meakin nodded, allowing himself a brief, self-satisfied smile. "Discretion. You have my word, prime minister."

The specialist nurse who joined them at Heathrow turned out to be a well-built, muscular man about the same age as Ryder. He blended with the security personnel which, as Margo said, was in fact his job: security of the health of the prime minister. Indeed, so well did he look the part that Margo wondered if he had served in the forces. Two for the price of one, she said: the man was probably as handy with a firearm as with a hypodermic. Ryder teased her that she fancied him, saying she would probably be very happy for this hulk of a man to be leaning over her attempting to extract grit from her eye or a fish-bone from her throat. Margo blushed, told him not to be so silly: the only man she fancied was right there, next to her. Ryder winced. An image of Ellie, borne on a wave of guilt, swept over him, and he felt ashamed.

Margo had leaped at the chance to accompany her husband to Washington. The White House had intimated that Ryder and his wife would be made especially welcome because of Margo's American origins: one of our own coming home, as it were. It was an opportunity, too, to spend time with Jim and Grace Murchison. They were flying in from San Diego and had been invited, as the parents of the British first lady, to the White House banquet to be held in Ryder's honour.

The only worry was Alistair and whether he would manage when restored, if only for a few days, to the questionable care of Marie-France. Ryder knew his son had made progress since Margo had moved back to Northaven. His attitude to his studies and, indeed, to life in general, had markedly improved. He was less moody, more polite, and the school reported favourably on his work. It was like the Alistair of old, who had blithely told his mother not to worry, to go off to Washington and do her first lady stuff, and to bring him back the latest iPad.

Margo's presence in Northaven, as Ryder realised, worked both ways. It was beneficial both to Alistair and to her. He knew Margo was glad to be away from the dingy flat in Downing Street, with its constant flow of unsolvable problems and unworkable solutions swirling over its threshold.

"You've got your politics," she had told him in a fit

of pique. "I guess you don't really need me. It'll be a relief to get away and spend time with Alistair."

Yes, Ryder thought. Even if it's several years too late.

***

You have to hand it to the Americans, Ryder told himself. The banquet might have been a disaster, with the guest of honour like a small child, unable to cope with the food, the courses barely touched, plates still laden, returned with apologies and excuses into the hands of those who had so recently served them. The menu, though, had been designed with Ryder, or rather his ailment, in mind. New England potato and chestnut soup, wild yellowtail flounder from Cape Cod, served in carrot puree, honey-glazed chicken, Hawaiian style, followed by homestead ice cream and cheese: nothing that required excessive cutting or chewing, and Ryder was grateful. He was even more touched when the president, proposing a toast, praised Ryder's courage in refusing to be beaten by ALS, as the Americans termed the disease, reminding his guests they were privileged to be in the presence of someone who truly deserved to be called a hero, one whose spirit, as in those dark days of the 1940s, refused to be dashed or daunted. The British prime minister, the president said, epitomised all that was fine and noble not only in his country but also in the human spirit. Ryder, surprised but elated by the eulogy, fervently hoped the television cameras had caught the president's words and were beaming them back to Britain. If this didn't sway the undecideds in the few remaining marginals, not yet persuaded of his policies to lift the country from its slough of double-dip recessions, then nothing would. In response to the president, Ryder, brandishing his stick, said he was a disciple of Franklin D. Roosevelt, not only because his policies helped get America back to work but also because of his dictum "Speak softly and carry a big stick: you will go far". This, Ryder said to appreciative laughter, was precisely what he was doing. In this way, he added, as the room erupted in applause, their two great nations could learn from one another and go from strength to strength.

If the banquet was a public triumph, then the talks with the president were, Ryder felt, something of a private victory. The two leaders were left alone while their wives, who from staunchly republican and staunchly democrat backgrounds nevertheless found common cause to transcend political divide, took themselves shopping. Ryder was concerned lest Margo be pictured ogling expensive clothing or other exclusive items that would give an impression of carefree extravagance at a time when the electorate was only just beginning to forget about austerity. His hosts, however, assured him that any shopping trip would be conducted away from paparazzi. We manage things differently, Ryder was told. It's a big country ... more places to hide, more malls to visit. Besides, we're not as hooked on personality as you guys in Europe. Ryder, not convinced, hoped they were right. Some of the British press who had come over on the plane were tenacious little bastards who would not be fobbed off by some smooth-talking spokesperson from the White House. Quite the contrary. They'd smell a rat anywhere, alive or dead, even doubly wrapped in cling-film, sealed in tupperware and entombed in the sepulchre of their own lost morality. But there was no point worrying about it. Ryder had more important issues to raise with the president.

It was the much vaunted special relationship that particularly exercised Ryder's mind. He began by adopting a position of humility, reminding his host that for decades the relationship had been essentially one way, of greater benefit to Britain rather than the USA. Behind the deceit of the so-called independent British nuclear deterrent lay transatlantic technology and know-how. Without Polaris and, later, Trident missiles, as well as American intelligence, Ryder said, Britain would be dependent on conventional weapons and denied its place at the military top table. The president demurred. Britain, he said, despite a certain difference of opinion towards the end of the eighteenth century, was one of America's oldest and most trusted allies. The country had provided crucial support, such as military bases and intelligence, throughout the cold war and, more recently, offered critical tactical and diplomatic support in more recent theatres such as those in the middle east. Moreover his people, the president said, held Britain in high regard, admiring her royal family, political institutions and rich history and heritage.

Ryder acknowledged the compliment and told the president his country was grateful for the benefits the special relationship bestowed. Accordingly, Ryder added, he wanted to explore ways it might be strengthened, to encompass not just military but also mercantile and commercial collaboration. The president frowned. What was Ryder suggesting? Surely he had his European Union, membership in a powerful trading bloc which, despite its inability to manage its internal affairs, nevertheless constituted one of the largest and wealthiest markets in the world?

Ryder chose his words carefully. It was partly because of the internal difficulties of the EU, he explained, that many of his countrymen wished to leave. A referendum would probably see Britain exit the union ... and, even assuming his popularity remained at

283

current levels, it would be unlikely he could influence a vote in favour of retaining membership because of years of anti-Brussels sentiment. An exit would leave Britain isolated, disadvantaged in markets to which previously it enjoyed free and open access. What he was proposing, he told the president, was a form of economic union with the USA to the mutual advantage of both their countries.

The president raised an eyebrow and, leaning forward in his seat, gazed not without pity at Ryder. "I guess what you are proposing, mister prime minister, is not just economic union. You're asking, in fact, to become the 51st state."

Ryder smiled. "Something like that," he said. "Yes ... the state of New New England."

***

Ryder was woken by an insistent knocking. It was a dull, dead sound, and seemed to emanate from beyond the bed, from a distance. But it was becoming louder, more urgent, and as Ryder struggled to haul himself from under the duvet he remembered where he was: the British Embassy in Washington. But surely it wasn't time to get up. The room was still in semi-darkness: it seemed too early for any wake-up call ... what was the time? He leaned over to the bedside table to consult his watch, bringing it to his still bleary eyes. Just after six. He replaced the watch and, so doing, managed to overturn his glass of water.

"Damn," he said, aware that Margo next to him was beginning to stir. And that the knocking, now more a drum roll, was being played out on the door to the sitting room of the embassy guest suite.

"Come in," he croaked, cursing that he had decanted his water onto the embassy carpet. His throat was furred and feathered, and he had to repeat the instruction before the thumping ceased and he heard the outer door open.

"What is it?" Margo asked, her voice husky and heavy with sleep.

"No idea," Ryder said testily, hauling himself to a sitting position and drawing the duvet round him. "Third world war, for all I know."

A young man was padding across the carpet whom Ryder recognised as a junior embassy official.

"Apologies, prime minister," the man said, "but I've been asked to give you this."

He handed Ryder a folded sheet of paper, at the same time bending to switch on the bedside light. For a moment he paused, startled, as he squelched onto sodden carpet at the base of the table.

"Sorry," Ryder mumbled, noting his consternation. "Slight mishap."

"No permanent damage, I'm sure," the man said smoothly, turning away. "If you need me I'll be outside."

Ryder nodded, and unfolded the paper, rapidly running his eye over the page.

"Oh, no. For pity's sake, no ..."

The words tailed away, though his lips still moved, the sound choked by pain and anger.

"Honey ... what is it? You okay ...?"

Staring before him into the crepuscular room, into the shadows beyond the light cast by the table lamp, he thrust the note, with trembling hand, at Margo.

"My god," his breathing was short and rasped. "How could we let this happen?"

***

The gremlin, Ryder decided, with grim fatality, loved

foreign travel. Or else loathed it. Either way, as in Brussels, it was when he was tired, beyond his usual comfort zone, that it chose to remind him of its presence. At other times he could spite it, by working round it, immersing himself in affairs of state, leaving the gremlin to sulk, ever-present but neglected, though biding its time. Now, however, with his defences weakened, and his mind wrestling with the implications of the message delivered to him in that embassy guest room, the gremlin seized its chance. On leaving the bed, to cross to the bathroom, splash cold water onto his face, shock his brain into action, he stumbled, falling heavily to the floor. He cursed, growling for Margo to help lift him, bring his stick ... but the words were sullen and slurred. She helped him to the bathroom, saying she would ring for a doctor, at least for the nurse the neurologist insisted travel with them, but Ryder refused.

"It'll pass," he insisted. "Just give me a few moments."

Banging the bathroom door shut, Ryder flopped onto the toilet. This is what it was coming to. His body was not his own or, at any rate if it was, it was being hollowed out before his very eyes. It was akin to living in a husk, likely at any moment to implode, disintegrate, its remnants scattered to the winds. All that would remain was a brain, its cognitive faculties unimpaired, but a brain destitute, naked. He wondered if there was any way to keep a brain in a test tube, or a petrie jar, perhaps feed it with its own recycled blood, not that this would be much of a life. Wasn't there a Dahl short story in which a husband's brain, along with an eye, was kept alive, only for his vengeful widow to blow cigarette smoke at it because the husband, in life, disapproved of her nicotine addiction?

And now this. Sick with worry, Ryder went over the

contents of the message. The facts were few, but beyond doubt. Alistair was missing ... and with him Marie-France. The boy, apparently, had been at school on the previous day, when he attended the first lesson. After that no one could recall seeing him. One of his friends reported he had with him a large backpack but she had thought nothing of it, assuming he was returning books to the school library. Then, when he failed to show up on the following day, and it became clear no one had seen him for twenty-four hours, the school grew anxious. A phone call to the house received no reply and the headteacher, mindful of security, given this was the prime minister's son, rang the police. A car was dispatched to Ryder's home which was found to be securely locked and with no one there. At this point the police contacted SO1, responsible for the safety of the prime minister and his family. An alert was issued for the missing persons, including a call to ports and airports, and within an hour came the news that the couple had passed through customs at St Pancras on the previous evening and left the country on a Eurostar bound for Paris. CCTV confirmed their presence at the station.

Ryder leaned back on the toilet seat, and shut his eyes. They would have to leave Washington at once: Margo would want that, to be near the people coordinating the search for her son, to know what was going on, to welcome him home when he came back. If he came back. Ryder shuddered. What had driven Alistair to this? Were they such bad parents that their son couldn't stand them? Worse, preferred the company of a frumpish French nanny ... though, he recalled with a start, she had been looking more presentable of late, slimmer, trimmer ... but nevertheless a woman almost twice his age? Christ ... all the signs had been there. When he came back, after Christmas, had seen them together, emerging from the flat ... it was so obvious. With hindsight, of course. But he should have thought, done something ... and angrily he clenched his fists. But only in his mind. His brain registered the attempt, sent the appropriate signal, but the muscles were unresponsive, powerless, and his fingers hung helplessly from his hobbled hand. A roar, of frustration, rage, filled the bathroom, which brought Margo rushing to the door which she pushed open.

"Honey ..."

Ryder staggered to his feet, supporting himself on his stick and on the washbasin. He felt suddenly like an old man and he knew Margo thought so, too. The colour drained from her face as she saw him, moved towards him to assist. Channelling his anger into action, he barged past her, his breathing heavy, laboured. He stood in the middle of the room, swaying slightly, fighting with words reluctant to form.

"I blame myself," he managed. "For all this ..."

"Honey ..." Margo moved towards him, catching him in an embrace before he could fall again. "It's not your fault. If anyone ... it's ours. Together. But now ... we've got to deal with it. Sort it. And we shall."

She was holding Ryder, tightly, to try and stop the convulsions with which his body was racked. And, like a child distraught, the tears were flowing.

***

A call from the embassy to the White House, explaining that the prime minister would need to cancel engagements for the remaining twenty-four hours of his visit, was met with understanding and sympathy. The president had children, two daughters, and fully grasped the urgency of the situation. As embassy officials were rapidly ringing airlines to get the Ryders onto the first flight to London, a call came from the Pentagon that a military transport was about to leave for Ramstein, in Germany, from a nearby airbase. The Ryders could be accommodated on this flight, if they wished, which would divert to Britain to discharge its VIP passengers. They accepted at once and, within minutes, found themselves whisked through Washington streets, waking to rush hour traffic, as they headed away from the city to the waiting transport.

Ryder spent the flight fretting ... fretting over his relationship with Alistair and the boy's disappearance, and how this would play in the country. The press never stopped teasing Margaret Thatcher after her playboy son got lost during a car rally in the desert and mummy had to bale him out. True, the circumstances were different, but the subtext was the same: if the prime minister can't look after his kids, how can he look after the country? The timing couldn't be worse: with an election in a little over a month the last thing Ryder wanted was sniping from the press and from political opponents. The sooner he was back in London, could speak to the people in charge of ensuring Alistair's safety, and bringing him back home, the better.

Margo had wanted Meakin's nurse to join them on the flight but there was no time to collect him from his hotel or have him meet them at the airbase. The plane was waiting, ready for take-off, and it would have been diplomatically unacceptable to delay it longer. The crew strapped Ryder, Margo next to him, into an adequate, but hardly comfortable seat, where his head yawed from side to side as the aircraft, grappling with gravity, gathered speed along the runway. It was easier once they were airborne, less vibration, but the cabin was noisy. Ryder took Margo's hand, and held it loosely between fingers bony and brittle. Eventually he fell into a fretful sleep, muttering to himself, and Margo, relieved, reclaimed her hand.

Later, relaxed after his slumber, Ryder rallied when someone brought him a cheeseburger and, probably against regulations, a large whisky. His mood switched, though, when fat from the burger squirted into his face and over his shirt. As Margo tried to clean him up, he let it be known in tones fractured and faint that the only decent thing to come out of this whole business was the thought of the journos, back in Washington, kicking their heels with nothing to do except wait for their flight back home the following day. Presumably, though, they'd be fishing for news of his reaction to his missing son. He hoped the embassy staff could be relied on to preserve a diplomatic silence. If not, he'd fire the lot of them.

Afterwards, when the whisky took effect, he fell into a profound sleep, his head tilted, mouth half-open, saliva gently percolating at one corner, and snoring. He remained like this until the transport touched down at RAF Lakenheath where a car was waiting, with a clean shirt, to whisk them to London.

London. March 2015.

Commander Rachel Hewlatt was forthright and firm.

"I can fill you in on where we're up to," she said. "But I need to create a profile of the missing persons. The more information you can give me the sooner we can achieve what we all want."

"Bugger the profile," Ryder rasped. "Just get my son back."

"Honey ..."

"I'm sorry," Ryder breathed an immediate apology. "I know you're doing your best. It's just ..."

His voice trailed away.

"I understand, Mr Ryder," Hewlatt said. "It's a long flight. Now ... if we can get down to business."

They were in the white drawing room at number 10, the Ryders perched uncomfortably on the sofa facing the police officer in charge of operation Dewdrop. Quite why the name Dewdrop had been selected in the quest to restore Alistair to his parents was unclear: if Ryder had been told he had forgotten. Likewise, all he recalled about Hewlatt before he had been introduced to her was that she was regarded as a high-flyer and spoke French, having studied at the Sorbonne.

"We're working on the assumption they've gone back to the Auvergne where, you say, this woman has connections. Obviously an address would be helpful ..."

"All we know is that it's Saint-Nectaire or thereabouts," Margo said. "She was always going on about the cheese. I guess her folks ... not that she got on with them ... were into cheese-making. We might have an address for her back home, of course. But I'm not sure."

"Our colleagues in Clermont-Ferrand are checking addresses. I have to say, though, despite the particular circumstances of this case ... and, it must be said, the security implications ..."

"Oh my god," Margo's hand shot to her mouth. "No, please ..."

"We have to face facts, Mrs Ryder. I wouldn't be doing my duty if I didn't mention that there are certain risks we have to bear in mind. But, as I was saying, I'm not persuaded the French authorities are treating this matter with the seriousness it deserves."

"What do you mean?" Ryder leaned forward.

"There has been a reluctance to get involved on account of Alistair's age."

"What ...?" Ryder thumped the floor with his stick. "He's a minor ... not yet eighteen."

"While we have no indication there have been sexual relations ..."

Ryder snorted.

"The age of consent in France is fifteen. The French are saying if there's been no coercion ..."

"That woman kidnapped my son," Margo interjected. "Took him against his will."

"There's no evidence of that. The CCTV pictures ..."

"She forced him. Made him ... made him behave normally."

Hewlatt sniffed. "That's something we shall look at. In the meantime ..."

"It doesn't matter he's over the age of consent," Ryder spoke carefully and deliberately. "That's not the point. She's in a position of trust ... and she's abused that trust. Under British law ... and I imagine the French have something similar ..."

"French law prohibits sexual relations between someone under eighteen and a person in authority. But ..."

"Then we've got her," Ryder's voice was strained. "Find her ... throw the book at her. And bring Alistair back home."

"Unfortunately it's not as simple as that. The French are saying she's not in a position of authority. She might be employed as a nanny over here but they're claiming because of his age that's pretty tenuous in France. In other words ... you'll pardon me, Mrs Ryder ... if they are having sex then they're consenting adults."

"The devil they are," Ryder snapped, forcing himself, leaning heavily on his stick, to stand up and hobble to the door of the drawing room. Dragging it open, and summoning as much of an imperative as a dry and constricted throat would allow, he called into the space beyond.

"Get me the French ambassador. On the phone. White drawing room. Now."

He turned back unsteadily into the room.

"And now, Commander Hewlatt, while we're waiting for that call, I think you might explain what your people were doing when they were supposed to be protecting my son."

***

As Ryder feared, the red tops were taking a salacious interest in the disappearance of the prime minister's son and the "nympho nanny" (Daily Star) with the "frisky Frog legs" (The Sun). They had discovered that Alistair was probably in the Auvergne and they had descended on the area in droves. Ryder imagined the arrival of the British press in this bucolic part of France was as much a shock to the locals as it was to him. How had the newspapers known where to look, he wanted to know. Had someone in the police tipped them off? Commander Hewlatt assured him this was not the case. No one on her team would speak to the press, she told him, without her knowledge. Still less would anyone accept cash from a journalist in return for information.

"Those days are over," she said. "Post Elveden we've learned our lesson."

"I doubt it," Ryder spoke with difficulty, struggling to articulate every syllable. "The press will pay for gossip as long as people are prepared to sell it. And that includes the police."

Margo directed an apologetic smile at Hewlatt. "I guess we've a lot to put up with where the papers are concerned. You'll understand we're wary."

"Wary," Ryder snorted. "The understatement of the year."

It was not just the reporting of the hunt for Alistair that troubled him. The more serious newspapers were running stories on the problem of professional parents neglecting their offspring. There was no shortage of so-called experts ready to claim that children suffered serious psychological damage when parents chose financial, rather than familial, well-being. In the word "career" was also the word "care", one wise-crack academic pointed out, but all too often the care in career was ignored. None of the commentators mentioned Ryder by name. Propriety or, in its current guise, political correctness, saw to it there was no direct criticism of a someone afflicted with a terminal illness. All the same, Ryder had taken the comments as oblique criticism of himself.

The newspaper columns, however, were a model of restraint in comparison with the tweet that went viral towards the end of the second day of Alistair's disappearance. With the hashtag ryderloverat it read: PM screws own kid also exgirlfriend does wife know???

The tabloids pounced on the tweet with unrestrained glee. The writer, they soon discovered, was a nurse who used to work at a health centre in Manchester which Ryder had visited apparently for clandestine encounters with his former student sweetheart. A taxi driver then came forward to say he had taken Ryder, whom he remembered as a tight-fisted toff who gave no tip, to this place for treating sexually transmitted diseases with no questions asked. Within hours there were pictures across the electronic media of Ellie, looking startled outside her Raby Street practice, and cast in the role either as prime ministerial mistress or as back-street quack dealing dodgy drugs and other risqué remedies. In some instances she was both. Ryder, in turn, was a serial womaniser who treated his marriage vows, in the words of one commentator, "like political promises to be broken at the earliest opportunity". One blogger even went so far as to suggest the motor neurone disease was a myth to mask the degenerative effects of untreated syphilis.

Ryder was livid. He was incoherent, choking, coughing, wheezing instructions in monosyllabic gasps. He demanded the presence of Blenhesket. Blenhesket would sort those yahoos. He'd done it before. He'd do it again. But not just threaten. Sue them. Sue the hide off the bastards. And tell Ellie. Tell her he'd make it right. Damages for her, too. Monstrous damages, the fattest the courts could find. And Margo ... she knew it wasn't true. This business about betrayal ... and syphilis. All lies. To bring him down. Bring down the government. But where was Margo? He wanted her ... wanted her now.

Margo was in an adjacent room telephoning the consultant, Mr Henderson. She told him to come at once. He arrived within the hour to administer a sedative and a promise to return the following day. A semblance of tranquillity descended on Downing Street.

***

In the event, and despite the promised intervention of the embassy, it was not the French police but the British press who located Alistair. Four days after the disappearance the Daily Mirror published a grey and grainy picture of Alistair and Marie-France peering from the window of a tumbledown farmhouse some ten kilometres from Saint-Nectaire. What looked under scrutiny like a ruin had been transformed, with editorial inevitability, into a "cosy love nest". The reporter who discovered them, according to the front page splash, had been unable to speak to the "fly-away love birds" because he was chased off by a farmer armed with a shotgun and an apparent hatred of trespassers.

Commander Hewlatt, updating the Ryders, said within half an hour of publication of the photograph the farmhouse was under siege from reporters. The local police, she added, were in attendance.

Ryder, still on medication prescribed by Mr Henderson, mumbled his relief that his son had been found and was going nowhere. Evading police protection was easy, he said, scowling at Commander Hewlatt: avoiding the British press an impossibility. And the reporters would not be deterred by a farmer with a shotgun. Even if the fellow discharged both barrels at the slavering newshounds, Ryder said, they would see it merely as the price to pay for a good story and would claim lavish expenses by way of compensation.

Margo said she would go to France at once to bring Alistair home. Hewlatt advised against it. The case was already high-profile and the presence of the prime minister's wife, and distraught mother, would hinder rather than help. Everything was under control. The embassy in Paris was monitoring the situation and Marie-France would be placed by police under investigation, pending further enquiries as a prelude to being formally charged.

"What with?" Ryder wanted to know.

"Abduction, kidnap," Hewlatt replied. "They'll find something. And then, when the police have done with him, taken statements, that sort of thing, someone from the embassy will escort Alistair back to London."

"When?" Margo asked.

"I can't say," Hewlatt shook her head. "The police will want as full as picture as they can get, especially if they are to charge this woman. The embassy people will be with him, make sure he's properly represented, and speed things up as much as they can."

"Good," Margo said. "We want him back as soon as possible."

***

Later that evening Ryder was in the study in Downing Street, trying to focus on the final draft of the manifesto with which he would launch the party's election campaign. He'd read it numerous times before, in its earlier versions, but now the words and ideas were confused, jumbled, a scrambled scrabble of double letters and triple word scores ... or double-dip recession and triple A credit-ratings. Or double A credit and ... but no. He shook his head to clear the confusion clouding his mind. It was the medication, the damned medication, on top of all else ...

He was roused by a knock at the door. He opened his eyes in time to see Blenhesket enter but stop when he caught sight of Ryder.

"I'll come back another time," Blenhesket said. "That is ... when you're ..."

"I'm fine," Ryder coughed, trying to straighten up, as manifesto papers scattered on the floor around him.

"With respect ... I think it would be better if I ..."

"I'm fine, I said. Just a bit ... run down. A difficult week. Still is."

"It's good news about your son. You must be relieved."

Ryder cleared his throat. "It could be a couple of days. Formalities. Until then ..."

He shrugged, and the rest of the sentence was lost.

Blenhesket frowned, unsure whether to stay or to go. But Ryder's mouth was moving again. The words came with effort, in short bursts, brief and breathy. Blenhesket, feeling on balance he should remain, bent low, straining to hear.

"Have you got them nailed ... those bloggers, floggers ... spreading lies about the innocent ... ruining reputations? Ellie ... the doctor. I've been in touch. This business ... wrecked her relationship. Some fellow she was seeing ... going to get married. Not any more. Well ...?"

"The attorney general's office feels it would be unwise at this particular time ..."

"Bugger ... bugger the attorney general's office."

"With an election coming up ... making unnecessary waves ..."

"Not unnecessary waves. The opposite."

"It's a question of priorities. For instance ... there are other things."

Blenhesket paused and looked at Ryder.

"It'll do tomorrow."

"No. Now."

Blenhesket straightened up, studying Ryder's drawn and haggard countenance. He took a deep breath.

"Okay. You recall that bomb attack. The middle east ..."

"No. Which bomb attack? The middle east is nothing but bombs. And sand."

"The one in which our peace-keepers were killed. The day you flew to Washington."

"That. Yes."

"French newspapers ..."

"I've had enough of the French."

"French newspapers are saying these were British explosives."

"We have never supplied ..."

"British ordnance. In other words, from a British base. What the papers are saying is that a faction in the British military caused the explosion to highlight the dangers our troops face out there and to direct more resources to the area."

"Bullshit." Ryder tried to raise himself from his seat.

"It's being said this is part of a campaign to increase overall defence spending and that Miller's behind it."

Ryder sank back, coughing, almost choking, his frame convulsed, contorted.

"A response is needed from number 10."

Ryder shook his head, which jerked to one side, and flapped a hand at Blenhesket. His voice was almost inaudible.

"Deal with it. Do something. I ... I can't. Not now. I mean ..."

"Prime minister ..."

"It's too much. Just leave me."

"I don't think ..."

"Please. Just go."

"I'm going to fetch someone. You need ..."

Ryder, writhing, waved him away.

"Nothing. Nothing at all. No point."

Blenhesket was at the door when he heard a cough, almost a rattle, from behind. He turned to see Ryder looking at him, two eyes, still bright, still penetrating, staring from a countenance gaunt and greyed. His voice was low, but surprisingly clear.

"Sir Wesley ... you've been good to me. Very good. I hope ... I hope I haven't been a disappointment. So ... thank you. From the bottom of my heart ... thank you."

Northaven. April 2015.

The crematorium chapel was packed. Margo wondered if it was still technically a chapel since they had asked for the cross to be taken from the wall. This was a humanist funeral, a celebration of a life painfully, pointlessly ended, and one in which god, particularly at the end, had played no part. Or, if there was divine intervention, it was the work of a smiteful, spiteful old-testament god, callous, cruel and vengeful.

A cordon of police prevented the television crews, the reporters, the curious and the rubberneckers from entering the crematorium grounds. They gathered at the main gate and lined the low wall that separated the gardens of rest, with their lofty trees, silent glades and mildewed monuments, from the busy main road leading out of Northaven. A sign by the entrance exhorted visitors to drive slowly and to watch out for red squirrels. Life, even in this place of the dead, was hallowed.

In the absence of hymns and prayers, of sermonising and biblical readings, the service was relatively informal. More do-it-yourself than do-it-for-god, the celebrant said, an opportunity to personalise proceedings to reflect the life, rather than any afterlife, of the deceased. Margo, in shock, skewed by the suddenness of events, left the arrangements largely to the celebrant. Her only input was the music. Even then her contribution was random, unfocused. She had found a CD in his room, probably the last piece of music to which he had listened, and handed it over to be played at the service. She had no idea what it was, didn't know if it would be appropriate, didn't care. Didn't care because it didn't matter. Nothing mattered. Not any more. Not now.

The celebrant had read a poem, of which Margo had

registered not a word, and now it was her turn to step to the lectern and speak. At first she had dismissed the idea. I can't, she told the celebrant. What I want to say is here ... and she touched her heart ... and it's too late. But at the last minute she changed her mind, told the celebrant she would like to say something, thought it might help her if she could address her grief in this way. The celebrant altered the order of service accordingly.

Clutching her notes, Margo stood and crossed to the front of the chapel. She placed the papers on the lectern, glanced down at them, then up, out across the rows of those who had come to pay their last respects, but the images before her shivered, shimmered, in the watery April sun shafting into the chapel. All she could distinguish was the lustre of buffed brass fittings on the coffin and the steely glint of rollers to slide it to the fiery nothingness beyond. She shuddered, averting her gaze, grasping the lectern for support, and was comforted to feel an arm round her shoulders, a tissue thrust into her hand.

"If you don't feel you can ..." the celebrant began.

"I'm okay. Just ... just give me a moment."

The celebrant withdrew. Margo dabbed at her eyes, looked again at her notes, and realised what she had written, what she had prepared, was not what she wanted to say. Wiping away a final tear, feeling calmer, more collected, she began to talk. The words tumbled out, haphazardly, at first slowly, haltingly, but then more quickly, confidently. What they lacked in structure, they gained in resonance.

This was a life, she said, of promise and hope. Of promise unfulfilled, of hope dashed. A life that had barely begun to make sense of the complexities of the world. But a life, nevertheless, with the courage to kick against a past perceived as cold and harsh, wanting in compassion, and in which those who should have cared, should have understood, were found lacking in love and human charity. This was a spirit that created its own values, realised them in its own way, to circumvent the infelicities foisted upon it. Perhaps the chosen path was wrong, had its doubters, its deniers, for it had caused pain, anguish. But that was nothing compared with the pain and anguish of the person in whose name they were gathered today, that person with so much to give, and whose best, whose potential, had been surely yet to come. His passing left the world a poorer place ...

Stop it, Ryder thought, crumpled in his wheelchair, isolated, at the front of the chapel. Please ... enough. This is maudlin, sentimental. A grieving mother must be allowed to mourn, but self-recrimination should play no part. Today is not about you, but about Alistair ... the son who, less than a week after returning, under protest, from France, stepped onto a live rail outside Northaven station, having left a note saying at least in his short life he had known love, true love, and if this were denied him he could see no point living. What a waste, Ryder reminded himself yet again, a stupid and tragic waste.

Or was it? Since Alistair's suicide Ryder had felt a strange strength in his broken body. True, the neurologist had recommended, indeed insisted on, the wheelchair, as more of his patient's everyday functions deserted him. Yet Ryder, in a perverse way, liked the wheelchair. It was a chariot, in which he felt safe, protected, but in which, at the same time, he could sally forth to slay enemies and slaughter foes. If he could only learn to operate it, make it go forwards, backwards, in the direction he wanted, then it would become his nerve centre, replacing those faculties the gremlin had stolen from him.

Ah ... the gremlin. Since Alistair's suicide Ryder had

known something within him had changed. It was as if the gremlin, having ravaged a body, claimed a life, was content, had withdrawn, abandoned him. That the ravaged body was not the one that died seemed not to matter to the gremlin. Its task was complete. It had wrought suffering, brought death, fulfilled its evil purpose and moved on. Where it was Ryder knew not, cared even less. But all his senses, his entire being, told him it was no longer with him. Told him ... and this was his guilty secret, shared with no one; a secret irrational and ludicrous, yet he knew it was so ... that the son had died so the father might live. Of course, it was wrong. All wrong. If sacrifice were required it should be the other way round. The father for the son, the older for the younger. But this disease was savage, played its own warped, capricious game. And now it had stopped, leaving him, Ryder, the bloodied, broken victor. From this victory he drew strength, strength for the battles that lay ahead. And in which he would be equally triumphant.

Around him, people were stirring. The service seemed to be over. Lost in his thoughts, his guilt, his elation, he had missed the closing part of the ceremony. How had Margo finished her eulogy, if that's what it was? Had there been another poem, more music? If there had, it had passed him by. He looked up. The celebrant seemed to be indicating they should file out past the coffin, through a side door and into the walled quadrangle where, Ryder remembered, flowers from family and others were displayed. Now he could feel people behind him, waiting for him to lead the procession. He twisted in his chair, as far as he could, to look round, see if Margo was coming to join him. But she was still seated, next to Jim Murchison, who had flown over for the funeral of his grandson. They were conferring, checking watches. Of course. They had a flight to catch. Margo was returning with her father to La Jolla, to escape, as she said, the ghosts in the house at Northaven. And to avoid playing the part of the dutiful first lady in the imminent election campaign.

Ryder fiddled with the controls of the wheelchair. It was like the mobile phone he had never quite mastered. Too many buttons, switches. Eventually he'd get there. He'd have to. In the meantime ...

"It's all right. I'll push you."

Ryder looked up as he heard the familiar voice. He smiled. Ellie ...

"What are you doing here?"

"What do you think I'm doing here?"

Ryder blushed. "You didn't have to."

"Of course I did. You didn't think I'd ..."

Ryder extended an emaciated hand which she took, and gently squeezed.

"I'm sorry, Tim," she said. "Sorry for your loss."

Ryder nodded, tears in his eyes. "Alistair ... had things been different ... you know ... he might have been ours. That might have been you, up there, talking about your son ... our son."

"That's history. We have to move on."

"True," Ryder said, collecting himself, blinking away the tears, slowly removing his hand from hers. "We do. We have work to do. For now ... an election to win. Then, I think, the mourning."

"The mourning after."

"The mourning after. I like that. And then whatever else life might bring. But for the moment ... please, get me out of here. I've had enough."

Ellie nodded, leaning on the wheelchair to set it gently rolling, steering it past the waiting coffin out into the struggling sunlight beyond the chapel.

Ryder stared ahead, his mind fixed not on his

surroundings but on a distant point in the future. He could feel Ellie behind him, pushing, straining slightly. The wheelchair probably weighed as much as he did. But it would be all right. Absolutely all right. This was not an end, but a beginning.